Into the Heartland

Len Custer

*Best wishes to
Fred & Ellie Stein.*

Len Custer

iUniverse, Inc.
New York Bloomington

Into the Heartland

Copyright © 2009 by Len Custer

All rights reserved. No part of this book may be used or reproduced by any means, graphic, electronic, or mechanical, including photocopying, recording, taping or by any information storage retrieval system without the written permission of the publisher except in the case of brief quotations embodied in critical articles and reviews.

This is a work of fiction. All of the characters, names, incidents, organizations, and dialogue in this novel are either the products of the author's imagination or are used fictitiously.

iUniverse books may be ordered through booksellers or by contacting:

iUniverse
1663 Liberty Drive
Bloomington, IN 47403
www.iuniverse.com
1-800-Authors (1-800-288-4677)

Because of the dynamic nature of the Internet, any Web addresses or links contained in this book may have changed since publication and may no longer be valid. The views expressed in this work are solely those of the author and do not necessarily reflect the views of the publisher, and the publisher hereby disclaims any responsibility for them.

ISBN: 978-0-595-52945-2 (pbk)
ISBN: 978-0-595-52013-8 (cloth)
ISBN: 978-0-595-62997-8 (ebk)

Printed in the United States of America

iUniverse rev. date: 2/18/2009

Dedication

◆

This book is dedicated to William Henry Custer, my grandfather. His life experiences were my inspiration for writing *Into the Heartland*. There are many similarities between his early years and those of the protagonist, Will Curtis.

William Henry Custer

Contents

MARY	1
GOOD-BYE, CHILDHOOD	7
ANNOYING DELAY	16
RIVERBOAT MAN	21
WAR STORIES	28
NATTY	32
SUSPENDERS	41
MOSES	45
LAZARUS	51
GOOD-BYE *NELLEBELLE*	59
FAMILY SECRETS	63
MEDAL OF HONOR	71
KANSAS CITY	81
HEARTLAND	88
SODBUSTERS	95
NEIGHBORS	99
CONFRONTATION	104
THE LORD'S WORK	109
FOURTEEN	115
FAMILY TIES	120
TRAPPER AND HUNTER	126
PREMONITION	134
SEARCHING	141

MARTYRDOM	150
RETRIBUTION	159
ELISABETH COUSTEAU	165
MARY'S SECRET	172
PROSPERITY	181
FLEETING GOOD TIMES	185
TRACKING	194
FRONTIER JUSTICE	203
ZEKE SUFFERS	209
JOAN AND ESTER	215
BUDDING ROMANCE	223
ALMOST A MAN	229
FIRST TIME	234
OUT OF THE PAST	241
NOSTALGIA	247
HAWTHORN "SKEETER" CRANSTON	256
MAN OF MEANS	261
CRUEL REVENGE	267
KIDNAPPED	275
BETSY'S DILEMMA	281
GUN FIGHT	285
MARY'S ORDEAL	289
ZEKE'S STRATEGY	297
RITE OF PASSAGE	303

Acknowledgments

I'm very grateful to Charlotte Hayes, my talented daughter, for suggesting my book's title and for creating the cover design and artwork. Don Metzler and Leah Naess, long time friends and members of our writers group, provided timely encouragement and frank evaluations of this novel as it was being written. I owe them a heartfelt debt of gratitude for the many improvements they suggested. Leah's professional-quality editing services are especially appreciated.

Will Curtis
1872 Age 13
Art by Charlotte Hayes

CHAPTER 1

MARY

◆

With his tattered boots clutched in one hand, Will Curtis quietly backed down the loft ladder, hoping his Pa would still be sleeping. As his bare feet touched the cold kitchen floor, a gruff male voice resonated from the frosty gloom, verifying that Pa was up and grumpy.

"Is that you, Will? Go hitch my horse to the buggy."

"Ya-ya-yes, sirrr," Will's stressed thirteen-year-old vocal cords squeaked.

He stumbled backward to the hearth and his skinny butt hit the chilly stones hard. Those darn stiff boots weren't cooperating—got to force them onto cold bare feet; no time for socks. His socks had big holes in them anyway.

"Move along sharply, boy. I ain't got all day!"

"Yes, Pa."

Hobbling toward the cabin door while stomping on the last boot, Will gave wide berth to the large, dark shadow that had spoken. Grabbing his coat from a peg, he stumbled out into the crisp morning air. With a closed door between him and his volatile father, the apprehensive boy felt safe enough to stop and pull on the shabby coat. He removed a length of rope from one pocket and looped it around his waist because all of the buttons were missing.

At the dilapidated pole corral, he held out a handful of oats to attract Pa's large saddle horse, which sometimes doubled at pulling the buggy. Strong for his size, Will stood on his tiptoes to throw a heavy, stiff harness over the shying horse's back. With numb fingers, he soon had it strapped into place and the resisting critter was hitched to the ramshackle buggy. He'd made good time, but was it fast enough to satisfy his impatient Pa?

After leading the hitched horse to the front of the cabin, Will held tight to the bridle rein with trepidation. Pa approached out of the shadows into the dawn light. His gait and size reminded his son of a lumbering disgruntled bear. When the emerging form got closer, Will noticed his self-ordained minister Pa was wearing his black preacher suit. He wondered why—it wasn't Sunday.

Without speaking, Josh Curtis unwound the reins from the whip holder, stepped into the protesting buggy, and plunked his considerable bulk on the seat with a grunt. Will sighed, released his tenacious grip on the bridle, and stepped back from the horse.

"Mrs. Hinkle will be over with your sisters soon," the dark image on the buggy seat announced. The tense youngster flinched at the sudden brusque sound. "Tell her we'll be back by supper time. Mind you, finish them chores 'fore you go running off anywheres!"

Reins slapped the slouching horse's rump, and the buggy moved up the lane toward the rudimentary road that led to New Haven, West Virginia.

"Ya-ya-yes, sir," Will managed to shout before the squeaking buggy reached the gate.

Returning to the empty log house, the despondent boy hesitated just inside the door. Tentative fingers of early morning sunlight filtering through dirty window panes did nothing to dispel the gloom in the sparse room. For a fleeting moment, he expected to see his adored mother at the hearth of the once-cozy kitchen, cooking his breakfast, where she'd been every morning of his life until six months ago.

Reality slammed into his distressed mind. She couldn't be there—she'd died giving birth to his baby sister, Anne. Never again would he see her smiling face, feel her warm hugs, or have her brush back that unruly tuft of auburn hair that fell across his forehead. Tears welled. He clinched his jaw and blinked them away; be darned if he was going to keep crying like a baby. Besides, he had other things to worry about.

He'd been told the family would soon be moving to a homestead in faraway Kansas. Even more shattering, he'd overheard Pa tell his Uncle Zeke that he'd found a young replacement for Will's departed Ma from among his scattered religious flock. The resentful youngster guessed that was why Pa was wearing his preacher suit on a weekday. Likely, she was the other person in the "we" of his Pa's curt message: "We'll be back before suppertime." No one could ever replace his dear mother. He vowed to hate anyone that tried!

By late afternoon, with the chores finished, Will sat in his special spot under a majestic oak tree on the bank of the Ohio River, with bony knees pulled up under his chin. His old dog, Crusher, slept curled beside him, and his buddy since early childhood, Hawthorn "Skeeter" Cranston, sprawled nearby.

"I'd of come up and helped you with them chores if I'd knowed your Pa was gone," Skeeter said.

"It ain't fair that Pa thinks you're a heathen and a bad influence. I'm sure sorry he won't let you go to Kansas with us," Will lamented. "I'll bet Ma could have talked him into it if she was still here."

"Everybody knows your Pa's a religious nut," Skeeter declared.

Will agreed with that assessment, yet he felt obligated to defend his sanctimonious father. He'd heard the story many times of how Pa found his religion on the Bull Run battlefield, when his Union cavalry unit was facing annihilation.

"Well, Pa's got some problems, right enough, but Ma told me the war done that to him."

"Maybe it started in the war," Skeeter allowed, "but seems to me he's getting worse since your Ma departed."

"Yeah, I guess he is. Uncle Zeke says Pa's courting a gal that's *only eighteen years old*."

"Well now, that there just proves how crazy your Pa is—thinking he can replace your Ma with a gal what's only five years older 'n you!"

"Will-l, Will-l!" The sound roared through the trees and descended on the boys like the growl of an enraged grizzly bear. "Y'all come to the house—right now—to meet your new ma!"

Will lunged to his feet and his eyes darted toward the demanding voice.

"Oh my gosh—Pa's back! I'd sooner take a whoopin' than go meet his new wife, but I'd best hightail it 'fore he busts a gut."

"I hear ya-a-a, Pa-a-a-a," he hollered toward the house, fracturing the high notes. "I'm on my w-a-a-ay."

"Yeah, y'all better haul your butt." Skeeter's face took on a sad, hangdog look. "I'll—I'll be seeing you again 'fore you leave for Kansas, won't I?"

"I just may not go!" Will said as he started toward the house.

"You'll go alright, if your Pa wants you to, or he'll take your hide off," Skeeter shouted after his friend, who was now trotting up the path with Crusher close behind.

When he had skirted the hog pen, Will got his first glimpse of the young woman Pa had brought home. Standing beside his paunchy, middle-aged father, she looked very young and vulnerable. Will might have even felt sorry for her if his resentment hadn't run so deep.

They were all in the yard waiting for him. As he got closer, Pa's dark expression flashed a warning that he was irritated, likely because Will hadn't been at the house when they arrived. There'd be hell to pay if Pa knew he'd been jawing with Skeeter.

Mrs. Hinkle, a neighbor who was helping out, stood near the kitchen door holding his baby sister, Anne. Jeanie, Will's six-year-old sister, timidly peeked out from behind Mrs. Hinkle's skirt. A thumb was jammed in her mouth, her chin trembling, and tears overflowed from sad eyes. Concern for vulnerable, frightened Jeanie pushed aside Will's own trepidation for a moment.

"*Will!*" Pa's stern voice demanded his full attention. "Take off your hat and say howdy to Mary, your new ma."

God how he wished Pa hadn't called her *his ma*! He diverted his eyes, knowing they reflected hurt and anger. Doffing his tattered straw hat, he twisted it in sweaty hands. After a few awkward seconds, he forced a glance at the pretty, auburn-haired young woman standing just a couple of steps away. He intended for it to be a belligerent look so she'd know she wasn't welcome.

She returned a disarming wink and friendly smile. Be darned, if she hasn't misread my intent, he thought. Her broad smile revealed two rows of straight white teeth, lit up her pretty face, and caused her luminous brown eyes to sparkle. Will's fast-developing male hormones couldn't miss the obvious fact that she had the shapely, athletic body of a mature woman.

Flustered, he managed to stammer, "How-ow do, ma-ma'am."

"Pleased to meet you, Will Curtis." Mary's melodious voice suggested a bubbly personality and her diction was nearly devoid of the usual West Virginia twang. "I'm sure we're going to be *great* friends. Come here and let me give you a hug."

When he hesitated, she boldly stepped forward and pulled his skinny body against hers in a surprisingly strong bear hug. Moving one hand to the back of his head, she buried his face between her protruding breasts. The thrilling sensation that flashed from Will's mind to his groin was soon replaced with concern that he might suffocate. She released him and he stepped back, muted by confusion and embarrassment

"I didn't mean to embarrass you, Will," that enchanting voice said. "Just want to be friends with you and your sisters. You'll soon get to know my forward ways."

Will glanced at Pa, and tensed at the petulant scowl—a stern reminder Pa wasn't much for hugging, and never in public. Will's cheeks flushed. In the awkward silence, he felt obligated to reply to Mary.

"P-pleased to meet you," he managed to utter. "Ah-ah…" His befuddled mind hung up on what to call her. Would it be proper to call her Mary? He sure wasn't going to call her *Ma*!

She smiled back and gave him another wink with a slight nod of her head.

"Just call me Mary, Will." And then she took the pressure off of him by turning her soft brown eyes and warm smile on sad Jeanie.

Pa cleared his throat, "Hu-u-umph," which was his habit when displeased. "Let's go in and eat."

That evening, Will's troubled mind kept him awake. He stared at the reflection from the banked fire playing on smudged rafters, contemplating how he could keep from going to Kansas, and what to make of the mysterious young woman his Pa brought home. During the supper blessing, Pa had thanked God for bringing Mary into the family, but said nothing about where she came from. It seemed very unfair for Pa and his harsh God to expect him to accept an eighteen-year-old as his mother! Then, why didn't she share Pa's bed?

He conjured up a disturbing image of Mary, and he tried to evaluate those strange sensations he'd felt when his face was buried in her bosom. Soon, the memory of her firm, yet yielding, breasts against his cheeks caused an erection. Darn what's wrong with me, his confused mind demanded? I vowed to hate her—why does she make me feel this way?

CHAPTER 2

GOOD-BYE, CHILDHOOD

◆

The sun was just clearing the wooded hills to the east when Zeke Curtis reined in his horse at the rutted entrance to the old Curtis family farmstead. He shifted his weight in the saddle to his right hip and sadly shook his head as he surveyed the ramshackle log house, derelict outbuildings, and weed-chocked fields. Zeke recalled it having been a hard scramble farm when he lived there as a boy, but now it was hardly recognizable.

His brother Josh had inherited the farm, and rightly so in Zeke's opinion, because he'd earned it. He still felt a tinge of guilt for having left fifteen-year-old Josh to assist the old folks when wanderlust lured him westward at age seventeen. Actually, there was only eighteen months difference in their ages.

Other ghosts from Zeke's past lured him back to the area after he was discharged from the Union cavalry during the Civil War, and caused him to feel responsible for assisting his troubled, religious-fanatic brother and his family. In fact, they became his only family when the woman he married after the war died of consumption two years later, without bearing any children.

Before she died in childbirth, Will's mother, Marge, and Zeke had collaborated on a project to move the family to a Kansas homestead. Now that Marge was gone, Zeke felt even more obligated to follow though on the relocation that she hoped would improve her husband's deteriorating mental condition and the family's bare subsistence. As Zeke nudged his mount toward the cabin, he wondered if Josh's new eighteen-year-old wife would be a complication. He intended to forge ahead.

A big grin creased Zeke's tanned face and crinkled the smile lines at the corners of his penetrating green eyes when he noticed Will, his nephew, approaching the house with a milk pail.

"Hi, Willie," Zeke said affectionately, as he dismounted at the hitching rail with the happy grin still in place. "You suppose a hungry man could get some breakfast around here, now that there's a woman in the house?"

Only Uncle Zeke called him Willie. His given name was Willard, after his maternal grandfather who died before he was born. He had nothing against the grandpa he'd never known, but wasn't too happy with being called Willie. He made an exception for Uncle Zeke.

"I bet you could, Uncle Zeke. Mary was up and cooking 'fore I went out to milk Bessie. But I ain't seen hide or hair of Pa yet this morning."

"Well, likely your Pa's tuckered out, what with being a newly wed—an' all," Zeke said, with a wink and a knowing smile.

The innuendo went right over Will's head.

"Where'd Mary come from and why you 'spose she married a grumpy old man like Pa?" Will asked Zeke quietly, not wanting those in the cabin to hear.

"Only met her once and I wasn't invited to the wedding. Heard tell she was raised as a city girl over in Ohio. Got no idea how a bright young woman like her would hook up with the likes of Josh—not that your Pa ain't of good character, you understand."

"Wh-wh-why you suppose Mary don't sleep with Pa like Ma did?" Will stammered.

Zeke's eyebrows raised and he blinked a couple of times.

"Well—well now, can't rightly say I got the answer to that question. Maybe ol' Josh just snores too loud."

"I've never known him to snore very loud," the innocent youngster countered.

"Whatever the reason," Zeke said, "I've learned its best not to stick my nose into other people's private business. Suggest you take that advice, Willie boy."

"Gosh—don't mean no disrespect. I was just curious, that's all."

"T'was curiosity what killed the cat, my boy. You don't want to be a dead cat, do you?"

"Well, no-o-o."

The cabin door opened and Mary stepped out into the morning sunlight, shading her eyes with her hand.

"Thought I heard someone talking out here," her melodious voice said.

Will's face reddened. He glanced at his uncle; was he thinking the same thing? Sure hope she didn't hear what we were talking about, he thought. If she did, she didn't let on.

"Mornin' Mary," Zeke managed, while removing his hat. "Remember me? I'm Josh's brother Zeke."

"Why yes, Zeke, I remember you. How could I forget such a handsome man? Come on in, you're just in time for breakfast. Here, Will, let me take that milk."

Will noticed Zeke's face blush. Likely Mary was teasing, but Will wouldn't have been surprised if she meant the compliment. At age forty, Zeke Curtis's six-foot frame was firm and lean. A full mustache matched the texture and color of his slightly curly, rust-colored hair. The impressive mustache covered a scar on his upper lip and added character to his strong-featured, weathered face. Smile wrinkles at the corners of penetrating hazel eyes reflected his uncle's quick wit, of which Will was often the recipient. The youngster idolized his widowed and childless uncle. When people said that he resembled Zeke more than he did his father, it pleased Will, but he could tell it rankled Pa.

Zeke and Will followed Mary's shapely body into the cabin. Pa sat at the table with a mug of coffee in his big hand. His greeting was an ominous scowl.

"And a good morning to you too, Josh," Zeke said cheerfully. He seldom missed a chance to razz his somber brother. Will often wondered if it was intended to rile his Pa, or was just brotherly banter.

Whatever the intention, Zeke was the only person in the world that could get away with it.

Uninvited, Zeke plopped down at the place Mary had set for Will. Will sat on the hearth beside Jeanie. Mary put the milk pail on the sideboard and was juggling a big skillet of fried ham and eggs and a plate of hot soda biscuits as she moved toward the table when Pa finally spoke.

"What you doin' over here so early, Zeke?" he demanded.

"Don't you recall? We were gonna finalize our travel plans for going to Kansas today."

"Well, you wasted your time coming over. I've decided my family's not going!"

Mary nearly dropped the breakfast and Zeke stared at his brother, slack-jawed.

Will's feelings were ambiguous. On the one hand, he didn't want to go against his hero, Uncle Zeke, but on the other, he'd be very happy not to leave the only home he'd known, his buddy Skeeter, and the place where his dear mother was buried.

"Wha-what the hell you mean—you're not going? We had this all settled weeks ago," Zeke stammered. "We've both made deals to sell our farms and I've bought us a big Studebaker wagon and four new horses to help carry our extra things."

"That may be so, but I've had a message from God. He told me my flock needs me here, an' I'm not leaving 'em without a preacher. Anyways, this unholy venture has been your idea all along—not mine!"

"Josh, you'd better stick to our deal, or I'm packing out of here," Mary declared firmly.

What deal, Will wondered; this presented another mysterious aspect of Mary!

Will had to agree with Pa on one point; homesteading in Kansas was Zeke's project. He knew Zeke had learned that the part of the sprawling Osage Indian Reservation located in Kansas was going to be opened for homesteaders, and had traveled there last summer to check out the land. He was also aware that his mother had been in favor of the move. Now it looked like Mary, for whatever her reasons, was pushing it too.

"Where you gonna go? You ain't got no people," Pa said to Mary.

"I'm educated to be a teacher and there are other things I can do. I don't intend to dry up and grow old in these parts—but now that I've met them, I don't want to abandon these kids either," she declared. "Why don't you let Zeke tell us again about what he has lined up in Kansas?"

"Well! Look who's trying to tell me what to do," Josh sneered. "All right, Zeke, let's hear about that *heartland* of yours again."

He managed to make heartland sound like a dirty word. Zeke's jaw tightened, but he replied in an even tone.

"Being Union veterans, we had priority on picking claims and I got us two darn fine ones, Josh. All we gotta do is prove up on 'em in five years to get title," Zeke began. "They're only a mile apart. One borders on the Arkansas River and the other on the Walnut. You can have your pick."

"Hu-u-umph," Pa countered. "Being on rivers, they're likely covered with timber and brush and prone to flooding."

"Yeah, like I told you before, there's some timber and brush to be cleared all right, but each place has about equal acres of hillside grassland for pasture and hay, and good bottomland for all manner of row crops. Hell, clearing a little brush ain't gonna hurt us none, and we'll need trees for building. It's a damn sight better than being out on the windswept western Kansas prairie."

"No call for using sinful language," Josh said in his most pious manner.

"What I'm trying to tell you is that the good land is along the rivers, and that's what we'll have."

"All that may be well and good, but can I trust you to hang around long enough to help us get established, Zeke?" Pa blurted out.

Zeke's face flushed and he glared at his brother for several seconds. Will knew his adventurous uncle had the reputation of having been an irresponsible drifter in his youth. He'd heard Pa tell Ma how he resented being stuck with helping their folks on the farm when Zeke left to seek his fortune out West. Ma hadn't defended Zeke.

"Yes, Josh, the *family* can depend on me—my wandering days are over."

The brothers held heated eye contact for a few heartbeats before Josh spoke.

"Are there any settlements anywheres near where them wonderful homesteads are located?"

Zeke sighed deeply, his eyes softened and his voice was under control again when he answered.

"They're about ten miles southeast of the frontier village of Winfield, Kansas. We'll only be a mile north of the Osage Nation that's located in Oklahoma Indian Territory."

"Hum-m-m," Josh mused, "likely them Indians are all heathens, a fertile ground for God's work."

A faraway stare glazed his father's eyes and Will knew Pa was hooked on the idea of farming for Indian souls. The boy felt trapped. His only choices were to run away from home or go to Kansas with the family. If Ma was still here, going to that wild place with Pa wouldn't be so scary. He'd seen the hurt in her eyes sometimes, but she'd always been able to keep Pa under control.

Zeke had suggested they pool equipment and funds. Will suspected that was his uncle's unassuming way of financing the enterprise because Pa's evangelism kept them at bare subsistence. He was aware of many other times over the years that Zeke had quietly helped the family, being careful to keep it from his jealous and volatile brother.

Josh set off the next day to tell his scattered flock good-bye, leaving the others to do the heavy work of getting ready for the trip. Mary and Will spent considerable time together during the next two weeks. She earned his respect, efficiently cooking the meals, washing and mending their clothes, taking good care of the younger children, and packing the household goods. At first, he resented her badgering him to help get things ready for a move he didn't want to make, but he was shamed by her work ethic and finally pitched in to help.

Will noticed Mary soon captured the loyalty of Moses, an aging former slave who was an honorary member of the family. Little Jeanie began following her around like a love-starved puppy. Within a week, Jeanie stopped sucking her thumb. The pinched mouth and wide eyes of a startled doe also diminished, and there were even a few smiles. Formerly fussy Anne was a changed baby; she smiled, gurgled, and cooed when Mary held her, and her cheeks became plump and rosy. But Mary remained an enigma to Will, and she made no effort to satisfy his curiosity.

Pa returned in time for the final loading and seemed critical about everything. They'd be taking three canvas-covered wagons, a spare team, two saddle horses, and Bessie the milk cow. Two wagons were for all of their personal things. The third wagon, a four-horse hitch Zeke had bought, was loaded with tools and grain for feed and seed. They debated on what farm equipment to take in addition to the hand tools, and settled on only a large two-horse, moldboard plow, a five-sweep cultivator, and a single-row corn planter. Even so, the large wagon was loaded to capacity. Will witnessed a big argument between Pa and Mary about her taking a couple of boxes filled with her books and teaching materials. Mary stood her ground, and the boxes were loaded.

As the time to leave grew closer, Will's resentment grew stronger. It reached a breaking point when Pa gruffly informed him that he intended to shoot his faithful dog, Crusher, because he was too old for such a strenuous trip. Anger, mixed with anguish, bubbled up from deep within Will's soul. Anger won out and sent a red flash across his eyes.

"Moses is getting old, why don't you shoot him, too?" Will shouted belligerently, pointing to the aging former slave standing nearby.

Will knew how deeply his father cared for Moses. It was a touching story, how Pa purchased him from an army contractor's work gang at the beginning of the war, and gave him his freedom. The wise and kindly old black man had been an important part of Will's life since he was two years old. He loved Moses, too.

Pa's face flushed beet red. He drew back his huge hand to strike his impertinent son. Will didn't flinch, and before the blow fell, Moses courageously stepped between them. The scene froze in that muted posture for several seconds. Breathing heavily through flared nostrils, Pa slowly lowered his hand, turned on his heels, and strode away. Moses and Will watched him for a while before Moses turned his aging, yet penetrating, brown eyes on his trembling friend.

"Now y'all jus' simmer down young man," he instructed in his soothing southern drawl. "I knows you're concerned 'bout ol'

Crusher, but so's your Pa. He don't want the old dog to suffer none on that long trip we fixin' to take."

"I'm sorry I brought you into my problems with Pa," Will lamented, anger giving way to grief. "But-but I'll run away from home 'fore I'll let Pa kill Crusher."

"Now you knows you don't mean that, Masta Will. What we do without you?"

"I do mean it, Moses! I'm old enough to take care of myself. Pa refuses to let ol' Skeeter go with us, and it ain't right—he's dragging the family off to some wild place in the heartland!"

"You may thinks you man enough to look out for yourself, but you ain't! Just what you got in mind?"

"Skeeter will help me build a big raft and we'll float down the Ohio to the Mississippi. If we can't find jobs on a riverboat, we'll just head on out West. Uncle Zeke weren't much older than me the first time he went out West."

"Your Uncle Zeke weren't never crazy enough to try floatin' down the Ohio, during spring runoff time on no log raft. That just shows how dumb you are; you boys already near drowned trying that once before. Beside, your family needs you now more 'n ever."

Tears of frustration clouded Will's eyes. "Moses, I just gotta do something to save Crusher."

"Well now, Masta Will, I suggest you take 'im on over to your friend Skeeter's place. You knows he'd take good care of him."

That was the answer to the Crusher problem. Will knew the old dog was nearly as attached to Skeeter as he was to him. He begrudgingly conceded that Moses was probably right about his running away when the family needed him. He'd go to Kansas—but he didn't have to like it.

Early in the morning of March 1, 1872, the Curtis family was ready to leave for the boat landing where the stern-wheeler Zeke had chartered was docked. It would haul them down the Ohio River and up the Mississippi to St Louis. From there they would ride on trains as far as the railhead at Wichita, Kansas, and then drive the wagons the last sixty miles to their homesteads. There was no turning back. Everything was loaded and their chartered boat was waiting.

All except Will were committed. The gray, rainy day matched his depression.

The family was seated on the four-horse hitch wagon and Moses sat on the other wagon when Will trotted up, out of breath. His eyes were red, having been at his mother's grave telling her good-bye. Pa knew where he'd been, but gave him a critical glare anyway.

"Could I ride with Moses?" Will found the courage to ask his scowling Pa. "Maybe I can drive the team if he gets tired."

"No!" Pa curtly answered. "You spend too much time bothering Moses. I want you where I can see you. Get yourself up on this wagon!"

Without knowing where Pa intended him to sit, Will quickly climbed up and found a storage box to perch on, close behind Mary, but out of his father's reach.

The two wagons lumbered out of the gate from the old Curtis farm, land that had been handed down to Pa from two generations of Curtis'. Zeke would meet them at the Point Pleasant boat landing, some fifteen miles away.

Will resolved that he wouldn't look back, fearing it would be too painful. But as the wagons proceeded down the muddy, rutted road, his head overrode his willpower. It turned for a last glance. The sad sight wrenched at the youngster's heart. It hadn't always been a happy place, but, God, how he hated to leave his childhood home, mother's grave, Crusher, and Skeeter. There was no stopping the tears that rolled down his cheeks.

CHAPTER 3

ANNOYING DELAY

◆

They reached the Point Pleasant Ohio River wharf about mid-morning. The rain had stopped. Pale sunlight struggled to break through thinning clouds, but mist still shrouded the river. Zeke's canvas-covered wagon was parked at the top of the riverbank, beside the rutted road that snaked down the embankment to a rickety wooden landing where a derelict stern-wheeler riverboat was docked.

"Pull your rigs in behind mine," Zeke shouted, using his cupped hands as a megaphone. "Stay with your wagon, Moses, there'll be a little wait."

When Josh's four-horse hitch stopped, Zeke stepped on the driver's side front wheel hub and nimbly raised himself to Pa's eye level.

"The crew's doing some work on the boat," he said. "You folks just as well stay in the wagon 'til they're ready for us, and keep out of this mud and wet grass."

"I knew your *great* friend couldn't be depended on," Josh complained. "I'm still against using that sinner's worn-out boat for this trip. Them rivers are gonna be flooded and dangerous this time of year."

"Josh, there ain't no danger of you getting your big feet wet. You know darn well Jack Johnson is one of the best captains on the Ohio."

"I ain't so sure about that—everybody on the river knows he's a drunkard."

"Drunk or sober, he'll get us to St. Louie safe and sound, for a lot less money than them railroads."

Josh thrust out his prominent chin in defiance. "It's against my Christian judgment to depend on that heathen. I reckon we're stuck with him, seeing as how you done made all the commitments for this unholy venture—without consulting me."

"That's not so, and you know it, Josh. We been over this a half dozen times. You agreed to go to St Louis by riverboat. Just relax; a little wait won't hurt you none. I'm going to see to my stock and eat the lunch I packed. Any of you want to join me? I brought plenty."

"We don't need nothing from you," Josh grumbled. "Mary has fixings for us and Moses."

Zeke went back to his wagon. Mary removed the food basket from under the seat and handed out thick ham sandwiches and hardboiled eggs. She had given Moses his before they left the farm.

When they had finished the meal, there was still no word from the boat. Pa became fidgety. Will noticed Pa's thick neck turning red and his jaws tightening. He slipped out the back of the wagon and sidled up to where Uncle Zeke was pacing on the grass. A tinge of guilt touched his conscience. Unsuspecting Mary was left alone with the girls to deal with Pa's wrath that he knew would soon erupt.

Preoccupied, Zeke nodded at his nephew and continued pacing. Will fell in beside him and stretched his legs to match Zeke's bigger stride.

"Uncle Zeke, that little boat don't look much safer than the raft Skeeter and me built, what nearly drowned us when it broke up. Do you think there's room enough for all our wagons and stock? Where we gonna sleep?"

"Oh, ye of little faith. You're as bad as your Pa," Zeke said, throwing up his hands in a defensive gesture without slacking his pacing. "The *Nellebelle* don't look so pretty, but she's river-worthy. Why, she's a veteran of the war, just like your Pa and me. Now what else was you jawin' about?"

"Wel-l-l, I was wondering how we'd get everything aboard and where we'd sleep?"

"There'll be room that we won't even use. See the corrals on her stern? That's for the livestock. We'll tie up the wagon tongues so's we can bunch the three of 'em close together, probably forward of the deckhouse. As for sleeping, the womenfolk can use the wagons and us men can use the deck under 'em."

After a slight pause, Zeke stopped pacing and faced his nephew. A big grin creased his ruggedly handsome face.

"Don't worry none about missing your Saturday night bath. We'll tie a rope on you and pull you alone behind the boat 'til you're cleaner than a whistle."

"Well, can't say as how I was much worried 'bout my bath," Will said. He was pausing to ponder on a better response to his Uncle's joshing when they heard his Pa's angry voice, loud enough to carry over to the next county.

"Damnation, you stupid girl, can't you keep them screaming kids quiet? Ain't I got enough on my mind without having to put up with that infernal racket?"

Will guessed Pa stopped to take a breath, otherwise, Mary wouldn't have been able to shove in a response.

"*Mister Curtis*, these are good children. They're only uncomfortable and tired. You don't have leave to shout at them, or me, like-like *we were dumb animals*! You ever raise your voice to me again, I'll kick you right where it hurts."

She wasn't shouting, but her voice carried clearly to them, unintimidated and firm.

"Another thing, *don't you ever again* lay a hand on any part of my body, like you tried to do the other night. *That* wasn't part of the deal!"

There was no immediate response from Pa. Will envisioned him with a beet red face, puffed-out cheeks, and being dumbstruck that that slip of a girl had the audacity to stand up to his bullying.

"Good for you, Mary," he muttered, loud enough that Uncle Zeke heard him. Zeke grinned, nodded his head in agreement, and they exchanged quizzical looks.

"Nothing like overhearing people's domestic squabbles." Zeke sounded a little embarrassed. "But I'm thinking she's got the spunk to hold her own with that cantankerous old fart. Oops! Sorry, I shouldn't talk that way about your Pa."

"That's okay, Uncle Zeke. I know Pa's got some problems. Ma told me once that he wasn't always mad about everything. She said it was the war that done something bad to him."

Before Zeke could reply, they heard Pa's angry voice again.

"Well, ain't you the devil's helper? Get thee behind me, Satan! I'll not stay here and be talked to that way, by an immature girl," he roared. They could see that he was getting down from the wagon. His boot slipped on the damp grass and he nearly fell into the muddy road. Will snickered at the stocky man's flailing arms and ultimate ungainly recovery.

A fugitive smile also curled Zeke's mustache upward for a moment. "It ain't nice to wish ill for your Pa, Willie."

Once stable, Pa stomped down the slope toward the moored boat. Zeke took off trotting after him and spoke to Will over his shoulder.

"I'd best go keep him out of trouble or we'll lose our boat ride. You see if Mary needs any help. Try to make out like we didn't hear nothing."

When Will reached the family wagon, he found Mary calmly sitting on the seat, rocking the baby and comforting sobbing Jeanie. She greeted him with a bright smile, as though nothing unusual had happened.

"Well, there you are, Will. I was wondering where you'd gone off to."

He blushed and hesitated to speak because he hardly knew what to say.

"You probably heard your father and me talking," she volunteered. "I assure you, Will, our differences aren't any fault of yours. You can plan on me being around a long time to take care of all of you."

Will didn't understand why she'd make that kind of commitment, but God knew his little sisters needed some mothering.

"I-I believe you, Mary, and I'll be there to help you—all I can." His voice squeaked with emotion and almost broke.

"Bless you, Will. I know you mean that. I'm sure you and I will always be good friends. Now, why don't you come up here and tell Jeanie about the great adventure on which we're embarking."

He settled on the wagon seat beside her and she gave his leg a reassuring pat. The sincerity of her words, delivered with a warm smile, touched him, but he just couldn't bring himself to think of her as a replacement for his mother. Maybe she could be like an older sister to him—if it weren't for those strange groin sensations that seemed to happen every time she touched him. Darn, what's wrong with me? He thought.

CHAPTER 4

RIVERBOAT MAN

◆

Pa and Zeke returned in a few minutes. Pa sullenly climbed onto the wagon seat and Will scrambled to the back to make room.

"We can move on down and start loading now," Zeke said. "Will, if it's okay with your Pa, why don't you ride with Moses. He'll likely need some added pressure on the brake lever, going down this muddy slope."

Pa nodded slightly and Will lost no time scampering down and trotting to Moses's wagon.

There were still a few hours of daylight left when all was securely loaded. A deep baritone voice bellowed through a megaphone.

"Hoist in the gangway and cast off all lines."

The stern wheel churned muddy water as the stubby boat pushed away from the rickety dock. Three forlorn blasts of the steam whistle announced that the Curtis family had started on the first leg of a long journey to a new home in the raw Kansas heartland.

Will had seen many riverboats plying the upper reaches of the Ohio, but had never been aboard one. Black smoke belching from the tall smokestack and clanging sounds emanating from the engineering space stimulated his youthful sense of adventure and curiosity. He fantasized about being in control of the bulky vessel, making it go where he commanded. How was that accomplished?

As though Uncle Zeke read his mind, he invited Will to accompany him to the pilothouse where they met Captain Jack Johnson, owner and skipper of the *Nellebelle*. When they entered the surprisingly small pilothouse, three decks up, the captain stood with his big hands firmly gripping the spokes of the helm wheel, personally steering the boat. Captain Jack scrutinized them with hooded blue eyes from under a crumpled billed cap, jauntily cocked over his bushy right eyebrow. Only the man's weather-lined cheekbones and a sliver of forehead were visible between his graying beard, eyebrows, and a shaggy mane of kinky hair. The sturdy, middle-aged man acknowledged Zeke and his young companion with a nod and the warm grin of a friend. He spoke in a husky baritone voice that seemed to fit his nautical appearance.

"Hey, you broken down ol' horse soldier, did you get all your kit and tucker settled in on deck? I stayed out of sight so's not to rile that brother of yourn."

"Yeah, you pirate, we got it all lashed down, best we can on this rotten ol' tub." Zeke chuckled.

"Well, you never bad-mouthed the *Nellebelle* when I was carting your motley cavalry outfit down to Kentucky in 1861," Captain Jack said, feigning indignation.

"Now that you brought up that little trip—I ain't never forgive you for dumping me off down there at Pittsburgh Landing. Them rebs started shooting at me before sundown and didn't quit for two days. Could have got my tail shot off."

"I'm sure sorry, Zeke, but it weren't my fault. That little trip caused me a few problems too, you know."

"Yeah, I know," Zeke replied, turning serious.

"Well, what the heck, Zeke, them days is long gone. Now you're heading to be a sodbuster in Kansas, and I may beach ol' *Nellebelle* and move ashore after this trip. Who's this young buck you got with you?"

"That's why we come up here, wanted you to meet my nephew, Will Curtis. Will, this here's the notorious river pirate, Cap'n Jack Johnson."

Keeping one hand on the helm, Captain Jack took Will's hand in his big, calloused paw and shook it vigorously. Will's slim hand was stronger than it looked, but it took all his willpower not to wince. Surely the stout man hadn't intended to hurt him, he probably just didn't know his own strength.

"Pleased to meet you, Will. You're a good looking boy for having such an ugly ol' sidewinder for an uncle. I won't hold that against you 'cause a man can't pick his relatives."

"Pleased to meet you, sir," Will replied.

"I know your Pa, too. Heard he was a tough soldier during the war, and he's a good preacher—for them what needs some preaching," Jack volunteered.

It sounded sincere enough, yet Will judged the Captain didn't hold his Pa in the same high regard as he did his Uncle Zeke. But then most people didn't. Will couldn't think of an appropriate reply, so he just nodded.

"This your first time on a riverboat, Will?" Jack asked, breaking the awkward silence.

"Yes, sir. Me and my friend Skeeter been on the river though. Built a raft once, and floated it downriver a ways," Will answered. "I'm sure interested in learning all I can about steam boating though."

"You're one up on me there; rafting is something I ain't never done," Captain Jack said, nodding his head in recognition of that feat, and then he flashed a broad smile at Will.

"Seeing as how you could handle a raft on this wild river, I'll bet you could steer tame ol' *Nellebelle*."

Will's eyes bugged wide. "Gosh, sir, I-I don't know 'bout that. To tell the truth, I didn't do very good with the raft. After about twenty miles, she began to breakup and we had to beach her."

Will recalled his dear mother being worried sick and his having received a terrible whipping from his Pa for that little adventure. He'd been ordered by Pa to never again associate with that heathen, Skeeter, which wasn't fair because the raft had been Will's idea.

"Had the same problem with boats a few times myself," the smiling captain admitted. "But handling this ol' river's a lot like riding horses; you get dumped in the river, you just right the boat and get back in again. Come over here and take the wheel, boy, and we'll try you out as a helmsman."

That astounding offer hit Will with such force—he was both stunned and scared stiff. Surely, Captain Jack wasn't serious? He's just pulling my leg, Will reasoned, looking to his smiling uncle for guidance.

"Just as well give her a try, boy," Zeke said with a nod toward the helm wheel. "You ain't gonna get no better chance to run this ol' tub of Cap'n Jack's aground."

Uncle Zeke's left-handed reassurance gave Will enough courage to move hesitantly closer to the big helm wheel. He stood beside the burly Captain with trembling legs and his heart pumping a mile a minute.

"Take the wheel with both hands. Put them here and here, and grip her firm, so's you'll be in control," Jack instructed, in a calming voice.

Forcing his rubber legs to function, Will moved in front of the helm and grasped the designated wheel spokes. His thin fingers barely reached around them. Captain Jack removed his hands. Will nearly panicked when pressure from the river's current pushed against the rudder and passed through the helm to his hands.

His fists gripped so hard that his knuckles turned white and he stood as straight and tense as a wooden Indian, afraid to blink or breathe. It was cool in the pilothouse, but sweat trickled from under the brim of his tattered straw hat and his armpits. As Uncle Zeke was prone to say, "The pucker string on his butt was drawn tight!"

"Now, Will," the Captain continued, in a soothing tone, "line the pole on the bow up with that there big tree sticking out over the river. It's on the right bank—'bout half-mile downriver—you make it out?"

Will nodded, too petrified to speak.

"Good. Do you think you can steer right to it? 'Til I say otherwise."

"Ya-ya-yes, sir-r-r," Will stammered, embarrassed by his squeaking voice. He had to stand on tiptoes for an unobstructed view over the big helm.

Locking unblinking eyes on the target, mind and body were frozen in that uncomfortable position. Soon, the relentless current pushed the bow slightly to the starboard.

With trepidation, bordering on alarm, Will cautiously turned the wheel clockwise. When the bow-pole moved farther to the right of his target tree, panic gripped his throat, moved rapidly down to become a hard knot in his gut, and then strained his bladder. Quickly, he overcompensated counterclockwise and the bow moved to the left of his target. Lord, his mind pleaded, please don't let me piss my pants.

Captain Jack placed a gentle hand on Will's slim shoulder.

"You're doing just fine, Will." His natural booming voice was modulated and reassuring. "But you're working too abrupt. Takes awhile to get the feel, but she knows you're in charge—just nudge her gently, and she'll be proud to go where you steer her."

With that calming encouragement, Will succeeded in getting the big boat—it seemed much bigger now that he was steering it—lined up with the target tree again. Soon he felt secure enough to loosen his grip slightly, a great relief because his hands sweated and ached something fearful. A deep sigh relieved some of the pressure on his bladder. The muscles in his arms and shoulders were taut as fiddle strings, but excitement diminished that minor discomfort.

Will chanced a quick look at the deck below. Mary was pointing up at the pilothouse showing little Jeanie the great thing her big brother was doing. They both waved. Afraid to loosen his grip on the helm, the proud youngster acknowledge them with a nod and a smile. Only one thing would make this glorious moment better: having his doting mother there to see him control the mighty riverboat.

God, he felt good! Expanding his bony chest with pride, he glanced toward Uncle Zeke, who returned an empathetic smile, a wink, and a nod of approval. Were Zeke's eyes misty? Perhaps wind blowing into the open pilothouse window caused them to water?

"Your doing great, Will, but there's a tricky turn coming up," Captain Jack said. "Best let me take over."

The captain grasped the helm and Will stepped back "Thank you, sir, for letting me steer," Will said. A simple thank you didn't seem adequate for such a grand adventure.

"You're welcome, son," Jack replied. "We'll give you other chances to steer ol' *Nellebelle* before this trip is over."

It didn't take the gregarious youngster long to make friends with most of the boat's five-man crew, but the crusty old engineer, Pete, was a challenge. He and the Negro boiler-stoker, Joe, held superior dominion over the mysterious machinery. It took Will two days to con his way into those hallowed spaces.

The run-in Pete and Pa had didn't make it any easier for Will to gain the gruff engineer's confidence. While the family was eating breakfast the first morning, and the crew was busy getting the boat underway, Pete's voice came to them loud and clear through the open boil room hatch.

"God damn your hide, Joe, get off your lazy ass and throw some wood in that boiler or we'll never get up enough steam to get this ol' tub back on the river."

Pa dropped his fork in mid-trip to his mouth, sprang to his feet, surprisingly fast for a man his size, and rushed to the open hatch.

"How dare you use the Lord's name in vain, you heathen," he shouted through the hatch, puffed up like a pregnant frog.

"Take your preaching somewhere it's wanted, you goddamned Bible thumper," came roaring back from inside.

"You're lucky I'm a man of God, or I'd come in there and give you a good thrashing," Pa threatened.

"You'll need God if you step inside that hatch, fat man, 'cause I'll lay you out with this wrench," Pete replied in a tone that convinced Will he meant what he said. He was disappointed that he didn't get to find out. Zeke intervened by grabbing Pa's arm in a viselike grip and spinning him around. Not an easy feat for a man that outweighed him by fifty pounds.

"Josh, I suggest you save the preaching for Sunday services," Zeke's voice was low but firm. "Best we don't rile up the crew none. This is their boat, and we got a long trip ahead."

"Hu-u-umph, hu-u-umph," Pa grunted, pulling his arm loose from Zeke's grip with some effort. After glaring at his brother for several seconds, he stalked to the stern of the boat, where he sulked until lunchtime.

On first encounter, the heat, smoke, cinders, and grease of Pete's world intimidated the farm boy, but insatiable curiosity soon overcame apprehension. Surveying the cramped, machinery-filled cubical with nervous eyes, he tried to make intelligent conversation with Pete.

"This-this machinery sure seems to be working good," was all he could think to say. Actually, he had no idea what all that huffing, banging, and rattling machinery was, or what made it work, yet he was eager to learn.

"Hell, it oughta be working good, 'cause we're going downstream," Pete yelled back at him, over the rumble of the rack-and-pinion gear, the panting boiler, and hissing steam. "Wait 'til we go up against the killer spring current of the Mississippi. It'll take all the piss and sweat we can ring outta her to make headway upstream on that powerful ol' river!"

After a few more visits, Pete condescended to let Will relieve Joe throwing wood into the boiler's firebox, filling the oil cups and wicks on the machinery, and operating the bilge pump. The eager boy had to hump his slim back to make the big bilge pump spew the gunk overboard that accumulated in the bottom of the boat.

When Will emerged from the machinery room, he wore grease smudges on his hands, face, and clothes as badges of pride, because they identified him as an adopted member of the exclusive fraternity of riverboat engineers.

Mary refused to wash the grease-smeared overalls and wouldn't let him eat with them on. She made him scrub them himself and sit around in his long johns while they dried; a hard side of her he hadn't seen before. That was something his coddling mother wouldn't have done.

Just because Mary made his groin ache sometimes, it didn't give her the right to be so high and mighty. Obviously, she didn't realize what an important man he was aboard that boat, what with him being both a helmsman and an engineer.

CHAPTER 5

WAR STORIES
◆

While Uncle Zeke expressed concern about getting a crop in on their new land this spring, *Nellebelle's* slow progress down the Ohio at steerage speed of about ten miles per hour didn't bother Will. He was in no hurry to get to Kansas. Life on the river became a pleasant routine for the active youngster. He found new and exciting things, either on the boat or watching the passing scenery. Each day when the daylight began to fade, the captain found a safe place to tie up for the evening. If they were in an uninhabited area, Will explored along the bank and helped the crew gather firewood for cooking and the hungry boiler.

Will was thankful that after his altercation with Pete, Pa kept mostly to himself, brooding and reading his dog-eared Bible. Mary had her hands full caring for the girls and the family domestic chores. Will enjoyed her company, but he told himself that he'd have helped her with the heavy work anyway.

Uncle Zeke swapped stories and shared a few drinks with his old friend Captain Jack, when he wasn't busy repairing equipment and caring for the livestock. Often, they allowed Will to sit in on their bull sessions, something of a revelation for the naive boy.

One moonlit evening, while tied up on the Ohio side of the river, Captain Jack and Uncle Zeke leisurely passed Jack's jar of moonshine between them while swapping stories about unusual experiences during the war. Will listened intently. One of his greatest desires was to hear about his uncle's many adventures, especially as a cavalryman during the Civil War. Everyone said Zeke was a war hero, that he had been awarded the Congressional Medal of Honor, whatever that was. He knew little else about his uncle's war experiences because Zeke wasn't much for talking about himself.

The conversation lagged some before Zeke recaptured their attention with an embellished story about Colonel Ambrose McNeal, the commanding officer of his cavalry regiment during the war, and now governor of West Virginia.

"Jack, you recall that old windbag Ambrose McNeal was always looking to help himself politically during the war?" Zeke asked.

"Yeah, I recall how he liked to toot his own horn," Jack replied. "He was damn near as bad about looking for publicity as that young whippersnapper General Custer. Say, come to think of it, didn't Will's Pa ride with Custer when he commanded the Third Michigan Cavalry?"

"He sure did," Zeke confirmed. "And Custer was always looking for a fight. Josh's one of the few that rode with that blood-and-guts bastard and survived the war.

"But this here story is about ol' Ambrose McNeal. He'd crap his pants if he knew I was telling it on him, an' it probably wouldn't help the ol' guy's political image none if it got out."

"You're among friends here, Zeke. Let's hear the story," Jack urged.

"Well," Zeke snickered and began, "we was bivouacked near the Stones River in Tennessee, couple nights before the big fight down there. It was near midnight when some reb cavalry rode into our camp, likely trying to run off our horses. Them rebs was right on us, whooping, hollering, and shooting 'fore we got wind of 'em.

"Ol' Ambrose come tumbling out of his tent, hobbling around while stomping on his boots—you'll recall he was overweight, even then. Finally got them boots on, strapped on his pistol and saber belt, and slammed his hat on his head. Only other thing he had on were his red, long john underwear.

"Mounting one of the sentries' horses, he circled around in the camp a couple of times, hollering, 'Follow me, men,' then he rode off into the night, not knowing where he was headed or if anyone else was mounted up to follow him. He had a way of going kind of crazy when excited.

"Well, me being on duty as a dispatch rider, I was sleeping with my clothes and boots on. Had my horse saddled and tied next to my tent. I mounted up and took off after him, figuring I'd best round him up 'fore he hurt himself.

"Weren't hard to follow that red underwear. Before I could catch up, he led me smack-dab into a reb camp. We'd been scouting for the reb army for two days, but that was a damn dangerous way to find 'em.

"Guess a guy wearing red underwear, come riding through their camp, surprised them rebs some. They didn't fire a shot 'til we was riding hell-bent-for-leather back towards our camp. Be darned, if I didn't hear some of 'em laughing their fool heads off."

Zeke and Jack laughed so hard tears rolled down their cheeks. Will's lively imagination pictured a fat colonel charging through the night, wearing red underwear, but he didn't think it was all *that* funny. Of course, he didn't have any of the moonshine in his belly.

When their boisterous laughter subsided, Jack passed the moonshine jar to Zeke.

"Here, Zeke, you got to be darn dry after telling that long story. Best wet your whistle."

Will was aware his Pa had been in a lot of battles during the war, but it was news to him that he'd ridden with the famous General Custer. While he was curious to learn more about that, what was said next most excited his curiosity.

"Zeke, weren't it down there on the Stones River where you saved ol' Ambrose's life?"

"By God, Jack, you know that's something I don't talk about!"

"Can't see why the hell not to talk about it?" tipsy Jack blurted. "Way I heard it, you was a real hero. I'd think Ambrose should have shown his appreciation by at least giving you some soft state job when he got to be the governor."

"What the hell makes you think he didn't try buying me off?" Zeke snapped while abruptly pushing to his feet.

"I ain't no damn hero," he continued, glaring down at his well-meaning friend. "I sure don't need no charity from Ambrose McNeal, *or anyone else*! Don't want to talk about that war no more. I'm going to bed."

With that, he turned on his heels and stomped down the deck toward the wagons. His two companions stared after him, slack-jawed. Captain Jack shrugged his massive shoulders and broke the embarrassing silence.

"Didn't aim to get him all riled up, but I'll tell you one thing for sure, your Uncle Zeke has the reputation of being one helluva horse soldier. They don't give out them Congressional Medals of Honor for nothing. Must of been something happened between him and ol' Ambrose that still sticks in Zeke's craw." The large man grunted to his feet and stamped feeling into his legs. "Guess I'll go get some sleep. We'll be shoving off, come first light. You'd best hit the hay too, Will."

Jack wobbled down the deck toward his quarters. Will watched his receding back without replying, but remained sitting on the deck, deep in thought. A few minutes later he nodded and muttered to himself, "I'm sure what Captain Jack said has something to do with how Uncle Zeke earned that medal of honor. I want to hear that story some day. I just got to catch him in the right mood."

CHAPTER 6

NATTY

◆

At first, Will resisted Mary's attempt to apply her teaching skills on him. He considered it okay for Jeanie. She was only six and hadn't been to school, but his mother had made sure he could read and write and do basic arithmetic. What more did a farm boy need to know? However, Mary had a way of presenting things that captured his interest, in spite of his reluctance.

Maps in her geography book especially interested him. One evening they sat close together on stools made from firewood, tracing the route for their journey down the Ohio.

"Cin-cin-nat-ee," Will read, pointing at a large dot on the Ohio side of the river. "I'll bet that name came from some Indian tribe."

"Well, a lot of people think that, but actually it was named by the first northwest territorial governor, after the name of a society that a group of Revolutionary War officers formed," Mary replied, sounding slightly smug.

That bit of information wasn't of much interest to Will, but her extensive knowledge impressed him.

"How do you know about so many things?"

"I read about them. You could learn things like that, too, if you'd get interested in reading books."

"I guess it's nice to know all that stuff, but what's it good for? I'd just as soon learn something useful."

"You've got a good point there, smarty pants. That sounds just like your Uncle Zeke talking," she responded with a chuckle, gently patting his cheek and then playfully ruffling his hair. Her leg pressed against his and one of her firm breasts brushed his arm.

Will felt a tingle in his groin area, ducked his head, and blushed. Self-conscious about the resulting sexual arousal, he crossed his legs and changed the subject.

"Boy, I'd sure like to spend some time in Cincinnati. It looks like a big city on the map."

"It is the largest city on the Ohio River," Mary confirmed. "You may get your wish. I overheard Captain Jack telling Zeke we'll be at Cincinnati early tomorrow morning and he intends to take on firewood. Zeke said he was going to ask for a stopover anyway because he had some business to take care of around there."

When Pa heard about the intended delay, he wasn't pleased.

"Zeke, you best forget about visiting one of them houses for soiled doves in Cincinnati," Will heard him declare.

"That's easy enough for you, seeing as how you've got a young wife. You just stick to your business, Josh, and I'll take care of mine," Zeke replied and walked away from his sputtering brother.

Will was uncertain about what "a house for soiled doves" was, but he suspected it had something to do with women. He knew his uncle liked women because he was always polite to them, and most of them seemed to like him.

That evening Captain Jack promised he would show Mary, Jeanie, and Will around the big city after he finished arranging for the wood. To everyone's amazement, Pa agreed he'd stay on board with baby Anne. Moses said he'd be staying aboard too because he had no desire to see all those people.

Thrilled with anticipation, Will hardly slept that night. At first light, he rushed to the bow and sat on the anchor chain locker. In about an hour, a panoramic view of the Cincinnati waterfront appeared. Boats of all manner and size seemed to be going every which away on the broad river. Captain Jack skillfully maneuvered their boat through the traffic, and nudged her into the woodlot dock.

Uncle Zeke had saddled his horse, and as soon as the gangway connected with the dock, he rode off alone, telling no one where he was going. It wasn't like Zeke to be so secretive. Will suspected he might really be headed to one of those houses for soiled doves.

After arranging for the fuel, the captain gathered Mary, Jeanie, and Will for the trip to Cincinnati's business district. Just beyond the warehouses and railroad tracks, Will was in for the first of many surprises. They boarded what Captain Jack called a streetcar—an enclosed, horse-drawn carriage with windows and a row of seats on each side of an aisle, wide enough to allow people to get in and out of the seats. Most amazing, it ran on two steel rail tracks that were embedded in the brick-paved street.

Captain Jack seemed to nearly burst with pride, showing the wide-eyed young people many wondrous sights along the way uptown. They got off the streetcar and walked for a few blocks. Jack pointed out displays in shop windows until they reached a two-story building that covered half a block—the biggest building Will had ever seen, or imagined. A huge sign over the corner entrance read "Ohio Mercantile Emporium."

Their enthusiastic guide led them through the swinging double doors, looking as proud as if he owned the place. Stopping just inside, they stood for several seconds, mesmerized by aisles crammed with all manner of merchandise.

"Holy cow, this store must have everything in the whole world in it," Will exclaimed.

"Sure looks like it," Mary agreed.

They walked through the aisles on both floors, bumping into other shoppers and ogling the cornucopia of merchandise. On the second time around the circuit, Mary stopped in the fabric and sewing materials section, where Captain Jack excused himself saying he'd meet them later at the main store entrance.

"Bet he's going to one of them saloons for a drink," Will speculated to Mary.

"Well, he seems a civil man. I don't think a drink or two will hurt him any," Mary replied.

Before they left the boat, Pa gave Mary some money to buy dress material for her and the girls, but had forbid her to buy ready-made clothes because they were too expensive. After purchasing enough material to make everyday dresses for her and the girls and shirts for the men, she took Will and Jeanie to the ready-made department. Mary confided to Will she had money of her own and intended to use some of it to buy them things that probably would be hard to obtain once they were on the Kansas frontier.

They selected a frilly, pink dress for Jeanie, her first ready-made dress. Jeanie pleaded with Mary to leave it on. Even though she knew there would be a ruckus when Pa saw it, Mary couldn't refuse the excited little girl's request.

Mary selected a blue dress for Anne, big enough to last her until she was at least three. Finally, she decided to find something for herself. After considerable indecision, she settled on a soft yellow, simply styled party dress, with a fitted bodice. The style accentuated her trim figure and the color complimented her shoulder length auburn hair, and dark eyes.

"G-g-gosh, Mary you're beautiful!" Will uttered when she came out of the dressing room to model the dress.

She flung her arms around him, planted a big kiss on his cheek that brushed his lips, and twittered like a delighted schoolgirl. Will's face turned crimson. Three or four city men stood nearby staring at Mary with unabashed admiration. He couldn't' blame them because she surely was a beauty. For the umpteenth time, he wondered how such an attractive young woman got tangled up with a crotchety old man like his pa.

"Thank you. Thank you for the compliment. It's special coming from such a handsome young man. I think I'll just leave the dress on until we get back to the boat. Heaven knows when I'll have another chance to wear it."

They moved on to the men's and boys' clothing department where Mary bought five identical pairs of suspenders with wide, red straps.

"Who you buying all them 'spenders for?" Will asked.

"Why, they're for the men in my life—your pa, Zeke, Moses, Captain Jack, and a pair for you too, Will."

"Gosh, Mary, that's nice of you, but I'm not sure they'll wear 'em." He didn't want to hurt her feelings, but thought she ought to know. "I ain't even got any waist high pants."

"I think they look good on men, especially ones with big bellies. You don't have that problem yet, do you Will?"

She grinned and playfully patted his flat stomach, and then lightly swatted his skinny rear.

"Or they even help young men hold up their pants who don't have much of a butt yet."

Will blushed and glanced around to check if anyone had seen that lighthearted display of familiarity. Mary laughed loudly, apparently enjoying his adolescent embarrassment.

"You'll see; they'll all be wearing them by the time we leave the boat. As for you, my little buddy, we're going to buy you a new pair of pants right now. Then you can wear your new suspenders."

She was obviously enjoying herself and Jeanie was in a giggly mood with her. This was a different side of Mary, and he wasn't sure how to take her being silly out in public like this. Pa would have a conniption fit if he'd witnessed her behavior. What the heck, Mary deserved a little relaxation and fun, he decided. God knew she'd only experienced hard work and confrontation since becoming part of the Curtis family.

Before they left the men's department, Mary bought Will the promised pair of city-dude pants and a new pair of heavy pull-on work boots, both items a size too big so he'd have room to grow into them.

On their way to the front entrance, they passed through the book department, and Mary was drawn to the many publications on the shelves.

"I hope you'll grow to love books as much as I do, Will," she said. "You can travel all over the world and live many adventures by just reading books. Let's buy us some new ones. God only knows when we'll have a chance to be in a bookstore again. You pick out one, I'll pick out one, and we'll select a new reader for Jeanie, one that's got some pictures."

Will settled on a book titled *Gulliver's Travels* because he was interested in traveling. Mary chose a thick volume of the selected works of some Englishman named Shakespeare. She told him they were classic stories that she hoped he'd someday enjoy reading. He was more interested in Jeanie's new illustrated reader.

Captain Jack gave the girls sincere compliments on their new dresses when they met at the entrance. Maybe it was because he enjoyed the company of pretty women that he insisted on taking them to a restaurant for lunch. It would be a first time experience for Jeanie and Will. Mary confessed it was only the third time she had eaten in a restaurant. When they boarded the streetcar for the return trip to the riverfront, Will was a very happy young man, with a full belly.

The captain shared a double seat with Will and after they were settled, he fumbled in his peacoat pocket and came out with a small package. He handed it to Will with a big grin on his bushy face.

"Here's a little something for all the hard work you've been doing on the *Nellebelle*. It's from all the crew. Even Pete chipped in," he said. "Just wanted you to know we appreciate your help."

Will hadn't received many presents in his young life. His eager fingers trembled as he fumbled with the tight box lid. When he succeeded in getting it open, he found the finest pocketknife he'd ever seen, with two cutting blades and a leather punch. His eyes misted and he bit his lower lip to keep from blubbering. Darn, he thought, why are people always doing things for me that make me want to cry?

"Th-thank you, sir. It's the best knife I ever saw and I ain't never owned one before. But-but you sure didn't owe me nothing. Tell you the truth, what I been doing has been fun," he felt compelled to confess.

"If you say so, Will, but we still want you to know you've been a big help on this trip. Anyways, you'll have something to remember the ol' *Nellebelle* by."

"Boy, I'll never forget this trip. I'll keep this great knife forever. I sure do thank you, sir, for the knife and-and—*everything*," his voice trailed off into a near sob.

"That's okay, Will. It's been a pleasure to meet my good friend Zeke's nephew. You just grow up to be half the man your uncle is, and you'll be all right."

The burly riverboat captain patted Will on the knee, and turned to look out the window. Will glanced across the aisle and saw a warm smile on Mary's pretty face before she too turned toward the window. The cuff of his old coat brushed away the tear or two that had escaped to trickle down his cheeks.

When the tired but happy group returned to the boat, Uncle Zeke met them with a smug grin on his tanned face.

"Come on back to the corrals," he said to Will. "Got something I want to show you."

They moved aft while the crew cast off the mooring lines. Pa followed along, even though he wasn't invited. He'd been taking a nap when Zeke had arrived back aboard earlier. When they reached the corral, Zeke pointed to a sleek sorrel mare and a shaggy, long-legged, buckskin male colt munching hay in a partitioned-off section.

"Whata you guys think of that pair?" Zeke asked, with considerable pride.

"The mare's good looking horse flesh," Pa admitted civilly. "By chance did you buy her from Westerbrook? Looks like his line."

"Sure did," Zeke replied. "Wrote and told him to cut me out a good brood mare so's I could pick her up on the way down river."

"What good's a high-bred and temperamental racehorse mare gonna be to you on a Kansas farm?" Pa asked, dripping sarcasm.

"Plan on raising me some good saddle stock in Kansas. Mendy's gonna start the Zeke Curtis Line," Zeke replied, unruffled.

"Hu-u-umph," Pa responded. "Why'd you waste your money on bringing along that spindly colt? He's past old enough to be weaned."

"Coulda left the colt, but didn't want to break 'em up. I saw his sire. With his beautiful ma, and such a grand papa, this guy's gonna be one mighty fine horse." He turned to Will. "What do you think about that frisky little fellow, Will?"

"Why, I think that's the best looking colt I've ever seen, Uncle Zeke! Does he have a name?"

"It's going to be up to you to name him—*because he's yours!*" Zeke's eyes twinkled and the toothy smile turning his mustache upward at the corners. "All I ask is that you loan him to me for breeding mares sometimes when he grows up."

Will stared at the colt and then at Zeke, spellbound and tongue-tied. Pa butted in.

"He can't have it! I'll see that he gets a good horse when I figure he's responsible enough to take care of one."

Pa turned to walk away. Zeke clamped a restraining hand on his arm.

"Just one damn minute, Josh, 'til I've had my say. It sure ain't my intention to come between a boy and his father, but you'd best know, I intend to give that buckskin colt *to my nephew!*"

Pa's normally ruddy complexion darkened a shade.

"You keep forgetting Will's *my son*, Zeke," Pa growled like an enraged bear. "I'm saying he ain't grown up enough to take proper care of his own horse. That spindly colt will never be worth a bucket of spit anyway."

"You don't know a damn thing about horses, if you can't see the potential in that colt. And you don't know a damn thing about Will, if you can't see he's well on the way to growing into a better man than either of us."

Zeke held heated eye contact with the younger, but bigger, man. Pa's eyes blazed and his breath came fast through flared nostrils, but he was first to blink.

"Well, damnation, Zeke. You've been jealous of me ever since Marge chose me over you," Pa shouted, his voice cracking with anger. "Go ahead, be the big man, and give her boy the horse, but that ain't going to make up for running out on her when she needed you!"

"You ain't got no call to bring Marge into this discussion, after all these years."

Zeke spoke in a curt manner.

"Hu-u-u-mph," Pa grunted. "Have it your own way, Zeke. You always did because you're the oldest—except when it counted with Marge—I won her!" He turned and walked forward toward the wagons.

Zeke watched his angry brother's back for a moment before turning his attention to his visibly shaken nephew.

"Sorry 'bout that, Will. I don't want to go against your Pa, but I intend you to have that buckskin. When I first laid eyes on that perky little critter, I felt it in my bones; he's just the horse for you. The two of you are on the spindly side now, but you've both got the makings of something special."

A jumble of emotions surged trough Will. What was that about his Ma? There was something between Pa and Zeke he'd not witnessed before. He'd always had a good rapport with his uncle, yet Zeke never talked to him before with such affection. Was the wonderful colt going to cause an irreconcilable riff between the two brothers?

"Gar-osh, Uncle Zeke, he-he's just beautiful. I never figured to have a horse like him. I hope you and Pa can patch things up. He's sure got enough troubles without getting any more from us."

"You're right," his uncle answered, putting an arm gently around the perceptive youngster's shoulders and giving him a squeeze, something else he'd never done before.

"I'll make my peace with him. We've had worse tangles than this one, and we're still blood kin. Now, let's take a closer look at that horse of yours. Got any ideas for a name?"

Will wrinkled his forehead and squinted at the colt for a moment before replying.

"Yeah, I'm thinking Cincy, after Cincinnati. What do you think?"

"Guess that'd be a different kind of name, but folks might get it mixed up with Cindy, and think he's a girl horse." Zeke pulled at his earlobe, a habit of his when pondering on something. Will often copied that gesture.

"How does Natty grab you, Will? Has to do with Cincinnati, and says how sharp he looks at the same time. That's still kind of a sissy name for a stud horse, but I think he'll grow big and strong enough that no one will dare snicker at his moniker."

"That sure fits him," Will agreed. "He's one darn neat horse and he's from Cincinnati. That's it, we'll name him Natty. Yeah, that sounds good, Nat-e-e-e!" It rolled off his tongue in a special loving way.

Uncle and nephew leaned on the top corral rail, admiring the sleek sorrel mare and her beautiful buckskin foul. "Nat-e-e-e," Will said again. The buckskin colt picked up his ears, whinnied, and stared back with big brown, intelligent eyes.

CHAPTER 7

SUSPENDERS

◆

Mary presented Captain Jack with the pair of red suspenders she'd bought for him while the other men were looking at the horses.

"Thanks for the wonderful day," Mary exclaimed, standing on her tiptoes and planting a peck on his whiskered cheek. "These are just a little gift to show my appreciation."

The bear of a man gave her a hug that pulled her off her feet and squeezed the air out of her lungs. Dropping her back down, he removed his coat and put on the bright red suspenders—right there on deck.

Crusty engineer Pete observed the friendly exchange from the open engine room door. "You look like the pian-e-e player in a Cincinnati whorehouse," he scoffed to the proud captain.

"You're just jealous because this sweet little gal didn't give you any 'spenders," Jack countered.

Pete snorted in reply and ducked back into his machinery-filled sanctuary.

Mary waited until the evening meal was finished before presenting the men in her family with their suspenders.

Pa responded with his usual nervous "hu-u-u-mph," deeper than usual, sounding like he was hawking a big goober. "You shouldn't of wasted your money on these foolish things. Since it's too late to take 'em back, I'll keep 'em to wear with my preacher pants," he grumbled after several seconds of embarrassing silence.

That's a darn weak thank you if I ever heard one, Will thought. But it didn't seem to bother smiling Mary.

Zeke showed sincere surprise and pleasure when she handed him a pair. He embraced Mary with a hug that made her grunt, while planting a big audible kiss on her flushed cheek.

"By gosh, Mary," Zeke said, "these darn things are beautiful. Always wanted a pair of flashy 'spenders, but been too darn tight to buy 'em. Thank you, thank you kindly, little princess!"

She giggled like a schoolgirl and gave Zeke a return hug, provoking another "hu-u-u-mph" from Pa.

Mary insisted that Will put on his new clothes and show them off to everyone. He reluctantly retired to the family wagon. It took a while to hook the suspenders to the buttons on the stiff new pants. When he finally succeeded and pulled them on, it was obvious the pants were way too big. Self-conscious, he delayed leaving the protection of the wagon cover.

"I'm coming in there after you, Will, if you don't come on out and show us," Mary threatened.

Darn that gal. She's just saucy enough to do it, Will lamented. I best go out and face them. Ain't no way she's going to let me off the hook. He mustered his courage, parted the canvas flaps, and reluctantly stepped down into the lantern light. His checks reddened when he noticed most of the boat crew had also gathered around to see the fashion show. They had become kind of like extended family.

With a mischievous smile, Mary turned him around for a thorough inspection. He felt like a pig in baggy pants roasting on a spit.

"Don't worry about the pants being too long, Will, there's plenty of room for adjustments on the suspenders," she cheerfully stated, while commencing to shorten them.

Before she was satisfied, the waistband was nearly to his armpits. He could have lived with that ungainly inconvenience if the crotch hadn't pinched his private parts in front and tucked into the crack of his skinny butt in the rear.

"Ha, ha, ha," Zeke roared when Mary stepped back to observe her alterations. "By gosh, Will, you ain't got no waist but you sure got a cute butt, har, har, har." He slapped his leg and doubled over laughing.

Some of the others in the attentive audience laughed with Zeke, others snickered, Pa scowled at the nonsense, and Mary covered her mouth with her hand. Her shoulders shook. Laughter induced tears rolled down Zeke's cheeks.

"Mary, Mary," he scoffed. "Quick—slack off on them 'spenders some, you're about to geld him! Haw, haw, haw."

Mary stomped her foot, feigning furry at Zeke's hurrahing, but Will could tell she was about to bust a gut trying to keep from laughing herself.

"Now Zeke, you know he'll soon grow into those pants," she managed to utter. "Anyway, he looks very handsome to me. Best you quit joshing him before he gets down on himself."

Zeke threw up both hands and answered through fits of mirth.

"Whoa there, miz mama-hen, I don't mean the boy no harm. I love him, even if he does look like a stork that's wearing red spenders. Haw, haw, haw."

When things quieted down, Mary took the last pair of suspenders from the paper sack and handed them to Moses, who smiled, but hadn't joined in with the joshing of his young friend.

"Here, these are for you, Moses," she said, and in her enthusiasm, she gave him a quick hug.

The slight black man, dressed in a patched shirt, baggy overalls, and boots run-over at the heels, visibly stiffened his body. Mary seemed disappointed at his reserved response to her spontaneous and lighthearted display of affection. Will understood the problem. Moses had told him about seeing black men lynched for lesser offenses.

"I—I's thanks ya most kindly for the fine 'spenders, Miz Ma-Mary," he managed to stammer. "They beautiful. But-but, I ain't got no pants to wear 'em with."

Will felt sadness for both Mary and his friend and mentor, Moses. Darn it, I know she meant well. Who could blame a girl like Mary, apparently raised in an Ohio city, for not knowing the problem of a white girl hugging a black man? Or that a pair of fancy suspenders would be useless to a man with Moses's meager wardrobe? Will felt bad that he'd let her down. He should have told her those facts before she got into this embarrassing situation. But then, she must have known by now that the rest of evangelistic preacher Josh Curtis's family had little more.

Mary blinked back tears and seemed at a loss for words. A strained, awkward silence hung over the previously jolly group until Zeke spoke.

"Hey, Moses, we can fix that little problem darn quick. I got a pair of pants I seldom wear that'll fit you with a little shortening. They've got 'spenders buttons on 'em, too. You're welcome to 'em," he offered cheerfully.

Will was so pleased with his thoughtful uncle that he immediately forgave him for the hurrahing about his crotch-pinching pants.

"I'd be happy to shorten them for you, Moses," Mary quickly offered.

"Thank you, Miz Mary, an' I thanks you kindly too, Masta Zeke for the offer of them pants," Moses replied, a big smile replacing the pained expression. "I'm sure gonna be mighty proud to put 'em on with these here fine red 'spenders what Miz Mary done give me."

CHAPTER 8

MOSES

◆

The following day, Captain Jack put into Louisville. They tarried only long enough to load wood for the hungry boiler because the trip down the Ohio was taking longer than planned. Will overheard a conversation between his pa and uncle.

"We've been on th' river a week, and there's still a long ways to go," Pa complained. "This ol' boat you chartered is just too slow."

"I share your concern, Josh," Zeke agreed. "Cap'n Jack hasn't felt it's safe to travel on the river at night. Now that it's widened out considerable, maybe he'd agree to push on, at least on moonlit nights. I'll talk to 'im about it."

"You do that, Zeke," Pa demanded. "Tell that heathen we ain't going to pay him if he don't get us to St. Louis by March fifteenth."

"I'll talk to him all right, but I don't aim to threaten him. He's a good man and will do the best he can for us."

Will tagged along when Zeke broached the subject with Captain Jack

"I'll do it, weather permitting, but we'll have to feel our way along after dark. There's lots of things on this river that could snag ol' *Nellebelle*, or put her on a sandbar," the captain replied."

For the moonlight steaming, the deck lookouts were doubled and a leadsman was on duty to check water depth where sandbars or rapids made the channel hard to read. Will was pressed into service as a bow lookout from 8:00 PM to midnight.

"You can share the bow lookout duty with Will," Captain Jack suggested to Moses. "Two sets of eyes are better than one, and you can keep each other awake." Will welcomed Moses's company. It gave him and his old friend an opportunity to catch up on visiting.

"What you suppose it'll be like out there in that wild heartland?" Will asked Moses one evening.

"Probably different 'n we ever known before. But we gonna be just fine 'cause we is together." Moses always had a way of putting a positive slant on things. Just talking with him usually raised Will's spirits.

"Anyways," Moses continued, "you got a nice new ma to look out for you. She one fine lady and she likes you a lot."

"Yeah, she's okay, but she ain't that much older 'n me. Tell you for sure, she ain't never going to take the place of my real ma!"

"Well now, Masta Will, that be asking a lot. Ain't nobody in the whole world gonna be as nice as your ma was."

"The girls sure like Mary though, and she's good to them. I just can't figure out why she married grumpy ol' Pa?"

"Now you knows your Pa weren't always grumpy. Were that terrible war, what harmed him."

"Yeah, that's what Ma told me, but I can't help wishing he was more like Uncle Zeke. They're so different it's kind of hard to believe they're brothers."

"Masta Zeke a good man, right enough, and we lucky he going with us to Kansas. There was a time they was more like brothers. The war and other things I don't knows about done come between 'em. We best keep on praying it'll be set right."

"Moses, you knew Pa before he fought in all those Civil War battles. What was he like?"

Moses's watery eyes brightened for a moment, and then glazed over. It was several seconds before the pensive, old black man spoke.

"First I laid eyes on your Pa, he were a tall, handsome redheaded sergeant in the U.S. cavalry. It were right after the white folks commenced that Civil War. He were in charge of us slaves what was digging places for big guns to protect Washington City from them southern soldiers."

"I thought you grew up on a plantation down in Virginia," Will said. "How'd it happen that you were up in Washington when the war started?"

"That right," Moses confirmed. "I born and live on a plantation down near Richmond, Virginee, 'til I were 'bout the age your pa is now. But when I met your pa, I belonged to a farmer what lived in Maryland, near Washington City. He done hired his few slaves out to the Union Army for diggin.'"

In the moonlight, Will noticed Moses's broad brow wrinkle and his eyes take on the faraway look of a man remembering difficult times.

"I recollect hearing Pa talking about looking for your family. How'd you lose 'em?" Will blurted out thoughtlessly.

"That a kind of sad story. You sure you wants to hear it?" Moses's usually steady voice trembled slightly.

"Not if it's too hurtful for you, Moses."

"Well, you is my friend and gettin' old enough you should know what bad things people do sometimes," Moses answered with a shrug of his slender shoulders.

Will leaned closer, wanting to give his friend moral support, while being sure he didn't miss a word of the former slave's story. When he was younger, Will's mother had cautioned him not to ask Moses about his life as a slave or how he came to be with the family. He only knew that his pa had bought Moses and set him free.

"Like I told you, I grow up on a big Virginee plantation, down there near Richmond. I were a household worker. Old masta, Cornwall, an' his misses always good to us, but they had a spoiled-rotten son what give his folks and me a lot of grief."

Moses paused and sadly shook his fuzzy, cotton-topped head.

"Then when I was about thirty, I marry the prettiest, nicest gal on the plantation, praising the Lord for my good fortune." There was a disbelieving shake of the head before Moses's mind slowly returned to the story.

"She was Miz Cornwall's personal maid, an' ten years younger 'n me. If you saw her, it would be hard for you to believe a skinny house slave like me won her affection. She were very pretty, with lighter skin than most us black folks. People say old masta were her pappy. If that so, she be young masta's half sister."

It wasn't hard for Will to understand what the pretty, young woman would see in his congenial, loyal, and sensitive mentor.

"Soon God give us a strong boy child and two pretty little girls. Our life were good 'til old masta an' Miz Cornwall both dies, within a month of one another. The plantation and all us slaves then belong to that worthless son. He had become a drunkard and a gambler, and soon lose all his pappy leaved for 'im. When he sell off us slaves, made no mind to him if them slave traders break up families."

"Geez," Will said heatedly, "he sounds like a terrible man."

"Well-well, he were a bad man, but he weren't much different from most them slave owners down there in the old South." A catch constricted Moses's throat and he blinked back bitter tears. "We was just animals to 'em!"

"Di-did he break up you and your family, Moses?"

In two heartbeats, Moses's normally placid eyes flashed angrily, and Will read a frightening urge to kill in them. The practiced, deferential drawl disappeared and his language became brusque and more articulate. The severity and suddenness of the transformation caused a chill to run down Will's spine; in a moment, his placid friend was transformed into a black avenging angel!

"That miserable son-of-a-bitch done sold my wife and children without me included. A mean-looking rice plantation owner from South Carolina bought 'em. Said he don't want me 'cause he was gonna breed my lovely wife to a big black buck he already owned. Planning to raise strong field hands. If any of 'em were girls, he said, they'd likely be good looking, and fetch a lot as whores. Bragged about his inhuman plans—right there in front of me and all them uncaring white folks at that slave auction!"

Pent-up anger seemed to overwhelm Moses. He sat mute, trembling and panting like an enraged bull. Will wisely held his tongue. It seemed a long time before Moses spoke again—perhaps two or three strained minutes had passed.

"Told that bastard, young Cornwall, he was selling his own sister to become a brood mare. He hit me. I fought back, but two white trash held me 'til he beat me unconscious. When I come to, my family was gone! I was being carted off by a Maryland farmer. He'd bought what was left of me for a pittance, thinking I might not live."

Now Will was angry. "By God, I'd of hunted him down and killed 'im," Will shouted.

"Not if you were an injured slave—*white boy!*" Moses snapped. The venom in Moses's voice caused Will to shiver. At that moment, he was afraid of his friend Moses and ashamed to be white. A couple of more minutes passed before the volcano in Moses's soul seemed to subside. His countenance slowly reverted back into his ex-slave, subservient persona.

"I see your point, Moses," Will muttered. "Maybe some of them mean people got what they had coming when Pa, Uncle Zeke, and all them other Union soldiers won the war. I'm sure glad they freed all you slaves."

"Well," Moses replied, sounding more like his old self, "I was luckier than some. Your pa set me free at the start of the war, and done his best to help me find my family after the war was over."

"Care to tell me how that come about?" Will asked.

"Sure, I be proud to. That's what I started this story to tell you. My new masta hire me out to dig fortifications for the Union Army. Your pa was in change of my gang an' he done paid one hundred dollars for me. Said that was all th' money he got, money what he saved to send to Miz Marge and his little boy. That be you."

"Ma told me that Pa would have bought all the slaves in your work gang if he'd had the money," Will said.

"Your Pa a good man! He hate slavery, and fight in that terrible war to free all of 'em," Moses confirmed. "That why I love 'im so much, and feels terrible sorry for the trouble what is in his head now."

"I was only two when you come to live with us, but I remember you was very sick. Seemed like you slept for a week when you first got to our farm. How'd you get all that way from Washington to West Virginia?"

"Masta Sergeant done bought me a train ticket to Charleston. I walks the rest of the way. Was nigh on a hundred miles. Were a terrible trip through the mountains. Your pa drawed me a map, but I get lost anyways."

"Gosh, how long did it take you?"

"Were about two months," Moses responded after several seconds of meditation. His frail body shuddered.

"What were you doing all that time?"

"First, I wandered 'round, lost in them mountains, eating roots an' such, for about a week. Then some white trash people, what live deep in them mountains making moonshine whiskey, caught me. They say I'm a runaway slave, an' they gonna keep me. I get away from 'em, after 'bout a month. They put the dogs on me, but I lose 'em when I run a long way in the water of a cold creek. Then I don't know which way to go."

"Geez, there ain't many people living in them mountains. How'd you manage to stay alive and find your way out?"

"Good Lord done sent a angel for me," Moses stated firmly.

"A-ah *angel*?"

"He were an angel, right enough," Moses repeated. "He done come riding out of the mist on a mule. Yeah, he say he a traveling preacher, but I know he were a angel. I were so hungry an' sick, I had done just laid down to die."

Will shook his head in amazement. "What did he do?"

"He dismounted from his skinny mule and say in a voice like thunder, 'Hold on, you child of God. He don't intend you die in this here wilderness!'"

Moses stopped talking and meditated so long that Will thought he had finished his story before he finally continued.

"That angel give me food, an' asked me if I were a lost sheep. I say, 'yes.' He say, 'Well, tell me who your flock is, an' I'll take you to them.' I tell him, 'I going to Masta Sergeant Josh Curtis's farm.' He say, 'I know the place. It's only a day's ride from here.' He put me on the mule behind him and takes me to your pa's farm."

"I was just a little tike then, but I don't remember anyone bringing you to the farm," Will countered.

"That right," Moses agreed. "The angel let me off at the gate, and I kind of stumble from the road to the cabin door. By the time Miz Marge answer my knock, he gone, but he were a angel, right enough!

"I done told him 'bout my lost family. He gonna get us back together one of these days, that for sure, 'cause he promised!"

"I sure hope he does, Moses," Will said with misty eyes. "You deserve it!"

CHAPTER 9

LAZARUS

◆

Moses' story affected Will deeply, and telling it seemed to have exhausted the former slave. The friends sat silently, immersed in their emotions, while *Nellebelle* continued to cruise cautiously down the Ohio.

The huge, nearly submerged rock loomed in the river like some prehistoric monster. Their boat was bearing down on a collision course with it before either of the distracted bow lookouts spotted the danger. Moses saw it first. Lunging from his packing box seat, he gripped the bow rail for a few heartbeats before his brain activated his voice.

"There's a big-g-g rock out there!"

Will jumped to Moses's side, adding his excited, high-pitched voice to the warning.

"Big rock—turn left—turn left. Now!" he screamed.

The helmsmen whirled the big helm hard port and called for the engine room to reverse the stern wheel. Will and Moses gripped the rail, mesmerized, as the ungainly boat continued downstream, crawfishing sideways toward the menacing rock. In seconds, *Nellebelle's* starboard side bounced off the solid object with gut-rending impact and sickening splintering sounds. Will and Moses flew over the low rail like two limp rag dolls.

Being a strong swimmer, Will bobbed to the surface near the boat and grabbed a dangling rope as the boat floated past him. Instinctively, he clutched it with both hands, and pulled himself back aboard before anyone knew he and Moses were overboard. Sprawled on deck, panting for air, he recalled that Moses feared water and had never learned to swim.

"Moses is in the river. Help him—help him!" he shouted the moment he was able to suck enough air into his aching lungs.

Captain Jack heard him and ordered the skiff launched. Zeke physically restrained Will from getting into the search boat. There was only room for the two experienced crewmen. Will cussed and kicked at his uncle until the boat moved away from the stern-wheeler.

While the search proceeded, *Nellebelle* tied up on the Ohio side of the river, where the captain surveyed her damage. Externally, a few feet of starboard fender planking were splintered and things on deck were in disarray, but below, her tough old oak hull remained sound.

The search for Moses continued all night without success. When daylight arrived, they scoured both banks for five miles downstream. By noon, hope faded for finding him alive, but the melancholy search for his body continued until dusk.

Darkness descended on the river, shrouding the Curtis family in gloom. Captain Jack reluctantly advised they continue their journey the next morning. Will's mind rebelled and wouldn't accept the heartbreaking fact that his friend was gone.

"No! No!" he shouted and ran to a secluded spot near the corral that held his buckskin colt, Natty. He threw himself face down on some feed sacks, sobbing into his arms with self-incrimination. Why hadn't he paid closer attention to the river? Why hadn't he prevented Moses from falling overboard? And why hadn't he tried to save him in the river?

After a somber supper, Pa arranged a lantern lit memorial service for Moses on *Nellebelle's* deck. Both Pa and Zeke had good singing voices, but it was Mary who led them with some of Moses's favorite hymns. The boat crew joined in, and mournful renditions of "The Old Rugged Cross," "Rock of Ages," and "Swing Low Sweet Chariot" resonated for a mile up and down the river.

Will sang as loud as he could with his immature, soprano voice. He knew Moses was a little hard of hearing and he sure wanted his friend to hear him up there in heaven. While he was a skeptic about

Pa's vengeful God, Will felt sure his dear friend had gone to heaven because that's what Moses and his ma had taught him to believe.

Uncle Zeke strained to keep his voice from cracking when he recited from memory the Twenty-Third Psalm. That message was of some comfort to Will, especially coming from his Uncle Zeke, but it caused a few more tears to trickle down his cheeks.

Pa's usually steady and strong baritone preaching voice quivered before he finished his sermon, which was heavy on salvation for a good man and believer like Moses. His heartfelt personal prayer concluded the service.

> "Oh most merciful God, we pray for you to receive your loyal servant, Moses, into your heavenly kingdom.
>
> In your wisdom, Lord, you made Moses's worldly body a slave for most of his life, but we thank you for giving him a free spirit. You know he dedicated his body and soul to you, Lord, and that his spirit was never a slave to any man.
>
> We also thank you, dear Lord, for allowing us to know Moses in this life. You made him a great inspiration and blessing to all who knew him here on earth. We are comforted in knowing he is now a blessing to your angels in heaven.
>
> It is our most fervent prayer to you, heavenly Father, that someday you will reunite in heaven your servant Moses with his lost family.
>
> In Jesus' name, we pray for Moses' immortal soul. Amen."

There wasn't a dry eye within hearing of Pa's voice, and Will was never more proud of his troubled father.

During the night, sleepless and grief-stricken, Will left his pallet and huddled fully clothed near his new friend, the buckskin colt Natty. Exhaustion finally overcame grief and he drifted into a troubled sleep, only to be awakened in a couple of hours by cold, drizzling rain. Damp and chilled, he returned to his usual sleeping spot under the wagon beside his Uncle Zeke and shivered in his damp clothes.

Arrival of the wet, gray dawn did nothing to disperse the gloomy pall shrouding *Nellebelle*. Without a body to bury, it was difficult to accept closure for Moses's death. Everyone in the family, except Pa, was reluctant to leave the place where Moses had disappeared.

Pa told the others, "We held services for Moses, and God accepted our prayers on behalf of his soul—therefore, *he is dead!*"

When Mary started the cooking fire in the portable iron stove, Will moved close to it. While partially warming his chilled body and drying his damp clothes, its warmth did not penetrate into the deep sorrow in his heart. Mary didn't question what caused his bedraggled appearance. She took a moment from her cooking to give the despondent boy a hug and reassuring pat on the back. He discerned her tender empathy, though no words passed between them.

About 9:00 AM, the fog lifted slightly and Captain Jack ordered the mooring lines cast off. Seemingly as reluctant to leave Moses as her passengers were, the battered *Nellebelle* slowly slipped back into the Ohio River current. She still hugged the Ohio bank, gathering steerageway speed, when a man appeared on the river bank about a quarter of a mile downstream. He frantically waved his arms and those on deck heard him shout, "Did y'all lose a nigger off your boat?"

"Yeah, our friend Moses fell overboard, night before last," Zeke yelled back through cupped hands. "Have you seen his body?"

"Got 'im at my place—beat up some—but still alive when I left to hunt for your boat," the man yelled back.

Captain Jack overheard the bellowed conversation and quickly steered the boat back to shore, while calling for the stern-wheel to be reversed. *Nellebelle*'s bow nudged against the bank near to where the bedraggled man stood. The gangway no sooner touched shore before the entire Curtis family scrambled across to bombard the bearer of wonderful news with questions.

Water dripped from the brim of the gray-whiskered man's drooping felt hat and his tattered, black wool coat was saturated, but he looked as bright and divine to them as the Angel Gabriel.

"My name's Hank Jordan," the man managed to slide in between the rapid-fire questions. "My farms 'bout ten miles down river. I been traipsing up river all night looking for you folks. I'm half-froze and plumb tuckered out. If you'll put me next to a warm fire an' give me a mug o' coffee, I'll tell y'all about your nigger."

"Oh, we're right sorry for forgetting our manners and abusing you, Mr. Jordan," Zeke apologized. "Please come aboard, come aboard."

They all returned to the boat's deck and when Hank Jordan was seated near the cook fire with a blanket over his shoulders, replacing the dripping coat, Zeke spoke to spellbound Mary.

"Would you please get this good man some hot grub and coffee, Mary? His story can wait until his belly's full and he's thawed out some."

While Mary dished up leftover breakfast and poured coffee for Mr. Jordan, Zeke asked, "Is there a place near your farm where we can safely tie up this boat?"

"Sure is," he replied. "I got a dock that's big enough for this here boat, not a hundred yards from my cabin."

With that information, Captain Jack ordered the gangway pulled in and he guided *Nellebelle* back into the river current. Between chewing food and gulping hot coffee, Hank Jordan managed to tell the story of Moses's miraculous rescue before they reached his landing.

He began, "It were about daylight yesterday when I went to feed my hogs. They're in a pen, what I fixed right there on the riverbank, so's them hogs can wallow and drink in the backwash.

"That's when I heard some groaning from the upstream side of the hog pen. I took a look and there were that skinny, cotton-topped nigger. A darn good-sized log, that he'd probably been floating down river on, had him pinned to the fence. You see, that hog pen fence runs out some into the river there when it's runnin' high," he explained.

"I seen he were still alive. Got the log off him and fetched him to the barn where I made a pallet for 'im with some hay. He 'peared near froze and waterlogged. Got my ol' woman down there and we warmed him up with some blankets. Then he come around some, and we got hot coffee and a mite o' food down his gullet until he were strong enough to tell us about falling off a stern-wheeler called th' *Nellebelle*. He were sure you folks would come a looking for him.

"Figured as how you'd be showing up, I kept an eye on the river all day. Come dark last night, my ol' woman weren't gonna give me no peace 'til I come a lookin' for that nigger's people. I took off up river with my lantern. She'll be happy I found you 'cause she kind of took a liking to that ol' nigger."

Pa spoke up with fire and brimstone in his voice. "Moses ain't just a ol' nigger! He's been a free man since before the war ended. He's—he's—well, he's a beloved member of my family! But that ain't Moses you got anyway, 'cause he's *dead*!"

"Geez, I sure don't aim to rile you none," Mr. Jordan stammered. "No disrespect meant, sir, but that nig-ah-ah, that Negro says his name is Moses, and he sure enough was alive an' kicking when I left him last night. And if my wife has her way, he's soon gonna eat me into the poorhouse."

"Hu-u-u-mph," Pa grunted. Before he could respond further, Zeke spoke up.

"I'm sure my brother and the rest of Moses's family are beholden to you for helping him. How bad 's he hurt, Mr. Jordan?"

"Just call me Hank. Well, this feller, whoever he is, must of taken one helluva beating, what with floating down that cold river for nigh-on ten miles, holding on to a log. But once we got him warmed up and dried out, he didn't have much more 'n cuts, bruises, and maybe a broken arm. Can't tell how bad the arm's hurt, but he can't move it."

As Will listened to the unfolding story, his heart jumped for joy. He had difficulty resisting the urge to run around the deck screaming at the top of his lungs, *Moses is alive! Moses is alive! There's a God after all*! But he settled for screaming it in his mind and being hilariously happy. Mary gave him a big hug and kiss.

Hank directed them to his landing and before the crew had secured the mooring lines, the entire Curtis family and Captain Jack jumped to the rickety dock. Approaching the barn, they heard Moses speaking in his slow, soft manner.

"I sure enough like them vittles you done fixed me, Miz Jordan, but I'm just as full as a tick. Couldn't eat another bite."

They found Moses sitting on a pile of hay with his back propped against a wall. He was dressed in better clothes than he had on when he fell overboard, but he still wore his red suspenders to hold up the baggy pants that the Jordans had given him. A blanket was draped over his shoulders.

Plump Mrs. Jordan knelt beside him, urging him to eat one more bite of the thick beef stew. It looked like he'd been working on it diligently, but apparently the stout, good woman thought the frail, black man needed fattening up. She was doing her best to force one more bite down him.

Seeing the smiling faces of his loving family and his new friend Captain Jack crowded around him, Moses grinned back at them like a Cheshire cat. Mary pushed the others aside and knelt to embrace him while planting a kiss on his cheek. This time he didn't resist her show of affection. Anne cooed and tried to reach him from her perch in Mary's other arm and shy little Jeanie hugged him too.

Will had an urge to hug him and never let go, but he figured it wouldn't be a very manly thing to do. He settled for gawking, beaming, and generally understating his pure joy.

"Gosh, it's swell to see you Moses. We thought you was dead, so we had a service for you," he said.

Tough Zeke wasn't bothered about trying to look manly. He knelt beside his dear friend, tears moistened his eyes, and he practically smothered the slight black man in a bear hug.

"That sure nice, Masta Zeke," Moses said weakly, with a grimace, "but you kind of hurting my banged-up arm."

Zeke pulled back like he'd touched a hot coal and stammered, "Oh my gosh, Moses. I sure didn't aim to hurt you none. Here let me take a look at that arm."

Pa abruptly knelt, elbowed Zeke aside, and roughly placed both big hands on Moses's cotton-white, kinky hair, squeezing his head in a vise-like grip.

"Thank you good and gracious Lord for bringing Moses back to life—just like you done Lazarus!" he shouted to the heavens. "Fall down on your knees, ye undeserving heathens, and thank God for this miracle."

His startled audience fell to their knees, even Captain Jack.

Seeing that his flock had obeyed, Pa continued.

"Hallelujah! Hallelujah! Thank you, God, for bringing Moses back from the dead. It's a miracle!"

The recipient's eyes bugged, and when Pa paused for a breath Moses muttered, "I sure enough does thank God for saving me, Masta Sergeant. I do appreciates your blessing an-and your helping me to say thanks to God—*but I weren't ever dead.*"

"Oh, yes, you were dead, Moses!" Pa insisted. "You had to have been dead because we held a service for you. God accepted my prayer for your soul. You were dead, Moses, and you've been resurrected— you are another Lazarus!"

"Yes, sir, Masta Sergeant, if you says I were dead, I were dead," Moses agreed, trying to put an end to the embarrassing ranting of his friend and patron.

Zeke interrupted his possessed brother by insisting on tending to Moses's injured arm. With help from Captain Jack, he set the simple fracture, applied a splint, and bound it up with strips of cloth from an old petticoat Mrs. Jordan supplied.

The Jordan's steadfastly refused to accept any payment for saving and feeding Moses, but Mary left a package on their table, which contained enough cotton material for portly Mrs. Jordan to make herself a new petticoat.

By noon, with resurrected Moses safely back aboard, a happy *Nellebelle* cruised once again on the river.

Will went aft to tell Natty the good news. Making sure no one was near, he spoke softly to the colt, "There really is a God, Natty. I'm thinking even Pa saw God's kinder side. He says God brought Moses back from the dead, like he done some guy named Lazarus in the Bible. Makes no difference how he done it—Moses is alive! He'll be here to help me train you. You're going to learn to love him as much as I do."

Natty whinnied and nuzzled the boy who often gave him a sweet carrot.

CHAPTER 10

GOOD-BYE NELLEBELLE

◆

It was mid-afternoon when Captain Jack announced they had reached the confluence of the Ohio and the mighty Mississippi. He nudged *Nellebelle* crosscurrent toward the Cairo woodlot dock. All Will could see off the port beam was a broad expanse of water that faded into the mist. His active imagination conjured up the possibility they had taken a wrong turn and would be steaming into a vast ocean if their little boat ventured out there.

Titus Turner, a Mississippi River pilot and old friend of Captain Jack's, boarded shortly after the boat docked. Though retired, he would pilot the battered *Nellebelle* to St Louis as a favor to his friend. His services were needed because Captain Jack's pilot license was only valid on the Ohio.

By the time they finished loading boiler wood and grain for the stock, it was dusk. Predicting a misty, moonless night, Captain Titus decided to wait at the dock until morning. At first light the next day, *Nellebelle* backed away from the Cairo woodlot dock and slipped downstream on the Ohio, hugging the Illinois shore. Across the broad expanse of water, Will discerned a vague outline on the western horizon that he assumed was the Missouri shore.

The little stern-wheeler shuddered as she nosed into the full force of the mighty Mississippi. The aging river pilot spun her helm hard starboard, and held it there with the engine throttle wide open and the boiler panting. Torrents of cold water flooded across the deck. *Nellebelle* strained, shook, and rumbled. Her stern wheel foamed the water, yet the wallowing boat continued to slide sidewise downstream. To the uninitiated Curtis family, the struggle took on the appearance of an eternal standoff, which their valiant little boat might lose at any moment. Pa prayed for divine intervention, and on this occasion, Will appreciated his prayers.

Ever so slowly, the *Nellebelle's* blunt bow nudged to starboard until it was finally pointed upstream. In a few more minutes, she was making straining headway at a top speed of about five knots per hour. Captain Titus told them that barring unforeseen calamities, they could expect to reach the dock in St. Louis in three days. As it turned out, they approached the port of St. Louis about noon of the fourth day. The worthy, seasoned river pilot guided their boat safely through a myriad of river traffic, which increased to congested proportions as they passed a long line of occupied wharves. Will's mouth was agape with awe. Would marvels never end? This great river port made Cincinnati look like a village.

Captain Titus maneuvered the battered boat past about five miles of dock area without finding an empty public berth. They had passed upstream to beyond the railroad bridge that was under construction before making a U-turn in the wide channel and starting back downstream. Just as hope faded that they'd find a berth near the city, the alert pilot spotted one, barely big enough for *Nellebelle*. With considerable skill, he nudged her into the dock, and the Curtis family's river odyssey was over.

Arrangements had been made by mail to ship their wagons and stock to Kansas City on the Katy Line, as the locals called the Missouri–Kansas–Texas Railroad. Zeke suggested he reconnoiter a route to the Katy freight yard before unloading the wagons. Pa scoffed at the delay, but in his usual contrary way insisted on going with Zeke.

Moses and Will were instructed to exercise the horses in the dock area to prepare the teams for a possible hard pull to the train depot. First, they took the placid work teams down the gangway, and in manageable groups, led them around the congested dock area. When finished with the teams, Will suggested they give Uncle Zeke's mare and Natty some freedom. They had separated the willful colt from his mother to wean him a few days before, and had taught him to accept a halter, but there hadn't been much opportunity to work with him to be led in the confines of the boat corrals.

"Masta Will, that's a good idea, but we best take 'em off the boat separate times," Moses cautioned.

"We can't get Natty out without going through his ma's corral," Will said. "I'll take her over to the dock first and tie her out of the way, then come back and help you get Natty off."

"Alright," Moses agreed, skeptically.

The plan worked fine until they reached the dock with Natty. The gangling colt caught sight of his ma. It seemed there was no force on earth that was going to keep the stout animal from her inviting udder. Moses dropped the halter rope from his one good hand to prevent being dragged, but stubborn Will held on and was pulled along the dock like a feather. Natty soon reached his mother, grabbed one of her teats in his mouth, and nudged her utter. She tried to kick him away, yet Natty persisted, even after a couple of *Nellebelle's* crewmen arrived on the scene to help Will tug on the halter rope. At Moses's suggestion, they harnessed one of the work horses, snubbed the resisting colt's halter rope to one of the hames, and literally drug him back aboard.

By the time Zeke and Pa returned to the boat, there wasn't enough daylight left to unload and move the wagons over the ten-mile circuitous route they had selected. Uncle Zeke offered to buy supper for the family, Captain Jack, and Captain Titus at a café near the waterfront to celebrate their safe arrival. It was also his plan to buy the family breakfast the next morning, so that all of the cooking utensils and the portable stove could be loaded that evening. Hard working Mary was pleased. Pa refused to go with them, wanting no association with the sinful city, and Moses also declined the invitation.

When they returned to the boat from their pleasant meal, they had brought with them some food for Pa and Moses. Before beginning to eat, Pa issued a curt command.

"Since Moses's arm is injured, Mary will drive my team to the Katy depot tomorrow."

"Mary has no experience handling a farm team hitched to an overloaded wagon. Besides, she'll have her hands full looking after the girls," Zeke pointed out. "It's time we let Will show us what he can do."

"It's my wagon and my family!" Pa countered, puffing up like a toad.

"Its okay, Zeke," Mary said. "I-I think I can handle the team. Moses can ride with me in case the baby gets fussy or I need help."

"Josh, there's no damn need for Mary to take on that job. Will can do it," Zeke insisted. "We'll let Mary and the girls ride with him in case he needs more help than Moses can give him with that bad arm. *And that's the way it's gonna be!*"

For several seconds, the tension could have been cut with a knife. Pa's face turned redder and he uttered "Hu-u-u-mph" three times before he turned and stomped away, leaving his supper untouched.

Zeke had won another round in the ongoing test of wills between the two brothers. But, at what price? His concerned nephew wondered.

Disembarkation began at first light. By 9:00 AM, the Curtis's worldly possessions were all on the St. Louis dock, with the teams hitched to the wagons. After a touching good-bye to the *Nellebelle* and her crew, they were off to the Katy freight depot. Will held the reins in a white-knuckled grip. With sweaty palms and heart palpitating in his throat, he resolved to give it his best effort. The team pranced and snorted in the unfamiliar environment as the three-wagon caravan, trailing a milk cow, five extra horses, and one rebellious colt, proceeded along the roundabout route that Pa and Zeke had scouted.

CHAPTER 11

FAMILY SECRETS

◆

When they reached the Katy freight yard, it was swarming with activity and challenged Will's stamina to his limits. He relinquished the team with a sigh of relief when Zeke took over to help the railroad men spot the wagons for loading. It was tight, but by removing the tongues and angling the three wagons slightly on the flatbed the Katy loaders succeeded in fitting all three on one car.

With their work finished, the draft horses were returned to the stockyard and loaded into a slatted livestock car with the rest of the stock. Partitions separated the animals into groups at each end of the car, leaving space in the center for feed, water barrels, harnesses, and sleeping pallets for Zeke and Will. Pa and Moses intended to ride with the wagons. Mary and the girls would be given space in the caboose, with the conductor and brakeman. The train that included their cars was scheduled to leave the depot about 8:00 PM, allowing them plenty of time to get their noon meal at a nearby restaurant.

"Since our stuff's safely stowed aboard them railroad cars, I'm going with you to eat," Pa announced, the only communications other than curt nods and grunts they'd heard from him since leaving the boat.

"What's the matter, Josh," Zeke taunted, "did your hungry gut get the best of your pouting?" There were times when Will suspected his uncle deliberately baited his disturbed father, and this was one of them.

"Hu-u-umph, since when do I have to get your permission to eat with *my* family?" Pa retorted.

Pa's sullen presence, which this time was partly caused by Zeke's goading, stifled casual conversation during the meal.

Because they'd packed the portable cooking stove the prior evening, Mary wasn't able to prepare adequate food for the trip. She suggested they stop at a nearby grocery store to purchase what they'd need for and evening meal and breakfast the following morning. Without consulting Pa, she and Zeke selected crackers, cheese, canned meat, and sardines. When those purchases were paid for, Zeke instructed the storekeeper to fill a small bag with hard candy.

"Good Lord knows we ain't got money to fritter away on the likes of store-bought sweets!" Pa blurted out, glaring at the bag in Zeke's hand.

"Well now, Josh, for your information, I ain't buying this candy with family money. This here's from my private poke that I keep for sinning purposes. Way I see it, what I spend for candy will keep me from using it for worse sins."

The red flush started at the base of Pa's neck and soon spread to his heavy jowls. Zeke pressed on.

"Besides, I intended giving you some to sweeten up your sour disposition. Here take a couple pieces and let's see if it works."

Zeke held out the sack. Pa stared at the benign brown bag as though it was Lucifer himself. He raised his hand as though to slap it away, glared at his taunting brother for a few seconds, turned on his heels, and stomped out of the store.

Mary sighed sadly, gave Zeke a disapproving look, and shook her head slowly. Zeke shrugged his shoulders, as though dismissing the incident. Will was disappointed with Zeke's behavior, too, but hid his feelings.

By the time they returned to the depot area, the two railroad cars loaded with their worldly possessions were part of a ten-car train sitting on a siding track.

"This train won't have the right-of-way until about dusk, so you people got plenty of time to settle in," the conductor informed them. "If all goes well, we'll pull into the Kansas City, Missouri depot around eight tomorrow morning."

Will and Zeke made sure Mary and the girls were settled safely in the cramped caboose before they proceeded up the track to find the stock car. Abreast the flatbed loaded with their wagons, Zeke called out to Pa three times. When he didn't get a response, he climbed the short ladder and called out again. "Josh, are you there?"

"Quit your bellowing," Pa responded from inside one of the wagons, sounding like a martyr. "Don't worry none about me. I'm here with my Bible and the Lord. Go see to the stock!"

"Damn it, Josh, no need to bite our heads off. Just wanted to make sure you was all set to go. We'll sure see to the stock. Where's Moses?"

"None of your business, but if you must know everything, I sent him after some water."

"I'm leaving some of the food here by the wagon wheel for you and Moses," Zeke said. "Come on, Will, let's go make a nest with the stock. They'll be better company than we'll get here 'bouts."

Will sure didn't intend to take sides, but he figured this time Pa had a right to be grumpy with Zeke.

They walked along the tracks to the stock car without further conversation. Zeke boosted Will through the open door and scrambled up beside him. A quick check of the animals found all secure with the sturdy partitions in place. Some animals were already lying down, settled in for the trip.

Natty and Bessie were in the same section, leisurely munching hay. Will milked Bessie and took the milk back to the caboose, while Zeke watered the animals.

Will stayed for a while to visit with Mary. He'd said hi to Moses on his way back, but there was no sign of his Pa. The sun was low in the west when he returned. After scrambling back into the stock car, he and Zeke sat with feet dangling from the open door and ate cold rations in silence. Store-bought potted ham, crackers, and cheese seemed a gourmet meal to Will. He wasn't much for sardines, but he and Zeke shared one tin of the little, olive oil packed fish, while also enjoying a fiery sunset.

Zeke produced three bottles of Anheuser beer, clandestinely purchased and stashed in his coat pocket. Although warm, he disposed of the first bottle with gusto. Will considered his uncle a very moderate drinker, even though he had the reputation of having been a rounder in his youth. When Zeke opened the second bottle, he nursed it more judiciously with his food, even giving Will a swig to show him how it tasted.

"Thanks for the taste, but if it's all the same to you, I'll just settle for water," Will said, puckering his mouth and wrinkling his nose.

"Ah-ha, my boy, can't say that I blame you," Zeke said, without mirth. "Alcoholic drink is an acquired taste, and you'll be better off never to acquire it. I've seen a lot of good men lose life and soul sucking on a beer or whiskey bottle."

By the time they'd finished the leisurely meal, uncle and nephew were in an expansive mood, enjoying their camaraderie and the warm glow of comfortable full stomachs. Zeke was slightly more relaxed than Will because of the two bottles of beer in him; he'd saved one bottle for later.

They bunched the straw toward the center of the car, spread their bedrolls, and sat facing each other, with their backs leaning on the wooden partitions. It thrilled Will when Natty reached his nose over the partition and nudged him on the shoulder. He gently rubbed the colt's head.

A broad smile spread across Zeke's face, pushing his bushy, roan mustache in a half-moon shape and crinkling the lines at the corners of his sparkling hazel eyes. Will was pleased to see his Uncle Zeke in such a mellow mood. *Maybe this will be a good time to learn more about his war experience*, the inquisitive youngster thought. He put that possibility aside when the conversation took an unexpected turn.

"Guess you don't like that little critter much, do you Will?"

"I sure enough do like him, Uncle Zeke, and I thank you again for giving him to me. But-but it's sure hard to figure why Pa was so riled when you done it. Why don't he like Natty? Why's he's so mad about most everything?"

Zeke pondered on Will's sincere questions for several seconds.

"Well now, there just ain't no simple answers to your concerns," he mused. "If I knew how, I'd sure fix it, but it ain't easy to get inside another person's head. Tell you for sure, though, your pa may be grumpy at times, but loves you."

"I-I sure wish I could help him. Moses says something come between you and him; can you tell me what it was?" the youngster pleaded.

"It ain't proper for me to be telling you things about your pa, Will, especially when he ain't here to tell his side of things."

Will sensed his uncle anguishing over the matter and remained quiet. In a few seconds, Zeke hesitantly continued.

"But—but there again, how you ever gonna learn some of the reasons for things 'less I tell you, best I can?"

There was another awkward silence. While Zeke collected his thoughts, he removed the cork from his last bottle of beer and took a long drag.

" First off," he said in a reflective tone, "I worry about your pa, too. After all, he is my little brother. When we were just young tikes, Ma made me promise I'd always look out for him. I would have tried anyways because he's family."

Will sat quiet as a mouse while Zeke stared at the sinking sun, so long that the curious youngster feared his uncle had said all he was going to.

"Th-the way I recall," Zeke continued, picking his words carefully, "it's been in your pa's nature to have a jealous streak since we was boys. I'm as much at fault as he is. We never were much alike. I was kind of restless and he was serious and reliable—no, we never was much alike."

Zeke bogged down again, and took another long swig from his beer bottle. Will chanced prompting him.

"Yeah, I've always known you and Pa are different in lots of ways."

"Yeah—yeah, but that's only part of it," Zeke responded.

"It sure didn't make ol' Josh happy when I took off gallivanting out West! I was seventeen at the time, feeling the wanderlust like a disease. He was about sixteen, and a serious kid. He had no choice but to stay home and help our ailing folks on the farm. I—I kind of done him dirty."

That admission seemed hard for Zeke to admit. Will always admired his uncle's adventurous nature, and never thought that it might have made him an irresponsible youth.

"Way things worked out between us later, and what happened to him in the war, only made matters worse. An-and then he come home with that hellfire religion stuff."

Zeke choked up, sat looking at his scuffed boots with a pained expression for several seconds, and finally made a couple of "hu-u-umph" sounds, clearing his obstructed throat.

"You-your ma dying, like she did—it-it just kind of all piled up on him—an-and maybe pushed his mind on over the cliff."

"Yeah," Will said softly, giving his obviously overwrought uncle time to regain his composure. "I already figured out some of that stuff. But why'd he bring up my ma when he argued with you about giving me Natty? Can't see where she's got anything to do with you giving me a horse."

Zeke's facial muscles tightened, he worried his lower lip with his teeth, and his eyes became misty.

"Now—now that there is a subject I'd just as soon not talk about," he managed to stammer and then studied the toes of his scuffed boots again for several seconds before looking up at Will with a strained expression on his weathered face.

"But there again, I reckon if I don't give you the facts, you'll likely chaw on it the rest of your life, and come up with wrong answers." His uncle's voice reflected mental anguish such as Will had never before witnessed in him.

Zeke finished the beer before speaking again. It seemed to fortify his courage.

"It's like this: I—I courted your ma before your pa did." He looked at Will as though debating in his mind if he should continue on such a sensitive subject.

"We got kind of serious about getting hitched. I—I loved Marge and was all for the idea, but I figured there was a problem. You see, your pa had the family farm—*and rightly so*—rightly so, because he'd earned it! What with all my gallivanting around, wasting my youth, I sure didn't have much to offer a gal. Was my aim to go out to the Colorado gold fields and get us a grubstake, before I married Marge.

"She wasn't much for the delay and would have gone with me, but I knew it'd be hard scrabble and took off alone. Didn't strike it rich, but after a while, I found some color. Was little over a year before the claim petered out. Figured I had enough money to get us started, so I quit the gold fields and went back home to claim my bride."

The stressed storyteller abruptly stopped talking and his eyes reflected a vacant stare. While sensitive to Zeke's anguish, Will's consuming need to know wouldn't allow him to let his uncle off the hook.

"What happen then, Uncle Zeke?" His maturing voice came out more demanding than he'd intended, but it got his uncle's attention and the vacant eyes focused back on him.

"Well, I weren't much for writin', and Marge didn't know how to get hold of me, so-so I-I didn't know she'd already married your pa, just a couple of months after I left. Now—now mind you, I couldn't blame her all that much, or your pa. It weren't like I didn't know all along that Josh was sweet on her, too."

Zeke stared directly into the attentive boys eyes, "She was a good woman. I had my chance and pissed it away—that's all there were to it!"

His uncle picked up the water bottle and took a big drink. Will spoke, just a little louder than a whisper.

"Gosh, I never knew that."

Will was touched by the warm and caring look Zeke gave him.

"You—you had come along right away and, well-er-ah, anyways it looked to me like the war with the rebs was gonna start soon. The western counties of Virginia broke away and formed the separate state of West Virginia when it looked like Virginia was going to secede from the Union. I packed up and joined the first company of West Virginia cavalry that was raised for the Union Army."

"Did Pa join up about the same time?"

"That's something that's still hard for me to figure," Zeke said. "I thought your pa—with a wife and a young son depending on him—would have had enough sense to stay out of the mess. But, damned if he didn't join up about six months later. His outfit was sent back East, right off, to become part of the Army of the Potomac. He didn't get home again in nigh-on four years."

"Don't you have any idea why he done that?" Will asked, incredulously.

"He never told me why, but I'm guessing that was one time he just wasn't going to let his big brother leave him behind, and he was dead set against slavery.

"Only time during the war I got to talk to him about it, I gave him holy hell for leaving you and your ma alone. He said it was none of my damn business. Guess he was right, except I was worried about you and your ma. That's why I come right back to West Virginia when they forced me out of the Union cavalry in the summer of 1863, and I stayed there ever since to kind of help watch over th' family."

With three blasts of the whistle, the puffing engine jerked their car forward and they heard the car connections clanging down the line. They were on their way to Kansas City.

Chapter 12

MEDAL OF HONOR

◆

Uncle Zeke seemed talked out. He took a drink of water and stared out the open cattle-car door into the growing darkness. The things he'd revealed whetted Will's desire to hear more about the family's secrets and intensified his long-held obsession to learn about Zeke's war experiences—especially how he'd earned the Congressional Medal of Honor. With his uncle in a rare pensive mood, he judged now was his best opportunity, one that may never arise again. He took a chance and interrupted Zeke's reverie.

"Did you or Pa get hurt in the war, Uncle Zeke?"

Those vacant eyes focused back on his nephew and Zeke's mind seemed to return to the railroad car through time and space from wherever it had been.

"Well now, depends on what you call *hurt*. I recollect your pa telling about his horse getting killed, and him being blowed ass-over-teakettle by a cannon shell. He's had bad headaches ever since. Maybe that kind of scrambled his brains because he sure ain't been the same since he come home."

Zeke shook his head, as though clearing away suppressed unpleasant thoughts, and reached for the nearby kerosene lantern.

"I'm gonna light the lantern. Maybe we can play some cards before bedtime."

That was the last thing Will wanted to do. After the lantern flame fluttered to life, Zeke closed the globe and sat it on the gently rocking floor between them. Will tried again to prime his uncle's memory well.

"What about you, Uncle Zeke? I heard tell you did a lot of fighting. Did you get wounded?"

The youngster feared he'd gone too far when Zeke's jaw tightened. He sighed with relief when after a few reflective seconds, his uncle replied in a calm, almost jovial, manner.

"Talking about my war wound is kind of embarrassing, but I been known to show the scars to some of the gals, haw-haw-haw."

"Gosh, Uncle Zeke, them scars must be hidden real good. I ain't never seen 'em."

"If you must know, I'm usually sitting on them scars," Zeke confessed. "I was shot clean through the left cheek of my butt when I stuck it up too high in a fight down on the Stones River in Tennessee."

"I'll bet that sure hurt like the blue blazes!" Will said, eyes as big as saucers and voice full of empathy. It kind of made his rear end pucker just thinking about it.

Reacting to Will's enthusiasm, Zeke continued with his story.

"Well, it were a darn inconvenient place to get shot. Slept on my belly and stood up to eat for nigh-on three months, ha-ha-ha." And then seriously, "Weren't no fun though. What good is a cavalryman that can't sit in a saddle?"

"Did they take good care of you in the army hospital, Uncle Zeke?"

Zeke's eyes flashed hot and his expression darkened. The previous jovial tone took on a sharp edge. "Took too damn good care of me! Forced me out of the army on a trumped-up medical discharge. Was that damned Colonel Ambrose McNeal, trying to buy me off by getting me discharged in the summer of '63 as a wounded hero. Made out like it was for my own good, just because I got infection and loss some weight 'fore my butt healed."

Falling silent again, Zeke focused his eyes somewhere over Will's head. His nephew, sensitive beyond his years, read anger and torment in them. There was also something else there—perhaps a compelling need to get a festering story out of his craw?

"Gosh, Uncle Zeke, I thought you and Colonel McNeal was friends. Didn't Captain Jack say something about you saving the colonel's life?"

The glazed eyes moved back to focus on Will.

"Guess Ambrose and me was friends once," he said, his tone now almost wistful. "Knew him before the war, and then we saw some tough times together during that darn war. You see, as top sergeant of the regiment, and in charge of scouts and dispatch riders, I was mostly right beside the colonel. As for saving his life, that's an exaggeration. What really happened has been eating at my guts all these years. Maybe it's high time I talked about it. It ain't a pretty story; you sure you want to hear it?"

"I sure do, Uncle Zeke. If you feel right about telling it to me."

Zeke warmed to the subject, seemingly compelled to tell it to the audience of fifteen horses, one colt, one cow, and a very attentive nephew.

"Wel-l-l, to understand what happened, you got to know something about the people, and how they got where they were. Ambrose McNeal got elected governor of West Virginia mostly on his war record. Maybe that's what galls me most. Ambrose was a prominent horse breeder and a Virginia State Senator from up Parkersburg way. He was one of the main supporters for West Virginia breaking away from Virginia and staying with the Union. I'll give him that!

"I'd done jobs for him over the years, training his horses and the like. When he started putting together a volunteer Union cavalry regiment, he offered me the rank of major. For personal reason's, I did join his outfit and I talked a lot of the local boys into joining up from around Mason County. But I told him I wasn't qualified to be an officer. He insisted on at least making me the regiment's sergeant major."

There was a pause while Zeke wetted his parched throat with a drink from the water jug. His face contorted and he continued in a wistful tone. Will sat as quiet as a church mouse.

"There—there was this skinny, redheaded, freckle-faced boy named Otis Crammer. He was only about sixteen. His pa had been a friend of mine before he died when Otis was a little shaver. I felt sorry for Otis and his ma, and tried to help them out some because it was hardscrabble for 'em to make a living. Otis had got hold of a beat-up bugle and taught himself to play it darn good. Begged me to take him with us. His ma said he could go—if I'd promise to look out after him. I bought him a horse and he went along; made a damn fine soldier, too."

"You probably don't remember your Aunt Dorothy, who was Otis's mother. I married her after I come home from the war, but she died of the consumption when you was still a little guy. She was a good woman."

"I vaguely remember her, but I didn't know she had a son," Will replied. He felt a tinge of jealousy for that redheaded bugler boy whose memory made his hero uncle's voice quiver, and wondered what had happened to him?

"Ah-ah, well, after we trained some, we was rushed down to Paducah, Kentucky. The regiment fought our first battles near there, helping to capture rebel-held Fort Donnellson and Fort Henry. Right away, it were obvious Ambrose was more politician than cavalry officer, but he usually let better men make the tough decisions.

"We followed the rebs on down the Tennessee River to Pittsburg Landing, where we fought a big battle called Shiloh. That slaughter lasted for three days. The outfit saw our share of hard fighting. Way too many of my friends got killed.

"After that fight, we followed the rebs into Mississippi, and did a lot of raiding and scouting around a place called Corinth during the next six months. We found out for sure that them reb cavalrymen were damn tough fighters!

"Come winter of '62, they was working up for a big fight over in central Tennessee. Ol' Grant sent our outfit and Sherman's infantry division over there to help out. The rumors had it that there was a big reb army south of us somewheres. Our cavalry regiment was assigned to locate them.

"Four days later, we found the main body of reb troops, about ten miles north of Murfreesboro, Tennessee. Ambrose sent me to report that information to General Rosecrans. The general pushed his forty-five thousand troops into a battle line that very afternoon, close to a half mile north of where he figured them rebs would hole up for the night. Couldn't tell exactly where they was because most of 'em had good cover in dense cedar timber. Our outfit was ordered to a position close behind Sheridan's infantry division. We got there just before dark. Any fool could see our position weren't very darn good—out in the open—on a little rise, with them thick stands of cedars in front of our infantry, and more timber on our right. We found out the hard way later that them trees were growing amongst limestone rocks. It was th' best darn cover them rebs could hope for."

The storyteller paused. Will envisioned that battlefield clearly in his mind's eye. Mesmerized, he absorbed every word without moving a muscle. After another deep drag from the water jug, Zeke continued.

"Like I said, the First Cavalry was ordered to picket our horses in a muddy, half-frozen cotton field on that exposed knoll, about two hundred yards behind Sheridan's battle line. We made a cold camp—a damned cold camp!"

Empathy for those freezing soldiers caused Will to shiver.

"Well, we lived through the night. Come daylight, thousands of screaming Johnny Rebs come a running out of them cedar trees, attacking Sheridan's line. Had a scrap on their hands, but held. We caught a few stray shots but couldn't fire back for fear of hitting our own men. Waiting is the hardest darn thing to do in a battle! About noon we started taking reb artillery shells. Rumors circulated that the rebs was rolling up our right flank. We was ordered to stand fast and let the fight come to us; a damn hard thing to do when you're getting shelled and holding defensive positions. Hell, all we wanted to do was to mount up and charge something. But we darn sure couldn't ride through them dense cedar trees where the enemy was.

"Firing got heavy from the woods to our right; damned close by, and coming our way. Ambrose ordered us to fall back. One of Rosecrans's staff officers rode in about then. 'Have your men formed into a battle line, quick march them on foot into those trees on the right, and engage the enemy!' the man said and then turned his horse and rode away.

"Ambrose stood with his mouth agape, doing nothing. Major Wellington—a darn good man—spoke to me, 'Send orders to the battalion commanders to leave the horses with every fourth man, and form a skirmish line on us. They're to move out at a quick march when our bugler blows the charge.'

"Well, I done that and the battle line was formed in short order. Wellington spoke to little Otis, 'Blow the charge.' Ambrose seemed to get his wits back. 'I'll say when my men will charge,' he said to Wellington, and then to Otis, 'Sound the charge.'

"Otis blew his heart out. Was bitter hard for us cavalrymen to leave our horses, but the line began to move out at quick march. When we reached them thick cedar woods, a bunch of our own retreating infantry damn near trampled us—running for their lives, every man for himself!

"Ol' Ambrose got mighty excited, but we kept on pushing through them thick trees and the panicked Union troops best we could. It weren't long before we lost contact with all our men that were more 'n twenty feet away. Bug-eyed Ambrose ordered Otis to sound recall! Otis did what he was ordered and quicker 'n you could say scat, a horde of screaming rebs come crashing through the trees all around us. It became a root-hog-or-die kind of fight. I shouted to Otis for him to stay near me and I was trying to stay close to Ambrose. Our little bugler was fighting hard, but Ambrose just hunkered down behind a tree. It were only a few minutes later, when out of the corner of my eye I saw our commanding officer turn tail and run—and he weren't looking back.

"He didn't get far 'fore I saw him tumble head-over-ass and disappear. I figured he got shot. There come a little lull in the fighting near where we was. I pulled shell-shocked Otis along toward where Ambrose went down. We found him in a big pothole, kind of like a limestone cave in the ground. It was hard to see down into it because it was partly covered by a big windfall cedar tree. I hollered, 'Are you hurt, Ambrose?' and got no answer. Bullets was still flying through them trees like riled-up bees. Otis got his wits about him and shot a couple of them rebs that was coming after us. I shot a couple more, and then told Otis to hunker down and cover me while I checked on the colonel.

"I found Ambrose unconscious, but didn't see no blood on him. Before I could check him out for wounds, I heard Otis scream, and poked my head out of the hole. He was kicking around on the ground, holding his gut with both hands. Some rebs were heading our way through the trees and there wasn't another standing Union soldier in sight. It looked like our best chance was to hide out in that hole until the rebs passed on.

"I crawled out and had Otis in my arms when something slapped my ass—like I'd been kicked by a mule. By the time I got Otis in that hole, my butt commenced to hurt like crazy. After laying Otis down, I dropped my pants and discovered I'd been shot clean through the left cheek.

"Sure enough, Otis was gut-shot. It looked bad. Tears rolled down his cheeks and he pleaded, 'Help me, Zeke! Help me, Zeke!' Hell, I wanted to cry for the poor little guy 'cause weren't many survived a gut-shot—how the hell could I help him? I took off my shirt and made a compress to press against his wound out of half of it and stuffed the other half in the seat of my torn pants. There didn't seem to be any of my bones broken.

"Ambrose come around about then. He wasn't shot; likely he'd tripped and fell into that hole. He only had a sprained ankle and an egg-sized bump on his head, but he was putting on like he was dying.

"It was getting dark. Things had quieted down outside, but we could hear distant artillery fire and the pitiful pleading of hundreds of wounded men out among them rocks and cedar trees. Ambrose wanted me to find some rebs that we could surrender to. Made out like it would be the best thing for Otis. I wouldn't have nothing to do with that idea.

"Later that night, I crawled out, wanting to scrounge some water, blankets, and food. Most of the wounded had either died or given up hope. When I heard some low talking off to my right, I thought they might be reb medics picking up their wounded. Hoping I could capture one and make him patch up Otis, I decided to sneak up on them. It turns out they was the worst kind of scum: reb deserters robbing the dead and wounded. I saw them bash a wounded Union soldier's head in with the butt of his own rifle while he pleaded for a drink of water.

"By God, I splattered both them sons-of-bitches' brains all over that goddamned battlefield!"

Zeke shouted, so viciously and vindictively that it sent an involuntary chill down Will's spine. Good Lord, he thought, Uncle

Zeke most have been a cold-blooded killer on the battlefield! After a few seconds of breathing hard through flared nostrils and taking a long drink of water, Zeke was able to continue his story.

"Well—well, I realized them shots would likely bring others like them down on me. I scampered out of there, picking up a couple canteens, some grub, and three blankets on the way back to our hiding hole. What with them grave robbers working the battlefield, I knew we was considerable behind the reb lines. I judged we'd best just hunker down for the night, and get our bearings come daylight."

Zeke's countenance abruptly changed from anger to grief-stricken. A mournful, gut-wrenching "aw-w-w-w, aw-w-w-w" emanated from deep within his tortured soul. With a stifled sob, he said, "Just—just before first light, my-my buddy, Otis Crammer, died in my arms! A great spasm of pain grabbed at him. He-he said 'Mama' softly a couple of times. Guess she come to him in that stinking hole—to tell him good-bye. He squeezed my hand, sighed, and closed his eyes. I knew the Good Lord had come for him.

"I—I ain't ashamed to tell you, I cried for that boy. His life hadn't been much, but he was sure proud of being a U.S. cavalryman. I'll be forever thankful I gave him that chance—even if-if I did get him killed."

Misty eyes and a clogged throat prevented the storyteller from speaking for several seconds. Will suffered from the same problem.

"Well—well, come full light, we had to get out of there. I had another run-in with Ambrose. He ordered me to leave Otis's body and help him to walk. Hell, I was probably hurt more than he was. I cut the bastard a crutch from a forked limb and told him that come hell or high water, Otis was going with us! I-I carried that boy for nigh on three miles. But we made it!

"He was buried down there in Tennessee, with full military honors befitting a U.S. cavalryman. I saw to that before they hauled me off to the damn hospital. I-I know where he is, and I'm going back to visit him one day soon. I'm sure glad his ma got to see where he was buried before she died. I paid for her trip right after the war, but I wasn't quite up to going back just then."

Zeke abruptly stopped, as thought the story was ended. Will knew there was more. Sorely wanting to hear about the Congressional

Medal of Honor, he took a chance on prompting his emotionally drained uncle one more time.

"You said Colonel McNeal got you discharged. How'd that happen?"

That caused Zeke's eyes to flash hot again.

"Ol' Ambrose hobbled out, leaning on me. When it looked like we was going to make it, he started buttering me up. 'We should forget what was said in the stress of the time'—stuff like that. He said what a good soldier I'd been from the get-go; how much he depended on me; he'd see me decorated for my bravery.

"I told him, I didn't want no damn decoration. What happened out there was between him and me. I didn't intend to tell anyone about it. And I ain't told nobody, 'til now!

"Last thing I said to Colonel Ambrose McNeal was, 'I got no respect for you, and I ain't gonna ever serve with you again.' Well he wouldn't leave it that way. Told a big story about how I stood over him fighting off the rebs and saved his life. How I risked my life and got wounded, pulling his courageous wounded bugler out of danger— told it like he believed it. There wasn't much I could do without making him out as a big liar. Looking back, maybe I should have shut him up, but I just kept my fool mouth shut, thinking nothing would come of it. Anyhow, I was busy seeing to burying Otis.

"After my wound got infected, I was sent to a hospital up near Washington City. I'd been there about two months when President Abe Lincoln, himself, showed up with ol' General Grant. Lincoln made a little talk about the new decoration that Congress had recently created called the Medal of Honor, and then he hung one around my neck.

"I liked Lincoln and wasn't going to embarrass him with the true story. Told him I was accepting the honor for my little buddy Otis. When I got home, I give it to his ma. She didn't want to take it, but I told her Otis was a good soldier and he had earned it with his life— and he damn well had!"

As though in confirmation, Zeke stopped talking and nodded his head a couple of times. After a few seconds, his troubled mind seemed to have returned from that desperate struggle to the rumbling train chugging across Missouri. His sad eyes focused on Will.

"That's enough war stories for now," Zeke stated. "I'd just as soon you keep what I told you to yourself."

His nephew was choked up, and had to clear his tight throat before he could reply.

"Th-thank you for telling it to me, Uncle Zeke. I sure enough will keep it to myself."

Zeke extinguished the lantern and rolled into his blankets. A few minutes later, Will heard what might have been muffled sobs coming from his uncle's bedroll.

"I was scared to death, and only stayed in that stinking hole for Otis's sake," the strained voice muttered. "I would have probably run off too—if I could have. I sure as hell didn't deserve no medal!"

Will didn't believe his uncle's pained confession, but he made no comment. After that, the only sounds in the cattle car were the rhythmic puffing of the locomotive, the click-clack of the train's steel wheels on the rails, and the heavy breathing of the sleeping animals.

Overloaded emotions kept Will awake for a long time. In his mind, Uncle Zeke was truly a hero to be proud of, but then he'd always been proud of his uncle.

CHAPTER 13

KANSAS CITY

◆

Will suddenly snapped to a sitting position in his rumpled bedroll. "No-o-o, no-o-o," he shouted. Startled eyes opened wide and darted around the rocking stock car. Intermittent flashes of morning sunlight streamed through the cattle car slats. His eyelids fluttered, accentuating the fearful expression on his face.

Zeke nearly dropped the bucket he was using to water the stock. "What—what's wrong with you, Will? A bear get after you in your dreams?"

Brought back to reality by Zeke's voice, Will's darting eyes focused on his uncle. Seeing him up and around and filling out the seat of his pants quite well was a great relief. Thank God he wasn't really lying dead, face down on that bleak battlefield with his rear end missing. It had only been a horrible nightmare.

"S-s-something like that, Uncle Zeke," he managed to stammer through labored breaths. "Guess I just didn't know where I was for a while."

"Well, whatever it was, quit lollygagging and milk ol' Bessie. We'll soon be rolling into Kansas City."

"Okay, Uncle Zeke, but I got to pee first."

"Best you get it done then, if you don't want to piss your pants."

They were finished with their chores and were munching on leftovers from their supper when the train jerked to a halt on a siding at the Kansas City–Missouri–Katy depot. Stock and wagons were unloaded and the teams were hitched to the wagons by midmorning. Zeke had returned from checking out a route from the Katy depot to the Santa Fe Railroad depot that was located on the Kansas side of the river. Again, it fell to Will to drive his pa's second team. It wasn't comforting to learn that the five-mile trip would be along busy streets and cross a half-mile long, plank-decked bridge.

The trip proved tougher than he'd feared. His skittish, steel-shoed horses snorted and pranced along the cobbled streets. Tense and sweating, Will strained to prevent the big farm animals from trampling pedestrians or colliding with one of the hundreds of buggies and horseback riders who darted in and out of congested traffic.

At the approach to the long, two-lane bridge, Zeke pulled his leading wagon to the side and tethered the team. Will and Pa pulled to a halt in tandem behind Zeke's wagon, creating a traffic hazard. As he walked back to confer with Pa, Zeke ignored the shouted complaints from irate teamsters who had to pull around them.

"Josh, I got to thinking; them goosey farm horses ain't ever been on a plank bridge before. Likely, they'll spook and fight the reins all the way across. Best you pull around Will and cross with me. I'll ride one of the saddle horses back over and drive Will's team across."

"That'd slow us down too much," Pa snapped. "You was the one making out like he was man enough to handle that team. Since you're the big leader, why don't you quit your jawing and lead on across that bridge."

Will overheard the loud exchange. Pa had no confidence in him; now it seemed even Uncle Zeke had doubts. Humiliated, he ducked his head and bit his quivering lower lip. Mary gave him a reassuring pat on the shoulder, but didn't speak.

"It be alright, Masta Will, y'all can handle that team just fine," Moses assured him in his soft manner, but it didn't help much. Maybe Zeke was right, Will allowed. That bridge sure looked narrow, long, and full of traffic going both ways.

Zeke clinched his jaw, stared in heated silence at his unreasonable brother for a few seconds, turned on his heels, and walked away. He stopped beside Will's wagon, stepped up on the wheel hub, winked at Mary, and gave Will a reassuring pat on his knee.

"Will, them horses might act up some and shy sideways when they hear the hollow sound of their hooves clopping on them bridge planks. Just take it slow and easy with even, firm reins. Don't whipsaw 'em and you'll be alright."

He grinned warmly, gave Will another pat on his knee, stepped down, and walked briskly to his wagon.

As soon as they were on the dreaded bridge, Will's team reacted just as Zeke predicted. With great effort, he kept them under prancing control until they were near the middle, where he met an oversized freight wagon being pulled by three yokes of oxen. Abreast the big rig, the nervous horses shied away from the unfamiliar oxen. Will pulled hard on the left rein to keep them from jamming against the right guardrail. The skittish team overreacted to their left, causing the rear wheel hubs of the wagons to sideswipe.

No damage was done, and Will would have likely regained control if the bull-whacker hadn't chosen that moment to snap his long whip over the oxen. It resonated like a rifle shot. Will's team went berserk, causing the horse on the right side to slam against the guardrail. The panicked youngster yanked hard on the left rein. Both wild-eyed horses leapt across the oncoming traffic lane, jamming themselves and the wagon's tongue into the left guardrail. The heavily laden wagon jack-knifed across both lanes and tipped precariously. In seconds, the thrashing team became tangled in the doubletree, singe trees, and tug straps. Fortunately, a break in the oncoming traffic prevented a collision, and the undamaged oxen rig plodded on its way.

While scared out of his wits, Will refrained from shouting at the panicked horses and from yanking on the reins. Coolheaded Moses spoke to the team soothingly, "Whoa, boys—easy there, horses—whoa, there." Moments later, the traumatized team stopped struggling and stood trembling in the tangled mess.

Traffic on the busy bridge began backing up in both directions. Pa left his four-horse hitch unattended. Wild-eyed, those horses pawed at the bridge planks while Pa rushed in a rage to the stalled wagon. Because Zeke took time to tie his nervous team's hitch rein to the bridge rail, it took a little longer for him to reach the chaotic scene. Pa halted in front of the jackknifed wagon, raving like a madman. Looking down into Pa's enraged eyes, Will's shock turned to stark fear. Instinctively, he cringed against Mary, fully expecting a lash from the horsewhip Pa held in his raised right hand. Mary pushed her upper body between Will and his pa, and threw her arms around the trembling youngster.

"It wasn't his fault, Josh. For God's sake, don't strike him with that whip!" she shouted.

Moses put out his good arm in a feeble attempt to protect them both.

The madman glared at them for a few terrifying heartbeats, and then turned his venom on the defenseless horses. He commenced to beat them unmercifully with the whip. Terrified, Jeanie wailed, and baby Anne added her shrill cry to the bedlam. The frantic horses shrieked and fought to escape the sharp blows by rearing and flailing their front legs over the three-foot high guardrail. Bruised and bloodied, they came precariously close to tumbling into the raging water below before Zeke succeeded in wrestling the whip from his enraged bigger brother's strong grip. He lithely sidestepped Pa's furious lumbering charge toward him. Pa tripped and sprawled on the bridge's floor. The air puffed from his lungs in a loud, "o-o-o-fff." Zeke straddled the panting, semiconscious man, pinning him facedown against the rough bridge planks.

"My God, Josh, have you lost your mind altogether? Best you just stay where you are until you simmer down some," Zeke commanded.

Pa wheezed, gasping for air, and in a few seconds, his lungs filled enough for him to begin struggling. While heavier than Zeke, he was out of condition and probably had never been as strong as his older brother. Zeke kept him pinned, while speaking firmly.

"I don't mean you no harm, Josh, but I don't aim to let you up until you simmer down." There was no reply from the struggling man. While keeping Pa pinned, Zeke shouted to the wagon.

"Will, get down quick. Go see to your pa's team. Mary, ease down with the girls and stay back with Will until we get this mess untangled. Moses, see what you can do for that poor team."

Wide-eyed people gathered around. All except one man gave the scuffling men and the tangled mess plenty of space. A well-dressed young man moved in and unobtrusively helped Moses calm the team. Soon the two of them had the pitiful horses backed off the guardrail. When he was sure Will, Mary, and the girls were safely out of the fray, Zeke eased up on Pa slightly and spoke to him quietly.

"Josh, I'm going to let you up now. We ain't got time for anymore of this foolishness. Got to get our rig straightened out so this traffic can move. Do you hear me?"

"Yeah, I hear you. Just get off me, you darn fool." Pa had quit struggling under Zeke's weight. Yet, he was still out of breath and talked in grunts.

Cautiously, Zeke eased off of Pa. Josh laboriously pushed himself to his hands and knees, and puffed for a few seconds before rising stiffly to his feet. His eyes were blazing and he breathed heavily through flared nostrils, reminding Will of an enraged bull. For a precarious moment, the brothers' eyes were locked in an unwavering stare.

"Weren't no call for you holding me down like that, Zeke. Let's get these wagons off this infernal bridge," Pa grunted, sounding more humiliated than angry. Zeke seemed relieved.

"Sorry about that, Josh," Zeke replied in a reconciliatory tone. "Guess I just lost my head in the excitement. Why don't you check the team for injuries and hold them here while I drive mine on over? I'll come back for this wagon."

By that time, the helpful stranger and Moses had the team untangled and over on the right side of the bridge. The young stranger spoke to them.

"Gentlemen, I don't mean to interfere, but may I offer my assistance in driving one of the teams for you? My associate can handle our gentle buggy team. That way we can clear the bridge quicker for the backed-up traffic."

"That's right neighborly of you, mister," Zeke said and stuck out his hand. "I'm Zeke Curtis and this here is my brother, Reverend Josh Curtis."

"Pleased to meet you, gentlemen. My name is Randy Briddle. If my offer is agreeable, let's get these wagons moving and we'll visit on the other side of the bridge. There's a wide spot over there where we can park all the rigs."

"That makes sense to me," Zeke stated. "Any objections, Josh?"

Pa hadn't offered his hand to the handsome stranger. He shook his head no and walked sullenly away toward his four-horse hitch without speaking. Mr. Briddle motioned to his colleague in the buggy that was halted directly behind Pa's wagon, and then climbed to the seat of the stalled wagon. When they reached the other side, as Mr. Briddle had predicted, there was room enough to park all the rigs without obstructing traffic.

Pa hadn't spoken to Mary or Will during the time it took them to get off the bridge. The moment Pa's wagon came to a halt, Mary and Will both jumped down without asking his permission, leaving him and Moses to care for the girls. When they reached where Zeke and the Good Samaritan were talking, Zeke introduced them. Mr. Briddle raised an eyebrow when he was told that Mary was Pa's wife, but recovered quickly and graciously shook her hand.

"May I ask where you folks are headed with these heavily loaded wagons?" Mr. Briddle said.

"Well, first we're going to the Santa Fe freight depot to put them on a train to Wichita, and then from Wichita we're going to drive them to our homesteads southeast of Winfield, Kansas," Zeke answered.

Mr. Briddle's eyes widened. "Well now, I'd call that a coincidence. It just happens that I own the general store in Winfield. I'm up here buying supplies."

Engaged in their animated conversation, they didn't notice Pa approach just in time to hear the stranger say to Mary, with a big friendly smile, "Why, it looks like we'll practically be neighbors. Did I understand Zeke to say you're the reverend's wife?"

Before Mary could reply, Pa snarled, "Yes, mister, Mary's my wife!"

"Reverend Curtis, please accept my apologies if I have unintentionally offended you," Mr. Briddle stammered.

Pa grunted, "Hum-m-mph," and glared at the stranger.

"Will you be staying in Kansas City long, Mr. Briddle?" Zeke asked, anxious to change the subject.

Briddle turned his attention away from the angry preacher and calmly responded to Zeke's question.

"No, I've completed my purchases and plan to leave for Wichita on tomorrow's passenger train. Perhaps we'll be riding on the same train?"

Pa's angry voice bellowed, "Not likely! We'll be riding with our outfit an' stock on a freight train."

"It's a long hard ten-hour freight train ride with lots of stops, Reverend Curtis," the merchant replied in a sincere, friendly manner. "Perhaps you would consider sending your wife and daughters on the more comfortable passenger train. I'd be pleased to look after them until you're ready to press on by wagon from Wichita."

"Yeah, I *bet* you'd take care of my wife!" Pa's voice dripped with sarcasm. "My family goes where I go—and that's on the freight train."

Pa turned and stomped away before anyone else could speak. Once again, Will felt embarrassed by his father's erratic actions.

Mr. Briddle stared at Pa's retreating back for a moment, and then turned to Mary with a quizzical expression. "I'm sorry if I offended your husband, Mrs. Curtis. It certainly wasn't my intention."

"Please don't worry about it, Mr. Briddle," she replied in her melodious voice. "He's been under a lot of stress and takes offense quite easily. You've been very kind. My family and I thank you."

"My friends call me Randy," he replied. "I hope you–er, that is, you folks will be my friends, Mrs. Curtis."

"I'm sure we'll be seeing more of you, Randy, since we'll be settling near Winfield. Please call me Mary." She extended her hand to him.

"I—I sure hope so, Mary," Randy stammered like a moonstruck schoolboy and engulfed her hand firmly in both of his.

In Will's opinion, the handsome stranger gripped Mary's hand too long and too warmly. It made him suspect Randy Briddle's motives, but he didn't recognize his concern as jealousy.

CHAPTER 14

HEARTLAND

◆

When the Curtis entourage reached the bustling Santa Fe freight yard, they were instructed to proceed to a loading ramp where the flatbed car assigned for their wagons was spotted. By midafternoon, everything was loaded, much as it had been on the Katy train, except that two stock cars were allocated for their animals. The train was scheduled to leave at 7:00 PM.

Uncle Zeke gathered the family for the short walk to a nearby restaurant. Pa and Moses stayed to watch the stock and wagons. Pa seemed to still be smarting from the bridge incident, and Will thought Moses probably didn't join them because he wouldn't feel welcome in a restaurant full of white people. Zeke honored Moses's unspoken concern, but told Will he didn't like leaving Moses out of family functions because of other people's bigotry.

About sundown, the train chugged out of the Kansas City depot. Will and Moses rode in one livestock car and Zeke in the other. Mary and the girls were in the caboose again, and Pa rode with the wagons.

Even though he was bushed, Will experienced another difficult night. About the time he'd drop off to sleep, the train would come to a screeching halt, twice on sidings for northeast bound trains to pass, and perhaps another five times to unload or take on freight. He woke with the morning sun shining in his eyes. The train was stopped on a siding at Newton, Kansas, still some thirty miles from Wichita. He'd learned that the new Santa Fe railroad line forked at Newton. The mainline went west toward Colorado and the Rocky Mountains, but the one they'd be taking was a new branch line that went south, terminating at Wichita.

Zeke walked up to their car and said they'd be waiting on the siding for about an hour. It was an opportunity to water and feed the stock, and for Will to milk old Bessie. Baby Anne needed fresh milk.

Two hours later, the train slowly approached the new Wichita depot. The raw frontier town didn't impress Will much compared to the big cities he'd seen the last few days. However, the massive network of stock pens under construction near the depot whetted his curious nature. Uncle Zeke explained that Wichita was now the southern-most railhead and during the summer the pens would be filled with longhorn cattle driven up from Texas,

Pa demanded they press on to their destination, but Zeke insisted they utilize the rest of the day to getting organized for the sixty-mile wagon trip still ahead. With Josh grumbling, the family established a camp on the outskirts of town in a grove of trees on the Arkansas riverbank. At Zeke's suggestion, Mary and Will took one of the workhorses to pack the staples they intended to purchase at the general store. Zeke rode off looking for some breeding stock to buy. Pa left the girls with Moses and walked the quarter mile into the clapboard and tent town, saying he was going to do some saloon or street corner preaching. Will and Mary were back in camp with their purchases about an hour before Zeke rode into camp.

"Help me harness my spare team," he said to Will. "I've made a good buy on a light spring-mounted wagon, a brood hog, and some young cattle. I'll need you to drive the team and wagon back while I herd the cattle."

When Will returned driving the team hitched to a nearly new light wagon, Pa was back in camp. A huge sow hog in a sturdy slated crate nearly filled the wagon box. Zeke herded eight young heifers and a bull. When the procession stopped, Pa walked over and stared disdainfully at the purchases. He countenance warned Will that another confrontation between the brothers was likely.

"Where'd you get that dilapidated wagon, the mangy hog, and them skinny cattle?" Pa sneered. Color rose in Zeke's neck.

"Will stole 'em," Zeke replied. "If the law shows up, I'm innocent 'cause I only helped him drive 'em over here."

"I ain't in the mood for any of your smart talk, Zeke. Seems to me a fool thing to haul livestock all the way down to our homestead, when we ain't got no feed or place to keep 'em."

"I got a darn good buy for them critters," Zeke retorted. "The sow's going to have a litter soon. Plenty of brush where we're going; won't take no time to build some temporary corrals."

"Hu-u-umph," Josh grunted. "Well, why'd you buy another wagon? We got three already. Who's going to drive the team for it? Did you think about them things, Mr. Big Shot Leader?"

"Yeah, Josh, I thought about them things. Figured Mary could drive that extra team of mine hitched to the light wagon. They're gentle and we'll be in open country. What do you think, Mary?"

"Why, yes," Mary quickly replied. "I can do that, and we can use the extra space in the new wagon for the camp things. It'll be a lot handier."

"That's great," Zeke said. "I'm thinking the rig will be good for you going to town shopping and such, once we get settled on our homesteads."

"If my wife needed a wagon, I'd of bought her one!" Pa said. It seemed to Will that Pa's hackles were raised higher than usual.

"Hell, I wasn't giving it to her. The wagon's for family use. If we waited for you to do something, we'd still be back in West Virginia."

Pa sputtered some more, but Zeke ignored him and turned away to help Will. Mary returned to the campfire to serve up supper and Moses went for some rope to make a temporary corral for the tame cattle. Pa stomped over to the riverbank and knelt to pray, making a lonesome and pitiful sight in the gathering dusk. Will was sure that Pa's loud petitions to the Lord could probably be heard by the people in town.

They'd had breakfast, were packed, and on the way to Winfield by sunup. The well-defined, but rutted and dusty, road followed the Arkansas River south. Zeke suggested they make camp about 5:00 PM. Will agreed with that decision. He was bushed.

"Why you stopping now? We got another two hours of daylight," Pa complained.

"These horses are out of condition. Why push 'em? We can make Winfield easy by tomorrow evening," Zeke explained.

"My horses are just fine. Carting that fool hog and herding them skinny cattle is what's slowing us down."

"Hell, Josh, all the horses are tired, and so are we. The rest of us are camping here; you're welcome to press on if you like."

Those senseless arguments made Will cringe, and he noticed Zeke gritting his teeth, struggling mightily to contain his anger. The sensitive youngster sighed with relief when Zeke walked away and Pa got down from his wagon to unhitch the horses.

The next afternoon the weary travelers reached the frontier village of Winfield, located on the bank of the Walnut River. Will was disappointed with the place. On one side of the dirt street was a log cabin and a large tent with boarded up sides. A freshly painted sign hung over the tent's entrance, announcing to the world that this was "Rosie's Place." Further, down the street, a larger, peeled-log building, with raw pole corrals in back, was signed as a blacksmith and livery stable. Beyond it, two smaller tents were probably someone's living quarters. Three unpainted, store-fronted buildings and three tents lined the other side of the rutted street. One tent was identified as a café and the other two as saloons. An "Eats and Rooms" sign adorned the front of one two-story building and a new single-story building was unsigned. The other two-story building was the most impressive. Bright with a recent white paint job, it had a board front walk and a covered entrance. It's neatly painted sign read, "Briddle General Store."

Zeke pulled his team to a halt beside the trail on the outskirts of the settlement and motioned the others to stop nearby. Pa didn't step down from his wagon seat, making Zeke walk over to confer with him.

"Our land is about ten miles further south. Best we camp here and press on in the morning. Why don't you folks pull over to that grove of trees on the riverbank and start making camp. I'll walk over to Randy's store to let him know we got here okay."

"We got no time for socializing with a high-binder, the likes of Briddle. I'm going on to my land, *right now*," Pa stated, with an irritated toss of his head toward the south.

Zeke's eyes narrowed. "Well now, seems to me being friendly with our new neighbors ain't going to hurt us none. Besides, I kind of took a liking to Randy."

Turning away without waiting for his contrary brother to reply, Zeke spoke to Mary and Will, still sitting on the seats of their wagons. "Why don't you two come with me to see Randy and his store? And bring the girls. Moses, we won't be gone long. Will you help Josh watch our outfit until we get back?"

Moses took a nervous glance at his angry benefactor before he timidly replied to Zeke. "Yes, sir, I'll help Masta Sergeant look after things."

Randy appeared sincerely pleased to see them, but Will thought Mary received most of his attention. Using a plotted map of Cowley County, Kansas, on the wall of Randy's office, Zeke showed Will and Mary the exact locations their homesteads.

"Gosh," Will said, "we'll be right on the northern border of the Osage Reservation and the Oklahoma Indian Territory."

"Yep," Zeke confirmed. "The line is only about a mile from us, but there ain't no Osage camps nearer than twenty miles. Except for timber and brush along the Arkansas, and some creeks, there ain't much out there in Indian country but rolling grass-covered hills. It's some of the best cattle grazing country I ever saw."

"Do the Osages have cattle?"

"Darn few, but the time will come when they will. Buffalo have about all been slaughtered and most of them hills ain't much good for farming."

They purchased a few things from Randy's well-stocked store and returned to the wagons. Camp was established and supper finished before nightfall. Most of the village residents stopped by to introduce themselves and wish the new settlers welcome.

At first light on March 15, 1872, the homesteaders left Winfield on the last leg of the long journey from West Virginia. Will was ambivalent. While pleased the trip would soon be over, he felt they were leaving the last outpost of civilization. In his mind, they were headed into an unknown wilderness. Zeke led them almost due south over a wagon-track trail along the east bank of the Walnut River. About noon they forded the Walnut. An hour later, he stopped his team on a grassy knoll above a wide bend in the river. He got down from his wagon and motioned for the others to pull beside him. A half-mile expanse of the wooded river valley was visible below them and they could see the timber-lined track of the larger Arkansas River off to their right. He didn't speak until they had all gathered around.

"Well, folks, we made it!" he announced proudly. "This here is the northeast corner of one of our claims. The line runs south along the Walnut River, down there on the left, for about a mile, then she goes west across them hills for a half mile before doubling back north. We're just a short distance from the confluence of the Walnut and the Arkansas."

This is truly the heartland Will thought. They hadn't seen a living soul since leaving Winfield. It was hardly worth the trip halfway across the country. He kept his reservations to himself, not wanting to hurt his enthusiastic uncle's feelings. Pa didn't seem to have the same inhibitions.

"Where's all that good farmland you bragged about? This is nothing but wilderness!"

"Well, what the hell did you expect?" Zeke's voice trembled. Will judged him both hurt and angry. "I told you all along it was raw land that's got to be cleared and broke out. That bottomland you see down there will grow all manner of row crops, forever—if it's farmed right."

Pa surveyed the surroundings again with a frown on his face. "Hu-u-umph. Where's the other claim? Maybe it'll look better."

"It's about a mile west of here, over along the east bank of the Arkansas," Zeke replied. "I picked these two locations so each claim would have some timber, some hillside grassland, and some river bottomland. Mount up and I'll direct you to the other place. You can have your pick."

After making camp in a pleasant grove of pecan trees on the Arkansas, Zeke and Pa conducted a thorough inspection of both claims with Will tagging along. Pa complaining and grumbling for a couple of days, finally chose the claim located on the Arkansas.

Will would live on the bank of a river again, but regardless of his uncle's enthusiasm, he was disappointed with both rivers. With the exception of a few clearings, like the one they were camped in, dense underbrush lined the two-hundred-yard-wide riverbed of the Arkansas, which looked to Will like it was more sand than water. The shallow, one-hundred-foot-wide stream of muddy water seemed only a trickle compared to the swift, full-flowing Ohio. He didn't want to side with his pa against Uncle Zeke, but he felt the need to share his disappointment with someone.

"This place sure looks like the end of the world," he lamented to Mary. "And there ain't going to be no river boats traveling on that shallow, muddy river."

"Zeke says it'll be running full, bank to bank, in a month or so when the snow in the Rocky Mountains begins to melt," Mary offered cheerfully. She gave him a warm smile and a comforting hug of reassurance. "I'm sure we're going to make a good home here, Will."

If Mary and Uncle Zeke were both optimistic about their future in this wilderness, he guessed he could live with it. Pondering on how to get his friend Skeeter out here with him and the chirping of crickets kept the weary youngster awake for over an hour that first night at his new home. No ready answer to the Skeeter problem came to mind, but just before fatigue took over, he resolved to find a way, and soon. *I ain't going to tell him that ol' river is a half-mile wide and only a foot deep.*

CHAPTER 15

SODBUSTERS

◆

Standing on the rounded crest of a low hill, looking southwest, the Curtis men could see about a mile of the Arkansas River Valley. It was decision-making time.

"There may be better places to build your improvements than in that low bend of the river," Zeke told his argumentative brother.

"I'm telling you Zeke, my house is going to be built right there in that grove of trees where we're camped," Pa insisted. "It'll be cooler in the summer and warmer in the winter—and it's handy to river water."

"You're right on them points, but it could all wash away first time the Arkansas gets at flood stage," Zeke countered.

"We'll build the house up on blocks and the other stuff, further up on this here hill," Pa rationalized.

"With the house down there and the stock up above, the crap's going to drain down 'round your house when it rains. Seems to me, it's best to build everything except the corrals higher up."

"Well, we're talking about my house! I'm going to build it right in them trees. That's my final word on the matter!"

Zeke emitted a long sigh.

"Okay! Just don't blame me when your stuff ends up down in Indian Territory. But I insist we clear out at least ten acres of the bottomland for row crops, since our survival depends on harvesting a decent crop of corn this fall."

"Why can't we grow everything we need on these hillsides?" Josh quipped.

"Damn it, Josh. Stands to reason if we plow all the grass under on these hills for row crops, the topsoil will wash away in a few years."

"Well damnation, what's it good for then?"

"Look where you're standing, man! It's still winter brown now, but can't you tell how lush all that good natural grass will look by summer. It'll be great for grazing and making hay. Some of the gentler slopes will probably grow good wheat and oat crops though."

"Hu-u-umph," Josh growled from deep in his throat. "If you want to mess with clearing all that pucker-brush near the river, go right ahead. I ain't going to have nothing to do with it."

"If you don't intend to help clear the land, what will you be doing, Josh?"

As usual, Pa ignored Zeke's disdain. "Why, soon as we get a roof over our heads, I'm going down to the Indian Territory and bring th' Lord to them heathens. That's the work God sent me here to do."

"Well, I'll be damned if you wouldn't let your family starve while you go preach to a bunch of Indians."

"The Lord's work comes first. He'll see to our needs, Zeke."

"He sure as hell will, if we work our asses off before snow flies this winter. I've heard tell he helps those most who helps themselves."

Zeke turned and stomped down the hill toward camp.

"Best we get started," he snapped over his shoulder to Will and Moses. "It don't look like Josh and his hard-assed God is going to give us much help."

Moses glanced at Pa, ducked his head, and followed Zeke. Will trudged close behind, leaving Pa standing alone.

For the next couple of days, they all worked at cutting logs and hewing them to make floors for two tents they formed by stretching wagon canvases over wooden frames. Once those temporary sleeping quarters were completed, Will and Zeke began the arduous task of clearing thick groves of sumac, dogwood, and black oak brush from bottomland located in a wide bend in the river. Josh and Moses worked on building a two-room sod house.

After three weeks of backbreaking effort, only five acres were cleared and planted with corn. The spring planting season was fast slipping away. Zeke concluded that they'd best concentrate on plowing under some of the hillside sod to seed wheat and oats. On a bright spring morning, he hitched their strongest team to the big moldboard plow, intending to lay out a proposed field on the gentle hillside, and then turning the plowing over to Will while he continued clearing underbrush near the river.

Zeke was demonstrating to Will how to handle the plow when aggravation soon turned to frustration. He couldn't force the plow's angled share deep enough to dig under the thick mat of grass roots. When he did manage to hold the plow steady for a few yards, the moldboard wasn't curved enough to turn under all the thick foliage. Having no near neighbors to ask for advice, Zeke went to Winfield to discuss the problem with Randy Briddle. Randy sold him a specially designed sod-plow with a blunter shear and a larger, more curved moldboard that worked much better. But strong, firm hands were required on the handles to keep the plow upright and following straight behind the team.

The curved plow handles, designed for the height and grip of a grown man, stood as high as Will's armpits. After watching his slight-built nephew suffer through frustrating failures, Zeke suggested that Will stay with grubbing underbrush and he'd do the sod busting.

"There's a lot of sod to turn, so I'd best learn how to do it," Will stated, with chin thrust forward in bulldog determination. "Let me try for a couple more hours."

"Okay, if it means that much to you," Zeke agreed. "But there's no need to strain your gut. It sure ain't your fault that plow is too much for you."

By trial and error, Will developed a technique for controlling the monster by gripping the rod that separated the two plow handles. Exhausted, but determined, he stayed with the job until he could guide the huge plow at a constant depth with a straight furrow. There was a sense of accomplishment in seeing the matted grass roll under, exposing the rich brown soil to the air and sunshine in a nearly unbroken ribbon.

When Zeke bragged at the supper table about Will's tenacious sod busting ability, Mary gave him a congratulatory hug and Moses smiled from ear to ear.

"Ain't no big thing to be a sodbuster," Pa stated.

"It sure is when you're only thirteen and as light as Will," Zeke countered. "That boy's got gumption!"

By the first of July, the family had ten acres each of wheat and oats flourishing on gentle hillside slopes. Ten acres of dark green corn plants stood knee-high on cleared bottomland. Besides cooking, washing, and mending their clothes, and tending to the baby, Mary and willing little Jeanie had managed to plant and tend a large flourishing vegetable garden

.A rough, but serviceable, two-room sod cabin had also been completed. The larger room, with a rock fireplace and hearth, served as kitchen, dining room, and family gathering place. The other room was for storage and a bedroom for Mary and the girls. The men had done a good job of hewing red oak logs and fitting them tightly together to create a relatively smooth floor for both rooms. They had purchased and installed two glass windows from Randy's store, which provided a miniscule amount of daytime light.

Will and Uncle Zeke continued to share one of the sleeping tents. Pa used the other one and Moses remained in the comfortable bedroom he'd fixed up in one of the wagon boxes.

It was a good start, but they all realized, except perhaps Pa, that a lot more had to be done if they and their animals were to survive the coming winter.

CHAPTER 16

NEIGHBORS
◆

Will was beginning to wonder if his hard-pressing Uncle Zeke realized that there were limits to human durability. After having worked from daylight to dark, seven days a week for three and a half months, he knew the others were as tuckered out as he was. Faith in his uncle was restored when at the supper table on the evening of July second, Zeke announced his intention to take the family to Winfield for an Independence Day celebration. True to form, Pa denounced the idea as foolish and a sinful waste of time.

"Do what you like, Josh," Zeke stated. "The rest of us are going to Winfield tomorrow morning. We'll camp a couple of nights and be back the morning of the fifth."

It took them until midmorning to get the chores done and things packed for a two-day trip. Pa didn't come out of his sleeping tent to help or to see them off. The others didn't let his petulant attitude dampen their festive mood. Just in case there might be some racing, Zeke trailed his prize mare, Mendy, behind the wagon.

About half way to Winfield, Zeke pulled over to a grassy and shady place along the Walnut so they could eat the picnic lunch Mary had prepared. She had just finished spreading the food on the tailgate when a dilapidated wagon stopped beside theirs. A plump, red-faced man, wearing patched bib overalls stretched tight over his barrel-shaped upper body and a battered straw hat on his baldhead, stepped down and stuck out a pudgy hand to Zeke.

"Name's Buck Sommers," he volunteered, with a tobacco-stained, gap-tooth expression that was more sneer than smile.

With a cursory flip of his dirty hand toward the wagon, he continued, "Them there's my ol' woman, Joan, an' our two younguns, Homer and Emily."

Will's attention was drawn to the man's thin, bonneted wife and the pretty daughter, a plumper, younger copy of her mother. In their worn but clean clothes, they didn't seem to fit the image of the man and his gangling, redheaded son. When Homer climbed down from the wagon, Will judged him about three inches taller and a couple of years older than him.

The shabbily dressed beanpole eyeballed Will with an arrogant scowl. Will though he looked like a freckled-faced stork wearing patched overalls that were six inches too short. His stringy red hair was cut the same length all the way around his head. It resembled a frayed, red skullcap protruding from under a floppy-brimmed felt hat that was pulled down so far it made his large, jug-handle ears stick out.

"Pleased to meet you, Mr. Sommers," Zeke replied, shaking Buck's hand. "I'm Zeke Curtis."

Zeke nodded to the two children, removed his hat, reached up toward Joan Sommer's hand, and cordially said, "It's also a pleasure to meet you, Miz Sommers."

With an anxious glance at her husband, she hesitantly extended her slim hand, pulled it back quickly after barely touching Zeke's, and nodded without speaking. Her tired eyes made momentary contact with Zeke's, then focused back on her lap. The clean, well-brushed dark hair was pulled back severely, causing her slim face to seem undernourished. But there was concealed beauty there. Will noticed Zeke kept his eyes on her longer than a casual greeting required, which wasn't lost on her scowling husband.

"These other folks are all members of my brother's family," Zeke said. He introduced each one by name, including Moses.

Buck Sommers frowned at Moses for a few seconds, and then focused his beady eyes on Mary, with curiosity bordering on rudeness. Moving closer, he took her un-offered hand in both of his filthy, chubby paws. His attempted smile looked more lecherous than friendly.

"Pleased to meet you, Mr. Sommers," she said with a slight edge to her voice and pulled her hand free from his two-handed grip.

"Just call me Buck. I answer best to that name."

Turning to Zeke he said, "Your brother must be a lot younger than y'all, judging by his pretty young wife. Is he away somewheres?"

"Well, he's some older than Mary, but younger 'n me. He stayed home to watch the place." Zeke answered, making unwavering eye contact with the crude man. "Do you folks live around these parts?"

"Sure do," Buck said. "Got a place 'bout five miles east o' here. Been there over a year. Might not be there much longer though. Crops burned up last year, and looks bad again this year. We're thinking 'bout pulling out and heading on west."

"I'm sorry to hear that," Zeke said. It sounded polite enough, but Will detected a chill in the voice.

"Mind if we visit with you folks for a spell?" Buck asked. "We're headed to Winfield for the Fourth of July festivities."

"That's where we're headed, too. You're welcome to join us," Zeke offered. "Looks like we're practically neighbors—our places are about five miles southeast, between the Walnut and the Arkansas."

"Well now, don't that beat all? These here people is our neighbors," Buck chortled to his wife. "Get down Ma, so's we can get aquatinted with our neighbors."

Will thought he detected her cringe slightly. The haunted look in her sad, blue eyes and the haggard expression on her gaunt face struck him as odd. Zeke stepped forward to give her a hand and was rewarded with an attractive fleeting smile. She stepped down very ladylike.

"How do," she said to Mary in a friendly but weary voice, and then ducked her head when her husband gave her a disapproving look. Will could tell that the flagrant example of intimidation didn't sit well with Mary.

Homer ambled over by Will. "How old are you?" he demanded in an irritating, high-pitched voice.

"Hi," Will said, offering his hand. "I'll be fourteen on September twelfth."

The gangling youngster looked down on Will with an intimidating smirk, ignoring the offered hand. Uncle Zeke had told Will there were only two reasons why a man would refuse to shake your sincerely offered hand: he either considered himself better than you, or he intended to be your enemy. After a few seconds, Will dropped his hand, wondering which of the two reasons this red-topped stork had for not accepting his friendly offered hand.

"Where'd you get them sissy red 'spenders?" Homer sneered. "Them must be nigger 'spenders. They look just like them that old nigger's wearing."

Will held unwavering eye contact until the bigger boy blinked. His impulse was to tie into the insulting stranger, but he resisted the growing anger. Maybe Homer's just ignorant and hasn't been taught any manners, he reasoned. Whatever the reason, he wasn't going to let an insult to Moses go unchallenged.

"My—my pa's wife give these 'spenders to me and *my friend*, Moses. We both like 'em just fine." Hoping to change the subject to something less antagonistic, he added, "I best go eat."

Will turned and walked away before Homer could reply. The gangling, freckle-faced youngster scowled for a moment, and then followed in a disjointed gait.

Emily Sommers smiled shyly at Will and he smiled back, a little embarrassed because Mary was watching. She sure seemed a lot friendlier than her brother. He noticed she didn't resemble Homer or her pa a bit.

After Mary finished serving her family, she politely asked the Sommers family if they'd care to join them.

"Thank you, but we've already eaten our noon meal," Joan answered shyly.

"Well now, Ma, it ain't poo-lite to turn down our neighbor's hoss-po-tal-a-tee," pudgy Buck rebuked her.

He and Homer moved to the tailgate and helped themselves to big portions of the food, and proceeded to wolf it down. Joan and Emily held back, seemingly embarrassed. There wasn't a scrap left when Buck and Homer finished.

Buck reciprocated the hospitality by offering Zeke a drink out of his quart jar of white-lighting whiskey. Will judged it must have been good because it brought tears to Zeke's eyes, and he took a second swig when it was offered.

The two families drove on to Winfield in tandem, and made camp near each other on the bank of the Walnut River. About twenty other groups had already set up camps.

Will was disappointed with the new neighbors and didn't want anything more to do with arrogant Homer Sommers. He sure wasn't a Skeeter Cranston. Missing ol' Skeeter put a damper on his earlier festive enthusiasm.

CHAPTER 17

CONFRONTATION

◆

Randy Briddle and other business people in the growing village of Winfield organized contests and festivities for the Fourth of July celebration, including horse races. Riding his mare, Mendy, Zeke won all three of the races. Randy Briddle came in second, riding a large, dapple-gray gelding. He was a gracious loser, even though he'd missed out on the fifty dollar prize purse and lost a ten dollar side bet to Zeke on each race.

Other contests included separate burlap-sack races for the men, women, girls, and boys. Zeke's horse racing competitor, Randy, won the men's sack race. Will speculated his uncle probably had a couple too many swigs of moonshine whiskey before participating because he got winded before the finish line and came in second. Mort McCracken, a big, good-natured homesteader from up north of Winfield, came in third. Mary won the women's sack race by two yards, but then she had the advantage of being the youngest of the contestants. There were a couple of good-natured complaints from losers that she should have competed with the girls.

Will was humiliated when he lost the boys' sack race to his incipient antagonist, Homer Sommers. Long-legged Homer hopped to victory, while Will, using the short step technique, fell on his face. He resolved to practice and beat gloating Homer next year.

Pretty Emily Sommers won the girls' burlap-sack race and the girls' foot race. Will was pleased for her and impressed that she hiked up her long skirt and ran like the wind. Everybody saw her flour sack bloomers, with the brand name still imprinted on them, but she didn't seem to care. Will was sure that's something Mary would have done, if there had been a women's foot race. But, as far as he knew though, Mary didn't have any underwear made out of flour sack material.

The boys' footrace was restricted to those under sixteen. Ten competitors lined up, with Will being the smallest. The liveryman supervising the race disqualified one tall boy after he admitted being sixteen. He questioned Homer's age, but allowed him to participate when Buck said his son was only fifteen. Will didn't believe him. When the starting gun sounded, Will took off like a deer and stayed in the lead to the finish line. Gawky Homer, loping like a drunken stork, came in a close second. Uncle Zeke pounded Will on the back, whooping and hollering like a wild man. Mary nearly smothered him with a hug that buried his chin in her bosom. He'd grow enough that his nose wasn't covered now by that kind of hug. Before he could claim the prizes of a silver dollar and a sheath knife, Homer, backed up by Buck, complained that Will had started before the signal gun was fired.

"Like hell he did! He won because he's faster than them other boys," Uncle Zeke stated loudly. "Will's even fast enough to out run most of the men here."

The liveryman sought the opinions of a few people who had been standing near the starting line. All agreed Will hadn't started early, and he was awarded the prizes. After graciously thanking the judges, he walked away to find a drink of water. Disgruntled, Homer followed him. When they were hidden from most of the crowd by some bushes, he grabbed Will's arm and tried to twist it behind his back.

"I would of won that race if you hadn't cheated, you little skunk," Homer snarled. "Give me them prizes or I'll stomp the crap out of you!"

Unintimidated, Will wrenched his arm out of Homer's grip and stood his ground.

"I don't want no trouble with you Homer. I won these prizes fair and square. I intend to keep them!"

Homer grabbed the arm again, but seeing Mary watching them from the fringe of the crowd, he turned Will loose.

"That bitch, what says she's married to your pa, is watching now, but I'll get you later," Homer hissed and roughly pushed Will.

A few heartbeats later, the "bitch" insult to Mary registered in Will's brain as a red hot flash. He rushed Homer like an enraged bull—intent on beating that smirking, freckled face to a pulp.

His bigger opponent hit the ground on his back with Will astride him, hammering the hated face with repeated blows. The bully suffered substantial damage before Mary arrived and pulled Will off. It took all her strength to jerk the flailing youngster upright and pin his arms to his side. Will struggled to break free while kicking at his injured reclining foe. Scarcely able to restrain him, Mary shouted in his anger-deafened ear.

"Stop it, Will! Stop it, Will, before you kill him!"

Zeke and Buck arrived on the scene at about the same time. Zeke took Will from exhausted Mary's embrace and restrained him in his strong grip, while Buck managed to get his battered and blubbering son to a sitting position. One ear was smashed, an eye began to swell, and blood from his battered nose splattered on the front of his dirty, tattered shirt.

"What happened, Homer? Did that cheating kid sneak up and cold-cock you?"

"That's just what he done Pa," Homer panted between sobs. "He jumped me from behind and tried to kill me!"

The red film was starting to recede, but Will still snorted angrily.

"That—that's a lie! I told him I didn't want any trouble when he threatened to beat me up and take my prizes," Will hissed through clenched jaws. "When he called Mary a *bitch*, I intended to make 'im eat them words. Let me go, Uncle Zeke, and I'll finish off the bastard."

"Whoa there, Will, just simmer down. Looks like you done enough damage to cause him to watch his mouth in the future," Zeke counseled. And then he turned to Buck.

"I'm sorry these boys got into a fight, but if Homer called Mary a bitch, it's lucky we got to Will before Homer was hurt even worse." His voice had an unmistakable hard edge. "Best we keep 'em apart for a while, until they simmer down."

"That ain't good enough," Buck snapped at Zeke. "That cheating nephew of yourn ought to be horse-whipped for what he done to my boy—sneaking up on him from behind. If you don't aim to whoop him, I'll do it."

With eyes hard as steel, Zeke released Will and took the two steps that separated him from the red-faced man.

"Buck, you're making too much out of a couple of boys having a fight—but lets get one thing straight, if I had heard your boy call Mary a bitch, I'd have taken his hide off myself." Zeke's firm voice would have chilled a campfire coal. "I don't fault Will for doing what I'd of done. If you ever put a hand on him, I'll likely kill you."

After pausing for a moment, with his hot eyes boring into those of the out-of-condition slob who outweighed him by fifty pounds, Zeke threw down the gauntlet. "If you want satisfaction from me, just say the word, or make your move."

Buck fidgeted, ducked his head, and swallowed hard.

"Don't want no trouble with you, Zeke," he muttered, his voice squeaking with tension. "I-I just got carried away with concern for my boy."

"Well, I can understand that," Zeke replied evenly. "But you best teach him to watch his mouth before he gets himself into a heap more trouble. Now, unless you want to take this further, let's put it behind us and get back to the festivities."

"Yeah," Buck said, "let's do that." He got his battered son to his feet and they walked away toward their camp.

Will had cooled down and was feeling remorseful for having caused trouble. But he knew in his heart he'd do it again to anyone that bad-mouthed a member his family.

"Gosh, Uncle Zeke, I'm sorry. I don't know what come over me. There for a while, I wanted to kill ol' Homer."

"I know what come over you, Will," Zeke responded in a somber tone. "You've been cursed with a bad temper—just like mine. If you don't learn how to control it, you'll sure enough kill somebody one of these times."

Mary spoke sternly. "Will, I appreciate your sticking up for my virtue, but I've been called worse things than a bitch. It sure wasn't worth killing anyone for. I-I just saw a dangerous side of your nature, and I want you to promise me, here and now, that you'll curb that terrible temper in the future."

"I–I'll sure will try, Mary, but Uncle Zeke has told me a man should only allow himself to be pushed just so far, then he's got to stand up and be counted."

"Yeah, I've told you that, Will," Zeke admitted. "But for God's sake, don't keep your fuse too short and be sure the situation merits the consequences.

"Take what happened today. We've made some enemies and haven't heard the last of this little fracas. We'll have to be on guard. I judge Buck as the sneaky type. It'll be just a matter of time before he finds an underhanded way to try and get back at us. Men like him usually operate that way."

"Geez, I'm really sorry," Will lamented. "But I just had to lay into Homer when he bad-mouthed Mary."

Shaking his head slowly, Zeke had the last word. "I know how it is, Will. You're stuck with being too damn much like me, and it's going to cause some rough spots in your life."

Will considered his uncle's comment more of a compliment than a reprimand. That's what he wanted out of life—to be just like his Uncle Zeke!

CHAPTER 18

THE LORD'S WORK

◆

When the rest of the family returned to the homestead, they discovered that Pa, along with some supplies and his big saddle horse were missing. Also, the hole behind a loose rock in the hearth where they hid the family partnership funds was empty.

"Damn, I reckon Josh is serving notice he's breaking up our family partnership," Zeke muttered, more to himself than to the family. "All the cash I had, except what I just won horse racing, was in our partnership stash. How am I going to pay for the newfangled McCormack mowing machine I've ordered from Randy?"

Will agonized, watching Zeke silently fume for several seconds, before he spoke again.

"By God, if Josh doesn't come back with our money by the first of August, I'm taking his team and wagon into Winfield and selling 'em. It won't near cover what I put into this partnership, but I'll settle for it if there's enough to buy that mower."

One hot sunny day in late July, Will and Uncle Zeke stood on the hilltop above the valley surveying the parched fields below. Zeke slowly shook his head, reluctant to voice his concern, but the rest of the family had a right to know.

"We just ain't had enough rain for our crops to mature right," he blurted to Will.

Will already knew there was a serious problem because he had noticed his uncle's usually optimistic attitude wilt a little more each day as they watched once hardy plants wilt in the merciless sunshine.

"How bad you think it is, Uncle Zeke? Will we lose everything?"

"Well, maybe not everything. Thank God, we planted some corn in that bottomland. It may draw enough moisture from the river to make part of a crop, but there's not much chance for the oats and wheat heading out without more rain. We might get some hay from the native grass, but we'll have to cut it soon."

After pondering for a few seconds, Zeke expressed the obvious, "That mechanical mower is going to be needed more than ever."

Pa hadn't returned and there was no word of his whereabouts by August first. Zeke hitched two of the weakest horses to Pa's wagon and headed for Winfield. Mary and the girls accompanied him in the light wagon. Zeke considered Randy's offer for the team and wagon more than fair, so he didn't bother getting an offer from the livery stable owner. He was greatly relieved that the proceeds covered the cost of the mower, with money left over. He spent all the extra funds on a dozen laying hens, a rooster, and enough grain to see the hogs and chickens through until some corn could be harvested, if any of it matured.

Randy informed them the mower should arrive at the Wichita depot within the week. He'd send his men to pick it up and deliver it to their farm.

It was nearly dark when they arrived back at the farm. Mary jumped down from the wagon seat with the girls and hurried in to the sod cabin to start supper. Moses and Will came from the tack shed to help with the team. Zeke got down to assist.

"Pa's back!" Will said.

"Damn," Zeke replied, "He would show up on the day I sold his team and wagon."

Moses started toward the corral with the team. Will stayed to help Zeke remove the chicken coop from the wagon bed. It was Will that first saw Pa lumbering toward them from the cabin, carrying a lantern.

"Here he comes," Will said.

"Go help Moses with the horses," Zeke ordered brusquely.

Will started in that direction, but stopped in the shadows on the far side of the wagon, curious and concerned about the confrontation that was surely coming.

Pa reached the wagon and set the lantern down on the end of the open wagon box, as though freeing his hands to do battle. Will could clearly see the two brothers standing toe-to-toe and staring at each other in the pool of yellow light. Tension, thick enough to be cut with a knife, permeated the still summer night air. It seemed an eternity before Pa spoke first.

"Moses told me you took *my* wagon and team to Winfield to sell them," he fumed. "Who give you permission to sell *my* property?"

"The same guy that gave you permission to take our cash and run off, leaving us broke and with all the work to do. *That's who the hell gave me permission!*"

"I doubt that. God directs me," Pa exclaimed, raising his eyes to the sky and putting both hands up in a gesture of reaching toward his God.

"Hell's fire, what makes you so damn sure you're the only one God directs?" Zeke answered sarcastically. "For your information, you still owe me. Your team and wagon only brought about half as much as I put into that cash box you took. God told me to spend it on giving the family a chance to survive the hard winter that's fast coming down on us."

"Watch your blasphemous mouth, Zeke," the righteous preacher demanded of the sinner, as he clinched his fists. "God's gonna make you feel his wrath for taking his name in vain. He could strike you down where you stand!"

"That may be so," Zeke said, holding hot eye contact with the bigger man. "I'll take my chances."

"Well! I hear you squandered the money on one of them newfangled mowing machines," Pa accused. "Since when did you get too darn lazy to cut grain and hay with a scythe, like we've always done?"

"Ain't a matter of being lazy. We just flat out ain't got enough time to get it done that way before the snow flies. Of course, you don't give a tinker's damn about that; if you did, you wouldn't of been down in the Indian Territory, shirking your obligations as husband and father."

"I have an obligation to a higher authority, and I aim to keep it. You're the one what's shirking by preventing me doing God's will."

"*I'm shirking?*" Zeke roared. "Can't you get it through your thick head? The family needed that money you took, without nary a word to any of us."

"That money is being used in God's service. I'm building a mission for the Indian heathens," Pa said. "Was my intention to use *my* wagon and team to cart tools I need down to *my* mission. Now that you done sold it, I'll just have to take the big Studebaker wagon."

"Damn it man, have you lost your mind, altogether?" Zeke seemed furious, but struggling to stay civil. "You know we ain't got no tools to spare and we'll need both big wagons to haul in what we can harvest from our burning up crops."

Pa looked at his fuming brother with a quizzical expression. Zeke sucked in a couple of deep breaths.

"Josh., I'm telling you straight out that I've put up with all your goddamned foolishness I'm going to. If you try to take what this family needs to survive for some damn fool mission that the Indians don't need, and likely don't want, you'll have to whip my ass to get it!"

Will could see Zeke tense and clinch his fists. Pa's eyes bugged and his mouth dropped open. He stood muted with that startled look on his broad face for a few anxious seconds. And then his big body slumped as though he'd been hit in the gut.

"Zeke, brother Zeke, what are we doing here? The good Lord don't want his children fighting over him, least of all us brothers." His voice trembled, sounding sad and conciliatory.

"Have you forgot that I'm your brother? Would you stand in the way of my fulfilling the commitment I made to God on that awful battlefield, in return for him sparing my life? He done his part of the bargain, protecting me through all those other frightful battles when thousands were being slaughtered all around me. Now I have no choice, I *must* do his will!"

Josh's quivering, pleading voice failed him for a moment and tears rolled down his cheeks. Zeke seemed too stunned to speak. Will resisted an urge to rush to his hurting father and consol him. After a short period of poignant silence, Josh got his emotions under control enough to continue.

"P-a-a-paying that debt is all I'm trying to do. That's all I'm trying to do, *best I know how*." The tears flowed again.

Zeke put his arms around his suffering brother and gently patted his back.

"I know Josh, I know. It's got to be hard for you."

Soon Josh stifled his sobs. Zeke released him and stepped back.

"You're plumb worn out, Josh. Why don't you get a good night's sleep under your own roof? Things will likely look better in the morning. We'll work something out."

"Yeah, I'm very tired Zeke, but I got to go back. The Lord needs me down there in the Indian Territory. He's called me to help those poor people. I just *know* he has!"

"I *know* you believe that, but I'm telling you, your family needs you, too. God surely don't expect you to abandon your family, does he Josh?" Zeke's voice was calm and pleading.

"He says to forsake all others for him," Josh earnestly replied. "He's provided you and Mary to take care of the family. They don't need me and God tells me those pitiful Indians do."

Josh paused for a few seconds, apparently gathering his thoughts. His usually domineering loud voice was soft, little more than a whisper, when he next spoke.

"Anyways, God and both of us know there is some question about Will."

Will couldn't be sure of what he'd heard. What question? He strained to make out Zeke's response.

Zeke diverted his eyes from his anguished brother and sighed deeply. There were a few seconds of strained silence before he replied.

"That—that stuff about Will is all in your mind, Josh, but I ain't going to argue with you about things anymore. I'm just telling you that I think you're wrong about what God expects from you. Why don't you pray and ponder on it some more, before going off to the Indians again."

"I will, Zeke, I will." Pa's voice was now calm and his demeanor almost serene. He put his hand on his shorter brother's shoulder. "Whatever happens, I know the family is in good hands. They all love you, Zeke. God loves you, and I do too."

He picked up the lantern and handed it to Zeke, turned, and walked slowly toward the house. Zeke watched his brother's receding back until the image faded into the gathering darkness. And then he followed him to the sod house.

From his place in the shadows, tears rolled down Will's cheeks. He stood for a long time, stunned and pondering on what he had witnessed. What was the question about him that Pa had mentioned and Uncle Zeke evaded? He dried his eyes and ambled to the sod house. Somehow, he'd have to face both men and the rest of the family without letting on what he'd heard and seen.

The family awoke early the next morning to find that sometime during the night Josh had left again. All he'd taken with him this time was his saddle horse, a bedroll, a few supplies, the Curtis family Bible, and his Dragoon .44 caliber pistol, a gun he'd used in many Civil War battles, but hadn't touched since.

CHAPTER 19

FOURTEEN

◆

Randy Briddle delivered the new mower personally, along with presents for Mary and the girls. There was also a package for Zeke, which Zeke hustled into his living quarters tent. Mary's present was a book titled, *Little Women*, by Louisa May Alcott. Somehow, Randy had learned she admired Alcott's writing, but hadn't read much of her work. Mary showed her appreciation with a smile and a friendly hug. Randy blushed. Intellectually, Will realized he had no right to be peeved about the budding friendship between Mary and Mr. Briddle, but emotionally he had to admit to being jealous.

After giving the girls their presents, Randy turned toward taciturn Will.

"I notice you've been eyeballing this dog I brought with me," he said. "How do you like him?"

"He's a fine looking dog, Mr. Briddle. Is he a collie?"

"He sure is. Actually, he's a Scottish collie. That breed is considerably larger than the border collies sheepherders prefer. He's only two years old. When he reaches full maturity, he'll likely weigh over seventy-five pounds."

"Boy, he's a beauty."

"I've been told your pa wouldn't let you bring your dog from West Virginia. Do you think he'd let you keep this dog, if I was to give it to you?"

Will couldn't believe his ears. How in the world did Randy know he'd had to leave his dog in West Virginia and that he was aching for another one? He guessed it was Mary that told him. First, he looked to Mary for guidance. She responded with her usual warm smile, but didn't comment.

He turned a questioning expression toward his congenial uncle. "Do you think Pa would let me keep 'im, Uncle Zeke?" .

"Don't see no reason why not. Since Josh's not here, it's up to us to make the decision. We sure enough need a farm dog on the place and he looks like he'd make a good one."

"Well, he's yours then, Will," Randy said, "I've been calling him Rex, but he's still young enough that you could change it."

"Thank you—thank you, Mr. Briddle, I think Rex is a good name," Will exclaimed, breathless with excitement. "I bet Rex and Natty will be good friends. Could I take him down to the corral and show him to Natty?"

"You sure can, Will. He's all yours. Consider him an early birthday present. I understand you're going to be fourteen years old soon."

"Yeah, I sure am," Will answered with pride. "Rex is a great birthday present. I can't think of anything I'd like better, unless it was for my friend Skeeter to show up from West Virginia."

"I'm glad you like Rex. Best you keep a rope on him for a few days," Randy suggested. "Until he gets to know you, he might want to find his way back to his old home."

"Thanks again, Mr. Briddle," the happy boy shouted over his shoulder as he dashed toward the corrals. Rex loped behind him as though he already knew Will was his new master, and approved.

By August 30, there had been no substantial rain for over four weeks. It was time for hard decisions.

"There's lots of stem and blade growth on our grain, but looks like the heads just won't mature proper this year," Zeke lamented to Will and Moses. "Best we cut the grain fields for hay. Thank goodness for our new mowing machine. I'll cut the native hay with it, but how'd you like to give it a try on the grain, Will. Do you think you can handle that contraption?"

"I'll sure give it a try. Only thing I'm scared of is being too light to raise the sickle bar with that foot-lever, for turning and such."

"Well, we won't know 'til you try. Better keep an eye on that dog of yours so's he don't get a leg cut off."

"I'll keep a close watch on him. He learns fast and does what I tell him."

Will had grown at least two inches and put on about fifteen pounds of hard muscle since the spring plowing. He had no trouble handling the mowing machine. Boy, it was fun to see that grain fall in four-foot-wide swathes, but it had to be bunched with hand rakes and loaded on the wagons with pitchforks—darn hard work in the late summer heat. In less than three weeks, they had three large rounded stacks of hay neatly piled near the stock corrals: one each of oats and wheat, and a larger one of blue-stemmed native grass. Two of the canvas wagon covers that were no longer needed as sleeping shelters were stretched over the wheat and oat stacks and tied down securely. When the job was done, the entire family stood looking at the result.

"I'd say it's a darn sight better than losing the crops altogether," Zeke commented. "It won't make our cattle and horses fat, but it should keep 'em alive until spring—if it ain't too slow in coming."

Will shook his head in agreement and felt pride in what they had accomplished so far, while realizing that the battle with nature wasn't over.

"What do you think we should do about the corn crop?" he quizzed Zeke.

"We'll cut some of the smallest cornstalks for fodder," Zeke replied. "If the weather cooperates for a few more weeks, we should shuck out enough mature corn to see the hogs and chickens through the winter. Maybe there'll even be enough so we can feed some to Mendy. She'll be with colt this winter from Randy's prize stud."

"Do you think we can get it all done 'fore the first snow?"

"Simple fact is, we got to, Will. We'll be able to live by butchering a hog and eating the canned produce from Mary and Jeanie's garden, but our stock has to have some grain to survive."

Mary and her willing little helper, Jeanie, had saved the garden by laboriously carrying water to it from the river.

It rained hard the day after the last load of grain hay had been put on the stack. Even though they had prayed for rain earlier, they were thankful it held off until the hay was in. It was Will's fourteenth birthday and Zeke declared a holiday.

With loving hands, Mary baked a big, fluffy angel food cake and splurged with their diminishing sugar supply to slap on thick white frosting. Having no small candles, she stuck fourteen kitchen matches into the frosting.

"Pucker up, Will, before I light these," she ordered. "You'll have to blow 'em out fast or the heat will melt and burn the icing."

"Ol' windy Will ain't going to have no trouble blowing out them matches," Zeke assured her. And Will proved his uncle right.

Mary presented Will with the shirt she had made for him and the cherished Shakespeare book she'd purchased in Cincinnati. She had helped Jeanie knit him a pair of wool socks. The exuberant seven-year-old gave them to her big brother and received a hug and kiss on the cheek in return. With great pride, Moses presented Will with a three-note flute he'd made out of a green, slippery willow branch.

"Does you recall me teaching you how to play a flute, back in West Virginie, Masta Will?"

"Sure do," Will replied. He put the tapered-reed end to his lips and produced a mournful screech. They all laughed at the sour notes.

"Guess you're out of practice and needs some more lessons," Moses chuckled. "I done made myself one too, so's we can play 'em together."

Zeke chimed in, "While we're on the subject of music, got something here I want to show you, Will."

He pulled a large package from behind his chair. Rather than hand it over to Will, he unwrapped it himself, revealing a shiny new guitar with a broad red and yellow shoulder strap. He leisurely strummed the strings a few times.

"How you like my new guitar, Will?"

"Gosh, Uncle Zeke, are you finally replacing that beat-up old guitar of yours?" Will asked in a kidding manner, thinking the old one was going to be his birthday present from Zeke.

"Well now, Willie, bad-mouthing my good ol' guitar does hurt me some," Zeke replied with a dead-pan expression, "after all them times you've begged me to let you strum it."

"Uncle Zeke, I like your old guitar fine. Now that you've got a new one, can I have it?" He overlooked his uncle calling him Willie, a name he hated more as he grew older.

"That dog just won't hunt, Willie boy. You done made fun of that fine instrument, like it weren't good enough for you." Zeke's tone and countenance were dead serious.

Will's smile was replaced with a confused expression. He really wanted that old guitar. Hoping he hadn't unintentionally hurt Zeke's feelings trying to be funny, Will pondered for a few seconds on how best to clarify his intentions.

"Guess there's no getting 'round it," Zeke drawled. "Now that you've made the old guitar mad, I'll just have to keep it and let you have this here new one."

The birthday boy stared speechless as Zeke handed the shiny guitar across the table to him. The forlorn expression changed to a broad smile. Little did he know that when he smiled in that way, he looked just like his Uncle Zeke. Only the mustache was missing.

Though overjoyed, Will lamented his own gullibility. Wouldn't he ever learn? He'd fallen for Uncle Zeke's joshing again, hook, line, and sinker. Finally, he found his voice, but it was chocked with emotion.

"Th-thanks, Uncle Zeke. I should have known you was pullin' my leg. Boy, this here is a beauty!"

The excited, budding musician strummed the strings for a few bars. It sounded better than his flute playing because Uncle Zeke had recently given him some lessons.

"Well, Willie, it's reassuring that even though you've reached the old age of fourteen, I can still get away with teasing you some," his uncle chuckled.

The happy boy could feel the pride and love projected toward him in his Uncle Zeke's toothy smile and sparkling hazel eyes, a grin and hazel eyes that were just like what he saw when he looked in a mirror and smiled.

CHAPTER 20

FAMILY TIES

◆

"Damn the Kansas weather! Where the hell was all this rain when we needed it?" Zeke shouted, turning toward Will and Moses.

The fall rain had deluged them for three weeks and the fields were a quagmire with over half their corn crop still not harvested. Just as Zeke had predicted, the buildings and corrals in the low area where Josh had insisted they be situated were threatened from the heavy hillside run-off and rising waters of the Arkansas. They'd done all they could to protect the meager stock feed supply already harvested.

"It's in the hands of the good Lord now, Masta Zeke. Ain't going to do no good to rant and rave about it," Moses counseled.

"You're probably right, Moses," Zeke agreed. "I just hope he knows that if we don't get that corn out of the field before it rots, our hogs and chickens can't survive the winter!"

"Are things that bad, Uncle Zeke?" Will lamented. Worry lines wrinkled his brow, barely visible under the dripping brim of his old black felt hat.

"They're bad all right, but I've seen worse," Zeke said, forcing a smile. "I think we got the hay and corncrib safe. Let's go see if darling Mary has some hot grub and coffee for us poor, miserable souls."

Will wanted to believe his uncle, but he really wasn't too sure as he eyeballed the water lapping the base of the two-foot-high earthen dam they'd thrown up around their vital stock feed supplies.

"It sure won't do us no harm to pray for the good Lord to bless us with some help in this time of need," Moses offered.

"You're probably right about that, Moses. But I've noticed the Lord helps them most who work hardest at helping themselves." Zeke rubbed a wet calloused hand over his whisker-stubble jaw and emitted a long sigh of resignation. "He surely must know how hard we been trying."

At the supper table, Moses, who usually said the blessing when Pa wasn't there, added a plea for better weather and suggested they all do the same before they went to sleep. Will intended to do that without Moses's urging. About midnight, the cursed rain stopped, and by morning, a cold front moved in. Will was willing to give Moses's God the credit.

Two days of freezing weather firmed the cornfield enough so they could get the wagons in without sinking to the hubs. Working in the wet, muddy mess from twilight to dusk, they salvaged the rest of the corn crop by week's end. Some was shucked and some was cut and put in shocks as fodder. Even Mary and little Jeanie helped, with year-old Anne riding bundled up on the wagon seat beside Moses. Zeke announced it'd be tight, but he judged there was enough to get their animals through the winter, if spring wasn't too long in coming. In celebration, Mary fixed chicken and dumplings for supper. After helping clean up the dishes, Zeke and Will picked out some cowboy and hoedown tunes on their guitars. Moses played the flute and the girls sang. The tight-knit, proud, and dog-tired family enjoyed a well-earned festive evening, having fought the fickle Kansas elements and won a slim victory. But was it enough to win the war?

Moses reminded them it couldn't have been done if God hadn't answered their prayers. Before they went off to their beckoning beds, the somber, old black man offered up a prayer of thanks for their salvation, and added a request for the good health and safety of Masta Sergeant, wherever he might be. They all said amen, but Will's was the loudest. He worried a lot about his pa.

Rumors came to them about a big, redheaded, ranting preacher that was wandering around down in the Indian Territory. They assumed it was Pa. One evening, Will shared his concern with Zeke.

"Do you think Pa's safe down there in the territory? You know he'll tie into anyone with his preaching. The cowboy that dropped by last week said the Territory is full of outlaws and all kinds of bad people. Some of 'em might not take kindly to Pa's pushy ways."

"I wouldn't worry too much about him, Will. Your pa's irritating and pushy, right enough, but he's also big and tough enough to take care of himself."

"But we'd never know if something bad happened to him. Maybe we should go down there and make sure he's okay."

"I was kind of giving some thought to that, too," Zeke admitted. "He'll likely show up here to spend Christmas with the family. Let's assume no news is good news and give it a little longer."

"Okay, but I just got a feeling in my gut that things aren't going good for him."

Before Christmas, they received the first cash earned by the farm. They sold the sow's litter to the butcher in Winfield, except for one young sow for future breeding and a large shoat for their own meat.

Butchering was a nasty job that Will hated, but the entire family had to pitch in. Every part of the carcass was utilized: The skin and fat were rendered into lard and some was made into lye soap. Residuals from rendered skin and deep-fried intestines were kept for cracklings and chitterlings snacks. Shoulders and haunches were cured for hams and the sides were salted for bacon.

In the fall, Zeke had announced his intention to leave his sleeping tent where it was for the winter, rather than move it over to his property. He winterized those quarters with a three-foot high log base, new waterproof canvas stretched over the weathered wagon-cover canvas, and the installation of a small stove. Will, who had been sleeping on a pallet beside the fireplace in the sod house since Pa left, asked to move in with him.

"You'd best stay in the house with the gals. You can help keep the fireplace stoked and such," Zeke advised. "If your pa shows up, I'll make room for you and he can do the fire stoking."

Actually, Will was pleased with that arrangement. It gave him special time with Mary. They were alone after Zeke had left for his tent and the girls had gone to bed. Moses slept in the tack room that was attached to the cowshed they had built. Often, Mary wore only her nightgown while sitting next to him during the lessons. Surely, she didn't realize how that affected him; yet, sometimes he wasn't so sure that she didn't.

During the long winter evenings, Will noticed Zeke spending more time with Jeanie, who never seemed to demand much from any of them. Zeke frequently mention how much he thought she looked like her mother. She found Zeke's lap a comfortable place and her uncle seemed to cherish the special bond that was developing between them. Sometimes toddler Anne vied with her sister for that special attention. When she lost out to her faster and pushy big sister, Will's lap was her second choice.

It didn't take Jeanie, a budding charmer, long to wangled Zeke into brushing her hair. It soon became their regular ritual. As her rugged uncle gently brushed her long, auburn locks, she breathlessly told him wild stories about many things. He'd listen dutifully, appropriately bugging his eyes in astonishment, nodding his head in agreement, and even emitting an occasional gasp.

One winter night, with the snow blowing outside and the fireplace cozily crackling inside, Jeanie sat contently on Zeke's lap. As usual, he gently stroked her hair with the brush and she earnestly related her latest fantasy.

"Uncle Zeke," she said in her pretend-grown-up little voice, "I saw a great big gray wolf behind the cowshed today." The two little arms spread as wide as they would reach to show that the imaginary wolf was indeed a big sucker. There were no wolves in that part of Kansas, just big coyotes, but she'd been reading about wolves in her studies and had seen pictures of the ferocious predators.

"Aw-w-w," Zeke gasped with his eyes bugged, "that sounds like a big one. What do you think he was doing there?"

"Most likely he was after Bessie's baby calf. Them wolves eat meat, and they're sneaky, you know!"

"Yeah, Jeanie, they sure are sneaky, and dangerous, too! Weren't you scared he might take after you?"

"Naw, I weren't scared, Uncle Zeke," the little girl replied with exaggerated bravado. "I just told Rex to sic 'em and he chased that wolf over the hill, going south. I'll bet that old wolf didn't stop until it was down in the Territory, where Pa is."

"Well, if he got that far, maybe your pa shot him and he'll bring you back the skin for a rug."

"Yeah, my pa's a good shot and he wouldn't be scared of any old wolf; would he, Uncle Zeke?" Jeanie earnestly queried.

"No, your pa sure wouldn't be scared of any wolf, little darling," Zeke assured the wide-eyed, little girl. "Your pa's a good shot all right, and there ain't much that scares him."

"Yeah, and you ain't scared of nothing either, are you, Uncle Zeke?" She stated that fact with certainty and confirmed it with a couple of exaggerated up and down shakes of her head and defiantly sticking out her cute little chin.

"When you reckon Pa's coming home?" she asked in a matter of fact tone.

Before Zeke had time to answer that difficult question, the exuberant youngster made eye contact with him and changed the subject.

"I love you, Uncle Zeke." She planted a kiss on his whisker-grizzled cheek and gently patted his bushy moustache with her slender little fingers for a moment before wiggling down from his lap to start her reading lessons with Mary.

"Hum-m-ph, hum-m-ph," he muttered and changed the subject in a failed effort to hide his emotions.

"You been putting them wild ideas about wolves in her pretty, little head, or does she just make up them stories on her own?" he asked Mary with bogus gruffness.

"They're mostly her own ideas, but then she just might be trying to top her Uncle Zeke in wild storytelling," Mary replied with twinkling eyes and a knowing smile. "I think she's heard a few whoppers from that source."

"Hum-m-mph," Zeke responded, sounding just like his brother Josh when he was frustrated about something. "Well-Well," he stammered, "I guess I'd best watch my language around these younguns from now on."

"Now, Zeke, I didn't intend to imply it was wrong for them to mimic their loving uncle. They could do a lot worse, and we're all lucky we've got you."

Mary walked over and planted a juicy kiss on Zeke's weathered cheek before turning to the task of helping Jeanie with her reading.

Will was busy over by the fireplace, struggling with his assigned multiplication and division problems. He produced a warm smile of appreciation for the intimate interplay between his family members.

Zeke cleared his throat again. "It's getting late and I best go turn in. See you folks in the morning."

CHAPTER 21

TRAPPER AND HUNTER

◆

"Will, did you do any animal trapping back in West Virginia?" Randy Briddle had asked while he was at the homestead delivering their mower.

"Yeah, some," Will replied." Me and Skeeter trapped a few rabbits."

"I was thinking more along the lines of critters like muskrats and otters. Those are the furs that are used for making lady's fancy coats, hats, and such."

"No, we never got any of them animals. But we hunted down a few opossums and skunks with my good old dog Crusher. Mr. Snyder, the man that owned the store in New Haven, gave us ten cents a skin if they were cured properly."

"I don't mess with those skins because the price they bring isn't worth the cost of shipping. But I take it you know how to skin, stretch, and dry hides?"

"Wel-l-l, yeah, but Moses helped us some with that," Will admitted.

"Reason I'm asking all these questions is because I was wondering if you'd be interested in partnering with me on a trapping venture this winter."

"Gosh, Mr. Briddle, I don't know nothing about trapping those critters you mentioned."

"I'll bet it wouldn't take a bright guy like you long to learn," Randy countered.

"I did some trapping for beaver out in the Rocky Mountains the first winter I was prospecting for gold," Zeke inserted. "I think I can remember enough to teach you the basics, Will, and there ain't no one better at skinning and curing green hides than Moses."

"What kind of deal did you have in mind, Mr. Briddle?" Will asked.

"For starters, if we're going to be partners, how about you calling me Randy. As to the deal, I have two dozen traps with me that I'll lend you. Come spring, I'll pay you 50 percent of the going wholesale rate, less freight costs to the Kansas City buyer, for all the muskrat, otter, or raccoon pelts you bring me that are properly stretched and cured."

"I sure appreciate the offer, Randy, but seeing as how I'd be doing all the work, seems to me 75 percent for my share would be fairer."

"Will, you've got the makings of a great businessman," Randy chuckled. "It's a deal; 75 percent for you. Here's my hand on it!"

They shook hands, as one businessman to another. Will was elated at the prospect of contributing some cash to the family's meager liquid assets. He would have settled for 50 percent, but was pleased with himself for having negotiated a better deal.

During the winter months, Will and Rex spent about four hours each day running the trap line that extended nearly two miles along the banks of the Walnut and Arkansas. After a slow start while learning, his catch improved to as many as four pelts a day. Most of them were muskrats, but a few were the more expensive, but elusive, otters. Moses helped him skin, scrape, and mount the hides on the stretching frames that he had helped Will fashion from willow branches.

Randy had told Will that coonskins were twice as valuable as otter pelts. Zeke informed him there was small chance of trapping a wily coon unless he happened to catch one in the hen house. Will asked Moses what he knew about hunting coons.

"My old Masta, down in Virginie, had a pack of special trained coon dogs," Moses told him. "I recalls many's a time them hounds chased coons all night long. When a big ol' coon see he can't outrun them dogs, he find a tree near water. Then he go out on a limb and jumps down in deep water. He better swimmer than any dog. When the dog follow him in, he pull that dog under and drown 'im."

"Well, I don't think any ol' coon could outrun Rex, or whoop him in a fight," Will asserted.

"Rex a strong dog alright, but-t-t, if he tree one of them full-grown he-coons you best get there quick to shoot 'im. He sure going to try to kill your dog; that's just their nature."

"Will you go coon hunting with me and Rex one of these nights, Moses?"

"I surely wish I could, Masta Will, but my old legs just couldn't keep up with you and Rex when he hot on the trail of a fast moving coon. Ask your Uncle Zeke to go with you. He were one fine hunter back home."

Zeke told him that chasing coons all night, after a hard day of cutting and fitting logs for the cabin he was building on his homestead, wasn't his idea of relaxation. But Will kept pestering until his uncle agreed to go with him and Rex—just one time—to show them how it was done.

Soon after dark, on a clear, cold, and moonlit night, they began their coon hunt on the hill east of the farmstead. Eager Rex sniffed and yapped, while ranging in an arc about two hundred yards out front. Will and Zeke trotted behind the dog in the general direction of the sound of his voice, encumbered with only a lantern and Will's small-caliber hunting rifle. Some three hours later, the hard working dog had led them to the bank of a substantial creek, about two miles north of the farm. They heard him bellow some distance off to their right.

"Best we hightail it," Zeke shouted over his shoulder, as he took off in a trot toward the sound. "He's cut a trail. Most likely it's a coon and he's moving fast."

Will followed in his Uncle's footsteps, trying to stay close because Zeke carried the lantern. During the next hour, the baying dog followed his prey in a wide circle, crossing the shallow creek twice. Rex seemed to work the hot scent like a seasoned coonhound. About midnight, the tenacious dog's bellowing settled in one place and changed tone. Frantic, loud, and mournful, it penetrated the otherwise still cold night air.

"He's got that critter treed, and he's telling us to come fast," Zeke grunted through labored breaths. "I'd judge he's a quarter mile away, over on the Walnut."

"Keep going," Will panted without breaking stride. "I'm right behind you. Darn coon ain't worth getting Rex hurt."

They moved toward the frantic sound as rapidly as they could over the rough terrain. It led them toward a large oak that stood alone on the edge of the riverbank with branches extending over the water. As they approached, Rex's bellowing abruptly changed to throaty growls, which were interspersed with eerie, high-pitched screeches, and sounds of splashing water.

The two breathless trackers came to an abrupt halt under the oak tree on the three-foot-high riverbank. What they saw in the ambient light of the full moon, supplemented by the feeble yellow glow of the lantern, chilled their blood. In about two feet of water, a life and death fight raged between Rex and a gigantic hissing coon. They seemed an even match. Rex maneuvered his ferocious adversary into shallow water for better footing. With his powerful jaws griping the big coon by the nape of his neck, Rex shook him like a rag doll. The equally determined coon raked Rex viciously on his neck, chest, and sides with razor-sharp claws. Though bleeding profusely, the courageous dog showed no signs of giving up the fight, nor did the coon. Frantic with concern, Will pushed past Zeke, intent on jumping into the water to help his endangered buddy. Zeke caught his arm in his strong grip just in time to prevent a potentially tragic error.

"Let me go. The coon's killing Rex!" Will screeched hysterically, struggling to break his uncle's hold."

"Will, listen to me!" Zeke shouted in his ear. "If you jump in there you'll only be in Rex's way. That coon will likely rip both of you to pieces."

"*What are we going do?*"

"We'll take a chance on shooting the coon without hitting Rex. Hand me your rifle. I'll do it."

Will twisted, trying to break away from his uncle, while holding his rifle at arm's length, out of Zeke's reach.

"*No!* He's my dog. I'll do it!" he insisted. Will seldom defied his uncle, but, by God, this was his dog.

"Okay, but you best simmer down and listen to me! You're only going to get one chance. Move in as close as you can."

He released his grip on Will's arm and picked up a stout piece of driftwood.

"I'll be right behind you with the lantern and this club. Get with it, boy!"

They both splashed into the near-freezing water. Zeke held the lantern as high as he could and Will maneuvered for a clear shot. The target bobbed and swirled. Zeke feared Will was taking too long when, as though he sensed that his life depended on it, Rex pinned the clawing coon up against the muddy riverbank and held him there between his front legs. For just a moment, the tangled fighters were relatively still. Will sucked in his breath and took his shot. The coon's body shuddered for a moment and then went limp. But the fight wasn't over for Rex. He held on to the dead coon tenaciously.

"Drop it, Rex," Zeke commanded. "Drop it, boy. You won!"

After failing to dislodge the lifeless body with his hands, Zeke picked up a stick, forced it between the determined dog's teeth, and applied pressure. Finally, the dead coon dropped at the water's edge. The injured dog collapsed into about a foot of muddy water.

Frantically, Zeke and Will lifted the inert, mud-caked dog and laid him on the riverbank. Will chocked back a sob when the lantern light revealed slashing wounds on his great dog's right side, head, and chest. The worse one was at the base of Rex's neck. Zeke ripped off his coat and then his shirt, which he used for a compress.

"We got a serious problem here, Will," Zeke lamented while holding the makeshift compress firmly against the neck wound and throwing his coat over the injured dog's wet body.

Shivering, with only his long underwear covering his upper body, Zeke looked into his nephew's worried eyes and told him the dreadful truth.

"He just ain't going to make it unless we get the bleeding stopped and warm him up—damn soon."

"I can see that!" Will screamed at his uncle. "Let's quit talking and start home with him."

"Settle down, Will, and listen to me. There's no way we can keep Rex warm and this compress in place while carrying the big fellow some two miles over rough country."

"What—what are we going do then? Are you going to just let him *die*?" Will screamed hysterically.

"Get hold of yourself, Will," Zeke demanded. "We're going to save this dog, but we got to stay calm. You hold this here compress firm on Rex's neck—but don't choke 'im—while I build a fire over beside them rocks."

With a plentiful supply of dry driftwood nearby, Zeke had a blazing fire going in a few minutes. Gently, they moved Rex, close enough to the fire for him to draw warmth without singing his hair. Steam rose from his wet fur emitting a pungent odor. Zeke cradled Rex's damaged head in his lap and gently rubbed the dog's wet, muddy body with his coat to stimulate circulation, while holding the compress to the neck wound with his other hand. Rex was conscious, but unresponsive.

"You run for the house and saddle Mendy. Grab a couple of old blankets out of my tent and that can o' Smith's Balm," Zeke instructed. "Oh, and you might ask Mary for some clean cloths so's we can bind up this compress and clean these other wounds, before we move him."

Will rose to his feet and stood there looking down compassionately at his suffering buddy.

"Will, did you hear me? You've got to go, *now*!" Zeke ordered harshly.

"I—I don't want to leave him this way," Will moaned.

"You've got to, if you want him to live. I'd go, but you're the faster runner. You know I'll do all I can for this ol' feller while you're gone."

"Yeah, I know you will, Uncle Zeke. Just keep him alive. I'll be back fast as I can."

Will removed his coat and draped it over his shivering uncle's underwear-clad shoulders, grabbed the lantern, and took off at a fast trot. Later, Zeke would swear Will flew to the farm. In very short time, he was back with everything Zeke ordered—plus Moses riding behind him on Mendy. The compassionate old black man wasn't about to be left behind when Will tearfully informed him that Rex was badly hurt.

"After all," he reminded Will, "I'm the family healer, and ol' Rex needs me. I ain't going to slow you down none."

Even in his weakened condition, Rex seemed to recognize Moses. He mustered enough strength to wag his tail slightly, as Moses cleaned his wounds and deftly applied soothing balm to them. He spoke softly as he worked.

"You going to be all right, you good ol' big dog. Moses here now, and he'll make you well. You just take it easy, good feller."

Will wondered if Moses's calm and confident reassurance didn't do more for his patient than the medication. It certainly was therapeutic for Will's shattered nerves. For the first time since they'd pulled the battered dog out of the river, he had real hope for Rex's recovery.

Zeke mounted Mendy and instructed Will and Moses to pass the limp dog up to him. While they struggled to lift him, the dog's involuntary whimpers wrenched their hearts, but it had to be done. Zeke cradled his blanket-wrapped patient against his stomach with one arm under his head and shoulders and the other under his rump. They bunched up another blanket to give Rex some protection from the saddle horn, but it was Zeke's intention to hold the heavy dog in his arms until they reached the farm.

Because it didn't seem right to Will that he should profit from something that almost got his buddy killed, he intended to leave the dead coon where it had fallen.

"Masta Will, your Rex near got himself killed getting you that coon—and that coon done fight hard for his life, too." Moses gently admonished Will. "It do seem a shame if his dying weren't put to some good use."

Moses was right, as usual, Will realized. He picked up the dead coon and was amazed at its size. Moses said it was one of the biggest he'd ever seen. No wonder he came so close to killing Rex. Will strapped the body behind his uncle's saddle, vowing that if God pulled Rex through this, he'd never ask him to hunt another coon.

While Will led the horse, Moses stumbled along beside, reaching up to help support Rex. Just his gifted, healing touch and soothing voice seemed comforting to the suffering patient. By the time they reached the farmstead, Will could tell that Zeke was functioning on sheer guts, but he hadn't ask for a halt. Mary and Jeanie were anxiously waiting in the yard and helped remove Rex from Zeke's desperate grip. Zeke remained in the saddle traumatized from fatigue, until Moses and Will helped him dismount. Mary suggested they take the wounded dog into the warmth of the sod house, but Moses insisted Rex be placed on a pallet in the tack shed near him. He had a little stove out there.

"I can keep him warm," he said. "My patient should be near his doctor."

They couldn't dispute Moses's healing touch; he was truly blessed. The family rejoiced when the mangled dog began to take nourishment within a week. Moses had him walking stiffly within two weeks and eager to go hunting with Will within a month. Yet, there were limits, even to Moses's great talents. As time passed, it became obvious that Rex had suffered some permanent damage to his shoulders. He would never recover his full youth and vigor. The coonskin had been costly!

CHAPTER 22

PREMONITION

◆

One day in mid-March 1873, Zeke, Will, and Moses stood on the same hill from which the family made the decision about where to place the house, out buildings, and corrals just a year before. From there, they had a clear view of the fields they had wrestled for the wilderness and the improvements they had built during that difficult first year. They had won a battle, if not the war, by bringing all the livestock through the hard winter alive, but lank. Now the fast approaching spring planting season presented another challenge.

"We'll have to face up to the problem of where we'll be getting the oat and wheat seed we'll need for this year's planting," Zeke stated with a wrinkled brow.

"Didn't Randy say he was shipping in some seed from northeast Kansas?" Will asked.

"Yeah, he did, and the price he set seems reasonable under the circumstances. But we haven't any cash," Zeke stated.

"Didn't Randy say he'd carry us until harvest?"

"Yes, but that means paying high interest, and it just goes against my principles to go into debt."

"I've got that bunch of hides from my trapping. How about we use whatever they bring to help pay for the seed?"

"That's your money, Will. You worked darn hard for it and that coon pelt nearly cost Rex his life."

"It's family money, way I see it. I think ol' Rex feels the same way—don't you, Rex?" The dog wagged his tail vigorously. "See, he said yes."

"Okay, if you're sure that's what you want," Zeke agreed. "We'll take 'em to Winfield tomorrow and see what they'll fetch."

Even though it was raining lightly the next morning, they loaded the sizable mound of cured pelts into the light wagon, covered them with a canvas, and departed for Winfield. Mary and the girls bundled up and went with Will and Zeke because they hadn't been off the farm in over two months.

Moses stayed home to watch the place. Some small things had come up missing around the farm and one of their pigs disappeared from the wallow they'd fixed down on the riverbank. Zeke said he suspected the Sommers clan might be involved, trying to get back at them for the beating Will had given Homer, but he couldn't find any proof.

"I count 'em to be ninety-seven muskrats, thirty-nine otters, and one raccoon," Will informed his partner Randy.

"This here's more pelts than I though you'd get for your first year trapping. But I knew you'd be a fast learner, Will," Randy replied to the proud youngster.

"The coon pelts darn near cost Rex his life," Will told Randy, pointing to the happily panting dog that they had brought along so he could visit with his mother and siblings.

"I'm sorry about your dog getting hurt, but it looks like Moses pulled him through all right," Randy commented.

"Yeah, he did a good doctoring job all right, but he says Rex probably has some permanent damage in his shoulders," Will said sadly.

"Sorry to hear that," Randy sympathized. He furrowed his brow and rubbed his chin a few seconds before continuing

"I've been told there's a financial panic starting back east," he said as much to Zeke as to Will.

"How you figure that'll affect us out here in the heartland?" Zeke asked.

"Well, for one thing, the Santa Fe railroad isn't going to start the extension south from Wichita this summer, like they promised. The reason I feel obliged to mention it now is because the fur buyers aren't offering as much for pelts as they paid last year."

"Gosh, Randy," Will said, disappointment showing in his voice. "We was hoping my furs would bring enough to pay for the wheat and oat seed we need."

"Well now, Will, I didn't say they were worthless. It's just that the market is soft. Let's take a closer look at what you've got."

They spread the pelts out on the floor of the storage shed behind Randy's store, sorted by species. Randy pursed his mouth and shook his head in approval while he carefully inspected each pelt.

"Those are darn good-looking skins. You've stretched and cured them better than the Indians do. Prime furs like these will fetch top dollar, even if the market is soft."

Self-conscious from the unabashed praise, Will's cheeks turned pink. While pleased with himself, he felt obligated to be honest.

"I—I had a lot of help from Moses, working those skins," he confessed. "He had experience from when he was a slave down in Virginnie–er–I mean, in Vir-gin-ia."

Will noticed Mary smiling broadly. She had been silently observing the proceedings. He assumed the warm smile was aimed at him as a reward for his grammar and elocution, which she'd been working on with him, as well as for his honesty. Whatever her reason, it always made him feel good to please Mary.

"Whatever, you've done well," Randy said. "Let's do a little arithmetic and figure out what you've got coming."

In Randy's tidy office, Will held his breath so long in anticipation that he nearly fainted while his partner calculated with pencil and paper. Finally, Randy spoke.

"Folks, the way I figure, Will has produced enough furs to pay for all that seed grain, plus $11.50."

Will felt like whooping with joy, but settled for saying, "Gee, that's great, Randy."

Zeke pounded Will on the back so hard it made his teeth rattle. Mary rewarded Randy with an especially big smile. Will sure didn't want to seem ungrateful, but he wondered if that warm of a smile was really called for. It seemed to rattle Randy for a moment. When he regained his wits, he took $11.50 from a desk drawer and counted it out into Will's hand. The elated youngster's hand shook, his eyes bugged at the pile of money, and he felt the urge to pee. The amount of $11.50 was a veritable fortune to a guy that had never had more cash money in his hands than the silver dollar he'd gotten last Fourth of July for winning the boy's foot race. He recalled that's what had caused the fight with ol' Homer Sommers, and wondered what had brought that disagreeable thought into his head at a happy time like this.

"Didn't you say that Moses helped you prepare those furs?" Randy quizzed.

"He sure did," Will confirmed emphatically. "Fact is, he did most of the work—and I almost stunk him out of his sleeping place when I put a couple of my first green skins in there with him."

"Well, seems to me we should give Moses a bonus for his work. You pick five dollars worth of goods that he might like from the store and take it to Moses with my compliments for a job well done."

"That's darn nice of you, Randy," Zeke commented. "Moses ain't got one helluva lot during his life. I know he'll appreciate what you're doing for him."

"Just assure him that I think he earned it," Randy insisted.

If he was trying to impress Mary, Will noticed that he seemed to have succeeded. Will liked Randy a lot, but it just wasn't fair that the man was so handsome—and rich, too. He wasn't really sure why that bothered him.

They picked out a pair of Levi pants for Moses that had buttons on them so he could use the special red suspenders Mary had given him. There was credit left for a flannel shirt and a wide-brimmed straw hat. Will added enough from his recently acquired wealth for a can of pipe tobacco and a bag of hard candy. Smoking his old corncob pipe in the evenings after supper was Moses's only vice, and he loved any kind of sweets. Will bought a separate bag of sweets for the girls.

Randy tactfully broached the subject of Josh's whereabouts.

"As far as we know, he's still down in the Indian Territory doing his preaching," Zeke replied. "I promised Will I'd go down there and check on him before we start plowing. I aim to start looking soon after we get back home."

Moses and Will had spent much of their free time during the winter training Natty, Will's spirited buckskin colt. They'd succeeded in getting him to follow where he was led if rewarded with a handful of grain. The day after returning from Winfield, the two horse trainers decided it was time to take the next step: putting a bridle on him and a bit in his mouth. With the stout horse snubbed to a post in the center of the corral, they worked on the project for half an hour without success. For the umpteenth time, Will tried to force the cold steel bit between the colt's clinched teeth. Moses stood nearby giving verbal encouragement.

From out of the blue, a ghostly likeness of his pa flashed into Will's mind. Pa's face was distorted in agony and he reached a clawed hand toward Will. The macabre scene faded as quickly as it had appeared. Had he heard the aberration moan, "Help me, son"? Will shuddered. The bridle slipped from his limp hands and dropped to the ground. Moses picked it up and tried handing it back. Will stared into space with sightless bugged eyes. Bewildered, Moses put his hand on the youngster's shoulder and gently shook him.

"Wha-wha-what!" Will stammered as though waking from a trance.

"You looks like you done seen a ghost, Masta Will," Moses said with a quizzical expression.

"I-I don't know as how it was a ghost, but I sure saw something scary," Will replied, still shaken, yet beginning to get back his wits.

"You want to tell me about it?"

"It was about Pa," Will confessed. "If you don't mind, I'd like to talk with Uncle Zeke first." Will didn't want to hurt his old friend's feelings, but he knew Moses was just too darn emotional and superstitious to rationally deal with a message like the one he'd received.

Moses raised one white eyebrow. "Go 'head. I think he working in the tack shed. I most likely have this bridle on that stubborn colt time you gets back, without you in my way."

Will entered the tack shed with a worried look on his face.

"What's up, Willie?" Zeke said lightheartedly. "You look like you're carrying the weight of the world on your shoulders."

"Most likely you'll think I'm crazy, but I just received a strange image of Pa."

"What kind of a image?"

"Like he was in trouble or something."

"Tell me about it," Zeke answered seriously. "I ain't going to think you're crazy because during the war I learned not to take revelations lightly."

"Tell you the truth; it's kind of hard to explain. All at once, I saw Pa with his face all in pain and he was reaching out to me. I—I think he called out to me, too." Will choked up.

"Sounds like a damn strong message. But I suggest we don't think the worst until we get some facts. It's time I go find your wayward pa anyway. I'll pack up and leave tomorrow."

"Can I go with you, Uncle Zeke?" Will pleaded. "Pa must need *me*. He had pleading eyes and he was reaching out to *me*."

"Sure would like your company, but if we both go, who'll look out for the family and get started on that brush grubbing on the new land we planned on opening up?"

"Moses and Mary can make out for awhile and that brush can wait," Will stated so firmly it caused Zeke to raise his eyebrows.

"Believe me, Will, I know how you feel, but there's two reasons I'm asking you to stay with the family. For one thing, there's a lot of rough people down the in the Territory. I don't know what would happen to the girls if we both got killed. Not that I intend to get myself killed, but there's always danger when traveling in lawless country.

"The main reason I haven't gone looking for Josh sooner is that I've been worried all along about them sneaky Sommers. Now I'm even more concerned. Randy told me Buck's been shooting off his big mouth about it being way past time that he got even with us."

"You're right," Will agreed. "One of us has got to stay and you'll do the best job looking for Pa."

"Sometimes, Will, it takes more guts to stay behind and take care of things than it does to go traipsing off looking for trouble. God knows, I'd feel better with you riding with me down there, but you made the right choice."

"Then you'll be leaving tomorrow?"

"I'll pack my tucker and leave at first light. Best we don't tell the girls about our conversation concerning them Sommers."

"I won't tell 'em, but I'm going to tell Moses so he can help me keep a sharp eye out."

"Tell him if you like. It won't change anything with him. He's been looking out for us for years, and will be until the good Lord takes him."

They were all out in the yard to see Zeke off the next morning. Jeanie hugged him long and hard.

Mary hugged him and kissed him on the cheek. "God go with you, Zeke Curtis. Come home safe. This family needs you," she said.

Toddler Anne gave him a hug and clung so tightly that Mary had to pry her away.

Moses held back until the last. He took Zeke's hand in both of his.

"I done said a prayer for you, Masta Zeke. I ask God keep you safe and help y'all find Masta Sergeant and brings him home to his 'n family."

"Thank you, Moses. I'll do my best."

The former cavalryman swung nimbly into his saddle and rode away without looking back.

CHAPTER 23

SEARCHING

◆

Zeke rode southeast across the bleak, rolling hills of the Osage Nation. He was cold and hungry. All he had to show for fifteen days of searching were frustrations and a saddle-sore butt. His elusive brother seemed to have disappeared into the vast Indian territory. If he'd followed through on his expressed intention to build a mission for the Indians, its location was well hidden.

A short, but violent, thunderstorm had passed through just before daylight, soaking him and his sparse camp. Giving up on starting a fire with wet wood on top of the soaked ashes, Zeke packed his damp tack and continued his trek without breakfast or even a hot cup of coffee.

"I've got a wet ass and a hungry gut," Zeke said to his mount. "How you feeling this fine morning, Mendy dear?"

She hadn't had any breakfast either, but the intrepid mare pressed on with her head ducked against the chilling crosswind. After days on the move, she still carried her rider at a steady mile-eating gait, but she was showing the need for rest and grain. Zeke worried about the foal she carried. Pregnant by Randy's big stud, she was expecting a colt in about three months.

If those Indians had given him good directions, Zeke anticipated reaching the Blackburn Trading Post a little after noon. Assuming he could buy oats and hay for Mendy there and some hot grub for himself, he intended to keep moving without taking a lunch break. Missing another meal wasn't a big deal for him, but he sure wanted something for Mendy.

When the trail went cold down in the Creek Nation four days ago, Zeke had reluctantly decided to give up. Maybe he'd try again when the crops were planted. If he rode hard, he'd decided, he could still be back at the farm within the two-week time limit he had set for himself. And then day before yesterday, while riding across the Osage Nation toward home, he came upon an Osage hunting party preparing their midday meal. They were a ragtag lot, but seemed friendly enough. The leader offered to share their lunch with him. Zeke gnawed on half-cooked venison, cold fry-bread, and enjoyed the weak, but hot, coffee, while the gaunt hunters ravaged their food with lip-smacking gusto and grunts. They were all working on a second cup of coffee before the taciturn leader spoke.

"You ride far?" he asked gutturally with a wave of his arm that encompassed the hills around them.

"Long trail," Zeke replied, mimicking the Indian's clipped English and hand signs. "Looking for lost brother in Cherokee and Creek nations."

"You find?"

"No. Go home, plant crops. Look more come summer."

"Brother hunter, trapper, trader?"

"No, he's a preacher." The Indians stared at each other and back at Zeke with blank expressions. Zeke tried again. "Teach Bible, black book, Jesus, white man God!"

They all nodded understanding. The spokesman responded, "He shout hal-ah-lu-ya? He say bad Indians burn in hell?"

Zeke brightened. "Yes, he shouts. You see white man that shouts like that?"

"This many," the leader grinned as he held up both hands with the fingers spread. "They all want save Indian from hellfire, devil. Say Indian great spirit no good! What brother look like?"

"Big, red hair, talks loud," Zeke replied.

"I see man like that, three, maybe four, moons ago, at Osage village near Blackburn Trader Post."

"Is he there now?"

"Maybe yes, maybe no. Is bad place. Trader bad man. Big, red hair man say he build mission; save drunk Indians. Two days ride. You go see?"

Zeke was torn by indecision. It seemed a good lead, but he was only two days ride from home and running late for his committed time for returning. There was a worried family and spring planting waiting for him. But they were all worried about Josh, too. Finally, an unwillingness to accept defeat won the mental debate. He turned Mendy onto the dim trail that the Indians said would take him to the Blackburn Trading Post.

About midafternoon, Zeke gazed down from a fifty-foot-high bluff at a disreputable looking establishment. A rambling, ramshackle log building, a pole-corral with a lean-to shed, a couple of smaller log structures, and two tattered tepees were sprawled in a flat area created by a bend in the river.

"That sorry-looking place must be the Blackburn Trading Post," Zeke speculated to Mendy. "It sure ain't big enough for much of an Osage village. There's a wisp of smoke coming out the biggest building's chimney. Someone must be home and they've got some company." Three saddled horses were tied to the hitching rail in front. Five unsaddled horses were in the corral.

Zeke felt uneasy, like an itch he couldn't reach to scratch, as he rode down the narrow, winding trail into the brush-covered valley. A faded "Blackburn Trading Post" sign hung on the front of the derelict log building. The tired and hungry traveler swung down from his saddle and tied Mendy to the hitching rail next to the other horses. The edgy feeling intensified and tightened Zeke's belly. He'd learned in the war to heed such warnings. Outside of the rough plank door, he unbuttoned his hip-length coat and pulled the right side back, exposing the butt of his holstered Navy Colt .44.

It took a firm push to open the sagging door. Quickly stepping inside, he moved to the right and closed the door with his left hand in one fluid movement. Without appearing threatening, he let his right hand casually hang near the butt of his pistol.

Stale air reeked of tobacco and wood smoke, unwashed human bodies, and raw whiskey. With his back to the cabin wall, Zeke's light-sensitive eyes scanned the dim interior. If someone intended to dry-gulch him, now was when it would happen. After a few critical seconds, his eyes adjusted enough to make out the images of three grubby white men sitting at a rough plank table near the center of the shabby room. A half-empty whiskey bottle sat in the table's center. Partially filled glasses were in front of the men. They held greasy playing cards in their hands and there was a small stack of poker chips in the center of the table.

In front of him and to his left, a large potbellied man with shaggy hair and a matching black beard sat slumped on a high stool behind a crude bar. Zeke's adjusting eyes picked up a slight movement in a darker corner of the room. On closer observation, he identified the object as a shabbily dressed Indian woman cowering on a pile of cured hides.

The unusually skimpy supply of trade goods caught his attention next. Non-descript garments hung from pegs on two of the walls and a few cans and boxes were on rough shelves to the right of the bar. Perhaps a dozen bottles of whiskey and two tapped beer kegs were on shelves behind the bar. Not much of a trading post, Zeke concluded. *Something else is going on here.*

The three men at the poker table eyeballed Zeke suspiciously. The expression on the face of the big man behind the bar resembled that of a snarling lobo wolf. The silence was ominous. Zeke's adrenaline level escalated and his senses went on full alert. An inner voice that had saved his life more than once spoke to him, "Keep your cool, Zeke, and stay alert!"

He assumed the hairy brute scowling at him from behind the bar was the proprietor of the miserable establishment. After drawing in a couple of breaths to settle his nerves, and forcing what he hoped would pass for a friendly smile, Zeke spoke to the sullen man.

"Is it okay for a tired and hungry traveler to come in out of the wind?"

"Don't see why not, lessen you're a nigger," the surly hulk snarled back at him with a white trash, southern accent. "If y'all want food, whiskey, or this here squaw for a hour or so, they're all for sale—cash up front."

"Well, that's right neighborly of you to offer the squaw, but it's some oats for my mare and hot grub for myself I prefer right now," Zeke replied lightheartedly.

"Sell you a gallon of oats for fifty cents and throw in a fork full of hay. Bowl of beef stew gonna cost you twenty-five cents more. A shot o' my best whiskey is another twenty-five cents. That'll be one damn Yankee dollar, upfront. You got that kind of money, stranger?"

"Does any bread, coffee, or refills come with the stew?" Zeke asked cheerfully.

"That'll cost you another two bits—and if you change your mind 'bout the squaw, that'll be another damn Yankee dollar."

"I'll pass on the woman because I ain't got much money," Zeke replied, struggling to keep his voice even as his anger level escalated.

With his eyesight adjusted to the bad light, he discerned that the cowering Indian female seemed to have a slender, well-developed body, even though she wore a tattered oversized dress. Her face and bare arms showed evidence of recent abuse. The piercing dark eyes darted between the trader and him, like those of a wounded doe's.

My God, he thought, she's little more than a girl and it looks like these yahoos have sure used her hard! He clinched his jaw, trying to control the rising rage.

Zeke carefully pulled a silver dollar and a quarter from his pocket, stepped forward, and placed it on the rough bar in front of the loathsome trader. All three of the scumbags at the table continued to scowl and eyeball him with hostility.

"I'll take the package, with coffee and refills because I ain't had no breakfast or dinner. Where can I feed my horse?"

"There's oats in the lean-to at the back of the store. You'll see an old washtub out there. Y'all can feed your crow-bait critter, right there at the hitching rail. Pitchfork is by the haystack. This here lazy squaw 'll have your grub ready when you get back in."

With that, the burly man heaved himself up from his stool and lumbered a couple of steps toward the Indian girl.

"You heard what I said, you dumb bitch! Get your lazy ass out there in the kitchen and dish up a bowl o' that stew. Bring the coffee pot and some fry-bread, too."

The intimidated girl jumped to her feet and scurried toward the back room like a startled quail. As she passed near the trader, he took a kick at her. Being young and agile, she managed to evade his vicious boot, which seemed to infuriate him.

Zeke came within a split second of drawing down on the bully, even though he realized that if he did, he'd likely have the three owl-hoots at the card table to deal with too. He gritted his teeth and turned toward the door.

While he loosened the saddle girth, removed Mendy's bit, and put out the feed for her, he continued to seethe, telling himself he was here for information and the odds were not in his favor for a fight.

"None of my damn business, is it, ol' gal?" he muttered to Mendy, with the muscles rippling in his clamped jaws. After giving him a quizzical look, she returned to munching her late breakfast.

"Yeah, I know you're right, my beauty. A thing like this is every decent man's business! But we're in enemy territory here without hope of reinforcements. Let's just play it cool 'til we get the lay of the battlefield. You know damn well I don't intend to leave that poor soul in such a mess!" he told the horse.

Zeke reentered the ominous building, alert and ready to draw his pistol at the slightest provocation. His breath released in an almost audible sigh when he saw the bowl of hot stew, an iron pot with more stew in it, two pieces of warm fry-bread, and a cup of coffee were sitting on a side table. He removed his coat and sat down to eat with his back to the wall.

Hungry as a wolf, he attacked the food and drank the coffee without speaking, while keeping a stealthy eye on the other men in the room. The hostility was pervasive. The Indian girl was nowhere in sight, dirty black-beard was perched back on his stool, hovering like a fat vulture, and the three hard cases made a pretense at playing cards.

"Damn, I didn't realize how hungry I was," he said when he'd finished off his second bowl of the surprisingly good beef stew. The fry-bread was tasty, too. That little Indian gal must be a good cook, he thought, but didn't say.

"Do you want that drink o' whiskey you bought now?" the trader growled.

Damn, but he's a surly bastard, Zeke thought. A smile would most likely break his pig-eyed face. Why in the hell is he pushing his rotgut whiskey? He really wasn't interested in a drink, but he figured he best not make these guys suspicious or rile them more than they already were.

"Well, since it's part of the package, I'll just as well have a snort." Zeke replied, in a faked pleasant manner that didn't quite ring true.

Zeke found it especially strange that the three men at the card table hadn't acknowledged his presence, much less spoken a word to him since he entered the place. He did notice them eyeballing the well-oiled .44 he wore, slung low and with the holster tied down in gunfighter style, more to keep it from flopping around when he rode than for a fast draw.

He sure didn't consider himself a killer or a fast-draw gunfighter, but he'd always had guts enough to stand up and be counted when there was no other way to settle matters. At least two dead men in his past, other than the uncounted numbers he'd killed in the war, validated that fact. But these hard cases wouldn't know that, he realized.

"You men look like Texas cowboys," he said toward the three men at the table. "Are you up here scouting out the trail for the cattle drive this summer?"

The men, as one, looked to the trader and he made a slight affirmative nod of his head before one of them gruffly replied to Zeke's question.

"Yeah, that's what we are. Just taking a little break from the trail."

Bullshit, Zeke thought, hoping his skepticism didn't show on his face. He wasn't very good at deception or lying.

The trader had returned to his perch behind the bar, after slamming a shot glass of whiskey on the table in front of Zeke. He spoke up before Zeke could speak again to the idlers at the card table.

"You look like a damn saddle tramp. What business you got around here?"

It wasn't said as a compliment, but Zeke managed a smile.

"Yeah, that pretty much describes me. I'm just passing through. Say, a bunch of Osages I saw on the trail said something about a preacher that has a mission here 'bouts. Do any of you guys know where it is?"

The three men at the poker table snapped their heads toward the trader, again in unison. Zeke thought they looked like he had just thrown a skunk into the room. The trader stood up abruptly and leaned toward Zeke, with one hand on the crude bar and the other poised near the hog-leg pistol he wore on his massive hip.

Zeke stiffened, sensing that the varmint intended to draw down on him. He couldn't take them all out, but by God, he'd sure put at least one slug into that buzzard's fat gut before they got him. The big man may have read Zeke's hard eyes. There was a moment of indecision before his ham-like hand moved slightly away from the butt of his six-shooter.

"What the hell you want to know 'bout a preacher for?" he barked out with venom. "Are you one of them damn Bible-thumping piss-ants, too?"

Tense as he was, Zeke managed to chuckle and answered in a steady voice.

"I been called a lot of things, but nobody ever accused me of being a preacher before. I was just curious because I saw a loud-mouthed, redheaded sky pilot down in the Creek Nation while back. They run 'im off down there and I wondered if he might of come up here."

The trader stared hard at Zeke for several unnerving seconds.

"There were a crazy bastard that fit that description, what spent some time in the Osage village, downriver a piece, but he took to messing with their women and they run 'im off."

If that was Josh, they had to be lying, Zeke thought. He may have problems, but he sure never messed with somebody's women.

"Well," Zeke said as he stood up. He stretched and reached for his coat, trying to act casual. "Now that I got my gut full and my ass warm, best I be moseying on. Nice to have met you gents."

None of them replied and the tension could have been cut with a knife. Zeke forced himself to walk casually to the door. He felt their collective eyes drilling into his back, expecting to hear the distinctive rustle of a pistol being drawn from holster leather at any moment.

Once outside, with the door closed behind him, he exhaled loudly, trying to purge his lungs of the stale air and his mind of debilitating blind rage. The quick gulps of fresh cool air he inhaled as he tightened the girth, replaced Mindy's bit, and untied the reins did more to settle his nerves than the drink of rotgut whiskey would have done that he'd left untouched on the table.

"I got a feeling those bastards know something about Josh that they don't want me to find out," he told Mendy as he reined her onto a well-traveled trail that headed downriver. "And, I'll bet you a bucket of oats to a shot of good whiskey that some of those hard cases will try to bushwhack us. We'll just find a good place to play out this hand, Mendy ol' gal."

CHAPTER 24

MARTYRDOM

◆

It was Zeke's assumption that the trail he followed downstream along the west bank of the Arkansas River would take him to the Osage Indian village he was looking for. About quarter-mile downriver, a twelve-foot-high rock outcrop choked the trail up against the riverbank so close that only one rider at a time could safely pass through. On the other side of the outcrop, the trail veered away from the river through dense growths of blackjack and sumac underbrush. Zeke's battlefield training told him that the top of the outcrop was a good place to observe his back trail and defend himself if necessary. He'd have to find a way up there and somewhere to conceal Mendy.

He dismounted on the downriver side of the outcrop and led his docile mare into the dense ten-foot-high brush at the base of the rock formations. It was tough going, but about twenty yards in, he came upon a small clearing. Nearby, there was a rockslide that would allow him access to the top of the outcrop.

After securing Mendy in the clearing, it took him only a few minutes to reach the top. Carefully working his way back toward the river along the ten-foot-wide crest, he came to a natural swale large enough to afford excellent concealment for a couple of people lying prone. That vantage point would give him a clear view of the back trail and two hundred yards of the downriver trail on the other side. Zeke unlimbered the telescoping spyglass he had liberated from a Confederate officer during the war. Properly focused, the back trail and rear of the trading post came clearly into view. His timing was perfect. In about five minutes, the three card players from the trading post appeared trotting their horses down the trail toward him. About thirty feet from where he lay concealed, they slowed their horses to pass single file through the trail's restricted point. Zeke's sharp ears picked up snatches of their conversation.

"The boss should have let us shoot that nosey stranger when he didn't drink that doctored shot of whiskey," one man said.

"Hell, he looked like a tough bastard to me. He might of got one of us if we'd of drawed on 'im. It's safer to bushwhack 'im and he'll be just as dead," another replied.

The man bringing up the rear grumbled, "Well, I don't like riding up on 'im on the trail. He might get suspicious, and be laying for us."

"He probably don't know the trail and ain't in no hurry. We'll loop around and bushwhack 'im at…"

The man's gruff voice faded away, as the riders disappeared from Zeke's view. They soon reappeared on the far side and spurred their horses into a lope.

"Ah ha, sure no doubt about what them yahoos are up to," Zeke muttered to himself. "They mean to do me in, and I don't even know why."

He remained in the rock notch for a few more minutes, trying to formulate a plan of action. For sure, he couldn't take this unfamiliar trail to the Indian camp. There was no telling where those hard cases would be waiting to dry-gulch him. His first inclination was to go back to the trading post, get the drop on that filthy trader, and force some answers out of him. But how to do that without getting shot or having to shoot the dirty bastard was the question. In his gut, he felt these strangers had something to do with Josh—and it wasn't good.

While pondering on the problem, he trained his spyglass back up-trail to reconnoiter the trading post. At that moment, the back door flew open. The Indian girl stumbled out and staggered toward him. Though obviously impaired, she seemed determined to get away. Frequently looking back, she gathered speed as she approached the trail's choke point.

A quick check of the cabin with his spyglass assured Zeke that no one had emerged in pursuit. He intended to speak to the desperate girl when she was through the choke point, but she surprised him by ducking into the dense brush on the other side so fast he failed to get her attention. Either she knew about a different trail or intended to hide there, he reasoned. And then it dawned on him that she'd likely stumble on Mendy. He scrambled down as fast as he could, intent on intercepting her before she got away with his horse and gear.

When he reached the clearing, the Indian girl was standing beside Mendy bewildered and frightened. Seeing him, she quickly darted away, like a startled deer. Zeke caught her when her shabby dress tangled in the bushes. He spoke kindly to her while gently trying to extract her without ripping the garment worse than it was. He could tell it was all she was wearing and it only partially covered her firm, shapely body. She fiercely resisted his efforts.

"I'm not going to hurt you none; just want to talk with you some."

She continued to struggle. Zeke lifted her off her feet in a restraining bear hug, trying not to hurt her. Surprisingly strong, the human tigress bit his hand, flailed at him with her fists, kicked his shins with her moccasin-clad feet, and tried to knee him in his groin.

"Easy there, gal. I mean you no harm. Just simmer down and I'll let you loose," Zeke pleaded, with the same soothing voice he'd use with a rebellious horse. He began to suspect she was either completely loco or didn't understand English. Suddenly, she quit the struggle and slumped in Zeke's tiring arms.

"Do you understand English?" Zeke asked, continuing to hold onto her, but more gently. She nodded her head affirmative.

"Now I'm not going to hurt you, little gal," he reassured her for the umpteenth time. "I'm just out here in this country looking for my brother and we might be able to help each other. I'll turn you loose if you'll promise not to run off, okay?"

"I promise," she replied in unexpected concise English.

Zeke eased her down to a sitting position on a windfall log. For the first time, he got a clear look at her. One eye was nearly swollen shut. Her long, dark hair was matted with blood from a contusion on the left side of her head. The left earlobe was partially ripped from her head. Zeke shuttered to think what damage was concealed by what was left of her torn filthy dress. He felt an overwhelming urge to go kill the miserable sons of bitches who had committed those atrocities on the young woman. Good Lord, she couldn't be any older than their Mary! The tough ex-cavalryman swallowed hard to fight down the lump that obstructed his throat. He removed his canteen from Mendy's saddle horn, wetted his bandana, and gently began cleaning her wounds. He noticed her complexion was lighter and her facial bone structure finer that those of most Osage women he'd seen. Maybe she was Cherokee?

"Don't you worry none, little gal. I'm going to take care of you. I won't let them bastards hurt you no more," he promised softly.

He tended to her visible wounds best he could, while realizing there were likely psychological wounds he couldn't touch. The battered girl relaxed slightly, and didn't resist his cleaning. There was the frantic gleam of a cornered animal in her visible eye, but no tears. After submitting to Zeke's tender treatment for a short time, she seemed to regain strength and spoke again.

"I'll be all right. Please, just let me go. I have to get away. McClure will find us and kill us both. He's a terrible man!"

"I think we're safe here until you can get your breath back," Zeke assured her, amazed at her literate English "I didn't see anyone follow you from the trading post. We're well hidden here. Tell me what happened and what we're up against."

"I knocked McClure out with a chunk of firewood, intending to kill him, even though I'm a Christian." She spoke with urgency, but wasn't hysterical. "I didn't take time to check on how badly I hurt him. He sent the others to kill you. They'll come back when they don't find you and start hunting for both of us."

"Why'd he send them men after me?" Zeke asked. "I never set eyes on any of them varmints before today."

"They're a bunch of cattle rustlers and robbers. The trading post is their hangout. They use it to cover up their stealing from ranches in the Cherokee and Creek nations. Sometimes they raid as far away as Kansas," she replied breathlessly. "They're suspicious of any strangers, but when you asked about a preacher mission, they were afraid you were interested in Pastor Curtis."

"What do you know about *Pastor Curtis*?" Zeke eagerly queried.

"I loved him," she responded emotionally. "He was a good man and he tried to save me from that filthy McClure."

"You said *was!* Do you know where he is now?" Zeke asked with both excitement and trepidation in his voice.

The girl gave Zeke a quizzical glance. "Did you know Pastor Curtis?"

"Yes, I know him—he's my brother. Tell me what you know about him," Zeke brusquely demanded.

The battered girl bowed her head and tented her hands in a praying gesture.

"I'm sorry, but—but he's dead. May his soul rest in peace," she muttered softly, showing sincere sadness and sympathy.

Zeke had tried to prepare himself for that dreaded possibility, yet it still hit him like a horse kick in the gut. He felt weak and helpless.

An image of two little boys happily playing together back on the West Virginia farm flashed into his mind. His eyes misted; he sat down limply beside the tattered, but empathetic young Indian girl and put his head in his hands. Pangs of guilt invaded his consciousness. He'd let his little brother get killed after he'd promised their mother he'd look out for Josh.

After a couple of painful minutes, Zeke regained enough composure to utter, "Wh–when? How–how'd it happen? Wh–where's he buried?"

It was the sensitive young woman's turn to console. She seemed to put aside her own distress and tenderly took his big, callused hand in hers.

"He was killed a couple of weeks ago by McClure and his gang after he rescued me from them. But—but it wasn't entirely because of me.

"Pastor Curtis had fearlessly confronted them many times before and they knew he intended to tell the authorities about their illegal activities. He made the mistake of telling them he was going to do it. That was a brave but foolish thing to do because it got him killed." She choked up and bit her lower lip.

"Yeah, that'd be just like Josh. He figured that hard-nosed God of his would always take care of him," Zeke replied bitterly.

"Yes, he certainly had a lot of faith, but I think he was also a good, brave man who was willing to give up his life for what he believed in," the young woman stated with conviction.

"He did wonders for my poor people. The men were all corrupted with McClure's rotgut whiskey before God sent Pastor Curtis to us. Many of them converted to Christianity and refused to buy anymore of that poison. That's another reason they killed him and burned down his mission."

"Then he really did have a mission?"

"Yes, he finished the building over a month ago with help from those people in my village he had converted to Christ."

"Do you feel up to telling me how that all happened?" he asked.

"Could I have a drink of water from that canteen?" she requested softly. After drinking deeply, she told the rest of the story in a clear, confident manner, though the memories were obviously very painful for her.

"Last summer, Pastor Curtis rode into our village and announced that he'd come to save the heathen Indians from hellfire and brimstone. When he saw the deplorable condition that our people were in from debauchery and whiskey, he told us he was here to stay and started building a log mission. At first, many thought he was crazy. I believed in him from the beginning, became his interpreter, and tried to help him in his ministry.

"You see, I was already a Christian. My father was a French Canadian and my mother an Osage. Papa sent me to boarding school at the Catholic mission, over in the Cherokee Nation, when I was eight years old. He was a Catholic and wanted me to receive a Christian education."

"That explains why you speak English so well," Zeke interrupted.

"Yes, but father died winter before last, when I was sixteen. I had to come back to my village to help my mother. Having married a white man, she was shunned after he died. She died too, during a cholera epidemic about a year ago. Many others in the camp died that terrible winter. I stayed because I really didn't have anywhere else to go."

"How'd McClure get hold of you?"

"About three weeks ago, Uncle Lonewolf, my mother's brother who became my guardian by tribal law, indentured me to McClure to work off his debt to him for whiskey and supplies. At least that's what he thought he was doing—but it soon became evident that McClure considered me his slave."

"How the hell would your people let McClure get away with something like that?" Zeke asked accusingly.

"You must not judge my people too harshly. Your brother understood and forgave them the many bad things the survivors did after most of the village leaders died in the epidemic. They were consumed with superstitious fears of the unknown killer and there was a breakdown of the tribal culture caused by the loss of leadership.

"Most of the men turned to using the rotgut whiskey as an escape from those perplexing problems. McClure was there to supply it to them. He had captured most of them—body and soul—until Pastor Curtis rode into the village."

"You said that Josh saved you before they killed him. How'd that come about?"

"When Pastor Curtis found out what my uncle had done, he confronted him and insisted he get me back. He even gave Uncle enough money to pay off his debt to McClure. And it wasn't the first time that he'd given money to people in the village who were in dire need." The distressed young woman paused and took another drink from the canteen.

Zeke's admiration for his brother's faith and apparent good works for the Osages grew as this intelligent and sincere young woman related the heroic story. *I guess Josh was putting our money he took to good use after all*, Zeke reasoned, *what with building those poor people a mission and trying to buy back a slave girl.*

"I take it that didn't work out?" He commented.

"No, it didn't! But my uncle died trying to get me back. I honor him for that. It was a horrible thing to see! McClure took his money then laughed at him while he gunned Uncle down—*in cold blood*. He was a feeble old man and wasn't even armed.

"I attempted to help him and McClure slapped and kicked me away. He snarled to his men, 'Guess I forgot to tell that dirty old Injun there were interest due.' They all had a big laugh before they dragged Uncle's body over to a steep bank and tossed it into the river, like some old dead dog." She choked up again and stopped for another drink from the canteen.

"Well, when Uncle failed to return to the village, Pastor Curtis rode over to the trading post looking for him. He walked right in and confronted McClure. Thank God, the rest of the gang had been sent out on a rustling job and McClure was alone. Even if they'd all been there, I don't think it would have stopped your brother. He demanded to know what had happened to Uncle Lonewolf. McClure snarled that he hadn't seen the mangy Injun and called Pastor Curtis a damn bible thumper.

"I screamed that I'd seen him kill Uncle. McClure reached for the gun he kept by the bar, but Pastor Curtis had his pistol out of the holster so fast I hardly saw him do it."

That didn't surprise Zeke because he and Josh had often practiced fast draws when they were young men. Big-handed Josh was always the fastest.

When the pause lengthened, Zeke prompted her, "Did Josh shoot?"

"No, but it was a near thing. For a moment, I saw a killer glaze in your brother's hard eyes. But just a heartbeat before pulling the trigger, he sighed and said McClure would surely be dead if Pastor wasn't a Christian. Then, he told that dreadful man that he was taking me with him, that I'd be under his and God's protection from then on. Pastor took McClure's guns and told him he'd leave them down the trail a ways. We got my horse and Uncle's out of the corral, and we rode back to the village."

The young woman choked slightly and stared into space. Zeke resisted the urge to press her for details of how his brother died. Soon her awareness returned to the thicket clearing. There was a catch in her voice when she continued.

"Ah—ah—the next day that—that wonderful man was shot from ambush. I heard the shots and rushed to where he lay badly wounded on the steps of his mission. McClure and his men had already poured kerosene on him and were inside pouring it over everything.

"All Pastor's work went up in flames and smoke. I struggled to drag Pastor Curtis far enough away to prevent him from being burned, but he was too heavy for me. McClure forced me onto my horse, which they had already stolen and saddled."

There was another painful pause. Zeke doubted she could continue. But, she did.

"Well—well, Pastor Curtis was dead and I was McClure's captive again. I nearly gave up hope—*and my faith*! That was over two weeks ago."

Zeke was visibly shaken. How could his brother have instilled a love that great in this young woman, and probably many others in the Osage village? Was it really divine guidance? A sudden memory caused a chill down his spine.

"My God," he muttered, "Josh must have been killed at the exact moment Will got that premonition his Pa was in trouble."

"What did you say?" the girl asked.

"My brother has a fourteen-year-old son named Will. I was just thinking how hard this is going to be on him," he said,

At that moment, Zeke made a solemn silent vow: Before I go home to tell Will about how Josh died, I aim to finish the job my brother started. Every one of those bastards will pay!

CHAPTER 25

RETRIBUTION

◆

"Thank you for telling me about my brother, young lady. He was fortunate to have a good friend like you," Zeke said, his mind returning to the situation at hand. *I've got to figure out a plan to deal with those scumbags,* he thought, *but how do I keep this abused young woman safe while I'm doing it?*

"I'm very sorry I had to give you such bad news," the young woman replied. "Pastor Curtis died for what he believed, and—and he was doing God's work. I think he'd want you to know that and be pleased for him."

"I'm very proud of Josh," Zeke assured her. "The rest of his family will be proud, too, when I tell them what he was doing and how he died.

"My name is Zeke. What do they call you?"

The young woman enthusiastically reached out her hand. "Pleased to meet you, Zeke. My white name is Elizabeth Cousteau. Friends call me Betsy. I hope Pastor Curtis' brother will be my friend."

"You can plan on that, Betsy," Zeke promised, engulfing her thin hand in his work-hardened grip, surprised at the firmness of her returned clasp and the fire that had returned to her good eye. *This damaged rose is no potted plant,* he concluded.

Their conversation was disrupted by the sound of a loping horse approaching from the other side of the outcrop, slowing, and then picking up again on the downstream side. Zeke suspected it was McClure looking for Betsy, figuring she'd head for her village. He cussed himself for spending so much time talking with her that he'd missed his chance to deal with McClure while he was alone. Now he'd likely have to confront all four of the hard cases at the same time.

"Betsy, how far is it to your village?" Zeke asked.

"Nearly four miles on fairly level ground. It's more than an hour's ride at fast walk, forty-five minutes at a lope."

"Is this the only trail to the village?"

"It's the most direct, but a couple of other prominent trails branch off of it between here and the village that could be confusing to a stranger."

"I'm betting those skunks will be back past here when they can't find hide nor hair of us between here and the village. They'll likely figure we're either hid out along the trail or took one of those branch trails. Either way, it'll be dark soon so they'll likely come back to the trading post for supplies and wait for daylight to try tracking us."

Zeke's cavalry scouting experience was driving his thinking as he warmed to the subject. He'd made up his mind to include the spunky young woman in his attack plans. She'd be safer with him that hiding out on her own.

"This outcrop's probably the best place to confront them. If they don't show by dark, we'll make a cold camp on top of the outcrop until morning. If they ain't come back by then, we'll burn down their damn rotten nest. Maybe the smoke will bring 'em to us."

"That sounds like a good plan," Betsy agreed enthusiastically. "I'll help you all I can."

"I should water Mendy, and it'd be nice if she had some more oats. There may be hard riding ahead, 'specially if we have to ride double," Zeke said. "Why don't you stay here while I get some oats and grub at the cabin?"

"There's no need for us to ride double, my horse and Uncle Lonewolf's are in the trading post corral. I know where things are located in that hateful place. I'll go with you."

"Okay, but we'd better hurry. Can't plan on McClure having to ride all the way to the village before he meets up with his three henchmen," Zeke pointed out.

In less than half an hour, they had saddle Betsy's dapple-gray mare, watered and fed Mendy, eaten some cold food at the cabin, and thrown supplies into a sack for later. Betsy also grabbed a couple of blankets and a coat that fit her. They quickly returned the horses to the secluded clearing and climbed to the top of the outcrop with their weapons, a couple of blankets, and a water canteen. Armament consisted of Zeke's Winchester rife and a Colt .44 pistol, against four men that would likely be armed to the teeth. Zeke wished he had taken time to search for more weapons in the trading post, but it was too late now. As they settled in to watch down trail, Zeke didn't think of his ten-inch sheathed knife that he carried on his pants belt as also being a useful weapon in such a fight as he expected.

"Betsy, can you fire a handgun?" he queried.

"I'm a good pistol shot, but better with a rifle. My father taught me to shoot and I hunted for the Catholic mission's meat when I was in school," she replied with pride.

"That's good to hear," Zeke said. "We may need all the firepower we can get if them bastards have guts enough to put up a fight. I'll keep the rifle and let you use my Colt .44."

"Thanks, you can plan on me using it. If I were you, I'd shoot them as soon as they come into range. They're all trained killers!"

"As bad as I'd like to see 'em all dead, in respect for Josh's beliefs, I'm going to give them one chance to surrender," Zeke told his vindictive companion. "But if any one of 'em goes for his gun, it's open season. Shoot to kill! Will your Christian beliefs allow you to do that, Betsy?"

"*Yes!*" she replied with conviction. "The Bible says an eye for an eye and a tooth for a tooth. I want those men dead after what they did to Pastor Curtis, Uncle Lonewolf, and—and *to me!*"

It sounded as though that if left to her there sure wouldn't be any prisoners taken. Zeke judged that was the Osage Indian part of her speaking, but then he'd heard that French Canadians were darn tough people, too. Her small right hand firmly griped the big pistol's butt, with a finger on the trigger. The other hand was poised to cock back the hammer. Zeke could sense her emitting the courage and determination of her Osage warrior heritage. He was pleased to have her as his ally.

Waiting was never easy for a man of action like Zeke. With his nerves poised for a fight, he squirmed in his prone position from discomfort and impatience. His ten-inch blade sheath knife dug into his side. He pulled it from the scabbard and laid it beside him. Betsy hardly moved a muscle or batted an eye. After a half hour passed, Zeke was gritting his teeth to keep from jumping up and riding down the trail looking for his prey. Yet Betsy remained perfectly still, lying on a hard and lumpy rock surface similar to what was giving Zeke fits.

The sun was slipping behind the western horizon when they finally heard riders coming. But there was still enough light to clearly see the four horsemen, riding two abreast, as they rounded the bend in the trail headed their way.

"Looks like they met up. I see four of 'em. Get ready, but hold your fire," he whispered to Betsy. "I'll call to them to surrender when they're within pistol range."

When the unsuspecting riders were about fifty feet from the outcrop, Zeke's top sergeant's voice shattered the still dusk air.

"Hold it right there, you dirty bastards, or we'll shoot you out of them saddles!"

All four horses shied. One man went for his pistol by reflex action, while trying to steady his horse. The gun cleared leather and the accomplished gunman snapped off one shot before Zeke's rifle bullet caught him full in the chest. Somersaulting backward out of his saddle, the man was probably dead before he hit the ground.

Another outlaw kicked his horse into a lope, trying to escape around the end of the outcrop. Zeke shot him out of his saddle when he came around to the other side. Betsy's first shot winged a third rider, knocking him off his horse. Though wounded, the man rose to a crouch and fired a shot in their direction. It came close enough for a rock splinter to gash Zeke's cheek. Betsy brought the outlaw down with her second shot.

The fourth rider, who they took to be McClure because of his size, pivoted his horse and rode hell-bent for leather downriver. Betsy fired the four rounds left in her gun at the hunched-over rider, but he was probably out of pistol range. Just before he rounded the bend, Zeke snapped off a shot that brought down the horse. The rider rolled free and scrambled on all fours for cover in the brush. Zeke was preoccupied for a few seconds, marking the spot in his mind where McClure had ducked into the thicket.

"I'll have to go smoke that son of a bitch McClure out of the brush, but he's afoot. Don't worry, he won't get away," Zeke said without looking Betsy's way. He rose stiffly and proceeded to stomp feeling back into his numb legs. When he turned to speak to Betsy again, she was gone—so was the ten-inch-blade knife he'd laid on the rock beside him. The empty pistol lay where Betsy had rested it to aim and shoot.

"That damn wild Indian gal has gone after McClure with only my knife," he muttered as he hurriedly scrambled down from the outcrop. "She'll likely get herself killed!"

Hugging the right side brush, with his rifle at the ready, Zeke cautiously moved down the trail. There was no sign of Betsy. He fought down an impulse to call out to her, realizing it was dangerous and useless. Guessing she'd be somewhere in the brush near where McClure disappeared, he reminded himself to be careful where he shot.

Damn, you crazy girl! He scolded Betsy in his mind. Be just my luck for that mean bastard to take you hostage—then what do I do?

When he came abreast of the man's wounded horse, a bloodcurdling scream from the thicket on his right raised the hair on the back of Zeke's neck. Fearful for Betsy, he recklessly plunged headlong through the thick foliage toward the sound. He'd forced his way through only a short distance when a gruesome sight brought him to an abrupt halt. Not three feet away, McClure's huge body was draped nearly upright over a sturdy blackjack bush. It stared in disbelief at Zeke, with bugging, sightless eyes. His big arms seemed to be reaching around the bush for help. The despicable man's thick throat was sliced from ear to ear!

McClure's lifeblood continued to spurt onto the bush, though a sizable pool had already collected at the base. Thick legs quivered for a few seconds, and then the corpse went limp. Zeke stared at the macabre scene, mesmerized.

Betsy stood calmly beside the body, holding Zeke's knife in her bloody right hand. The seemingly possessed Indian woman reached up and grabbed a handful of the dead man's dirty, matted hair and pulled his large bulk off the bush. The body landed sprawled on its back. Betsy knelt beside it and sliced open the fly of the greasy pants and dirty underwear with one pass of the bloody knife. Zeke came to his senses and grabbed the slender wrist just before she completed the second swipe with the sharp blade—this time it was aimed at the corpse's exposed manhood parts. Her one good eye blazed with more unadulterated hatred than he'd ever seen before in a man or woman.

"Let me go!" she screeched, fighting him like a demon.

"What are you doing, Betsy? He's dead! He can't hurt you ever again!"

"I'm going to cut off that son of a bitch's pecker and balls and stuff 'em in his filthy mouth."

The thought of that gory, barbaric image nearly turned Zeke's stomach. My God, he concluded, beneath that educated Christian veneer, she's still a savage.

"Betsy, leave him be! He's dead now. He can't ever hurt you again," he pleaded. "Keep this up and you'll be as bad as they were. *For God's sake, let it go!*"

In a few seconds, Betsy stopped struggling, dropped the knife, and collapsed against Zeke's chest. Great sobs that seemed to emanate from deep down in her tortured soul shook her slender body. The tough veteran of many battles held her as tenderly as he would one of his hurting nieces and stroked her tangled hair.

"It's all right now, Betsy," he whispered in her ear. "Everything is gonna be all right."

"Please ask God to forgive me for my sins, Pastor Curtis," she mumbled through her sobs.

Now she was the Christian French girl again. Did she think he was Josh, Zeke wondered, or was she pleading to his memory?

"God will forgive you Betsy. I'm sure he will," surrogate Pastor Curtis replied, his voice cracking with emotion.

CHAPTER 26

ELISABETH COUSTEAU

◆

By the time their tension subsided enough for Zeke and Betsy to consider what to do next, dusk rapidly gave way to darkness. Thunderclouds gathered, the temperature dropped, and it began to drizzle. Zeke confirmed from Betsy that she too didn't relish riding four miles in the rain to the Osage Village. Even though the thought was repugnant, Zeke decided the best option was to spend the night at the trading post. Betsy hesitated at the door, and then entered the hated place with clenched teeth.

"It stinks some, but beats the hell out of sleeping in the rain, and I been in worse places," Zeke commented lightheartedly, trying to alleviate Betsy's qualms.

"Well, I can't say that I have," Betsy replied with bitterness. "I really hate what happened to me here, but I guess the place didn't cause it."

Betsy explained to Zeke that McClure kept the meager trading stock in the cabin more for show than serious trading. There wasn't much variety, but she found a dress that fit her and slipped into it, after the luxury of bathing in the wooden tub of warm water Zeke prepared for her. The colorful calico dress accentuated her shapely, lithe body, drastically changing her appearance.

After dressing, Betsy sat on the edge of the hearth, drying, combing, and braiding her thick, slightly wavy dark hair, being careful with her head wound. Light from the crackling fire revealed attractive auburn highlights. Zeke assumed she'd inherited those striking characteristics from her French Canadian ancestry. He was captivated with her overall natural beauty, which showed through the contusions and burses.

With Betsy's physical and emotional state greatly improved by bath and grooming, she insisted on doing the cooking. Tired as they were, they lingered at the table, enjoying each other's company and second cups of coffee. The good food, blossoming friendship, and cheerful fire made the shabby cabin seemed almost cozy. Stresses of the day receded, replaced with a sense of comfort and well-being.

When the conversation lagged for a moment, Betsy fixed her one open eye on Zeke's rugged face and surprised him with a frank question.

"Zeke, do you have a woman waiting for you back on your Kansas farm?"

"No, Betsy, I don't," he replied. "I married a fine widow woman after I come back from the war. Her only child by he first husband was killed in the war, and we never had any before she died of the consumption."

When Zeke didn't volunteer more about his life, Betsy prompted, "And you didn't marry again?"

"Guess I ain't met another gal that'd have me. I already have a family because I kind of considered Josh's mine, too. Didn't see no reason to make another one."

"Well, your brother sure thought highly of you," Betsy stated sincerely. "He once told me that he'd left his family in your care so he could do God's work. He said, 'Thank God for Zeke. I know my family is in good hands.'"

Zeke diverted his eyes from Betsy until he had his overwrought emotions under control. It seemed he'd had enough sentimentality in the last twenty-four hours to last a lifetime. He was darn near emotionally rung out.

"Tell you the truth, Betsy, I figured Josh was touched in the head with all his religious stuff. Now, I've got to admit maybe he was called by God. But seems to me his God was extra hard on him and his family."

"It may have seemed hard to you, Zeke, but I'm sure Pastor Curtis was sent by God to help my people. I think you were called to finish the job. God bless you, Zeke Curtis, you saved my life and now it's yours!"

"You—you don't owe me nothing, Betsy," he stammered embarrassed. "I-I just done what any decent man would have done to help a gal in distress. And I was looking to get revenge for what they did to Josh."

"Maybe I don't owe you, but I meant what I said: my life is yours to do with it what you want. That's the Osage way."

Betsy paused for a moment and leaned across the table toward him before continuing in a soft, melodious voice.

"Zeke, I'd like to be your woman—starting right now—if you want! But I'll be better when I've had time to heal."

Her blunt offer caught Zeke off guard, but he considered it sincere. I suppose that's the Osage way, too, he thought. An involuntary spasm surged through his groin and for a fleeting moment, he was sorely tempted. It had been a long time since he'd been with a woman—and he liked women. Immediately, he was ashamed of himself for even thinking of such a thing, considering the living hell those depraved men had put her through—*and she is little more than a girl*!

Damn, but she's a good-looking gal, Zeke thought. Even in her battered condition, there's a vitality and earthiness about her. She's as pretty as Marge was, or Mary, in a darker complexioned way. She deserves a young man, after she's had time to heal, in body and soul—if the poor misused gal can ever heal her soul.

"Betsy, that's a mighty fine offer. A pretty gal like you is very tempting to an old man like me. But that there is the problem—I'm old enough to be your pa."

"You sure don't look or act like an old man, Zeke Curtis. The Osage women consider it an honor to mate with an older, proven warrior. I'd be much honored to share your bed and to care for you the rest of your life. And if you wanted, I'd give you a family of your own."

"I know you mean what you're saying, at least now, but it just wouldn't be right. You've been through a terrible ordeal that would have destroyed a lesser woman. Pretty gal like you deserves a young man to love and grow old with. There's surely a lot of young bucks among your people that'd fight for you to be their woman."

"Well, to begin with, there aren't many sober young men left in my village. Even if there were, an Osage man would have to be hard up to take me, even as a second or third wife, because I've been with white men."

She intently surveyed his face before speaking again. "Won't—won't you please take me home with you, Zeke? Maybe I could help you raise Pastor Curtis's family?"

"Josh has a young wife that's doing a good job with his kids, but if you ain't got anywhere else to go, you're welcome to come home with me. You and Mary, Josh's wife, would make great friends. I can't let you be my woman, but considering what you meant to Josh, you got a right to be part of the Curtis family. Would you like that, Betsy?"

"Yes," Betsy replied with conviction and relief. "If that's the way you want it, I'd be very proud to be a part of your family and I'd earn my keep."

"I know you will, young lady. Now that that's settled, let's get some sleep. This ol' man is plumb tuckered out."

"So's this young woman," Betsy replied. "Thank you Zeke for—for everything. I should have known you'd turn me down on the offer to be your woman because your brother did; saying the same thing you did about my age. But he didn't say anything about having a young wife. Just remember, Zeke Curtis, I'll always be here for you if you change your mind." She stood, moved around the table to him, and planted a warm kiss on his lips, and then busied herself banking the fire and preparing separate pallets for them in front of the hearth.

Mentally and physically exhausted, they both slept as if drugged, but they were awake at sunrise. While consuming a warm breakfast, they made plans to leave the place where Betsy was treated so badly.

"I'm going to take Uncle Lonewolf's horse and saddle and some other things I'll need," Betsy announced. "McClure owes me for what he took from Uncle when he killed him. And then I'm going to burn this varmint-infected place down!"

"Don't blame you there, but seems to me there's likely some things here your people could use. Maybe we should let them take what they want, and then they can have the pleasure of burning what's left.

"You say some of them are Christians; do you think they'd bury them skunks we killed? It just ain't in me to do it, but I hate to leave them for the critters."

"Yes, I think I can get some of my people to dispose of those worthless carcasses," Betsy replied. "You're right about my people needing anything they can salvage from here, but they'll have to be careful about being accused of stealing."

Betsy exchanged her dress for some small-sized men's clothes from McClure's stock to use for riding. After picking out another dress and some underwear, she was ready to leave the nightmarish place forever. Zeke felt that McClure also owed Josh's family, big time. From the trader's sparse stock, he took ammunition, a dress that he thought Mary might like, one that Jeanie would soon grow into, an outfit each for Moses and Will, and enough food supplies and oats to last them for the four-day trip home. They packed the goods on Uncle Lonewolf's skinny horse. Last thing, before leaving, they broke all the whiskey bottles and smashed the kegs.

"That damn McClure made slaves out of most of the males in my village with this horrible stuff," Betsy told Zeke as she swung an ax at the containers of rotgut poison. "If we left it here, they'd all be drunk for a month."

As they forced their skittish horses past the bloated corpses of the men they'd killed, Zeke was forced to look at them, thankful he didn't have to view McClure's body again. Killing men, even in the war, wrenched at his gut. He was never completely free of the trauma and regret it caused him. Zeke noticed Betsy stoically looked straight ahead, showing no emotion. *My God, but she's a cool one*, Zeke thought.

When they arrived at the village, Betsy called together the people and told them what had happened. The Indians seemed pleased that the hated McClure and his gang were dead, but one of the elders lamented that the Osages would probably be blamed for the deaths of the white men. After Betsy suggested that was a good reason why they should dispose of the bodies quickly, the village leaders agreed to take care of it.

While they were assembled near the burned-out hulk of the mission, which had been Josh Curtis's funeral pyre, Betsy asked the

Christians among them to join her in a makeshift memorial service for their revered pastor. She read a couple of Bible verses in the Osage language, led the group in the Lord's Prayer, and then she asked Zeke if he'd say a prayer for his brother.

Zeke searched his mind for words that would adequately express his ambivalent feelings about his brother's life and recent death. After clearing his throat—"hu-u-umph"—much like Josh used to do, he gave it his best.

> "You know, Lord, that I ain't ever been much for praying and preaching, but I'm going to try visiting with you a mite about my brother—your servant, Josh Curtis.
>
> I sure don't claim to understand what kind of deal you had with Josh. You already know that our parents raised us both as Christians, but after Josh found that different kind of religion during the war, he abandoned everything else. Seems to me you drove him hard. He sure done his best to follow your confusing directions.
>
> I do thank you, though, for finally directing him to this Osage village, and giving him a job he understood. Seems to me he done it damn—er—er darn good, too.
>
> I pray that you gave him some happiness and peace before he died. And that he and Marge are in heaven with you now.
>
> We both know he damn well earned it! Don't we, Lord?
>
> Amen."

Betsy translated what he said to the attentive Indians. Probably most of it went over their heads, but they all repeated, "Amen." Zeke's heart was touched by the outpouring of love those fifty or so souls expressed for Josh.

Only a couple of the older squaws, who had been friends of her mother's, seemed concerned about Betsy leaving. Zeke could see that there was no place for her in that village, now that her folks and her benefactor, Pastor Curtis, were dead. Perhaps the half-breed girl had always been something of an outsider, what with being educated in the white man's school, and all. He was more pleased than ever that she was coming with him. Likewise, Betsy didn't appear sorry to leave. She quickly added the things she wanted to keep from her lodge to those they had brought from the Blackburn Trading Post. The pitifully small bundle of her worldly possessions fit comfortably on Uncle Lonewolf's spotted horse.

By midafternoon, they were well out into the rolling Osage Hills, headed home—and to a promising new life for Betsy. She followed her new hero and benefactor at a respectful distance, as befitted a dutiful squaw. By chance, Betsy noticed a plume of black smoke curling into the sky over toward the Arkansas. Considering the direction and distance, they concluded it was the Blackburn Trading Post burning. Both riders halted their horses and silently watched the spiraling smoke.

Betsy broke the reverie. "I hope they threw those bastards' bodies into that fire so they'll burn just like those killers burned Pastor Curtis."

Her pretty, but battered, face hardened. She startled Zeke and the horses with a sudden war whoop into the clear crisp air, like an Osage warrior touting having settled the score with an enemy. "Burn in hell, you filthy varmints!" she shouted, and then reined her mare back onto the trail that would take her away from all of that. There wasn't a tear shed, or another backward glance.

Zeke figured the spunky girl considered the smoke they saw symbolic of burning the bridges to her past. He sure hoped she could soon put the Blackburn Trading Post parts of that life behind her.

CHAPTER 27

MARY'S SECRET

◆

Zeke and Betsy rode into the Curtis farmyard about noon, four days after leaving the Osage village, and three weeks after Zeke had left on his search for Josh. Mary and Jeanie were working in the garden. They rushed to meet Zeke and the unknown companion. Little Anne toddled along behind.

Mary laughed and cried while smothering Zeke with hugs and kisses. Excited Jeanie tugged at his hand and jumped up and down in glee. Toddler Anne cooed, "Uncle Keek—Uncle Keek." Zeke soaked in the affection, grinning from ear-to-ear. A smile came to Betsy's somber face.

"Thank the good Lord you're back, Zeke," Mary said through her happy laughter. "We were worried sick about you. Will wanted to go looking for you—but I made him stay with the plowing and grubbing brush in the new field."

"You did right, Mary. I didn't aim to worry you none, but it took a lot more time than I expected to find Josh and take care of things."

"Then you found him? Is he well? Does he intend to come home and help us with this work?"

Zeke held her gently by the shoulders at arms length.

"Mary, Josh is dead," he lamented, and then pulled her into his arms. "He was killed while trying to save this young woman from a bunch of very bad men. When we're all together, I'll tell you the details. But for now, I want you to know Josh died a hero, while doing what he believed his God wanted him to do."

Mary snuggled against Zeke's soft reversed sheepskin coat, but she didn't cry.

"I-I hope he didn't suffer and has found some peace. His God has been very demanding on him, ever since I first met him when I was a little girl," she mumbled with her pretty head pressed against his muscular chest. It was news to Zeke that Mary had known Josh when she was a child. But come to think of it, they'd learned very little about Mary's life before she came to live with them, or why she'd come, for that matter.

With a deep sigh, Mary gently pushed away from Zeke's embrace, looked up into his eyes, and uttered a disquieting comment.

"I'm sorry Josh is dead, but now my commitment to my father is over—*I'm a free woman!*"

Mary seemed full of surprises, but Zeke didn't dwell on the mystery long. Recalling he had a traveling companion, who was still mounted observing the tender exchange, he turned his attention to Betsy.

"This here's Betsy, Mary. She was helping Josh at the mission he built in her Osage village. Betsy has no family, so I brought her home to live with us.

"Betsy, this here is Mary, Josh's wife. That squirming gal is Josh's daughter, Jeanie, and the little tadpole there is Anne. She's two, going on twenty, and thinks she's the boss of the family."

Mary gave Betsy one of her radiant smiles, Jeanie eyed her warily, and Anne ignored her while trying to entice Uncle Keek to pick her up. He patted her head, preoccupied with seeing how Betsy and the rest of the family were going to hit it off.

"Welcome Betsy," Mary said, in her usual sincere manner. "It's a pleasure to meet you. Please get down and come with me to the house for something to eat and drink. You must be worn out from traveling with Zeke. Just because he has a calloused butt, he seems to think everyone else has one, too."

Geez, Zeke thought, Mary never talked about a *calloused butt* before. This frontier living has hardened her up some. Having another woman around the place to talk with will be good for her.

Betsy smiled back, dismounted, and put out her hand to Mary. "I'm pleased to meet you too, Mary. Zeke has told me a lot about you."

After a mutually firm handshake, Betsy turned her attention to Jeanie.

"Hi, Jeanie, I've heard about you too, but you're prettier and bigger than I'd imagined."

Usually shy, Jeanie boldly eyed the fascinating, battered young woman and blurted out, "Are you an Injun?"

Betsy threw back her head and emitted a hearty melodious laugh. It pleased Zeke to hear this stoic young woman laugh for the first time since he'd met her. Around these caring people, it wouldn't take long before she'd begin to heal, physically and emotionally. He was proud of his family. There was no doubt in his mind now—this was *his* family. Seeing how the girls reacted to her and how quickly she loosened up, he was reassured that bringing Betsy home with him was not only the right thing to do, it was also going to be good for them all.

Betsy stifled the spontaneous laughter and responded to the candid little girl. "Well now, little Jeanie, what makes you think I'm an Indian?"

"I guess you look some like an Injun, but I never saw one as pretty as you an'—and that talked so good."

"Thank you for the compliment, Jeanie," Betsy chuckled while reaching down and taking one of Jeanie's small hands in both of hers. "God gave me my looks and I'm thankful to Him for it—even though it's a curse sometimes. But, I learned to speak proper English at a school. I'll bet you're learning that in school, too."

"No, I don't go to school. Mary is a teacher, and she's teaching me and Will. Did Uncle Zeke hit you in the eye and on your head?"

Betsy laughed again and Zeke gave one of Jeanie's pigtails a playful tug. Mary blushed and intervened.

"Jeanie, watch your manners!"

"It's alright, Mary. I don't mind talking about it. No, Jeanie, your kind uncle would never do a thing like that. A very bad man did this to me. Your Uncle Zeke saved me from him.

"But I haven't answered your question about my being an Indian. I'm what people call a half-breed. My mother was an Osage Indian and my father was a French Canadian. My Christian name is Elizabeth Cousteau."

"What's a French Canadian?" inquisitive Jeanie asked.

Mary intervened again. "That's enough, Jeanie. We'll all soon get to know Betsy better."

"Where are Will and Moses?" Zeke asked Mary.

"They're both working down in the new field trying to get it ready for plowing."

"I'd rather take a beating than have to tell them about Josh, but it's got to be done," Zeke sighed. "Betsy, why don't you go on to the house with Mary and the girls. I'll unload your things and see to your horses before I ride out to the field."

Zeke read Betsy's look as a reminder to him that she considered it her job to take care of the horses. But she complied with his wishes without comment. She hadn't let him do any of the camp chores on the trail home. That kind of pampering could spoil a man, he reasoned, while enjoying every minute of being the recipient of her services.

Anne was still trying to get Uncle Keek's attention. He'd been engrossed in the conversations and paid her no mind. Betsy moved over and picked her up.

"Hi, Anne, old Uncle Keek seems to have other things on his mind. Is it alright if I carry you to the house?"

"Yeth," Anne replied, snuggling against Betsy's breasts, and stroking the soft, formfitting doeskin dress she has exchanged for her men's clothes this morning.

Zeke patted Anne on the head again and kissed her on the cheek.

"You're still my best girl, little darling," he assured her before turning to attend the horses.

As the women walked toward the house, Jeanie continued to chatter and held on to her new friend's free hand.

Zeke dropped the pack off Betsy's spare horse, tended to the horses, and then remounted Mendy for the ride to the field where Moses and Will were working. They were grubbing brush to enlarge the bottomland cornfield when he found them. The joyful reunion was cut short when he told them the sad news. There was no easy way, he just blurted out the facts. They both shed tears, but Will took the news more stoically than Zeke expected.

"I knew he wasn't ever coming back," Will commented matter-of-factly, and then changed the subject. "We been working in the fields or grubbing brush ever day we could, Uncle Zeke."

"You've done good, Will. I'll be helping you and Moses starting tomorrow morning. I think we should all take the rest of the day off today, in honor of your pa."

Perhaps Will felt he'd lost his father years before, or reconciled himself to the expected loss when he had his premonition, Zeke reasoned. It was typical for Will to keep his emotions bottled up inside, but it worried Zeke that he didn't want to talk about the loss or ask for more details. He wanted Will to understand and appreciate the circumstances of his father's death, and to be proud of his memory.

As Zeke expected, he could see that the bad news hit Moses hard. Zeke tried to find words to console the sensitive, old former slave. He sure wanted Moses to know the honorable way Josh had died. Perhaps he could also get through to Will by discussing Moses' deep sense of loss.

"Josh was a driven man, Moses. We should be pleased that he's at peace now. You and I'll have to remember him how he was before that damn war messed up his mind, and be proud of what he was doing that got him killed."

Moses was choked up and it wasn't easy for him to reply.

"Yes, sir, Masta Zeke, I'll remember him that way. He look like the Angel Gabriel, himself, when he done bought me and set me free, down there in Washington City."

"Yeah, he sure did the right thing by you, helping you look for your family and all. Josh's heart was always in the right place. His head just got scrambled some."

"I knows he had some troubles, but he always good to me. I wouldn't be alive if it weren't for Masta Sergeant."

"Damn it, Josh was a good man," Zeke vented his frustration. "It just ain't fair what his God demanded of him."

"Masta Zeke, it ain't *fair* for y'all to blame God for Masta Sergeant's troubles. God uses us all in different ways."

"Yeah! Yeah! I know that Moses. It's hard to know what's right sometimes. We'll all miss him. I keep thinking about how close we were and the fun we had when we were little tikes. You know he was always bigger than me even though I was eighteen months older than him."

The conversation with Moses was helping Zeke, too. There was some latent guilt there to work out. He patted the grieving old black man on his thin shoulder and changed the subject before he started crying.

"I brought a friend of Josh's home with me. Let's go on back to the house and meet her. When we're all together, I'll tell you about Josh's great work with the Osages."

By the time they reached the house and took care of the horses, Mary and Betsy had completed moving Betsy's things into the house and Will's out to Zeke's tent.

"You look a lot like your handsome Uncle Zeke, Will," she said, looking him direct in his eyes with her one open eye.

When introductions were finished, Zeke told Josh's story, leaving out some of the gory details about how he and Betsy exacted revenge. Suffice for them to know that Josh's killers and Betsy's tormentors would never again molest anyone. Zeke explained the gifts he brought as being payment in part for debts the trader owed Josh.

After the family finished their early breakfast the next morning, Zeke told Will and Moses he'd join them later because he had some things he needed to talk over with Mary. Betsy took the girls out to work in the garden. She'd been out earlier with her work clothes on to help the men with the chores.

When Mary and Zeke sat alone across the kitchen table from each other, with fresh cups of coffee in front of them, Zeke opened the conversation.

"Mary, I expect we'd best talk some about the family's business affairs. As Josh's widow, this farm is now yours. So is Josh's share of the partnership we agreed on, back in West Virginie."

"That would be correct, *if I was his widow*, Zeke. But now that he's gone, I can tell you the truth, I was never legally married to your brother."

"Not—not married, but—but both of you put on like you was." He paused to digest that startling bit of information for a few seconds.

When Mary didn't elaborate, he continued, a little embarrassed. "I-I have to admit thinking it strange you and Josh didn't share the same bed. And I've heard you mention some kind of deal a few times."

"No, we never shared the same bed. There was a deal, and that wasn't part of it," Mary calmly replied.

"Then the whole thing was some kind of deal?" Zeke uttered incredulously.

"Yes, it was a deal, or arrangement—if that sounds better to you. An arrangement that I made under coercion from my father on his death bed."

"What the hell possessed your pa to get you tied up in a lopsided, crappy deal like you got with Josh?" Zeke demanded to know.

"Well, Papa wasn't completely rational when the deal was made. But I think he sincerely thought he was doing us both a service. His pastor needed someone to care for his family and he felt that after he died, his headstrong eighteen-year-old daughter would need the care and protection of a Godly man.

"My father felt a debt to Josh, not only for bringing him to Christ, but also for having saved his life on the battlefield during the war. Papa was dying and there were no other living relatives for me to turn to. It's a little more complicated than that, but that's roughly how it happened."

"Am I to understand that your father insisted you make a marriage commitment to Josh?"

"No, the marriage was Josh's idea. He was afraid people would talk if a man of God took a young woman into his home without the benefit of holy matrimony. I steadfastly refused to legally marry him, or—or to agree to any bedding relationship. We compromised on pretending we were married. He promised never to expect any sexual favors, and he never did except for one minor indiscretion. Guess he figured it was better to live a lie than to have his parishioners think he might be living in sin."

"Then your father knew nothing about the sham marriage agreement?"

"That's right. Papa's deal was for me to make a ten-year commitment to help his widowed friend and pastor with his family. In return, he put the proceeds from the sale of his store and the rest of his estate into a Charleston Bank Trust with the provision that I could withdraw it when I was twenty-eight years old. It's a considerable amount of money."

"That sounds a helluva lot like blackmail to me," Zeke stated angrily. "Kind of like one old man selling his daughter to another.

Are you sure Josh didn't have some other kind of hold over your father?"

"Only that he felt that he owed his life to Josh. He swallowed Josh's hellfire brand of religion—hook, line, and sinker—and he could never understand why I didn't.

"Actually, Papa probably thought he was saving my soul by making me live with his pastor, who he was certain would some day succeed in converting me. Who knows, Papa may have also hoped I would marry his wonderful pastor, once I was converted and got to know him. That wouldn't have happened in a thousand years!

"In fairness to your brother, he wasn't the one pushing for the deal. My father insisted he take me in, for my own good. You see, he had raised me alone after Mother died when I was ten. He always considered me too willful, like my mother. Papa expected Josh to save me from my obstinate nature and to save my soul. I understood how important that was to Papa and agreed to the arrangement."

At that point, Mary sighed deeply, the only emotion she'd shown during her lengthy story. Zeke sensed that she was about talked out on the subject. He hardly knew where to go from there. It was his nature to ponder things before drawing any conclusions or forcing an issue, but his concern for the future caused him to plunge ahead in a wistful, almost pleading, tone.

"Mary, when you responded to me telling you that Josh was dead, you said, 'I'm a free woman.' Does that mean you intend on leaving us?"

Mary's eyes misted and she got up, walked around the table, and gave him a hug.

"Zeke, deal or no deal, I could never leave now. This is my family as much as it is yours! I meant that I was free from pretending I was Josh's wife."

And then she stepped back from Zeke, looked directly into his eyes, and lowered her voice.

"I'd be willing to marry you for real to get that job done, if you'd have me?"

Zeke returned Mary's gaze with love and affection, but it was the love of a big brother—or an uncle.

"That's a flattering offer, Mary, but you didn't say you'd marry me because you love me." When she blushed slightly, he rushed on. "No, you don't need another old man for a husband—make-believe or real. A young, exciting gal like you deserves a young man to love her passionately and to grow old with her. You'll find him someday. In the meantime, if you're willing, we'll just carry on like we've been. I'll see to it that you get title to Josh's land and remain a full partner in the family's farming business."

"God bless you! You're a wonderful man and it's a shame that you don't have a good woman to share your life with. I do love you, and certainly respect you! But you're probably right; it isn't the blinding, passionate kind of love on which a good marriage is based. I want you to know though Zeke Curtis you're one helluva man. I could do a lot worse."

She gave him a lingering, moist kiss with a light brush of her tongue on his lips—a kiss that he would long remember—and then she backed away. Zeke blushed deep crimson underneath his natural tan.

"Hum-m-mph, hum-m-mph," he stammered. "I-I best be gettin' to work. Will and Moses are likely tired of me slacking off. We—we all love you, Mary, and thank God he sent you to us."

With that, he headed for the field, thinking no need for the others to know anything about that conversation, unless Mary wants to tell them. He whistled cheerfully as he walked, with a spring in his step that belied his forty-one very active years.

You're a lucky man, Zeke ol' boy, having two beautiful young women offer to marry you, he told himself. A lesser man might let a thing like that go to his head, ha, ha, ha, but not a handsome ole dog like me!

CHAPTER 28
PROSPERITY

◆

In the caring environment provided by the Curtis family, Betsy healed fast, both physically and emotionally. Likewise, the complex young Indian woman was having a profound effect on the family.

She and Mary enjoyed each other's company from the outset. While from different backgrounds, they shared being near the same age and having independent spirits. As friends and confidants, they soon grew as close as the sister neither had had, but always wanted.

Jeanie adored Betsy and followed her everywhere. When Betsy took Zeke's place for the evening hair brushing and story telling sessions, Zeke joshed that Jeanie was fickle. He was only half-joking because he missed those special intimate times with his niece, but he recognized Betsy was bringing the shy girl out of her shell, even to the point of Jeanie becoming a chatterbox.

Anne seemed happy with the new arrangement, since it opened up Uncle Keek's lap for her. She reminded him that she had pretty hair too and it needed brushing. While Zeke loved the saucy little girl, she was at a disadvantage vying for his affections with her big sister. In fairness to her well-meaning uncle, he wasn't even aware that it was because Jeanie looked more like their mother—his first and only true love, Marge.

Will spent much of the time during those quiet evenings clandestinely ogling Betsy when he was supposed to be doing his lessons. He thought he cunningly concealed his growing fascination with the fawn-complexioned beauty, but it was obvious he had a near-terminal case of puppy love. He salved his conscience for being unfaithful to Mary by reassuring himself that she was still his true love. This thing for Betsy was more of a sensual attraction. His mind fanaticized and his body ached with desire, yet he didn't fully understand what was happening to him.

As seasons changed, life on the Curtis farm settled into the hard work of frontier farming. They expanded their acreage, the weather cooperated, and they produced bumper crops the second year. The numbers of marketable hogs and cattle increased. Zeke added bred mares for his future horse farm. He bought some of that newly developed barbed wire and used it to enclose a lush pasture for them on his homestead. The family prospered enough to hire a German immigrant to build them a simple two-bedroom clapboard house on Mary's place to supplement the crowded sod house.

Betsy was a big help. Dressed in rough boots and men's clothes, she did more than her share of the chores and worked beside the men in the fields when she wasn't helping Mary and Jeanie with the big garden. Her strong, young body and work ethic made her as tough and productive as any of the males.

"Betsy," Zeke said one evening when they had finished a good meal and were all in an expansive mood, "I never figured you for as good of a worker as you were a fighter when we were together down there at the Blackburn Trading Post."

A hurt expression momentarily crossed Betsy's usually placid face.

"I-I thought that's something we agreed not to talk about, Zeke."

The voice was strained just enough for Zeke to realize he had inadvertently hurt her by bringing up bad memories that were best left buried.

"You're right, Betsy, we did make that agreement. I only wanted to compliment you on your hard work. We all appreciate what you've done to help us."

"In that case, thank you. I'm just trying to carry my own weight, like I promised you."

"Well you're doing that and much more," Zeke stated.

"You sure are," Mary confirmed.

Will had grown six inches in a year. He'd also added thirty pounds of muscle, but he still looked gangling. Shortly before his fifteenth birthday, his voice stopped squeaking on the high notes. It was nearly as deep as Zeke's by the time of their third planting season. While still three inches shorter and perhaps thirty pounds lighter, he was fast developing into a replica of his uncle in appearance and disposition.

In October, two of Zeke's new brood mares disappeared from the pasture. He and Will followed a suspicious trail to the ford on the Walnut, and then lost it. Even though they hadn't seen much of the Sommers family since the run-in that Will had had with Homer, Zeke was suspicious Buck might be involved with the missing horses. There were rumors he and Homer sometimes rode with a gang of thugs from down in the Oklahoma Territory.

Cooperating spring weather, better organizing, a hired hand, and some new farming implements made planting a third crop much easier. They were able to double the corn, oats, and wheat acreage. During June, they began working on a new barn with a hayloft.

Zeke put a few pieces of furniture in the crude log cabin he had built on his place the prior year to satisfy the homestead "proving up" requirements. He stayed overnight there sometimes when a mare was foaling.

The morning of July 2, 1874, Zeke made a statement that pleased them all.

"You gals get things ready for the trip to Winfield. We'll leave in the morning to celebrate the Fourth of July with our friends."

"Uncle Zeke, can I take Natty and ride him in the horse races this year?"

"He's a big strong horse all right, but he's only three years old. You could hurt him by racing him too soon."

"But Uncle Zeke, we should have a horse representing our family in the races and Mendy can't do it because she's expecting soon."

"That's true, Will. Maybe Betsy would be interested in entering her mare, Blaze. She's a fast horse and Betsy can ride her like an Indian. Ha, ha, ha! She should be able to ride like an Indian, at least a half-Indian, shouldn't she?"

"I don't think of Betsy as an Indian, Uncle Zeke, and I don't think it's funny to call her one," Will reproached his thoughtless uncle.

"Well, that probably wouldn't be a good idea after all. There'll be a lot of drunk cowboys in town that wouldn't take kindly to having a young gal best 'em, especially one that's half-Osage. Of course, that wouldn't worry her none. She'd be game to compete with any of 'em. Best we don't mention it to Betsy."

"I think Betsy could beat 'em all if she was a mind to, but I think Natty's ready, at least for the shorter races. I'm betting he can outrun any horse in the county," Will replied with confidence.

"You're probably right, Will. Okay, let's take him with us. But, we'll only enter him in a couple of short races, nothing over a half mile. Do you agree to that?"

"Yahoo," Will shouted. "I agree. Thanks, Uncle Zeke. This is gonna be the best Fourth of July ever. I'll go get Natty ready."

In spite of the Santa Fe Railroad's failure to push their tracks south from Wichita, Winfield had grown considerably in the two years since the Curtis family had participated in their first Fourth of July celebration. The railroad was promised for the next spring. There were a number of new businesses in town, including a bank and another general store. Randy had competition. The city merchants were proud that a tent church and a one-room schoolhouse had been added to their town. Randy tried to hire Mary as the teacher, but she turned down the opportunity.

The Santa Fe Railroad had been given every other section of land on either side of their surveyed right-of-way by the government. They, in turn, sold much it to settlers at bargain prices, anticipating they would be prospective customers for the railroad when it was finally built. The railroad land agents had enticed a number of Russians to immigrate to Kansas with the promise of that cheap land. At least another hundred families settled within ten miles of Winfield.

"I'll be damned if this place ain't gonna outgrow Wichita. Getting so many people around it makes a man feel crowded," Zeke commented as they approached their usual camping area on the Walnut River. Curtis family had to settle for a different camping space. It was near the river, but the trees were too small to offer much shade. They stretched a twelve-foot square canvas from the covered wagon box to a couple of straggly trees for added weather protection.

Will noticed the Sommers camped about a hundred yards upriver. Before leaving the farm, as he had the year before, he promised Mary he'd do his best to stay clear of Homer Sommers.

CHAPTER 29

FLEETING GOOD TIMES

◆

They were still getting the camp in order when Randy Briddle showed up with a matched and spirited team of sorrel horses, hitched to a fancy red surrey. Randy had been aggressively courting Mary since he'd heard about her husband's death. Mary seemed to enjoy the attention, but had done nothing to encourage a romance.

"How do you like my new rig?" he asked Mary, proudly without seeming arrogant.

"Very nice, Randy. Aren't you concerned your customers will think you're getting too rich, at their expense?" Mary queried lightheartedly.

"Gosh," he stammered, with sincere concern in his voice, "I-I sure hope you don't feel that way, Mary."

"No, I was just kidding you, Randy.

"Mary, I'd be obliged if you'd take a ride with me," Randy asked. "I've got some new things in the store from Kansas City, and some new horses out at my ranch I'd like to show you."

"Gosh, I'd love to go riding with you; Randy, but we haven't finished setting up camp yet. Also, we've got to get some food prepared for our hungry guys."

"Go on with him, Mary. I'll see to things here," Betsy offered.

"Well, okay, if you really don't mind, Betsy," Mary agreed.

"Hey, what you think, I'm some kind of injun giver?" Betsy asked with a chuckle. "Go on before the good man changes his mind and asks me to go with him instead."

"I'm not worried about that, Betsy," Mary joshed, with a slight hint of sarcasm. "But I'll accept the kind offer." Turning to Randy she said, "Just give me a few minutes to put on something more presentable."

Mary hurriedly changing her clothes because as much as she like Betsy, she didn't what to expose her suitor to that natural beauty and exotic charm too long. But then what were her true feelings about Randy? While she liked him a lot and enjoyed his company, there wasn't that romantic spark that Randy obviously desired. Her woman's intuition told her that he would soon be proposing. She honestly didn't know what her answer would be. Betsy being her only female confidant, she had discussed her relationship dilemma with her and received some disquieting comments.

"If you're looking for a man, why wouldn't you marry him if he asked?" the practical side of Betsy queried. "He's good looking, rich, and seems kind."

"How about love?" Mary said.

"Well, if it's love you're after, you've got a bad problem because one of the males you love is too old and the other one is too young," Betsy stated.

"Who are you talking about?" Mary demanded, blushing.

"You know who!" was the terse reply. "If you really want my opinion, I'm betting you'll wait for the young one to grow up."

Will succeeded in staying clear of Homer Sommers until entries were being made for the first horse race. The Sommers entered a long-legged black horse that looked speedy. No one knew how the hardscrabble, disreputable farmer acquired such a fine looking animal. Homer strutted up to Will at the registration table.

"We got a horse that'll beat the hell out of your damn uncle's ol' mare this year," he boasted.

"Well, your horse sure looks fast, but we won't be racing Mendy this year. She's with foal. I'll be riding her son, Natty, in two of the short races."

"Natty's a shitty name for a horse. I saw your spindly-legged varmint over there by your camp. I'd say *Ratty* would be a better name for him. Har, har, har," Homer roared at his clever wit.

Will stared at the redhead with controlled fury. Zeke broke the tension by shouting from the racing officials' tent.

"Come along, Will. We got things to do before the first race."

As he turned to join Zeke, Will heard Homer say, "Yeah, that's it, go running to your piss-ant uncle. Someday, soon, my pa's gonna kick his butt, just for fun."

In deference to his promise to Mary, Will didn't honoring that stupid comment with a reply.

Natty won both the quarter-mile and the first half-mile races, going away. The Sommers' black horse, ridden by Homer, came in a close third in the quarter-mile race. It finished second in the half-mile, a neck ahead of Randy's horse. Homer's black horse had deliberately crowded the bunched field of five horses on the second turn. After the race, Randy dismounted and approached Buck Sommers with blood in his eyes.

"If that damn kid of yours ever tries to crowd me off a racetrack again, I will come looking for your worthless ass, Buck."

The pudgy, red-faced farmer backed away, stammering, "He-he didn't mean nothing, Mr. Briddle. That black thoroughbred horse is hard to control, that's all."

"Well, if that's so, you'd better get someone to ride the horse that can control him, or keep him out of the races. We're not going to put up with that kind of shenanigans in Winfield!"

"I'm too heavy for 'im, Mr. Briddle. If I tell Homer to keep 'im under control, would you let 'im run in the other two races? We're just poor farmers and sure do need some of that prize money. You wouldn't begrudge us that would you, Mr. Briddle?"

"Alright, Buck. We'll give him another chance, but I'm holding you personally responsible."

When it was announced Natty wouldn't be entered in the second half-mile, or the mile races, Homer sauntered up to Will again.

"What's the matter, you feared of running in a real race against my horse?"

Will's hot eyes bored into Homer until the lanky redhead flinched.

"Homer, I'm not afraid of you, or your horse. The reason we're not racing Natty anymore today is because he's young. We don't intend to hurt him by working him too hard."

"Hell that's a damn poor excuse for being scared to ride him against me."

"It'll be a cold day in hell before you ever scare me, Homer. I've got some free advice for you though: your horse is fast, but he'd be even better if you didn't whip him. It only distracts him."

"He's my horse. I'll beat the lazy bastard if I want to. It ain't none of your damn business."

"That's right, Homer, it isn't any of my business. I just hate to see a good horse misused."

"We'll be back next year with Natty entered in every race. Then we'll see which horse is the fastest," Will spoke over his shoulder as he walked away.

Randy's horse beat the Sommers' black horse in the second half-mile race by a nose. The sleek long-legged critter was fast. He obviously had racing experience because he paced himself, in spite of Homer's vicious whipping. The long-legged horse was coming on strong when they crossed the finish line.

Betting on the last race was brisk, about evenly divided between the two favorites. At the half-mile mark, Randy's horse pulled a length ahead, and then the big black made his move. They were neck and neck coming down the stretch. The rangy black reached down and made a last minute surge that won the race by a head.

Magnanimous Randy was the first to congratulate Buck and Homer. Will watched while the two blowhards strutted around like male peacocks at mating time. A group of newcomers, who didn't know Buck's reputation, crowded around him and his son offering congratulations and admiring the fast black horse.

Mort McCracken, a burly, successful farmer and cattleman, pushed his way through the group and got Buck's attention. His place was about five miles northeast of the Sommers'.

"Where'd you get an expensive horse like this black, Buck? I never seen him 'round your place before," the Scotsman demanded.

Buck's red face bleached from red to pink, to white, and then to chalk white.

"Bought 'im from a damn Injun, down in the nations, if it's any of your business," he managed to sputter.

Mort patted the horse's sweaty rump and examined the brand on his flank.

"That's sure a helluva funny looking brand. Looks to me like someone's used a running iron on it. Don't that blotched brand worry you none, Buck?" He spit out, *Buck*, like it was a dirty word that he was glad to get out of his mouth.

It was common knowledge there was bad blood between the men. Mort, who ran a substantial herd, had been losing cattle, two or three at a time. A couple of yearlings with his brand on their rumps were found in Buck's ramshackle corral. Buck got off by pleading they had wandered on to his land and he was just about to drive them back to Mort's range.

"That—that's one of them brands the damn Cherokees use," Buck whined. "I—I bought 'im down there in the Cherokee Nation, didn't I Homer? You was down there with me."

"Yeah, Pa, that's right. You paid that red bastard fifty dollars for 'im," Homer confirmed.

"Hell, his word don't mean crap," Mort spit out. "A mangy dog will lie and the cur pup'll swear to the lie."

Buck seemed to muster up a little courage. He hacked to clear his throat and replied in a nervous, high-pitched voice.

"No call for you to insult me, Mort. If you're accusing me of stealing this horse, you'd best have proof. You already falsely accused me of stealing some of your cattle."

"Well, I'm damn near sure you're guilty of rustling my cattle. When I do get my proof, you're a dead man, Buck Sommers. Only reason I let you off last time was 'cause you got a decent wife and a nice little girl."

With that, Mort McCracken pushed his way back through the crowd, which soon dispersed. Buck and Homer slinked away with their questionable horse.

Zeke prevented Will's temptation from overriding good judgment before they headed home after the celebration. Will wouldn't have admitted, even to himself, that the holstered pistols cowboys from down in the Cherokee Strip wore while they had friendly conversations with Betsy influenced his desire to part with twenty-five dollars of his winnings for a Colt .45 pistol and a holster from Randy's store.

"What do you need with a hand gun, Will?" Zeke asked.

"I want you to teach me how to use it to protect myself," Will replied.

"From what? That Winchester rifle I gave you for your last birthday should take care of anything you'll run across on the farm."

"I don't plan on being a farmer all my life," Will replied testily.

"That's your decision to make, but why don't you save your money until you need a handgun. I'll teach you how to draw and shoot with my old Colt .44," Zeke offered.

"Well, all right," Will agreed reluctantly. He sure liked the looks of that fine 45. Being a good salesman, Randy let him strap it on. It was hard for the youngster to take it off.

The Curtis family returned home from their third Fourth of July celebration in Kansas rejuvenated and happy. Will and Natty had done them proud. Because of Natty's speed, Will had one hundred dollars of prize money tucked in his pocket—a far cry from having to barter his entire winter catch of pelts for seed grain a little more than two years before. He dreamed of maybe quitting the farm, taking either Mary or Betsy with him—he couldn't decide which one—and making lots of money racing Natty. Zeke had told him there was a regular horse racing circuit back East.

Notoriously fickle Kansas weather continued to cooperate. Harvest from the expanded acreage was bountiful for a second year. By the end of the Indian summer, all the wheat and oats were in the granaries, except three wagonloads they consigned to Randy for shipment to Kansas City for sale. A bumper corn crop filled two cribs. Sweet, nourishing, blue-stemmed hay filled the hayloft of their new barn and there was a large stack near the corral over at Zeke's place. The horse-powered thrashing machine and hay rake they'd purchased helped with the grain harvest and haymaking. Having Betsy's assistance and a that of a hired man greatly sped up all of the work, especially corn shucking. Times were so favorable that one evening at supper, a contented and expansive Zeke tempted fate by wondering aloud about their superior good fortune.

"It must be Betsy that's brought us these good times. Things have sure improved since she come to live with us."

"If that's so, Zeke, it's the first time I've ever brought anyone good luck," the self-effacing young woman proclaimed. "My Osage mother taught me that people mostly make their own luck with hard work."

"That makes sense," Zeke agreed. "Trouble is, there's a time, like our first year here, when you work your butt off and things still don't go right. Got to be an element of luck in there somewheres."

"Maybe that's true," Betsy agreed. "My Osage mother had another saying that you might want to heed, Zeke: 'Good times are fleeting!'"

"Sounds like your ma was kind of on the pessimistic side," Zeke commented lightheartedly. "How'd she manage to raise such a practical daughter?"

Betsy's demeanor darkened.

"Osages weren't always pessimistic," she snapped back. "Things didn't start going bad for my people until the white men stole our land, crowded us on to a reservation, corrupted our men with rot gut whiskey, and debauched our women." This was a vindictive side of congenial Betsy that showed trough at times.

On September twelfth, the family celebrated Will's sixteenth birthday. Mary placed him and Zeke back-to-back, and announced he was just two inches shorter than his six-foot uncle.

"Now don't go getting the big head, Will, just 'cause you're damn near as tall as me. There's more than a couple of inches that makes the difference between a man and a boy, *sonny*. When you can grow a mustache what matches mine, well, then we'll have us a wrestling match to test you out."

"Gosh, Uncle Zeke," Will lamented. "I ain't in no hurry to have that wrestling match, but I sure would like a soup strainer like yours."

"You'll have one all too soon, Will," Zeke chuckled. "Then you either grow a beard or be shaving all the time." He paused for a moment, seemingly admiring his maturing nephew, and then continued on a more serious note.

"Just don't be in such an all-fired hurry to grow up. Once you're there, folks won't ever let you be a boy again. It's likely the best time you'll know because of all the new things you're learning and doing. Enjoy this time in your life."

It was the twentieth of October when the Curtis family awoke to find the first snow of the season had dusted the ground. Dropping temperatures and dark clouds on the northwest horizon forewarned of a possible blizzard. Zeke and Will left their sleeping quarters in the old sod house and met Moses near the tack shed where he slept, and the three walked together toward the horse corrals to begin the morning chores. Boris, the young Russian hired man who slept in the hayloft was taking a few days off to go see his folks.

"Sure looks like we're in for an early storm," Zeke commented. "Best we put off doing any fence building today. We'll work around here, putting down bedding and gathering the young stock into shelters. Way the weather looks, I'm darn glad we've already moved that bunch of horses here from the pasture at my place. Ain't good cover for them over there."

"That sure sounds like a good thing to do," Moses agreed. "I feels in my ol' bones there's a rip-roaring storm heading our way."

Zeke came to a sudden halt and Moses nearly bumped into him.

"Who left that gate open last night?" Zeke demanded. "All our horse are gone!"

"I closed it and wired it shut," Will stated.

They all rushed on toward the open gate. Zeke suddenly stopped again and put his arms out to restrain his two companions while closely observing the scuffed snow in the gate opening and the ground just beyond.

"Damn, look at them prints," he exclaimed. "Someone in high heel boots opened that gate and about three of the bastards run off all our horses. They must have roped one of then and was kind of dragging him along, probably Natty."

"Moses, you sleep closest to the corral, did you hear anything unusual last night?"

"No sir, I ain't heard nothing, but you knows I sleeps sound and don't hear all that good no more."

"If there were strangers around the place, why didn't Rex get wind of 'im and bark?" Will asked rhetorically, and then his voice took on a frantic tone. "Come to think about it, why didn't he meet us at the door this morning? Do—do you think something's happened to him too, Uncle Zeke?"

"I don't think he'd give up without a fight, and we'd have heard it," Zeke replied. "Let's take a look for him."

Ten minutes later, Will found his faithful dog. The stalwart hunter, buddy, and companion was lying in a pool of his own blood behind the corncrib with his throat cut. It hadn't happened too long ago. Will fell to his knees and cradled the limp dog in his arms. Tears ran down his cheeks.

"Aw-w-w, aw-w-w," he wailed from down deep in his gut. "Some bastard killed my dog and stole my horse. How you suppose they killed Rex without him putting up a fight?"

"Rex was a sucker for a hunk of beef. That likely distracted him long enough for some no-good bastard to cut his throat," Zeke answered.

"Poor ol' dog ain't really been right since that big coon almost done 'im in," Moses pointed out with a quivering voice. "Maybe that's why some bad man could of sneaked up and fooled 'im."

"We've got to get our horses back or we're done for," Zeke stated. "Damned if Betsy ain't right—*good times are fleeting!*"

CHAPTER 30

TRACKING

◆

Though Zeke was a fair tracker, anyone could have followed the trail left by a herd of horses in the light snow. It lead them to the northeast corner of the harvested cornfield, where Zeke read evidence of six or seven horses coming from the north and being held there for a short time. Those tracks merged with the dozen sets from their corral. From there, the conspicuous evidence went south over the hill toward a ford on the Walnut.

"Looks like they're headed for the Indian Territory," Zeke announced. "Probably intend to sell them horses down in the Osage or Cherokee Nation. I'll get my guns and tucker and follow 'em on foot. I'll have to hurry before the snow covers them tracks."

"Masta Zeke, does you think it a good idea to track them critters on foot?" Moses asked. "They done got a head start and, they got to be at least four of 'em."

"Hell, Moses, we ain't got no other choice. But I think there's a chance of catching up to them if I quit lollygagging and get started. They can't move that mob of horses very fast. Signs show they're having a lot of trouble with one of our horses. I'm betting its Natty. If it starts snowing hard they'll have to hole up somewhere." Zeke led off back toward the house at a fast pace.

"Yeah, I'm sure it's Natty giving 'em trouble," Will agreed, taking large strides to keep up with Zeke. "They'll have their hands full with Natty. Sure hope they don't hurt him none."

"Ha! More likely that young stud will be hurting them yahoos," Zeke answered. "It'll take at least two of 'em to control him and that'll slow them considerable. That may be just the edge I'll need."

"Just the edge *we'll* need," Will announced. "I'm going with you, Zeke!" It was a flat statement, not a request.

"I know how you feel, Will, but its better you stay and watch out for the family. No telling what's going on," Zeke replied without breaking stride. "Could be, them bastards are trying to lure us away, then swing back to rob our place, or worse."

Will thought about that possibility for a few paces.

"I think those scum were only after our horses. They won't think we'd be crazy enough to follow them on foot," Will replied with conviction. "I don't mean no disrespect, Zeke, but this time I'm going! They killed my dog and stole my horse. I aim to pay 'em back, *personally!*"

It didn't go unnoticed that Will had dropped the "uncle" from Zeke's name when he declared his intention.

"Okay, Will. It's gonna be a rough trip. I ain't cutting you no slack. Go tell Mary to throw some grub into a sack and put on your warmest coat. I'll swing by my storage tent to pick up my rifle and pistol. Leave your Winchester for the women and Moses. You can strap on my pistol. One long gun will be enough to carry. We'll have to be in close to take 'em anyway."

"Moses you go get your old rifle from your place and come running to the house. I don't want you to let any of the women out of your sight while we're gone, 'less they're sleeping or in the outhouse. Boris should be back tomorrow to give you some help with chores and watching the place."

Top Sergeant Zeke Curtis was barking orders. And the troops scamper to respond.

"Yes, sir!" Moses panted and veered off toward the tack shed, trotting as fast as his aging legs would carry him.

By the time Zeke reached the house, Mary had placed food, coffee, tin plates, and cups in a sugar sack. Some of it was packed in a gallon tin pail, which they could use to heat up food and boil coffee. Will had on his heavy coat and a scarf he could tie over his floppy brimmed felt hat to keep his ears warm. He was pulling on his gloves. While Zeke explained things to Mary, Betsy came out of the bedroom dressed in warm work clothes, heavy boots, and a hip-length, inverted sheepskin coat. A wool shawl was draped over her head, with the ends wrapped around her neck, squaw style.

"Now what the hell do you think you're doing?" Zeke barked.

"I'm going with you and Will," she replied calmly.

"Damn it, I want you to stay here to help Mary and Moses," Zeke ordered.

"If I was your woman, I'd be duty bound to obey you, but as a friend, I'm asking you to let me help. I'm a good tracker. Will says they're headed south. I know the country. I don't think I have to remind you, I can handle myself in a fight and keep up with you on the trail."

"But that leaves only Moses to look out for the girls until Boris gets back," Zeke pleaded.

"No! That leaves Mary and Moses to look out for the girls. You underestimate Mary," Betsy informed Zeke. "She can be a tough gal and shoots as good as any of the Curtis men."

"Well—well, I ain't got no gun for you," Zeke weakly argued. "I wanted to leave Will's Winchester for Mary and Moses."

"I wouldn't want to carry the heavy weapon anyway. Have you forgotten I can use a knife?" Betsy reminded him coolly, patting the large sheathed knife that was strapped to her trim waist under her coat.

"No—No, I ain't forgot," Zeke shuddered, in spite of himself, as the memory slammed into his mind of her slitting a man's throat as calmly as he would stick a butchering pig.

He turned abruptly to Mary and spoke gruffly in his frustration. "Is that all right with you, Mary?"

"Yes," Mary shot back. "They stole Betsy's horses, too. Just go get our horses back from those thieves. Moses and I can handle things here. The hired man will be back soon."

"If you're coming, let's get on the trail," Zeke grumbled, "before the snow covers their tracks and them horse thieves get plumb out of the country."

While they were talking, Mary stuffed in a slab of bacon, a loaf of freshly baked bread, and a small frying pan in another sugar sack and handed it to Betsy. She also had three blankets rolled up, each tied with cords for shoulder straps. Zeke wanted to travel light, but Mary insisted on the wool blankets and extra food.

Will strapped the cartridge belt and holster for Zeke's Colt .44 pistol around his slim waist under his coat. Pulled to the last hole, the belt fit him comfortably. Since Zeke had been giving him instructions as he had promised, Will knew how to use the surprisingly heavy weapon.

When he finished buttoning his coat, Mary abruptly embraced Will and kissed him on the lips while whispering in his ear. "Be careful, Will. You're very dear to me."

Seemingly embarrassed at her brash behavior in front of the others, she stammered, "All—all of you are precious to me; come back safely."

The three pursuers moved out of the door and followed Zeke's lead as he cut the thieves' yet prominent trail. At the brow of the hill that overlooked the Walnut ford, the tracks in the snow were mingled in confusion. When they took off south again, in a more orderly manner, one set dragged for a few yards, as though the horse was being pulled along against its will. For another hundred yards, those dragging hoof-marks became sharp imprints of a rearing or bucking horse.

"Here's where Natty tried to leave the herd and turn back," Zeke speculated. "The bastards were able to control him, probably by putting two ropes on him, snubbed to the saddles of two riders. He's slowed them fools down one helluva lot. Good horse! They'd be smart to let him go 'cause he won't stop fighting 'em. But, he's a valuable horse. I'm betting on their greed overriding their smarts. Hell, if they were smart, they wouldn't have messed with us!"

They forded the Walnut, about fifty feet wide and a foot or so deep at that point. No challenge for horses, but a cold, wet wade for the three pursuers on foot. Zeke offered to carry Will and Betsy across piggyback.

"We're in this together, Zeke," Betsy curtly replied. "Where you go, I go, and what you've got to do, I'll do." She splashed into the cold water with Will close behind. Zeke shook his head and plunged in behind them. An hour was lost building a fire and drying their boots and socks. Zeke chafed at the delay, but it was either that or frozen feet.

They were on the near side of a clear-running, shallow creek, well into the Osage Nation, before Zeke called another break. It was snowing harder by the minute and the brisk east wind plastered it against their left sides. The still-visible, but fading, markings indicated the horse herd stopped there for a drink. They also drank from the creek, and then sat on nearby rocks for a few minutes, gobbling down cold ham and biscuits.

"Let's hit the trail," Zeke said. "This snow's getting worse. If we ain't close to them when they go to ground, we could sure as hell lose 'em."

His weather forecast was accurate. By midafternoon, they trudged along in near white-out conditions. After another two hours of struggling through worsening conditions, the feeble daylight began to fade. Still, they shuffled on, following a trail that the accumulating snow made increasingly dimmer.

Zeke abruptly halted and turned his back to the blowing snow. Betsy stopped close by his side. He caught Will's coattail as he trotted by; otherwise, the cold, fatigue-mesmerized youth would have passed on by and soon been lost in the blizzard. Zeke cupped his hand to his mouth and shouted in Betsy's ear.

"What do you make of this, Betsy?"

She moved her head close to Zeke's ear and shouted back.

"Better find a place to ride out this storm, soon, or we'll be traveling in circles until we freeze to death."

"You got any idea where them bastards are headed?"

"Yes. I judge we're a mile or maybe two from a cabin with corrals that the contract grazers use when they bring their cattle to graze on Osage land. It's on the Arkansas."

"Why in th' hell didn't you tell me that sooner?" Zeke shouted.

"Because you didn't ask me," she shouted back. "Osage women know better than to try telling their men what to do."

"To hell with that!" Zeke replied. "You speak up when you're with me! Don't suppose you know where we can hole up until this blows over?"

"Yes. If we veer to our right, we'll hit the Arkansas in about half an hour. There are rock bluffs along the bank there with many cave-like overhangs. We should be able to find one near water that'll give us protection."

"Lead out then, Betsy. We'll follow close behind."

Without further comment, Betsy pointed to their right and moved off, setting a fast pace. Mercifully, they were now traveling with the wind to their backs. It was more like an hour, and visibility was almost gone, when she guided them down a ravine into a sheltered rock alcove below, not ten feet from the rushing water of the Arkansas.

It was a blessing to be protected from the windblown snow, and none too soon. Zeke and Will immediately plopped to the ground to catch their breath. Betsy disappeared into the curling snow that restricted vision beyond the lip of the alcove.

"Damnation!" Zeke said, between heaving breaths. "Where's that gal got off to now? She'll get lost out there in the dark."

Practical Will answered through the gulps of air he forced into his lungs. "Maybe she had to piss, Zeke. I've been busting my bladder for the last hour myself."

"Well, hell, if that was her problem, we would of turned our backs and she could of gone over there out of the wind. It's too damned dark to see anything anyways. Now that you mention it, I need to go, too. Best we take care of our needs before she gets back. That's just one more problem traveling with a damn woman!"

He pushed himself up wearily and moved to the far outside corner of their alcove. Will took the other corner, about ten feet away. They were buttoning up their pants when Betsy returned, dragging a small wind-fell tree.

"Well," Zeke stated sarcastically, "ain't that just like my Indian gal, to go out and drag in wood for her men."

Betsy broke off twigs to start a fire while replying. "I'm bushed and cold too, Zeke, but I figure first thing's first. I can hold my water until there's a fire going. While I get this started, now that you've taken a piss, you two bums can go drag in some bigger wood to bank the fire with after we finish cooking. There's a big pile of driftwood up against the cliff, about twenty feet to the right."

With a little chuckle she added, "Don't hurry back. I'll take care of *my needs* while you're out in the cold."

"Damn if you ain't way ahead of us again, Betsy. Could you just slow down some and let us catch our breath?"

"I just don't want to be a burden to you, Zeke," she replied demurely.

In a short time, Betsy had a small blaze going between two rocks. She had placed them in such a way that they would hold a frying pan for cooking or the gallon can directly above the controlled flames for boiling coffee. Once again, she had demonstrated her efficiency to Zeke.

"Come on, Will. You can see Betsy's got things under control, best we follow her orders."

They nearly froze their butts off, making sure they gave Betsy enough time to take care of her needs. She had to shout for them to return to the warmth of the fine fire she nurtured.

The next morning, breakfast was finished and the eager posse was packed to move out by the time it was light enough to make their way safely over the rocks and through the underbrush along the bank of the Arkansas. Betsy estimated the cabin where the thieves likely holed up for the night was only about a mile downstream.

Zeke discussed strategy with his cohorts before breaking camp.

"I'm assuming there are at least four of them horse thieves and they'll be well-armed. With only two guns, our only chance is to catch 'em by surprise and get the drop on 'em. They'll be thinking they're safe down here in the Territory. Maybe we'll get lucky and find 'em still asleep in the cabin. But I wouldn't bet on it."

The three pursuers moved cautiously. Thank goodness, it had stopped snowing sometime during the night. After they stumbled over rough terrain along the riverbank for about an hour, Betsy whispered, "The cabin is just beyond that grove of trees."

Zeke took the lead until he was in a position to see the corral and the rear of the one-room cabin. After observing the scene for a few seconds, he whispered to his companions.

"The bastards must be gone. No horses in the corral and only a whisk of smoke coming out of the chimney. You folks stay here and I'll sneak up for a closer look-see."

In a few minutes, Zeke appeared at the rear of the cabin and motioned Will and Betsy to come on in.

"They must have stayed here last night, but we just missed them." He pointed to the steaming horse-droppings in the pole corral. "Someone met them with grain and hay. They fed and bedded the horses down in the corral last night, all except one that was snubbed to a tree over there."

"That snubbed one must have been Natty," Will said proudly. "He's still fighting them."

"You're probably right. Wagon tracks take off south, along the river, but they took the horses east toward them hills." Zeke continued reading signs. "The tracks are pretty much in tandem. Must have gotten tired of herding the horses and roped them into two or three strings for leading."

"Let's get going," Will urged. "If they just left, and Natty's still giving them a bad time, we should be able to catch up to 'em soon."

"Don't think we want to catch up with 'em in broad daylight, Will," Zeke counseled. "I make out at least four sets of hoof prints that show heavier from having riders. Four to three odds, with us having only two guns, ain't very good. Best we follow along and look for a chance to get the drop on 'em when they camp tonight. Where you think they're headed, Betsy?"

"Could be the Cherokee Nation, which is over that way, but more likely they're headed to Pawhuska. There's a corrupt Indian agent there who trades in stolen stock. I overheard McClure say that's who was buying their rustled cattle, probably with government money, and he sells them back to the agency at exorbitant prices."

"Why the hell didn't you tell that to Josh, Betsy? He could have turned the crooked bastard in to the authorities," Zeke scolded.

"It wouldn't have done any good. That agent has been cheating the Osages for years and getting away with it because of powerful connections in the Bureau of Indian Affairs."

"Damn, that's rotten," Zeke fumed. "You got any ideas where these thieves might hole up tonight, Betsy?"

"They'll need water. About the only place they can get it, in the direction they're headed, is Bird Creek. That's normally about an eight-hour ride from here. I'm thinking it'll take them more like twelve hours, leading all those horses through foot-deep snow."

"And with Natty giving them trouble," Will added.

"That means it'll be dusk by the time they make camp. They'll be damned bushed by then. We'll catch 'em sleeping, sure as hell!" Zeke exclaimed.

"But we'll be walking, while they're riding," Will pointed out.

"It'll be a tough hike all right, but probably not as bad as their day's going to be," Betsy suggested. "Those horses will get hungry and thirstier as the day passes. That'll make 'em more contrary. On the other hand, they'll be tromping out a path through the snow for us to follow."

"That's the spirit, Betsy," Zeke said with admiration in his voice. "Let's move out and hope we can finish this job tonight."

CHAPTER 31

FRONTIER JUSTICE

◆

As Betsy predicted, the tandem horses left a well-defined trail, but the packed snow was slick underfoot for the hikers. A brisk wind kicked up about midday, occasionally slashing their faces with sharp snow crystals. They stopped about a half hour in the shelter of a rock cliff for a toilet break and a cold meal. Snow was their water source. Under heavy-laden skies, darkness came fast, catching them out in open country. They stumbled along having to check every step to be sure they remained on the horse-trampled trail. Sharp-eyed Betsy was first to detect the distant glow of a campfire against the black horizon.

"There's their camp," she said quietly, even though they were still some distance away. "They must be in a clearing beside Bird Creek."

"Good job, Betsy," Zeke replied. "That glow ain't easy to see. Do you know the lay of the land where they're camped?"

"Not exactly," she answered truthfully. "There are usually dense stands of black oak and sumac along the creeks in these parts. Also, there are rock canyons ten to twelve feet high in places. Can't tell you for sure about their spot, but I'll go find out."

She took a couple of steps before Zeke caught up to her and put a firm restraining hand on her shoulder.

"That's my job, Betsy! You and Will hole up over there by that big rock and I'll check out the varmints."

"As you wish, Zeke, but you know I'm half Osage and we're sneaky people."

"Sometimes I get the idea you're at least by half too damn sensitive about being part Indian," Zeke stated curtly. Then softer, "I know you'd do the job fine, but this is the thing I did in the war. I'll need to see the layout before I can make a battle plan."

He disappeared into the darkness without further comment. Will and Betsy moved over to the rock, brushed snow from a shelf, and eased their tired butts down onto it. Too tired to converse, they sat there, fighting to stay awake. Zeke returned in about a half hour.

"Them damn fools done got their balls in a nutcracker now! Oh, sorry about the language, Betsy," he stammered, always the gentleman.

"No problem, Zeke. I know all about balls and nutcrackers. Way you described the situation I get the picture. When do we hit them?"

"They're already hunkered down in their bedrolls, feeling safe enough to not even post a guard. No wonder you was able to see their fire; it lights up half the countryside. Best we wait until it dies down some before we try to capture 'em."

"Do you aim to give 'em a chance to surrender, Zeke?" Will asked, with an incredulous inflection in his voice.

"Yes, Will, I am. When I come home from the war, I took a pledge to myself that I'd never kill another human 'less there was no other way out. I've seen and done all the killing I want for a lifetime!"

"That's noble, Zeke, but that attitude could get us all killed. Remember what happened at Blackburn when you tried that?" Betsy curtly reminded him.

"Yeah, I remember I took some more lives in the heat of anger, Betsy. I wanted them to resist and that's how I feel about the scum we're trailing. But on the other hand, I know that if this country's ever going to be a decent place to raise a family, the time has got to come when we stop settling our own scores with guns, and let the law take over."

"That sounds good, Zeke. Call me bitter, but I've seen a lot of men that deserve to be killed, and the law's spread too darn thin to do much about it. Your brother thought like you and it got him killed."

"That's probably true, Betsy, but he died for what he believed in. I don't intend for us to take any unreasonable risks with those bastards. I'll just give 'em one chance to give up and face the law."

"Okay, I get your point," Betsy conceded. "How do we take them?"

"First, let's work our way down to a vantage point I picked out where we can make out the whole camp. It's downwind, so we shouldn't excite the horses that are picketed on the up-creek side of the fire. I think we can sneak up right close to them sleeping beauties."

A half hour later, they were peering around a rock outcrop, not more than thirty feet from the nearest mound that represented a sleeping horse thief. The huge fire had died down to flickering flames on a pile of bright embers, which still radiated shimmering light for a few feet. Zeke spoke in a hoarse whisper, which seemed loud in the still, cold night air.

"Count 'em. They're all spread out on this side of the fire. I made out four. Do you see any more?"

"No," Betsy whispered back. "But are you sure there isn't one on watch with the horses?" They could make out the dark outlines of a group of picketed horses just beyond the fire. Most were reclining but a few still stood.

"I ain't seen no movement over there, except for them tired horses. Here's the plan, troopers. See how them guys are spread out like the spokes of a wheel, with their heads to the fire. I'm going to work around to their right until I'm in position to cover them two furthest from the fire.

"Betsy, you wiggle straight ahead and put your knife against the next one to the left. Will, you work to the far left and draw down on that lone one over there. When we're all in position, I'll tell them to stay were they are. If shooting starts, find cover. Don't try to be no damn hero—*you got that, Will?*"

"Yes, sir," Will replied with a steady voice. "I'm ready." He drew the big pistol, pulled back the hammer, and cautiously moved toward his assigned position.

Soon Zeke was stared down at the two figures sleeping peacefully within three feet of each other between him and the fire. The glow from the once-blazing fire was still bright enough for him to make out that Will and Betsy were both in place. No one in the camp had moved a muscle.

"Stay where you're at, you skunks, or I'll blow your damn heads off." His voice was coarse, demanding, and loud.

The thief on his left set bolt upright and fumbled underneath his bedroll. The other man just grunted. For a split second, Zeke took his eyes off those men to check on Betsy and Will, and all hell broke loose. The fumbling thief cleared his gun from the bedroll and snapped off a shot that whizzed past Zeke's right ear. A point-blank shot from Zeke's Winchester slammed the man back, spread-eagled. Zeke jacked another shell into the chamber and pivoted to the other man, who was struggling to rise. His second short caught that man in the center of his chest and he fell backwards. Cavalry training caused Zeke to lever the third round into his Winchester's firing chamber before he turned his attention to Betsy and Will. Something slammed his raised rifle's stock and then went into his right armpit like a sledgehammer. He fell to his knees.

Betsy's man bolted to a sitting position with a pistol in his hand. Before he could get off a shot, the blade of her knife was buried under his left ribcage. He dropped the gun, clutched his chest, and fell back into his bedroll as a dying scream caught in his throat.

"You should have stayed put," Betsy muttered to the dead man. She was calmly cleaning her knife on his blanket when she detected a muzzle flash from the other side of the fire and saw Zeke fall to his knees.

Will's man didn't move until the shooting started, then was slow to sit up in his bedding. Will caught the muzzle flash from the other side of the fire out of the corner of his eye. With the speed of young reflexes, he turned the big .44 pistol toward the flash and snapped off a shot. A short, shrill scream was followed a split second later with the crack of a third shot from Zeke's direction. The shadow that had momentarily been outlined against the fire's glow had disappeared.

All that probably took less than thirty seconds. Will quickly turned his attention back to his original assignment that was now sitting up. A hair-trigger away from shooting the shadow, Will realized he was staring into the wild eyes of Homer Sommers. The startled redhead was fully clothed except for his tattered boots that stood in the trampled snow beside the bedroll.

"Don't shoot. I'm not armed. Please, don't shoot!" Homer blubbered with tears in his eyes.

The unwavering muzzle of Will's gun was within two feet of his archenemy's tempting temple.

"Damn you, Homer, if you move a muscle I'll blow away your horse-stealing, pea-size brain," Will shouted.

"I won't move—I won't move," Homer pleaded, throwing his hands into the air. "Plea-e-e-e-se don't shoot me!"

Will noticed Betsy moving toward Zeke. After finding and removing the redhead's holstered pistol from under his blankets, and figuring Homer too damned scared to move, Will cautiously circled the fire to check on what he'd shot. A body slumped on the ground, close enough to the fire for the clothes to smolder. When Will turned it over to make sure the bushwhacker was dead, he recognized Buck Sommers, with a bullet hole in the center of his forehead.

"Did I get the son of a bitch?" Zeke called out in a pained voice.

"You sure did, Zeke. He's dead as a stone, and it's Buck Sommers!" Will quickly decided there was no need to tell Zeke it was probably his bullet that hit Buck.

"Damn, I made a bad mistake not checking the other side of that fire better," Zeke grunted through clamped teeth. "Come close to getting Otis killed."

"There's no Otis here, Zeke," Betsy said as she knelt beside him. "But that don't matter now. Let me get a look at that shoulder. Come help me, Will, Zeke's been hit!"

For a few seconds, Will's eyes were locked onto Buck Sommers' body and the red pool of blood on the ground around his head. Shock from having participated in killing the man was soon pushed aside by concern for Zeke. He circled back to the other side of the fire to find Homer up on his knees staring toward where his father's body lay.

"Damn you, you killed my pa!" Homer whined. Will went ballistic!

"Damn you, too! You killed my dog! Your worthless pa stole our horses and shot Zeke! If Zeke dies, I'll blow your worthless ass off!"

Will shouted, while taking a roundhouse swipe at that repulsive red-haired head with the pistol in his hand. Homer saw it coming and ducked enough to escape the full impact. The pistol was drawn back for another swing at his prone, unconscious arch enemy when Betsy caught Will's arm.

"That's enough, Will. He's just a dumb kid that was probably only along for a lark. Zeke needs your help—*now!*" Betsy's harsh words got through the red glow of hatred.

Will moved with Betsy to his injured uncle's side, sparing Homer Sommers's life.

CHAPTER 32

ZEKE SUFFERS

◆

Zeke had managed to struggle to his feet. He stood wobbly and dazed, gripping his right shoulder with his left hand.

"Take it easy, Zeke," Betsy pleaded. "You've been shot. Sit down here so I can see to your wound." Betsy put her arm around his waist and eased him to a sitting position on one of the dead man's bedrolls, after she'd pulled the body aside.

While Will watched helplessly, Betsy gently helped Zeke remove his heavy coat and shirt. A blotch of blood stained the right side of his underwear from his armpit to his waist. His body shivered from the sudden cold and shock, yet beads of sweat dampened his bare forehead. A couple of oaths and low groans escaped through his clenched teeth.

"Sorry to be hurting you, Zeke," Betsy sympathized, "but I've got to get to that wound so I can clean it and stop the bleeding."

"Jus-just do what you've got to do," Zeke grunted in response.

"Stoke up that fire, and find something to boil some water in," she instructed Will in a calm but urgent tone.

Will jumped to the tasks of putting wood on the fire, dumping the contents of the blackened coffee pot, and stumbling through the dark the few yards to the creek for water. When he returned and placed the pot on a hot rock where the revived fire would heat it, Betsy had Zeke's underwear top off. In the improved light of the now blazing fire, an ugly purple hole was visible in the arm pit below Zeke's shoulder joint. Blood trickled down his side. The nasty looking wound mesmerized Will until his attention switched to Betsy as she frantically removed her upper garments. It wasn't until she had the halter part of her underwear off, revealing two firm brown breasts with protruding pink nipples, that it registered with him that she was providing bandage material for Zeke's wound. In her preoccupation with ministering to Zeke, Betsy was oblivious to Will's bug-eyed stare. His eyes seemed to have a life of their own and refused to be diverted from those glorious mounds. Betsy slipped her flannel shirt back on over bare shoulders and fastened the top three bottoms, breaking Will's hypnotic fascination.

Kneeling beside Zeke again, Betsy inspected the wound closer in the improving light of the crackling fire.

"Hum-m-m, this could have been a lot worse," she reassured Zeke. "Far as I can tell, the slug went clear through the flesh under your arm and didn't hit bone. If we can stop the bleeding and keep infection out, chances are good you'll recover without much damage."

"Well, that's reassuring," Zeke uttered, tight-jawed. "But, right now, I could use a stiff drink of brain-cracking whiskey more 'n doctoring."

Betsy chuckled at Zeke's attempt at levity while continuing her efforts to prepare bandage material from her underwear top.

"Doctoring is all I've got to offer you now, Zeke," she replied while cutting out the breast cups from her underwear top with her knife. "When we get you patched up, maybe we can find some rot gut in these horse thieves' tucker."

She was quiet for a moment, concentrating on her task. Will noticed a sly smile cross her face as she spoke without interrupting her bandage stripping.

"Then, when you get your strength back, my earlier offer is still open."

Even in his pain, Zeke nodded his head and forced a weak smile.

"That sure gives a man something to look forward to," Zeke grunted, his voice raspy with pain. The entire exchange went over Will's head, but it was reassuring that Zeke could still josh with Betsy.

After Betsy succeeded in separating the thick material of the cups from the rest of the garment, she pressed one firmly against the bullet's entry point between the armpit and the collar joint and other one over the exit, just under the shoulder blade. She was hoping no bone had been nicked.

Zeke had no way of knowing he was being treated by someone every bit as capable as most frontier doctors. Tending wounds and sickness wasn't new to Betsy. Many times, she'd been pressed into service as a nurse at the small clinic and hospital the sisters operated at the Catholic mission where she'd attended school. Except for offering her extensive knowledge of herbal medicines on occasion, this was the first time she'd had a chance to demonstrate her doctoring talents since arriving at the Curtis farm.

"Here, Will, come hold these firmly in place while I prepare more bandaging material."

Will slid his hands under Betsy's and firmly pressed the cups against the wounds. Zeke winced from the change in pressure, but endured the added pain without complaint. Betsy continued cutting strips from her underwear and the top of Zeke's long johns until she had enough material to fashion a shoulder bandage. She placed the pieces of cloth she intended to use as compresses into the coffee pot to sterilize them. Her assistant didn't understand why Betsy placed the blade of her knife in the coals beside the boiling pot, but he'd soon learn the gruesome reason. Zeke knew, and steeled himself.

When the tip of the knife blade glowed cherry red hot, she proceeded in a professional manner to cauterize the wounds. Large beads of sweat popped from Zeke's forehead, his jaws tightened over gnashed teeth, and he emitted a deep, mournful groan each time Betsy pressed the red-hot knife blade to the wound's entrance or exit point.

The stench of burning flesh nearly gagged her wide-eyed assistant, yet he stoically continued to help Betsy any way he could. When the cauterizing and bandaging were completed, they bundled Zeke into blankets and placed him near the fire.

Preoccupied with tending Zeke, Homer was ignored until they heard a running horse crashing through brush on the far side of the fire. Will took a quick look toward where he'd left Homer unconscious. It hit him like a sledgehammer that his nemesis wasn't there! Likely, he was escaping on one of the horses. Bitter gall rose in Will's throat. He jumped to his feet and dashed in the direction of the sounds.

"That damn Homer is trying to get away. I'm going after the bastard!" Will shouted over his shoulder as he crashed into the underbrush.

"Let him go," Zeke shouted back, as loud as his strained voice would project. "He's just a dumb kid. I don't want to see him killed for something his worthless pa got him into."

Will ignored his uncle's comment and continued to plunge frantically through the brush, desperate to get a shot at his escaping enemy. It was a futile effort. Homer Sommers had made his escape into the cold night, riding bareback on his own big, black horse with no coat or supplies. He had snatched his boots before sneaking away while Will and Betsy were preoccupied with ministering to Zeke.

The impetuous youth reluctantly gave up the chase, returned to the camp area, and turned to his attention to his horse, Natty. The noble animal was snubbed to a tree, so close it was impossible for him to lie down. Uncle Zeke wasn't the only casualty, but thank goodness, they were both alive. Will detected by feel and dim firelight raw whip marks on the young stud's withers and nasty rope burns on his neck and nose.

"We got all them outlaws that done this to you, Natty, except ol' Homer," Will informed the whinnying horse. "I swear to you, I'll catch that bastard someday, and he'll pay with his life for his part in this."

Natty rubbed Will with his sore nose. With tears of joy and empathy just below the surface, Will gently patted the horse's muscular neck.

"You're going to be all right now, good horse. Thank you, ol' buddy, for slowing them varmints down so we could catch them."

When Will returned to the other side of the fire, Betsy had lit a kerosene lantern she'd found in the thieves' gear and was preparing a meal. The efficient woman had also pulled the bodies into the bushes.

The three or four big swigs of the white lighting painkiller from the bottle Betsy had also located in the thieves' supplies seemed to have dulled Zeke's pain and put him in an expansive mood.

"Well, hot shot, I'm happy to see you didn't get lost out there, chasing on foot after a man on horseback," he teased Will. And then in a more serious manner, "Did you see to our horses?"

"Sure did, Zeke. They all seem okay, except for Natty. He's got nasty whip marks and rope burns."

"Figured he would," Zeke slurred. "I knew he'd fight them thieves all the way. If he hadn't slowed them down, we'd never of caught the varmints."

"Yeah," Will agreed, "I already told him so."

"Sure wish we had some feed for them horses," Zeke lamented.

"Maybe we should lay over here tomorrow and put them out on the hillside so they can dig out some dried gamma and buffalo grass from under the snow," Will suggested.

"That's a good idea," Betsy injected. "That'll give you some time to get your strength back, Zeke, before we hit the trail home. Now, you two dig into this food I've prepared, thanks to the supplies of the late Buck Sommers gang."

After spending the next day and night at the thieves' campsite, Zeke insisted he was well enough to ride. They packed and started on the journey home, with Will and Betsy each leading an unwieldy string of horses. Besides the three horses they rode, twelve more were theirs and four were those the dead horse thieves rode. There were two other good looking animals that must have been stolen from someone else. Zeke, who was an expert on such matters, didn't recognize the brand that was on both of them.

Will let Natty run free and rode one of Zeke's horses. It was great to be riding back instead of walking in the crunchy snow. He marveled at his gutsy uncle's ability to mount up, much less spend hours in the saddle. His doctor, Betsy, cautioned Zeke to take it easy, reminding him that he'd lost a lot of blood, but he steadfastly refused to lay over another day at the cattle herder cabin where they spent the night. Will understood that Zeke was more concerned for the condition of the horses and his traveling companions than himself. But he did seem overly anxious to get home, even if it killed him.

The evening of the third day after engaging the horse thieves, the bedraggled group straggled into the Curtis farmyard. The horses were gaunt. Zeke was slumped semiconscious and chalk-faced in his saddle. His two stalwart companions were so cold and bone-weary they had difficulty dismounting. Seeing that Zeke was badly hurt, Mary pried his clinched fingers from the saddle horn and eased him out of his saddle into her loving arms.

"Oh my God, Zeke, what have they done to you?" she moaned.

Mary half carried the semiconscious man into the house, striped him down to his long underwear, and bundled him in blankets in front of the fireplace. And then she frantically rubbed circulation back into Zeke's cold blue hands and feet, praying they didn't turn black from frostbite.

Left to fend for themselves, Will and Betsy left the horses for Moses and the hired man to tend and stiffly followed into the inviting warm house, looking more like walking dead than humans. After wearily removing frozen outer garments and boots, they slumped to the floor as close as they could get to the fire, without crowding Mary, who fussed over Zeke. Within minutes, the comrades were sound asleep, lying side-by-side. Betsy had taken Will's hand into hers. Mary directed Jeanie to throw blankets over them, and let them sleep where they lay.

CHAPTER 33

JOAN AND ESTER

◆

Even after consuming three swigs of whiskey that Mary administered, Zeke still seemed to be fighting sleep. He tried to raise on an elbow and turned his head from side to side in an agitated manner.

"Just relax, Zeke, everything's okay. You're home now. We're going to take good care of you," Mary cooed as she lovingly stroked his thick, wavy hair. Zeke persisted on trying to communicate with her in his semiconscious condition.

"Gotta check on Joan Sommers," him mutter. She leaned closer to his lips to hear the muffled words.

"Tell Joan—Buck dead—Homer on the run. Good woman. Know she needs help. Bring her and her daughter here," Zeke spoke in strained grunts while weakly tugging at Mary's sleeve with his good arm for emphasis.

"Okay, okay, Zeke, I hear you. I'll go see her first thing tomorrow. Now lay back and rest."

He sighed once, went to sleep, and didn't open his eyes again for twenty-four hours.

Early the next morning, Moses hitched a team to the light wagon. Mary hated to wake Will to find out how to get to the Sommers' farm. He had scouted the place trying to find evidence that Homer was pilfering pelts from his traps. The trip turned out to be about ten miles by snow-covered wagon trails. The weak sun was in mid-sky when Moses and Mary crested a small hill and saw an isolated, ramshackle cabin in the valley below.

"That has to be it, Moses," Mary said, "but it looks deserted. There's not a corral or outbuilding on the place."

"Maybe ol' Masta Buck done quit farming when he got to stealing horses and he chop up all the improvements for firewood," Moses suggested.

"That sounds like something the lazy bum would do," Mary agreed. "Must be someone home. There's a whisk of smoke coming out of the chimney. I hope it's not Homer. Will said he got away and is on the run."

She reached under the seat for the Winchester and cradled it in her lap. Moses drove the team down the winding track to the front of the pitiful excuse for a home.

There was no sign of a horse around the place. If Homer was there, he would have had to walk. Mary's curiosity deepened when she noticed there were no tracks of any kind in the snow that had fallen three days before.

"Moses, there's something fishy," Mary said. "You stay here with the rifle and cover me while I check out the cabin."

"Yes, ma'am," Moses replied. "I see hide or hair of that Homer Sommers, I put a hole in his mean carcass."

Mary rapped on the rough plank door and called out Joan's name three times before she heard slight movement inside. The door opened a crack. Red-rimmed, watering eyes in a skeleton-thin female face blinked at her from the gloomy interior. The woman put her hand to her forehead, shielding her eyes from the outside snow glare. She seemed either too exhausted or frightened to speak.

"M-my God, is—is that you, Joan?" Mary stammered.

The aberration inside the cabin continued to stare at Mary mutely for several more seconds before recognition crossed her face. Emaciated Joan Sommers threw open the door and fell into Mary's arms, sobbing hysterically.

"Dear God, Mary, what miracle brought you here?" her weak voice uttered through sobs. "Ester and I are in a terrible fix!"

Mary patted Joan's bony back while easing her back into the cabin. She could feel the shocking sharpness of Joan's protruding shoulder blades, even through the heavy shawl she wore. Good Lord, she thought, this woman is starving to death!

As Mary's eyes adjusted to the dim light inside, she recognized teenager Ester Sommers bundled in blankets and lying on a bed in front of the fireplace. Ester sat up and blinked.

"I'm Mary Curtis, Ester," Mary said, moving closer to the bed with sobbing Joan in tow. "I've come to see about you and your mother."

"Hi," Ester said, forcing a weak smile. Mary was relieved to see that Ester wasn't nearly as far gone as her mother, even though she was very thin. Obviously this is a case of the mother sacrificing herself to save the child, she told herself. Mixed feelings of admiration and pity for Joan Sommers bought a lump to Mary's throat.

Parts of a chair burned feebly in the fireplace, emitting weak light, but only a minuscule amount of heat. There wasn't another stick of furniture in the one-room cabin, other than the steel-framed bed.

"Oh, Mrs. Curtis, I'm so glad to see you. Please help us," Ester pleaded. "We just put our last piece of furniture on the fire. There's been no food for three days and very little for the last month. We're at our wits end because Mama and I are both too weak to chop any more wood."

"Buck didn't leave us with much when he and Homer left last month," Joan managed to add. "They were supposed to be back with supplies two weeks ago." It exhausted her to say that much.

"My God, that's terrible. I'm so sorry," Mary said, her voice breaking with emotion. "Moses and I are here to help you."

Mary eased Joan down onto the bed beside Ester. Daughter and mother clung to each other.

"Bring that lunch we packed in here, Moses," Mary shouted through the open door.

He soon appeared at the doorway with a wicker basket in his hand. His eyes grew big when he saw the cold, bare room and the two huddled, haggard females. He doffed his tattered hat and said, "How do, Miz Sommers."

Joan sat up as straight as she could, adjusted the shawl on her thin shoulders, and weakly answered, "Please come in, Moses. It's good to see you again."

Good Lord, Mary thought, the woman is starving to death and she's still thoughtful and courteous to a black man. No wonder Zeke is smitten with her.

While she removed the cold buttered biscuits and fried salt pork sandwiches from the basket, Mary instructed Moses to draw some water from the well and find wood. He soon returned with water and distressing news about the wood.

"I'll have to go into the timber to fetch firewood, Miz Mary. The sheds and corrals are all gone, not a stick left. I find a old ax out there, by where the woodpile was. I'll go chop some deadwood right quick now."

"Thank you, Moses, we won't need a lot. Just enough to get these folks warmed up," Mary said. Good Lord, she thought, we got here just in time! Ester wasn't exaggerating when she said they were burning their last stick of wood.

Joan and Ester wolfed down the sandwiches so fast Mary feared it would make them sick. Moses returned with wood and soon had a blazing warm fire burning in the fireplace. The food and warmth improved Joan's strength. She seemed eager to tell her woeful story. Once started, it flowed out like water from a breached dam.

"Buck and Homer have been off somewhere for a month. They left us very little firewood or food. Buck sold the farm team and wagon last month and they took both saddle horses. We considered trying to walk to your place or into town, but kept thinking they'd return. When the snowstorm hit, we were already too weak to attempt the trip.

"Thank God you showed up, Mary. We couldn't have lasted much longer. I don't know what's happened to Buck and Homer. They're often gone for long periods, but they always come back to eat, rest up, and to get their clothes washed and mended.

"Maybe they abandoned us this time. Buck threatened to just take off and leave us. You know, I'm his second wife. It wasn't a love match. My first husband died of consumption four years ago. I foolishly married Buck out of desperation. Homer isn't my son. Ester is my daughter by my first husband—he was a good man. Buck was a widower neighbor, back in Ohio. He wasn't such a degenerate then, and he made big promises.

"After talking me into selling my farm and the livestock my first husband and I had accumulated, he brought us out here to homestead. He was a terrible farmer, and when things went bad, he degenerated into the worthless person he is now. My only excuse for staying with him is that I have no money and nowhere to go. All my people were dead. I—I should've left him anyway, before Ester got this big. He's—he's a dirty, mean man and his son is growing up just like him!"

Ester cringed. The ugly image of what Joan meant by that statement was very clear in Mary's mind. Joan paused and stared into the crackling fire for a few moments. Mary felt it was time to tell her what had happened to the men in her family.

"Joan, the reason we came over today was to tell you Buck is dead and Homer is missing," she said softly.

Joan continued gazing into the fire emotionless. It was silent in the cabin for a couple of minutes before Joan's clear, piercing blue eyes focused on Mary.

"God forgive me, but *I'm glad he's dead*! I assume someone caught him stealing horses and shot him."

"Yes," Mary replied. "That's just what happened." She saw no reason to tell her that Buck had stolen all their horses and Zeke killed him while getting them back. She'd surely find that out soon enough.

"You said Homer is missing. Wasn't he with his pa? I know Buck took him along on his horse-stealing trips. He was becoming about as mean as his pa."

"I'm told that Homer was there, but escaped somehow. As far as we know, he's on the run down in the Territory."

"I just hope he doesn't try to come back here. So help me God, I'll shoot him myself if he does," Joan stated emphatically. Ester cringed again.

"There's not much chance he'll show up around here, Joan," Mary assured her. "He's a wanted man now. If he has any sense, he'll head out of this country."

Joan sighed. "That's his main problem. Besides having a natural mean streak like his pa, he doesn't have any sense. He's a bully who learned at a very young age to take whatever he wanted. His pa encouraged him. Ester and I will never be safe until he's dead!"

"If you feel strong enough Joan, let's pack up your things and get you out of here," Mary said.

"I have nowhere to go, Mary. About all we have are the clothes on our backs. There—there's just nowhere for us to go!"

Another sob hung up in her throat for a moment before Joan's voice broke. Her body shook as she wept hopelessly. Ester clung to her mother and cried with her. Mary put her arms around both sobbing females and gently patted Joan's skinny back

"You do have somewhere to go, Joan." Mary's voice was husky and replete with empathy. "You and Ester are coming home with me and you're welcome to stay as long as you like."

Joan stifled her forlorn tears.

"I couldn't impose on you folks, after the way Buck and Homer treated Zeke and Will," she replied. "What would Zeke think?"

"It was Zeke's idea. He was concerned about you, Joan. He'd have come himself, but he's recovering from a gunshot wound."

"Oh my God, did Buck shoot him? I've been mortally afraid he'd bushwhack Zeke some day. He boasted he was going to do it. I warned Zeke at last year's Fourth of July celebration in Winfield."

Mary told a white lie—not knowing why she did it, unless it was that she felt Zeke ought to be the one to tell her he killed Buck.

"Zeke didn't get bushwhacked. He got shot getting our horses back."

"Is he badly hurt?" Joan asked. "Will he recover?" Even in dull light, Mary could discern a pink blush on Joan's bony cheeks.

"He was struck in his armpit with a clean shot. Thankfully, the bullet didn't hit any bone. Baring infection, he should make a full recovery, given time," she replied.

Moses and Mary loaded the women's pitifully few personal possessions into the wagon, and prepared a warm pallet in the wagon box for Joan and Ester. They would have to hurry to make it back to the Curtis farm before dark.

As Mary tucked the quilts around Joan and Ester, Joan asked Mary if she'd do her a great favor before they left.

"If it's within my power," Mary replied. "What is it you want me to do?"

"Please—please, burn that miserable cabin!" she pleaded.

"Are you sure you want your home burned, Joan? As Buck's widow, you'll inherit the place. When you get back on your feet, you may want to move back here."

"Buck didn't have any papers for the place. We were just squatters. Even if I owned it, I'd never want to see the horrible cabin again. There's nothing here but heartaches and misery for my daughter and me. I'd burn it myself if I was strong enough. Please burn it down, Mary."

It wasn't something she relished doing, but Mary took coals from the fireplace and lit the straw-stuffed mattress. By the time the wagon reached the hillcrest overlooking the Sommers' former home, flames were leaping high into a cold, slate-colored sky.

Frail Joan pulled herself up high enough to see over the wagon box.

"I hope you're burning in hell, Buck Sommers, just like that horrible place where you kept us prisoners." After a brief pause, she added. "May God forgive me for letting you hurt my daughter." And then she reclined on the pallet, exhausted.

"God will forgive y'all, Miz Sommers," Moses said, "I'll pray for him to do that, too."

"Thank you, Moses. Please call me Joan. The Lord has saved me from Buck Sommers. I never want to answer to the name Mrs. Sommers again!"

"Yes ma'am, Miz Joan," Moses replied.

After Joan and Ester finished the first warm meal they'd had in days, Joan thanked Zeke profusely for taking them into his home.

"It—it weren't just me, our whole family welcomes you here," he managed to sputter self-consciously. "Anyways, this is actually Mary's home."

"Well then, Ester and I thank all of you," Joan replied, her voice still weak. "We'll be on our way as soon as we regain our strength."

"Don't worry none about that now. You ladies get yourselves some rest and we'll talk more about future plans when you're feeling stronger," Zeke offered.

Mary prepared beds in the old sod house for Joan and Ester while they were eating. She wanted Zeke to stay by the fireplace until he was stronger. Will fixed a pallet in Zeke's old sleeping tent, which was now being use for storage.

When Joan and Ester were bedded down, Mary shared with the family what Joan revealed about her relationship with Buck, and that she wasn't Homer's mother.

"Oh, and by the way, she wants to be called Mrs. Koster now, which was Ester's father's last name," Mary said.

Zeke pursed his lips and nodded his head thoughtfully.

"I just knew there had to be a reasonable explanation for why a good woman like Joan got mixed up with the likes of that scoundrel," he said.

"Yeah, knowing Mrs. Sommers and Ester ain't blood relations to Homer sure makes me feel better," Will agreed.

"It's, *isn't* any blood relation, Will," Mary corrected him in her ongoing effort to improve his elocution.

"Okay—whatever you say—I'm sure glad she isn't Homer's real ma."

CHAPTER 34

BUDDING ROMANCE

◆

Time, good food, and caring friends did wonders for Joan and Ester Koster. No one was more pleased about their metamorphic transformation than Zeke. One sunny spring day, after they'd been at the Curtis farm for about six months, Zeke glanced up from the repair job he and Will were doing on the horse corral. He noticed mother and daughter ambling across the barnyard from the garden. The attractive females leisurely chatted and laughed as they walked. It warmed the cockles of his heart to see the healthy couple so carefree and happy. The sunlight glistening on their almost identical shoulder-length brunette hair was most striking. When they had taken a few more paces toward the house, the angle of light filtering through their summer dresses outlined their trim figures. He didn't intend to ogle, but his eyes seemed to take command and refused to turn away.

Will looked up when he noticed Zeke had stopped driving the nail into a new corral rail he was patiently holding in place. His eyes followed Zeke's mesmerized stare and he, too, fixed his sight on the alluring spectacle.

"My gosh," Will exclaimed, "Ester's sure growing up. She's darn near as pretty as her ma."

It was not Ester that Zeke was watching, but the sound of Will's voice broke his reverie.

"Joan looks ten years younger now that she's got some meat on her bones," he blurted out, loud enough for his strong voice to attract Joan's and Ester's attention. They turned and waved cheerfully at Zeke and Will. Zeke blushed, and both admiring males waved back.

Everything about Joan had blossomed in the past few months. She was about two inches taller than either Betsy or Mary, with a well-proportioned, slender body. Her skin was tan and healthy, and her blue eyes complimented the naturally wavy, dark hair, which she now wore loose down to her shoulders. When Zeke first met her, he judged she was about his age. Now, she looked even younger than the thirty-six years she admitted to. He often found himself thinking of Joan in a romantic way, even though he still harbored guilt for having made her a widow.

A few days later, Joan and Zeke found themselves alone. She had volunteered to help him repair a set of harnesses by holding a tug strap steady while Zeke punched holes in it and secured the repair with rivets. Close proximity to that intelligent, fragrant, and very desirable woman was pleasant, yet so distracting he was in danger of hitting himself with the ball peen hammer.

At first, they talked about insignificant things. Later, Joan took the opportunity to broach the subject of her future. She had tried to talk to Zeke about the matter a couple of times before without much success.

"Zeke, I've been thinking it's time Ester and I find some place of our own."

When Zeke was slow to reply, Joan continued.

"I used to be a good seamstress before I took up with Buck. Mary and I have discussed the possibility of me moving into Winfield, or maybe even up to Wichita, and setting up a dressmaking shop."

Zeke had thought a lot about how he'd handle this dreaded moment, knowing it was coming sooner or later. His heart told him to ignore what she'd said and maybe it would go away. His mind knew he'd have to face up to his dilemma. On the one hand, he sure didn't want her to leave. On the other, for reasons he couldn't articulate, he wasn't ready to ask her to marry him.

"Who—who said you have to leave here?" he stammered, buying time, yet realizing she deserved a more definitive answer.

"No one has, Zeke," she replied truthfully. "But it certainly isn't right that we continue to live off of your hospitality indefinitely. You folks have been more than kind to us already."

"Well—well, now, I don't see it as a matter of us being kind, or you living off our hospitality. We've just been helping out a neighbor, same as you'd do for us. Anyway, since you and Ester got your strength back, you've more than earned your keep."

"That may be true, but I've got to find a new life somewhere. And see to my daughter's future."

"Don't you like it here with me—er—us?"

"Yes, you've made us feel very welcome. I'll always be beholden to you folks—and to you personally, Zeke."

"What is it you're looking for?"

"I don't know exactly. But I do know that in the past I've made a lot of mistakes. Getting tangled up with Buck was the worst. It's unforgivable and I should have known better."

"You're being too hard on yourself. We've all made mistakes. God knows, I've made my share."

"Perhaps you're right, but I let it go on too long. Anyway, I've got to keep trying for something better—for Ester's sake—if not my own. It's likely too late for me to ever have what I dream about—a family like yours that's kind and caring."

"No—no, Joan, it's never too late. Why—why, you and Ester are already part of this family. Can't you just stay on here, with us?" Zeke was touched and his voice sounded almost pleading.

"No offense meant, Zeke, but in what capacity would I be considered? Are you looking for an addition to the other two women in your household, who both adore you by the way?"

That question took Zeke back some. Betsy and Mary were like his daughters, which wasn't the kind of relationship he had in mind for Joan. But she'd made her point. This woman has pride and spunk, he thought. He mentally scolded himself for being so cautious about telling her how he felt. It's time to fish or cut bait, Zeke ol' boy. You won't get a better chance; go ahead and give it a try.

"That—that's not what I had in mind, Joan. It's just that any woman I ask to marry me will have to understand I've made a commitment to take care of Josh's family, and Betsy's part of it now 'cause Josh took her in before he was killed."

"Was that a proposal I just heard, Zeke?" Her eyes sparkled and her voice was almost playful.

Taken aback at the turn of events, it took a few seconds for Zeke to evaluate the ramifications and formulate a reply.

"Well, I'd—I'd say it was darn near one. I'm very fond of you and I know I want you, but I figure Buck's death puts kind of a dark cloud over us yet, and I'm thinking that you've still got some other things festering."

"You're a good man, Zeke, and I care deeply for you." She was serious now. "Yes, you're right about me having problems. I'm not sure if I can trust and love any man again. At least not yet, not the way I want to and should, if I'm going to make him a good wife."

A hint of tears appeared in her eyes before she lowered them and continued speaking. Her choked voice was so quiet; he had to strain forward to hear her.

"Maybe I don't deserve a decent man, after what I allowed Buck and his horrible son to do to me—and what I exposed my daughter to."

Zeke understood her meaning. The implications made him see red. He was even more thankful one of the guilty parties was already dead. Assuredly, he or Will would eventually get Homer Sommers. But would having the perpetrators dead help heal Joan's and her daughter's deep psychological wounds?

He cleared his constricted throat and spoke softly.

"Well, seems like we both have some things to deal with. As far as I'm concerned, you deserve the best. Don't let the past destroy your future happiness. Do you think it's worth working toward solutions, Joan?"

"Yes, I—I think so. And I truly hope so, but it'll take some time. Why don't we leave it where it is for now? Ester and I'll move into Winfield and find some way to make a living. We'll talk again, when things feel right."

"Guess that's the way it'll have to be. I'll sure miss your pretty face around here. Can I call on you wherever you settle?"

"Of course you can. I'd be hurt if you didn't."

Zeke bowed his head for a moment, and then said something he'd wanted to get off his chest since she'd come into his home.

"Before you leave, I—I just want you to know I'm sorry I was forced to kill your husband. It's been tearing my heart out."

"I realize that worries you, Zeke. I don't hold it against you. Killing Buck wasn't your fault. If it hadn't been you, someone else would have done it sooner or later. It's not a Christian way to feel, but I'm glad he's dead."

There was an uncomfortable pause for a few seconds. Joan smiled and her expressive blue eyes sparkled again. She took a step that brought her very close to him.

"Zeke Curtis, you're the finest man I've ever met and here is something for you to remember me by when we're gone."

She put her arms around him, pressed her body close to his, and planted a long and passionate kiss on his lips. He hungrily returned her hug and kiss. Fire shot through his groin. When he reluctantly released her, she was breathless. Without speaking, Joan turned and walked slowly toward the house, leaving him wanting more.

In Zeke's eyes, she didn't walk; she floated like an angel. The shoulder-length hair bounced and glistened in the afternoon sun. Her firm, supple hips swayed slightly, but very sensually. Zeke watched the back of her alluring, receding form, until she disappeared from sight, leaving him with overpowering sexual desires.

"Damn," he muttered to himself. "You'd be a fool to let that fine woman get away, Zeke ol' boy! Won't do to rush her though."

The next day, Mary drove Joan and Ester into Winfield, intending to help them get settled. Mary and Joan stopped at Randy Briddle's store to pick up the final payment from the sale of Joan's inherited outlaw estate. He had acted as Joan's agent in selling three of the horses ridden by Buck's gang, along with their tack and weapons that Zeke insisted belonged to her. Joan had kept one of the horses and a saddle for personal use.

When Mary told Randy that Ester and her daughter were moving into town and she was thinking about starting a dress shop, he surprised them with his quick response.

"Mrs. Koster, I think you were heaven sent to me today. I've been expanding the women's apparel section of my store and I'm in need of a knowledgeable woman to handle that department. Many of my lady customers don't feel comfortable talking about female undergarments with my male clerks. Would you be interested in the job?"

"Why, that sounds wonderful, if you'll have me," Joan exclaimed. "I could use my abilities as a seamstress to make alterations for the customers too, if you'd like. When would you want me to start?"

"Just as soon as you can," Randy answered. "I'll pay you the same wages that I pay my male clerks, fifty dollars per month, and a 10 percent discount on anything you buy from the store. Does that seem fair to you?"

"Yes—yes, that would be fine."

"Do you have a place for you and your daughter to live yet, Mrs. Koster?"

"Please, call me Joan," she requested. "No, Mary and I were going to see if Mrs. Baker had room for us in her boarding house."

"My name is Randy, Joan," he replied. "It just so happens I have three empty rooms above the store. I lived there before I built my house out on the ranch. I built out there hoping I'll find a wife one day soon."

"What kind of rent did you have in mind for those rooms?" an exuberant Joan answered, apparently missing Randy's questioning look toward Mary.

Randy wrinkled his brow in thought for a moment before answering.

"I'm thinking ten dollars per month would be about right, considering you're an employee, and you can use the store's wood supply for your cooking and heating stoves."

He turned toward Ester, who had been taking in the conversation, not showing much interest. Mary knew the girl had a crush on Will and wasn't happy about leaving their farm.

"Ester could probably make that much doing chores and running errands for the store at—say fifty cents a day when she's not in school—if she wants a job too. How does that sound to you ladies?"

"Just fine, Randy," Joan answered quickly. Ester shyly nodded her head in the affirmative.

"Well then, it's settled. Let's look at your prospective new home, Joan. If you find it satisfactory, we'll move you in right away and you can start your new job tomorrow."

"I'm sure it'll be like a mansion compared to what Ester and I lived in before Mary and Zeke took us in," Joan said with a happy grin on her pretty face.

Mary was very pleased for her friend, Joan, and Randy had made some favorable points with the woman he'd been courting.

CHAPTER 35

ALMOST A MAN

◆

Will was a busy young man during the winter after their fight with the horse thieves. For the third year, he ran a trap line. In the evenings, guitar lessons from Zeke alternated with academic lessons from Mary. Besides elocution, which she was on him about all the time, there were instructions in arithmetic, grammar, geography, history, and civics. She pressed him to read every book they owned. Sometimes his enthusiasm for the lessons lagged, but he always enjoyed the special times with the commensurate teacher, especially when she bent over his shoulder to help him with some difficult assignment and one of her breasts brushed the side of his face. It still embarrassed him when she affected him in that way—but he liked it.

Zeke often teased him about his educational efforts by saying such things as, "You keep this up, Will, and you're gonna be the smartest dumb farmer in Kansas." Actually, Will noticed Zeke listening in on a lot of the discussions, seemingly hungry to learn. His formal education had been rather spotty.

On the business side, Will had done so well with his trapping enterprise that he bought the traps Randy had loaned him, plus twenty more. Now he'd get the full market price for his pelts. It proved to be more than he could handle, and he felt guilty imposing on Moses for additional skinning help. The problem was solved by taking Betsy in as his partner. Her work ethic and experience proved invaluable. She efficiently handled most of the skinning and stretching of the hides and often ran the trap line with him and his new dog, Bounder.

Having a close relationship with an independent female, who was interested in the things he liked to do, was a new learning experience for Will. Also, it was disconcerting she could do most things as well, if not better, than him. His relationship with Betsy matured into esteem and friendship. Yet, her sexuality still caused the rapidly maturing youngster problems. Even when Betsy wore rough work clothes, he remained painfully aware of her desirable feminine body. His excess supply of testosterone often ran rampant when he was alone with her.

Once, his mind nearly exploded and his groin ached for hours when her loose man's work shirt gaped open while they were skinning an otter together. On that unseasonably warm day, she wore no upper undergarment. Absorbed in the task, she didn't seem to notice her firm tan breasts were exposed—or didn't care. Will sure noticed. Later, he considered himself lucky he hadn't cut off a thumb before they finished the skinning.

Will was showing other signs of manhood. Besides a deeper voice, scraggy rust-hued whiskers appeared on his tanned cheeks and chin. One evening, Zeke noticed his nephew's profile in the kerosene lamplight.

"Say, Will, is the lint off your blanket sticking to your face, or is it peach-fuzz? Ha, ha, ha."

The self-conscious youngster was mortified. Next day, he sneaked his uncle's shaving gear out to remove the fuzz, cutting his chin in the process. Things got worse.

"How'd you cut your chin, Will?" nosey little Jeanie blurted out at the supper table. The grown women smiled at Will's embarrassment.

In the fall, Will and Betsy were very busy getting ready for their second year as trapping partners and time got away from him. He was surprised when one evening Mary placed a thickly frosted white cake on the table, with seventeen candles blazing on top. My gosh, it's my birthday, he thought. The special attention made him self-conscious, but he was still kid enough it enjoy it.

Mary presented him with a new book, titled *Roughing It* by Mark Twain.

"This is Samuel Clemens's most recent book. I had Randy order it from Kansas City," Mary exclaimed proudly. "I want you to read it this winter as one of your English lesson assignments."

"Okay, Mary, I'll read it. Thank you for giving it to me," Will replied with shammed enthusiasm. It was a darn thick book.

Joan and Ester had borrowed Randy's team and buggy and driven out to be part of the birthday festivities. Joan had knitted him a stocking-style cap to wear on his trap line. Ester slyly presented him a matching wool muffler, which she had knitted. He gave them each a warm hug. Ester impulsively returned the hug and brazenly brushed his lips with a kiss.

Moses informed him his birthday gifts from him were a dozen new skin-stretching frames he'd made and stored in the tack shed.

"Thanks a lot, Moses. Boy, we can sure make good use of those, can't we Betsy?"

"Yes," she replied, rewarding both Will and their special friend, Moses, with one of her warmest smiles. "If our luck holds out, we'll need those and many more before the season is over."

"I'll sure be making whatever y'all needs. You just let ol' Moses know how many that 'll be," Moses answered, beaming with pride.

And then, Jeanie and Anne got into the act with buckskin moccasins and gloves they had made for their big brother, with Betsy's help.

Zeke deliberately held back until all the others, except Betsy, had presented Will with their presents. He pulled a shoebox size package from beneath his chair that was wrapped in brown paper. As he handed it across the table to him, Will recognized mischief coming his way in those twinkling eyes and the wily grin. He cautiously opened the package and removed a new shaving kit, complete with straight razor, soap mug and brush, and a sharpening strap.

"How you like them, Willie?" Zeke inquired when Will hesitated, waiting for the ribbing he was sure was coming.

"F-fine, Zeke," he replied cautiously.

"Well, I'm giving that shaving gear to you with two provisions."

"What are those provisions, *Uncle* Zeke?" He'd used "uncle" because he figured he could soften whatever was coming by showing deference. He'd played straight man for Zeke's shenanigans many times, and loved him for them.

"First, you've got to promise to quit using all that cream to persuade the cats to lick the fuzz off your face. We need it for churning butter for the family."

Zeke paused for a response from his audience and was rewarded with polite laughter from some, and snickers from the others.

"Second, you have to promise to not cut your throat with that there sharp, straight-edged razor like you almost did when you used mine. Har, har, har."

Zeke laughed till tears streamed from his eyes. The others either considered it funny, too, or Zeke's laugher was infectious. They joined in for a hearty laugh at Will's expense.

Darn, I've got a crazy family, Will thought, but I love them anyway. He responded with a grin and chuckle, so they wouldn't think he was a spoilsport.

After Zeke finally stopped laughing and dried his eyes, he moved to a dark corner of the room and retrieved a present that was more serious. He returned to the table holding a new Navy Colt .44, with holster and cartridge belt that he laid on the table in front of his startled nephew.

"You're almost a man now, Will. What with how you handled yourself when we was getting our stock back, I'm thinking you've earned the right to pack a man's weapon. I'm giving this to you with the understanding you'll never be the one that starts a ruckus, and you'll not ever pull down on another man less there's no other way out. Can you agree to them stipulations in good conscience?"

The lump in Will's throat made it difficult to answer. His well-meaning uncle still didn't know he was almost sure that he was the one who killed Buck. But there was no reason for any of them to know—ever.

"Ya-yes, Uncle Zeke, I can sure agree to those terms," was all he could manage to stammer before he choked up.

Betsy was the last to present Will a present: a scabbard for Will's Winchester rifle that she had made from beautifully worked buckskin. Straps were attached for either a shoulder-carrying sling, or to secure it to a saddle. Painted artistic diamond-shaped designs, zigzag lighting flashes, and stylized thunderbirds adorned the scabbard. All in all, it was an outstanding example of Indian art. Betsy had spent many loving hours producing it. She made her presentation with a light kiss on his lips that caused him to tingle down to his toes.

"Does this white man's weapon make you a man now?" she asked, with a provocative smile and wink.

"Well, not right away, I 'spose," Will replied sincerely. "Maybe I'll be one when I learn when and how to use it properly." Or make love to you, he thought. He blushed hoping the women folk couldn't read his mind.

"That's a good answer," Betsy replied seriously.

Uncle Zeke had said he was *almost* a man now. Will felt sure there was no *almost* about it. In his restless young mind, he was already a man!

CHAPTER 36

FIRST TIME

◆

"Gosh, Betsy, what little we've been catching in our traps lately is hardly worth running the trap line," Will complained to his partner.

"Well, greedy white boy, we've taken a lot of pelts out of this area the last two seasons," Betsy reminded him. "It's just trapped out."

"What do you suggest we do about that, partner? It's only March first; we still have a few weeks left in the trapping season."

"Only one thing we can do—find a better trapping area."

"Maybe so, but where's that going to be, Miz Smarty Pants? We're already setting traps so far away we can hardly get them all checked without camping overnight."

"It just so happens, Mr. Know-It-All, your worthy partner is half Osage, lest you've forgotten. I can trap anywhere on the reservation."

"Hey, that sounds like a great idea," Will exclaimed. "Do you know anywhere good that isn't too far away?"

"Unfortunately, no," Betsy said bitterly. "Your kind has already poached about every critter that walks or crawls within twenty-five miles of the boundary."

"What the hell do you mean, *my kind?*" Will snapped back. "I never poached one damn animal from the Osage Reservation, nor has anyone else in the Curtis family." Much as he liked Betsy, there were times when her Indian sarcasm got under his skin, and this was one of those times.

"I'm sorry, Will," she apologized contritely. "Sometimes I get carried away when I think about the deplorable condition my mother's people have fallen into. I know it's not your fault."

"I'm sorry too, Betsy," Will replied. "It's sure not fair, what happened to you or your people at the hands of some bad white men." Zeke hadn't told him the details about Betsy's ordeal, but he knew it had been horrific.

"That's okay, Will. Just ignore me when I get in one of those moods. I do know a very good trapping area that my French Canadian father showed me when I was a little girl. But it's about two-day's ride from here. If you're interested, I can take you there."

"That sounds good," Will said. "But if it's that far away, we'd have to camp there for a while to do any serious trapping."

"Yeah, that's right," Betsy agreed. "It's kind of an out-of-the-way place. I doubt if it's been trapped since my papa died. We could probably harvest a hundred prime muskrat and otter pelts in a couple of weeks. There may even be some beaver left."

"It'll be at least two weeks before we can get into the fields for plowing," Will pointed out, warming to the idea, not only because of the trapping potential, but mostly for the opportunity to spend two weeks camping with Betsy.

"Let's do it," he exclaimed.

The sun was shining, but the air was still nippy the morning Betsy and Will left on their trapping adventure. They led two packhorses, each lightly laden with traps, hide stretchers, food, and camping equipment. They'd need the extra packing capacity for the pelts if their venture was successful. All of the Curtis family members turned out to see them off.

"Don't do anything I wouldn't do," Zeke shouted after them.

"Thanks, Zeke," Betsy shouted back. "That leaves us a lot of latitude."

Yeah, Will thought, a hell of a lot of latitude!

They made a sparse camp in the Osage hills the first night, went to sleep early, and were back on the trail at daylight the next day. About sunset the second day, the weary travelers reached the stretch of the Arkansas Betsy had in mind. Light was fading, but they managed to establish a rough camp in a rock alcove on the bank of the river before it was too dark. Betsy cooked a hasty meal by lantern light and they settled into their bedrolls early.

"Tomorrow, I'll show you some of the best trapping spots this side of the Rockies," Betsy assured Will from her bedroll.

"We've come a long way so we'd better get some hides for our trouble," Will replied stifling a yawn.

"We will, we will, oh ye of little faith," Betsy mumbled and was soon fast asleep.

He should have been too tired to think about such things, yet he stayed awake long enough for his young male hormones to rage, hearing the soft steady breathing of that sensuous beauty only an arm's length away. Damn it, she could just as well be on the moon for all the good it's doing me, he lamented. I've got to quit thinking this way, or I'll explode.

The first day, they laid twenty-five traps in prime locations along the near bank of the river. Betsy was an expert at reading spoor, having learned from her trapping father. It was hard work, fighting through brush and setting traps in cold water. At dusk, the partners stumbled into their alcove campsite wet, hungry, and pooped. Will prepared the fire and Betsy warmed some food. They gobbled it down with little conversation, and then rolled into their separate blankets. In the few seconds before falling into an exhausted sleep, Will had a different kind of thought about Betsy—that woman can run my butt into the ground. I don't know where she gets all her strength and stamina.

The next day, they found prime fur-bearing critters in an unprecedented number of their traps. Working well together, they had the catch skinned and on stretchers before sunset. While Will cleaned up the skinning things and collected driftwood for the night fire, Betsy prepared a scrumptious meal. By the time darkness engulfed the campsite, they were relaxing with full stomachs and gratification for a successful day.

Conversation about the day's activities and planning for tomorrow soon ran its course. An awkward few minutes of silence was broken when Betsy got up from the log she'd been sitting on and sensually combing out her long, dark auburn hair, which she wore in two braids when she was working. As she yawned and stretched, the expanded fabric of the small man's shirt she wore revealed the outline of her braless bosom.

"Well, its bedtime," she said.

"Yeah," Will replied, "guess you're right. It'll be daylight again before we know it."

Damn, if I had any guts, I'd ask her if I could climb in with her. Worse that could happen is she'd say no. Considering how feisty she could be, his fear was that she'd more likely tell him, *"hell no,* you horny kid!"

"It's a little nippy," she said. "But I'm going down to the river and wash up some before I bed down. Do you mind me taking the lantern?"

Was there a suggestive note in her voice?

"No, I don't mind. Go ahead and take it. When you get back, I'll go wash some critter skinning crud off, too." She had a fetish for cleanliness. I'll have to smell good if I'll have any chance of getting close to her, he reasoned, even if it meant freezing off his manhood.

She was gone about fifteen minutes. Will sat staring into the fire wondering how she looked, stripped and glowing in the lantern light. Those carnal thoughts caused an erection. His entire groin area ached something frightful. It just wouldn't be right, and kind of childish, to sneak a look, he chastised himself. He'd never been a Peeping Tom, but he was sorely tempted.

Betsy returned with a blanket wrapped around her body, which she was having trouble keeping closed because she carried her soap, towel, clothes, and the lantern in her hands. She passed the lantern to Will, slipped off her untied boots, and quickly bundled herself into her bedroll, exposing a flash of light brown thigh in the process.

"It's your turn, Will," she said, in what he heard as a demure tone. "Be careful; that water's cold enough to shrivel things. If you're going to take a bath, I suggest you take a blanket and don't tarry to put your clothes back on down there."

She needn't have told him to hurry. Just in case she was sending some kind of coded message, he sure didn't want to waste any time freezing his butt off. After doing a quick dash through the brush to the water, he literally ripped off his clothes and boots, took a cold splash bath, and was back in camp in little more than ten minutes.

The lantern's yellow light fell across Betsy's bedroll. His overheated sexual passion became a lump of coal. She appeared asleep, with her back turned to him.

Damn, he muttered in his mind, she either didn't mean anything, or I messed around too long and she's gone to sleep. Either way, I've got to be the unluckiest guy in the world.

With libido cruelly deflated and sexual fantasy dashed, he pulled off his boots, blew out the lantern, and angrily started putting on his long underwear. There were rustling sounds in the direction of Betsy's bedroll. He subconsciously turned toward the sound and nearly fainted.

She had turned toward him and raised her blanket, exposing in the flickering firelight her sumptuous, tan-hued, naked body with firm, round breasts, flat stomach, and a thick patch of dark pubic hair—a lovely image that would be forever engraved in his mind.

"You must be cold, come on over here and I'll warm you up," the melodious voice invited.

Will was dumbstruck, afraid to believe his ears. Had she just given him the invitation he'd dreamed about for so long, or was he hallucinating? And then that sweet, beckoning voice spoke again, a little louder.

"Come here, *Will!*"

It was heavenly true! Reality of her invitation registered in his befuddled mind, and told his responding body to move. Like a flash, he was in her bed, pressing his eager naked body against hers, so violently that he knocked the breath out of her for a moment.

There was no more conversation. She regained her breath and welcomed him with a long juicy kiss, her searching tongue slipping between his lips and touching his tongue. In seconds his erection was nearly exploding. His taunt body quivered in anticipation. He endeavored to match her tongue movements while frantically pawing one of her breasts with one hand and searching between her spread legs with the other.

"That feels good, lover, but slow down," she whispered in his ear. "We've got all night!"

He heard her, but in his eager feverish mind, there were only seconds. His pent-up sexual desires controlled him, mind, body, and soul! She seemed to understand his urgency, pulled him on top of her, and guided his throbbing erection into her warm, moist cavity. Within seconds, he exploded with an ecstasy such as he'd never dreamed possible.

As Uncle Zeke would say, he'd been to see the elephant—and it was *marvelous*! But it sure hadn't lasted long.

Will panted and whispered hoarsely into her ear, as though there might be someone out there in the middle of the Osage Nation to overhear him.

"Th-thank you, Betsy. I'm sorry I was so fast and rough. I just couldn't stop myself. Did I hurt you?"

"No, you didn't hurt me," she chuckled, while caressing his back and buttocks, "but you'll like it better if you'll slow down some and kind of let things simmer. Anticipation is at least half the fun."

Will had hardly caught his breath when he was ready to go again. He allowed Betsy to guide and coach him this time and they both found ecstasy. After the third time, Betsy told her virile lover that they'd better get some sleep.

"You don't need to wear it out the first time. There'll be other chances."

"Do you promise, Betsy?" the little boy part of Will pleaded.

"Yes, I promise, but you've got to promise me our affair will remain between you and me. It would never do for your little sisters to find out what we're doing. Mary would be very disappointed with both of us, but mostly with you because she is very fond of you. We must be discreet, or I'll have to leave the Curtis farm. Do you understand that, Will?"

"Yeah, I understand Betsy, but don't ever leave because I love you, and when I'm old enough, I'm going marry you."

Those words were no sooner out of his mouth before a twinge of remorse, concerning Mary, squeezed into his mind, slightly dampening the afterglow euphoria he was experiencing.

"That's sweet, but it's not me you love," Betsy replied wistfully. "You love what we just did together. Someday, you'll find out the difference between having sex with someone you like, and real, lasting-a-lifetime-together love."

"But—but anything that feels this good must be real love," Will reasoned.

"I like you a lot, Will, or I wouldn't have shared my body with you, but I want you to understand I'm not in love with you, in the marrying way."

That message was hard for the sexually aroused youngster to accept, or understand, but he knew he would always remember her tenderly for having given him that marvelous first time.

CHAPTER 37

OUT OF THE PAST

◆

Since becoming the postmaster for Winfield, Kansas, Randy Briddle hadn't made a habit of delivering mail, but taking a letter to Zeke from an attorney in Parkersburg, West Virginia, gave him an opportunity to see Mary. He'd been doing his best to court her since hearing about her husband's death.

It was an unusual occasion for anyone in the family to receive a letter. Will had gotten three from his friend Skeeter Crandston during the four years they'd been apart, and Mary periodically received letters from a bank in Charleston, West Virginia, that were inexplicitly addressed to her maiden name.

Zeke was over at Mort McCracken's place doing some horse-trading. Because he came home hungry and supper was on the table, he delayed opening the fat, battered envelope until after suppertime. The curious family members were still sitting around the table lingering over second cups of coffee, waiting to get in on the mystery.

The recipient casually slit open the envelope with his table knife and removed a single sheet of paper and a smaller sealed envelope. The eyes of his inquisitive audience were all staring at him.

"I'll be damned if this letter ain't about ol' Ambrose McNeal!" Zeke uttered, staring at the paper in his hand for a few seconds before beginning to read the contents.

By the time he finished the short letter, Zeke had the appearance of a man who had just seen a horrifying ghost. His eyes moved from the page and he stared into space, slack-jawed, and seemingly lost in another world.

After a long scary silence, Mary spoke with concern in her voice.

"Talk to us, Zeke. What's in that letter that's causing you such distress?"

Slowly recovering from his stupor, Zeke's glazed eyes finally cleared enough to focus on Mary.

"Reading Ambrose McNeal's name, after all these years, kind of brought back some old bad memories that I'd just as soon stayed buried. What it's about is another shock," Zeke said sadly. "I'm—I'm okay now."

"Are you talking about the Ambrose McNeal that was governor of West Virginia for a few years?" Mary asked.

"Yes, he was," Zeke confirmed, "but my association with him goes back way before then."

"Is it something you can share it with us?" Mary inquired.

"Here, read it to the rest of the family. They should know what's in it because it could affect us all." He pushed the letter across the table to her. Mary picked up the single sheet of paper and read it aloud.

> June 5, 1876
> Parkersburg, West Virginia
>
> Dear Sir:
> If the addressee is former Top Sergeant Ezekiel W. Curtis, Headquarters Company, First West Virginia Volunteer Cavalry Regiment, as the executor for the estate of Colonel Ambrose McNeal, late governor of West Virginia, I write to inform you that under the terms of his last will and testament, you are bequeathed the amount of twenty-five thousand dollars in cash and five head of thoroughbred racehorses.
> To claim this bequeath, you must present yourself in my office, located at 445 Oak, Parkersburg, West Virginia, on or before July 1, 1876, prepared to

identify yourself with your discharge from the Union Army.

If you do not claim these inheritances, as provided for above, the assets will revert to the State of West Virginia at 12:01 a.m. July 2, 1876.

I am also enclosing a sealed envelope, which I understand contains a letter to you from Governor McNeal. His instructions were that it be presented to you after his death.

Your Obedient Servant,
Samuel S. Stokes, Attorney at Law

"My gosh, Zeke, the former governor for West Virginia has left you a fortune." Mary was breathless with excitement. "What's your connection to him?"

"I knew him before and during the war, but I have no idea why he'd feel obliged to leave me anything in his will. We weren't on the best of terms after the war," Zeke replied.

"Well, maybe you should read the letter Governor McNeal left for you," Mary suggested. "It'll likely shed some light on why he wanted you to have the money and horses. Gosh, it's like getting a message from beyond the grave."

"Yes," Zeke replied, seemingly not pleased with receiving that yet unknown message. He silently read the inscription on the envelope, recognizing his former commanding officer's scrawled handwriting.

To: Top Sergeant of Scouts and Couriers, Ezekiel Curtis.
Not to be opened until after my death.
From: Colonel Ambrose NcNeal, United States Volunteer Cavalry

It's just like the old windbag, he thought, to continue using military language and titles, even though the war had been over for eleven years. Zeke opened the envelope, unfolded the message with trepidation, and began reading it silently.

Dear Zeke

When you read this, I'll be dead. Please do an old dead man a favor and read it through before you throw it away.

Zeke, you made it clear many times since our difficulty down on the Stones River that you'd just as soon not hear from me or have anything to do with me because you consider me a coward and responsible for our bugler Otis Crammer's death.

I confess to being a coward that night when we were hiding from the rebs in that hole on the battlefield, but I'm not responsible for Otis's death and you aren't either. He took his chances just like the rest of us. It was that reb minnie ball what killed him. I'll admit I should have been more help to you in taking care of him after he was shot, but then I never was as strong a man as you, Zeke. There aren't many that were.

I'm writing this letter to try one more time to thank you for all you did for me and our troopers during the war, and for not telling people about our differences after the war when I was running for public office.

I know you're so damn hardheaded there's still a chance you'll consider my gifts to you and your family as trying to ease my conscience, or buy your respect or such, but that isn't the reason.

Figured maybe there'd be a chance you'd believe me after I'm dead and have no ax to grind. I just want to pay you a small part of the debt I owe you for all you've done for me. Before the war, you were like a son to me, and during that damn war, you stood by me in many a fight and steadied my nerves when I wanted to run away, before I did run out on you that one time. I have no excuse for doing that. I just went crazy and it cost me one of the things I most valued—your respect.

Please take the money and do with it what you will. Use the horses to produce an outstanding line, under your name. They're five of my best, a stud and four fine brood mares. I selected them special for you. Whatever else you think of me, you'll have to admit I've raised some damn fine horseflesh. You ought to know because you trained a lot of my horses before our falling out.

One thing more I want to make clear—you damned well earned the Congressional Medal of Honor and that's why it was given to you. It wasn't me that got it for you, but I was honored to endorse the recommendation. Many others witnessed your courage and bravery lots of times. It was them that got you the award, and you deserved it.

It would make me rest easier if you could forgive me for my weakness and for letting you down that once, so long ago. I want you to know I loved little Otis too, and mourned for him.

I consider you one of the finest men I've ever known, Top Sergeant Ezekiel Curtis.

Always Your Friend,
Ambrose NcNeal

When Zeke finished reading the letter, his eyes brimmed with tears and there was a lump in his throat as big as a wad of chewing tobacco. Praise was something he didn't handle well, whether or not it was justified. In this case, he still wasn't sure it was warranted. Hell, he'd only done his job. There were a lot braver men than him left on the battlefields. Little sixteen-year-old Otis Crammer was one of them!

With all that going through his troubled mind, Zeke impulsively crumpled the letter in his work-gnarled hand and threw it on the floor. His body shook from stifled emotions. Without speaking, he rose and left the room to find privacy in his bedroom. When secluded there, Zeke cried in great sobs for lost comrades, misguided judgments, and the soul of Ambrose McNeal. He spoke in his mind to the departed man, who indeed had once been his friend, hoping somehow he would get the belated, but heartfelt, message beyond the grave.

"I forgive you Ambrose, and it ain't because you left me that stuff. I can see now, I was way too damned self-righteous and hard-nosed back then, and have been all these years for not forgiving you a human frailty that I shared. Maybe I blamed you for my own fears.

"Tell you the truth, I'd lost my true love just before the war, and didn't think I had anything to live for. Much of what you may have thought was bravery, was actually don't-give-a-damn recklessness. Even so, I damn near run from that slaughter in the woods at Stones River too. I only stayed 'cause Otis was hit, and I'd promised his Ma I'd look out for him. That's why I don't deserve your respect, your gifts, or no damn medal!"

Zeke's loved ones sat staring at the door for a few seconds before Mary rose and retrieved the wrinkled pages, smoothed them out, and read a few sentences in silence.

"This is a very private message to Zeke, but I'm going to read it to all of you. It's something you should know about our Zeke and that modest man will probably never share it with you."

She read the letter to a very attentive group that included Moses. There wasn't a dry eye in the room when she was finished. Mary intended to keep the letter with her private papers for posterity, lest anyone, including the man himself, ever doubted that Ezekiel Curtis was a bona fide hero.

CHAPTER 38

NOSTALGIA

◆

The ruggedly handsome, broad-shouldered man, with penetrating hazel eyes and a bushy, sandy-colored mustache ambled down the brick-paved sidewalk. He wore well-tailored, western-style attire, including a string tie, high-heeled boots, and a Stetson hat. Zeke thought himself a successful Kansas horse rancher. He'd bought the new outfit from Randy's store, intending to dress the part for his nostalgic trip back to his old stomping ground.

Mary and Betsy had had a lot of fun helping him pick out the clothes from Randy's limited supply of dressy men's wear. There just wasn't much call for such clothing in Winfield, especially in the men's duds line. Zeke nearly balked on the string tie, but the women prevailed. When he modeled them for the family, Will couldn't resist ribbing him.

"Zeke you look like an eastern dude, play-acting as a cowboy."

"Now, Willie, you know it isn't nice to make fun of your old uncle. You'll give me some kind of a complex," Zeke replied.

"Ha, fat chance of that happening to a guy who thinks he's a lady killer," Betsy said. "Besides, you're about twenty-two jokes up on Will, and he'll never live long enough to catch up."

Will had asked to go back to West Virginia with Zeke so he could visit with his buddy Skeeter.

"Somebody has got to get started on the wheat harvest," Zeke told him. "Anyway, this is going to be a fast trip. I'll go see how ol' Skeeter is getting along and tell him hi for you."

Zeke noticed things had changed some in the five years since he'd last been to Parkersburg. He stopped to get his bearings in the shade of a large clock that hung from a bank building. Removing the hot Stetson and wiping the sweatband with his bandana, he glanced across Oak Street and spotted what he was looking for, number 445. There was a sign on an upper window that read, "Samuel S. Stokes Attorney at Law."

"That's the hombre I'm supposed to see," Zeke muttered. "I'll soon know if this inheritance thing ain't just a damn joke."

Zeke climbed the stairs, located a door with Samuel S. Stokes's name on it, and entered without knocking. His eyes soon adjusted to the dimmer light. There were shelves full of law books along one wall. The partially bald, smallish man sitting behind the desk perfectly fit Zeke's concept of a shyster lawyer. He was dressed in a gray suit with light pinstripes and a vest. A gold pocket-watch chain adorned his watermelon potbelly.

The officious-looking, pint-sized man glanced up from the papers on his cluttered desk and blinked at Zeke through thick reading glasses. His lack of a greeting and disgruntled facial expression sent the clear message that he resented being interrupted.

"Are you Lawyer Stokes?" Zeke queried in an even tone, although he already disliked this pompous-looking toad.

"Yes, I'm Samuel S. Stokes, attorney-at-law," the man replied, obviously trying to lower a high-pitched voice an octave or two for affect. "And who might you be, barging into my office without knocking?"

Zeke removed the man's letter from his shirt pocket and tossed it on the desk.

"My name is Ezekiel Curtis. You invited me to your office in that letter, mister."

He plunked himself down in the chair in front of the desk and gave the weasel his most intimidating glare. Zeke read alarm in the man's eyes at the mention of his name. Hell, he thought, I didn't intend to scare him that much. Just wanted to let him know I wasn't in any mood to take much of his big-shot crap.

The prissy man stared at the letter for a few seconds, and then looked up at Zeke over his reading glasses, with a frown that bordered on a scowl. After scrutinizing the rugged westerner for several more seconds, he finally spoke.

"Did you bring the required proof that you are Ezekiel Curtis?" he demanded.

Without comment, Zeke reached into his other shirt pocket, removed a folded document, unfolded it, and pushed it in front of the lawyer. The beady eyes focused on the creased paper through his thick glasses for a few seconds, then darted between it and Zeke for a few more.

"Well—well, this discharge paper seems authentic, but it says you were discharged for medical reasons. You look healthy to me."

"What the hell does the state of my health have to do with this?" Zeke growled. This pip-squeak was pushing the outer limits of Zeke's patience, probably not realizing what a dangerous thing that was.

"Your letter said I was to be here before July first and prove I was Ezekiel Curtis, by my discharge from the Union Army. It's June thirtieth and that's my discharge dated July 21, 1863, right there on your desk. *Now tell me if there's anything to this McNeal inheritance bunk.*"

Zeke figured the shyster attorney had more of a problem than just being naturally officious. Maybe he'd been raking off on Ambrose's estate, figuring the elusive Top Sergeant Ezekiel Curtis either couldn't be found or wouldn't show up in time. He'd sure cut the time short by mailing that letter so late. Zeke had found out Ambrose died April 20. Hell, Zeke thought, all the shady bastard would have to do is forge my signature and that money and them horses would be his.

"Well now, sir, as an officer of the court it's my fiduciary duty to make sure that Governor McNeal's estate goes where his will stipulates. How do I know this is your discharge? You could have stolen or forged it for all I know."

Zeke's eyes hardened. He slowly rose from the chair and leaned across the desk until his face was about a foot from the pretentious lawyer's nose.

"Where I come from, mister, it ain't healthy to question a man's word, lest you got good reason and are ready to back it up." Zeke's voice was gruff and his stare menacing.

"Now, I'm only going to tell you once more—*I'm Ezekiel Curtis!* You owe me twenty-five thousand dollars and five thoroughbred horses. I intend to get them without anymore bullshit out of you—or, I'll start taking it out of your scrawny hide."

The lawyer's eyes nearly bugged out of their sockets. Magnification from his glasses made him look like a hoot owl. Scrambling feet pushed his caster-mounted chair back, away from this irate cowboy, until it hit the wall behind him.

"You—you touch me and I'll have the sheriff on you for assault," he stammered, his voice squeaking from fright.

Zeke recognized a skunk when he saw one, especially if he was wearing a suit and said he was an attorney.

"You just do that, Mr. Samuel 'Shyster' Stokes, and we'll find out what kind of shenanigans you're trying to pull here."

"No—no need for that, Mr. Curtis. I'm prepared to accept your word that you're *the* Ezekiel Curtis," Stokes pleaded. "I'll have to arrange for some of the governor's estate funds to be transferred from one account to another. I'll take care of it right away. If you'll come back tomorrow afternoon, say about 2:00 PM, I'll have a twenty-five-thousand-dollar bank draft ready for you.

"The horses are out at the governor's horse farm. I'll give you a document that authorizes you to pick them up at your convenience."

Zeke snatched the letter and his discharge paper from the desk. "That's more like it. Give me the paper for the horses and I'll see you at two tomorrow."

With the attorney's authorization in his pocket, Zeke rented a horse from the livery stable and rode the four miles out to the McNeal Horse Farm. The ride brought back old memories. He'd spent many happy days there before the war.

Nostalgia engulfed him when he topped a rise that afforded a panoramic view of the expansive McNeal Horse Farm. It was much as he remembered, like a beautiful, breathtaking landscape painting. Across the rolling hills, a large, pastoral clearing was carved from the dense woods.

The crest and gentle slope of the closest hill were adorned with a palatial main house, three large white barns, tack sheds, and a training racetrack. Nearer to the road, he recognized the trim manager's cottage and a smaller barn. Beyond, a labyrinth of whitewashed board fences divided acres of lush, grass-covered fields into paddocks and larger pastures.

He knew the place well because as a young man he'd stayed there many times, working as a contract horse trainer for the man who later became his commanding officer during the war, and then after the war, was governor of West Virginia for six years. The place was impressive back then, but it was awesome now.

"Damn," Zeke said to the disinterested horse, "ol' Ambrose did alright for himself. But, he didn't have chick or child, so I wonder whose going to get this show-place?"

He clicked his tongue a couple of times to the horse and lightly nudged him in the ribs with the heel of his boot. The lazy mount trotted down the road. Zeke brought him to a halt again at the entrance of the quarter-mile-long lane that led to the main house. He remained there for a few minutes, admiring the vista once more. His thoughts went back to happier times, when he and his benefactor, Ambrose McNeal, had been close.

Zeke recalled a balmy summer evening when he and Ambrose leaned on a whitewashed-board paddock fence, watching young foals frisking around their sleek mothers. Out of the blue, Ambrose said, "Zeke, I'm going to be governor of this state some day. When I get there, I want you with me. You've got more character and common sense than any of the so-called educated men that I know."

At the time, Zeke took the compliment and offer of a job as some of Ambrose's typical hyperbole.

"If you ever get there, Ambrose, I'll be standing in line for one of them soft state jobs, with all the rest of your deadbeat friends," he had replied, half-joking.

After the war, Ambrose made good on his boast to become governor. He had offered his then estranged friend, Zeke, a high cabinet post in his administration. Zeke turned it down because he considered his former commander guilty of cowardliness and wanted noting to do with him.

Zeke shook his head, marveling at how things had worked out and returned his mind to the present. Rather than taking the lane to the main house, he directed his mount toward the attractive cottage, which he recalled being the farm manager's house. The manager saw him coming and met him at the gate to the cottage's well-tended yard.

The aging man squinted at the rider.

"My God, Top Sergeant Ezekiel Curtis, is that you?" he exclaimed.

Even with his graying hair and slowed gait, Zeke recognized the man as former Major Jefferson Wellington, who had been the farm manager for Ambrose for many years and served as an effective battalion commander in Colonel McNeal's First West Virginia Volunteer Cavalry Regiment. Zeke had warmhearted memories of this stalwart man, dating back some twenty years. Both men beamed, as Zeke swung down from his horse.

"Yeah, it's an older model of Zeke Curtis you're looking at, Jeff. How the hell are you?" Zeke stuck out his hand to his old boss and comrade-in-arms. Jeff engulfed it warmly, in both of his gnarled, work-hardened hands.

Seeing this long-time friend triggered mixed emotions in Zeke. Damn if this isn't like old times, he thought, except Ambrose ain't here for me to tell him that I was too hard on him for his having made just one mistake. God knows, I can see now that I sure as hell ain't always been prefect either.

"Come on in the house and let's have a couple of drinks and talk over old times," Jeff said, patting him on the shoulder. "God, but it's great to see you looking so damn good!"

As they walked along the flagstone-paved path to the kitchen door of the neat cottage, Jeff continued, "You remember my old lady, Martha, don't you? She's still kicking and hasn't run me off yet. She'll be glad to see you. Boy we used to have some great ol' times together, when you was a young stud breaking and training horses for us, didn't we?"

"Yeah, we sure did Jeff, and I remember Martha fondly. How could I forget a pretty gal like her, and all those fine meals she cooked for us?"

Martha met them just inside the kitchen door. With a little squeal of joy, she gave him a big hug and kiss on his cheek. She was older and plumper, but still an attractive woman. They'd enjoyed a bantering friendship over the years. Zeke greatly admired her.

After holding on to him for a few more seconds, she pushed him to arms length and looked him over.

"Where in tarnation have you been all these years, Zeke? My God, you're skinny as a rail, but still as handsome as a thoroughbred stud. You need some of my cooking. You're staying for supper—and that's final!" she demanded.

"Now, Martha, my love, you know I could never say no to you. Sure, I'll stay for supper. Why you think I rode all the way out here? It sure wasn't just to see this broken down ol' horse-soldier, Jeff."

"Zeke you're still as big a liar as you used to be. I know you come for them horses Ambrose left you. But I'm glad you come anyways. Now let me get to the cooking while the two of you drink some sipping whiskey and swap lies."

After Jeff poured them each half a glass of good Kentucky whiskey, they settled into a couple of comfortable, leather-covered chairs in Jeff's cozy office.

"I want you to know, Zeke, Ambrose was worried right up to the day he died that they couldn't track you down out there in Kansas to notify you about the horses and money he wanted you to have. He'll be resting better in his grave, now that he knows you got here in time. Weren't his idea to put a time limit on it. That shyster lawyer Stokes told him it wouldn't be legal if he didn't."

"What do you think caused Ambrose to leave me anything? Far 's I know, he never owed me no debts," Zeke asked.

"That's where you're wrong, Zeke. Probably won't get it through your thick head, but I'm going to tell you anyways. Ambrose might have been something of a blowhard politician, but he weren't no fool. He knew he owed you a lot for saving his bacon during the war—a number of times. Hell, it was always you that kept your head when all the rest of us was scared so bad we were running around like chickens with their heads cut off."

"Well—well, now Jeff, that ain't the way I recall them times. I ain't calling you a liar, but I think you've got things confused after all these years. Ever' body tried to do their duty, best they could. Sure, some did better than others, but it took us all to fight and win against them damn tough rebs!" Zeke respected the former major, but the unexpected praise embarrassed him.

"Damn your eyes, Zeke. You always was too damn modest, by half, for your own good. You know darn well that *you* was the *real* commanding officer of the First West Virginia Volunteer Cavalry, without proper rank. Hell, we all knew it, including Ambrose! Why do you think he kept you close to him all the time? It sure as hell wasn't 'cause of your pleasing personality.

"And another thing, after the war, he knew he cashed in on the wartime successes, what your abilities accomplished with the regiment, for his political gains

"Whatever else you might have thought of the old man, you have to know that he loved you like the son he never had. That friction that happened between the two of you, down there in Tennessee, haunted him to his grave. He told me a little about it and it's my opinion you was too damn hard on him. Hell, we was afoot and overrun; all scared out of our heads. It was one of them times that every man had to look out for himself. I ain't too damn proud of how I reacted, but I ain't let it eat my guts out."

Damn, Zeke thought, this guy always could be brutally blunt. His face flushed from embarrassment. Yeah, it was true, he'd let the thing fester and gnaw at his guts all these years.

Martha walked into the room and heard the last part of what her husband said. Being a blunt-spoken woman herself, she laid into Zeke too.

"Jeff's telling you like it is, Zeke. And I've heard other survivors of the regiment say the same thing. I'm sure you're aware they never fought again, as a unit, after you was discharged. They split up the survivors after the Stones River fight, and assigned them to other units. Ambrose finished out the war as a supply officer, procuring horses for remounts."

Zeke knew that was true, but didn't want to debate the more touchy things involved in those wartime internal conflicts with these old and well-meaning friends. He swallowed hard a couple of times to regain control of his emotions, and did his best to reply with some semblance of composure.

"You—you people are making too much out of what I did. I only tried to save my own carcass and make it back home in one piece. That—that's all I was doing. What—what can I say?"

"You ain't got to say nothing, Zeke. Just accept Ambrose's gifts an' figure he wanted you to have them because he thought you darn well earned them," Martha ordered. "Now both of you quit your yakking and come eat. Supper's ready!"

At the supper table, Zeke regained his composure and sincerely told Martha the excellent meal was only exceeded by her charming presence. She put him at ease with her typical response.

"I'm sure glad to see you're as full of bull as you always was. I was feared that being a sodbuster out in Kansas might have slowed you down some. Ha, ha, ha."

"Well, *you* sure haven't slowed down any, Martha, my true love," Zeke replied. "You can still cook a great meal and tell a guy what made the cow eat the cabbage!" Turning to Jeff, he asked a question that had been bothering him.

"Probably none of my business, but what's going to happen to you folks, now that Ambrose is gone?"

"We're planning on staying right where we are until we die," Jeff answered. "Course it ain't going to be the same, but we managed to put a little money away and this here house, the small barn, and twenty acres of land between here and the road belongs to me and Martha now. Ambrose give it to us.

"All the rest of the McNeal Horse Farm and his estate, that he ain't giving to you, goes to the State of West Virginia to become Governor McNeal State Park. Guess it was something ol' Ambrose wanted to give back to the state he helped create before the war."

"Well, I'll be damned," Zeke replied.

CHAPTER 39

HAWTHORN "SKEETER" CRANSTON

◆

After making arrangements for shipping his horses and picking up his check from Attorney Stokes, Zeke had a day left to see some of his friends around New Haven and say hello to Skeeter Cranston for Will. He learned Skeeter's worthless father had died, apparently in a drunken stupor when his dilapidated cabin burned.

Not that the two things had anything in common; Skeeter was serving a thirty-day jail sentence at hard labor for badly mauling one of the local young dandies in a fight. Zeke remembered Skeeter as a shiftless kid with no mother, and having received nothing but abuse from a drunkard pa. He didn't recall the gangling, personable youngster ever showing a violent nature. If fact, he'd always liked the boy.

The New Haven town marshal told Zeke what happened. Harry Blake, owner of the general store, had preferred charges against Skeeter for assaulting his son. Zeke didn't have much use for the penny-pinching merchant. The marshal said witnesses reported it was a fair fight, but the influential townsman pressed for prosecution, claming Skeeter had started it. Apparently, Skeeter did little to defend his actions.

Before getting into this trouble, the marshal said Skeeter had been sleeping in the livery stable in return for doing odd jobs for the owner. Zeke called on Ben Slocum, the liveryman, whom he recalled being a gruff man with a kind heart.

"Dag blame it," Ben spat out, along with volumes of tobacco juice, "that poor damn Skeeter can't win for losing. He was railroaded by ol' prissy Blake for whipping his big, blubbery kid in a fair fight. The Blake kid, and some of his stuck-up cronies, been hassling Skeeter for a long time. While I weren't there, and Skeeter ain't talking about it, I'm guessing he just had all he was going to take.

"I tried to get him off, but big-shot Blake wouldn't hear to it. He's got political pull, so Skeeter didn't have a chance. But, by God, it ain't right, and I told 'em so!"

"Yeah, poor old Skeeter hasn't had much of a chance in life," Zeke agreed. "I'll go over to the county jail and see if I can get him out. Sheriff Morgan is an old cavalry buddy of mine. I understand you've been giving Skeeter a place to stay. If I get him out, can he come back here?"

"Sure he can, but I don't think there's much future for him 'round here. Most of these God-fearing citizens look down their pointy noses at him, as though it's his fault who his folks was. Then, asshole Blake ain't ever going to get off his back," Ben stated, with a disgusted shake of his head.

"You're probably right, Ben. I kind of got a soft spot for that poor kid, too. You know, young Skeeter and my nephew, Will, grew up together, and were great buddies before we dragged Will off to Kansas. My sister-in-law, Marge, gave Skeeter about all the parenting he ever got—'fore she died," Zeke reminisced.

"Yeah, I recall what a wonderful women Marge Curtis was," Ben said. "We heard what happen to your brother. Sorry he met his end that way, out there in the Indian country."

"Thanks, Ben. It was a tragic thing, but he died doing what he felt his God had directed him to do," Zeke replied.

"He sure was a driven man, right enough," Ben allowed.

Reminiscing with Ben caused Zeke's mind to wonder for a few seconds. His brow wrinkled and he was hit by an inspiration. It was almost as though Marge had spoken to him. Pursing his lips and nodding his head in affirmation of his decision, he spoke more to himself than to Ben.

"I'll just take that boy back to Kansas with me," Zeke declared with conviction. "Damn if he ain't one of ours. I should have insisted that Josh let him come with us when we left. I sure ain't going to leave Skeeter behind again!"

"Now that's mighty decent of you, Zeke," grisly Ben said, with a toothless grin on his homely face. "But then, you always was the soft touch of the Curtis brothers."

Zeke noticed that Skeeter had grown from gangling, to slim. His sharp facial features that had produced the derogatory nickname, Skeeter, had fleshed out considerably. He was about the same height as Will, Zeke judged, but probably twenty pounds lighter.

Ten days after Zeke left for West Virginia to check on his inheritance, he proudly rode into the Curtis farmyard on a spirited, thoroughbred stallion, leading three sleek brood mares. Hawthorn "Skeeter" Cranston rode beside him on a fourth thoroughbred mare, leading a large male donkey with a pack on its back.

Will saw the two riders coming from considerable distance and recognized one of them as his uncle by the loose way he set in the saddle. He trotted from the cow shed toward the house, wondering who Zeke had with him. About ten yards from the riders, a crazy thought flashed though his mind—be damned if that guy don't look a lot like ol' Skeeter, some bigger and all duded up. A few more steps and he stopped to study the gangly rider closer. By some miracle, could it possibly be good old Skeeter Cranston? God, how he'd missed that freckled-faced beanpole. Moments later, Will's mind confirmed what his eyes were seeing, yet all he seemed capable of doing was to stand in the yard staring back at his grinning boyhood friend. The females in the family had heard the commotion and rushed out of the house to greet Zeke. They also stood mute, seemingly mesmerized by the unexpected spectacle.

Zeke hooked one leg over the saddle horn, pushed his hat back off his forehead, and remained mounted on his magnificent thoroughbred stud. There was a happy smile on his face.

"Well, if there ain't any of you glad to see me back, at least you could say howdy to our old friend Skeeter Cranston. He's going to be part of the family from now on."

Before they could respond, Zeke slipped down from the saddle. The womenfolk giggled at Zeke's shammed indignation and surrounded him, vying for hugs. Will came to his senses and was beside Skeeter's skittish mount in a few quick steps. He roughly pulled the youngster from his horse, knocking off his new hat in the process. They grappled in bear hugs, whooped, hollered, and danced around for a couple of minutes. And then, seemingly embarrassed about the public show of affection, they backed off a step and silently appraised each other.

"How'd—how'd *you* get here, Skeeter?" Will stammered.

"Why, I just rode on the train with Zeke and the horses to a place called Which-ta, then we rode them horses on down here," Skeeter drawled, as though he was stating an obvious fact any damn fool should have known.

Yeah, this is sure enough the same old smart-ass Skeeter, Will confirmed in his mind.

"Damn it, Skeeter, you haven't changed a bit. The place is called Wich-ah-taw. But I meant, how did you come to be with Zeke?"

"Maybe I ain't changed none, but y'all done changed! How'd *you* come to talk so funny?" Skeeter replied indignantly.

"I don't talk funny," Will insisted, feeling a little self-conscious because he hadn't realized Mary's efforts to improve his speech showed that much. "You're the one that talks like a West Virginia ridge-runner."

Seeing a hurt expression cross Skeeter's face, Will put his arm around his slim shoulders and said warmly, "Damn, it's good to see you, you ugly devil."

"Yeah, I'm glad to be here, too," Skeeter replied just as warmly. "I'd of still been in the Mason County jail if Zeke hadn't of busted me out."

"There's got to be a story behind that," Will answered with a chuckle. "Let's see to these fine horses and this here donkey, and then we'll start catching up on lost time."

"Well, I'm glad you two young peacocks finally remembered you used to be friends," Zeke commented. "Thought the two of you was going to get into a fistfight there for a moment. Oh, by the way, Skeeter, we have another member of the family since you last saw us. This here pretty maiden is Elisabeth Cousteau, known to family and friends as Betsy."

Skeeter's eyes nearly bugged out of his head. He gulped so violently Will thought his friend was in danger of swallowing his prominent Adam's apple.

"Paa-paa-leess-ed to met you, ma-ma'am," Skeeter stammered while staring at her like a gap-mouthed statue.

When Betsy put out her hand and shook his firmly, Skeeter's face turned beet red. He seemed to have trouble breathing.

Damn, she's smitten ol' Skeeter deaf and dumb, Will observed. He, of all people, could empathize with his friend, but he didn't intend to share any part of Betsy's affections. Nor did he intend to tell Skeeter about his and Betsy's special secret. There were some things you just didn't share, even with your best friend.

CHAPTER 40

MAN OF MEANS

◆

"Where's Moses?" Zeke asked.

"Moses has been feeling poorly. You know how he is, just won't quit. I put him to bed for some rest, but I'm having a heck of a time keeping him there," Mary replied. "He must be sleeping now or he'd be out here greeting you."

"He always works too hard. I'm going to see that he slows down," Zeke said. "Oh, by the way, I picked up a few little things for you folks during my travels."

He removed the bulging saddlebags from his horse, and then walked over to the donkey, untied the pack, and pulled out a large canvas bag. Will and Skeeter led the animals to the barn, while chattering like a couple of magpies. The others escorted the gift bearer into the house.

When they were all gathered in the kitchen having coffee and cake, Zeke began pulling paper-wrapped parcels from the saddlebags and canvas bag, seemingly a bottomless cornucopia.

"My gosh, Zeke, looks like you been spending money like a drunken sailor," Mary commented, about half serious. "Have you ever heard the old saying a fool and his money are soon parted?"

His hazel eyes sparkled and a toothy, prideful grin was plastered on his weathered face.

"Well, Miz Kill Joy, what good is there in having money if you don't spend it?" he asked. "Besides, I didn't do a darn thing to earn this money, so I plan on sharing it with the people I care about."

"I didn't mean to be a wet blanket, Zeke," Mary said seriously, "but I suggest you save something for a rainy day. Remember what happen last time we thought we were on our way to prosperity?"

"Yeah, I remember, Mary. And we're gonna be on guard to see that it don't happen again," Zeke assured her and the rest of his extended family. "Most of our new wealth is gonna be spent on better living conditions and setting us up to make our own prosperity in the future. Now, let's take a look at what I got here."

"Yeah, let's do, Uncle Zeke," excited Jeanie and Anne said, almost in unison. Having been taught good manners by Mary, they had stayed in the background during all that grownup talk.

Zeke's grin enlarged, turning up the ends of his barbershop-trimmed mustache and causing crinkles at the corners of his eyes. In the first big packages were new dresses for each of the females. Zeke anxiously awaited their reactions to the choices he had made, but he needn't have worried. They were the latest styles and if they didn't fit exactly, Mary could alter them. Next came five new books for Mary. He wasn't confident with his selection of titles either. The bookstore clerk in St Louis assured him they were all current best sellers by well-known authors.

Still imbued with his humble background, Zeke had to rationalize spending so much for books. He decided Mary would require Will to read them, and then later, Jeanie and Anne would also read them as part of their education. Who knows, Zeke conjectured, now that he was a man of means, he might find some time to improve his limited formal education by reading some of Mary's books, too. He considered Joan a cultured and educated woman and he didn't want her to be ashamed of him when they were married.

Yes, he intended to make her his wife. One lonely night on the train, he made the decision to ask Joan to marry him. It was just a matter of building up his courage for the right time and place. Joan and Ester had already received their presents when he stopped off in Winfield to show off his new horses and his stud donkey to Randy—actually, he stopped in Winfield mostly to see Joan. He'd missed her while he was gone!

In what seemed a never-ending flow of gifts, there was a set of clothes for Moses, who had joined the happy group, including a felt hat, a pair of cowboy boots, and a big tin of pipe tobacco.

He had bought life-size dolls for both girls, with wardrobes of clothes for each. In his extravagant mood, he'd added a number of illustrated reading books for eleven-year-old Jeanie, and large boxes of crayons, coloring books, and tablets and pencils for both girls to share. There were a dozen bright-colored, satin hair ribbons for five-year-old Anne. She squealed with joy. Now that he had money, when they were teenagers, he'd send those girls back east to school. He wanted them to have the best, even though it was difficult to think about being separated.

Finally, from the bottom of the canvas bag, he removed the things he brought for Will. First, he came out with a wide-brimmed felt hat that would need some steaming, and then a pair of new cowboy boots. The item he deliberately saved for last was a pair of Mexican-style chaps, with silver rosettes and buckskin ties.

"Gosh those chaps are great, but what's a farmer need fancy chaps for?" Will asked.

"From now on, Will, we're not gonna be sodbusters," Zeke replied seriously. "We're horse breeders and ranchers."

The evening of September 12, 1876, the family celebrated Will's and Skeeter's eighteenth birthdays on the same day. Skeeter had never had anyone celebrate his birthday. In fact, he didn't even know on what day he was born. He had figured the year he was born, and knew he was at least seventeen when he came to live with the Curtises. Zeke handled that little problem by decreeing Skeeter's birthday was the same day as Will's.

"Anyone can tell they're twins because they look so much alike," he joked, "except ol' Skeeter is a lot better looking than Will. They'll have to flip a coin to figure out which one was born first and is the oldest."

Both young men were pleased with the idea of having the same birthday, but Will argued the point of who was the best looking. He asked for a vote from the family, and gangling, freckle-faced Skeeter won.

Since they were now eighteen, and in Zeke's mind almost grown men, he shared a couple of shots of Kentucky whiskey with them. He also offered a drink to Mary, Betsy, and Moses. They all declined the offer, so the three "men" drank alone.

Zeke and Skeeter had moved into the cabin on Zeke's place soon after he returned from West Virginia. He figured that with the arrival of his thoroughbred horses, he should live closer to his stock. Since it was only a mile from Mary's house, the two bachelors continued to take most of their meals and spend their evenings with the rest of the family. The men continued to share the work on both places under Zeke's direction.

His expressed plans were to mate the sleek thoroughbred mares with Natty, and some of the best saddle mares with his new thoroughbred stud. Those offspring would combine the best characteristics of both ancestors—fast, yet durable. The donkey would be mated with their farm mares to produce large, sturdy mules. Zeke figured there would be a great demand for mules to do the heavy work of building the railroads that were coming very soon, and for clearing the thousands of acres in the Cherokee Strip and Unassigned Lands to the south, which would surely be settled in the next few years. He'd be right in the center of a big growing market for horses and mules.

Zeke needed more hay and pasture land for his intended enterprise. As a start on expansion, he purchased the one hundred sixty acres between his place and Mary's. He got it for a pittance because the man that registered the homestead never proved up on it. There were other parcels of land nearby that he would later acquire in the same manner.

Within a week after his return, Zeke had arranged with Herman Gunther and his oldest son to build a five-room house on his horse ranch. They were German immigrants who were accomplished carpenters. He also contracted with them for a three-room addition to Mary's house so the deteriorating sod house could be torn down.

With considerable tender loving care from both Mary and Betsy, Moses's health soon improved. He'd been joining them at the family breakfast table for a week without Zeke giving him a work assignment.

"Masta Zeke," Moses said one morning, "I'm well now, and ready to get back to work. Does you want me to go out with the boys?"

"Moses," he replied, knowing the old black man was willing, but too frail for fieldwork, "those young bucks could always use your help, but I've got another job for you, if you're interested."

"If old Moses can help you with that job, I'm sure enough interested," Moses replied earnestly. "What is it you wants me to do?"

"Well, it's like this—them foreign Germans are going to be building our houses. Except for people saying they know how to build real good, we don't know nothing about their character. What we need is a good man to kind of check their work; see that they got water, enough to eat, and the necessary materials on hand. Would you be willing to take on that chore?"

Moses puffed out his old chest as far as it would go.

"Yes sir, Masta Zeke, I'd be mighty proud to take on that job," he replied with enthusiasm.

That move proved a stroke of genius. Moses and the Gunthers hit it off from the get-go. Being emigrants, the Gunthers had no bigoted ideas about negroes. They seemed to accepted the congenial black man as a peer, and honor his position as their employer's representative. Moses soon returned to his usual optimistic, happy disposition and his health improved markedly.

Zeke situated his new house on the brow of a small rise, about two hundred yards from the west bank of the Walnut River, after asking Joan Koster for her advice. He ordered new furniture for the entire house from Kansas City, also with Joan's input. His prized purchase was a modern, wood-fired cook stove that came with internal pipes and a storage tank for heating water. He liked it so well he ordered an identical one for Mary.

The Gunthers did a fast and quality job. Both houses were completed by the last week of October. They stayed a week longer to remove the sod house.

While the building was underway, water wells were drilled on both places. They were encased and fitted with pumps that could be operated by hand or hooked to the windmills that Zeke ordered.

When they were moved into their new homes, Zeke was proud of his accomplishments. From his viewpoint, these were happy times and a new beginning. Now, thanks to Ambrose McNeal, he had some excellent breeding stock, good hay and pastureland, and for the first time in his life, a comfortable amount of money.

The future had never looked brighter—but he still didn't have a wife because he hadn't worked up enough courage to ask the woman he thought he loved to marry him. Joan Koster was on his mind a lot. He often found an excuse to go into Winfield to see her. She seemed receptive, but each time he was on the verge of popping the question, something came up that delayed his proposal. Was he just afraid of refusal, he wondered, or were there still some real obstacles standing in their way? He wasn't conscious of the possibility that much of his problem dated back to his youth, and a pretty girl named Marge.

CHAPTER 41

CRUEL REVENGE

◆

They retained the tent-bedroom that Zeke had used early on because Will preferred it to sleeping in the house. Actually, while he wasn't about to tell anyone, he wanted privacy for the times he could entice Betsy to sneak out and spend part of the night with him. To his consternation, those trysts were becoming less frequent.

"I don't like all this sneaking around. Our relationship isn't healthy for either one of us," Betsy told him. "I was taught by my mother how to count the days when I'm least fertile, but there's always a chance I could get pregnant. Or, one of the family is going to catch us. If we're not strong enough to stop this, I'll have to move away."

"Please don't leave, Betsy," Will pleaded. "If it comes to that, I'll go with you. I—I don't think I could live without you!"

"Oh, yes you can, Will. Sure, you'd miss me, and what we've been doing together; but it's like I've told you before, there will be other women in your life. If you're lucky, there'll be that very special one. It might even be Mary."

That unexpected comment got Will's attention.

"Why—why, she's a lot older than me. She'll be married to Randy before I'm old enough to marry her."

"She's not any older than me and you didn't let our age difference get in the way of your passion. Two or three years from now, that age difference will hardly be noticed. I'll take a bet she won't be married to Randy by then."

The last day of November, Will enticed Betsy to come to his sleeping tent after they hadn't been together for three weeks. Will's passions built to a crescendo, as he reveled in the fragrance, touch, and other exquisite pleasures of her lovely body. Still in rapture from the after-glow of their second mating, he passionately whispered in her ear how much she meant to him. Betsy rose on one elbow and shushed him by putting two fingers lightly on his lips.

"Now, I want you to listen to me, Will," Betsy said in a firm, but not unkind, tone. "I'm leaving now for my own bed, and this was our *last time*. I've told you before we can't go on deceiving the family or ourselves like this. It's my fault it got started, and I'm putting a stop to it before others get hurt."

She slipped from under the covers and hurried to put on her nightgown, boots, and coat in the cool tent.

Will reached for her and muttered, "But, I-I love you, Betsy! Please don't…"

She stopped him with a light kiss on his mouth and then pushed him away and held him at arms length with a hand on each shoulder.

"Don't make this more difficult for me than it already is, Will. We've been over this a number of times and you're not a boy any longer. You've got to start thinking with your head and not your crotch. You're very dear to me, and I've enjoyed our times together as much as you have, but it's got to stop—now! If you can't handle that, then I'll leave the farm."

His intellect told him she was right and that she meant it this time, but his heart felt like she'd plunged a knife into it. She said he was a man now, then why didn't she love him? In this moment of soul-wrenching disappointment, he sure didn't feel like a man. The little boy that still lingered in him wanted to cry.

"I-I know you're right, Betsy," he managed to reply. "It'll be hard, but I'll sure try to get along without what you've been giving me. I-I don't want you to leave the farm—the whole family loves you."

"Well then, that's it. We'll both have some fond memories and I hope we'll always be very good friends."

With that, she slipped through the tent flap into the night, gone from his bed forever. His world was crushed, leaving him too disturbed to sleep.

Over at Zeke's house, Zeke and Skeeter's sleep was shattered by two gunshots. Zeke was the first out of bed. He had his pants and boots on before sleep-drugged Skeeter emerged from his room. Zeke threw open the kitchen door and was greeted with a blazing haystack down by the corral, and the hoof beats of an undetermined number of horses running toward the southwest. He sprinted toward the horse corral with his Winchester ready.

"Oh, my God! Oooh, my God!" Zeke wailed at what the light of a full moon and burning hay revealed in the corral.

Seconds later, Skeeter came to a sliding halt beside him, and nearly gagged when he saw what had unhinged Zeke.

Will's buckskin horse, Natty, was down on his side. A pool of blood expanded around his head as his life drained into the manure. His strong legs kicked in a dying spasm. Mendy's most recent colt also lay dead a few feet away. Both beautiful horses had been shot.

Zeke put his head in his hands and moaned from deep in his soul, like a wounded animal.

"Aw-w-w, aw-w-w, good Lord, both of Mendy's wonderful sons have been shot! What low-life, miserable son of a bitch would do a thing like that?"

Skeeter noticed the white piece of paper stuck over a protruding nail head on the corral's gatepost. He pulled it loose. There was crude writing on it, in large printed letters. He couldn't make out what it said in the poor light. After determining that the haystack would burn out without jeopardizing any of the buildings, they went back to the house and lit a lamp.

The paper Skeeter retrieved was crumpled and the printing on it wiggly, but Zeke understood the vengeful message. He also knew who the deranged person was who wrote it. With unadulterated hatred in his voice, he read it out loud to Skeeter: "THIS HAR IS FOR MY PA."

"That cowardly bastard, Homer Sommers, done this," Zeke spat out. "I won't rest until the miserable son of a bitch is dead!"

Will had little time to wallow in his self-pity before a horse galloped into the yard. Zeke appeared at the tent flap and lit the lamp while Will struggled into his long john underwear that had been tossed aside for the lovemaking. The last arm went in just as the lamp illuminated his rumpled bed.

Boy, if Zeke would have shown up a half hour sooner he'd have caught Betsy and me in bed together, Will observed to himself.

Those frivolous thoughts were replaced with concern when he saw his uncle's grim face. Zeke sat on the bed beside Will and stared somberly at him for a moment. His eyes were watery and red-rimmed. Surely, he hasn't been crying, Will thought. What could have happened that would make a tough guy like Zeke cry? Zeke then studied the tent floor for several more seconds. Whatever the problem, he was having difficulty getting it out. His brow wrinkled and his jaws were clinched.

"My God," Will exclaimed, "what happened?"

"Will…," Zeke started, and then his unnatural, high-pitched voice broke. He looked toward the floor again, while swallowing hard. After a couple of deep breaths, he raised his head, looked directly into Will's questioning eyes, and delivered the dreadful message.

"Will, I'd rather take a licking than tell you this—but there ain't no easy way to say it—*Natty's dead!*"

When that horrible message registered in Will's mind, all the wind went out of him. He doubled over, as though punched in the gut. Panting for breath, his mind refused to accept what Zeke just told him. This is a horrific nightmare; it can't be real!

"Dead? When? Are you sure? How—how did it happen?"

"About a half hour ago, in the corral, over at my place," Zeke lamented. "You'll recall we took Natty over there to service that mare again that didn't stick the first time. God, I wish we'd left him over here, maybe he wouldn't have found him."

"Who wouldn't have found him? What happened to Natty?" Will screeched hysterically. "Damn it, Zeke, tell me what happened!"

"It had to have been that no good bastard, Homer Sommers, who shot him," Zeke angrily snarled while handing Will the crumpled, scribbled note. "Who else would leave a note like this? The scum has been laying in the weeds waiting for a chance to get back at us ever since you whipped his ass that Fourth of July. I swear to you Will, I'll get the bastard if it takes the rest of my life."

Will's jaws set. His eyes took on the glint of cold steel.

"No, Zeke, he's mine! I'm the one that'll take him down." Will's mature voice was determined, ruthless, and angry.

"I know how you feel, but I'm sure as hell not going to let you go after him alone. There's likely a gang of them because I heard a bunch of horses galloping away after the shots were fired. There were two shots. They shot Mendy's yearling, too."

"Okay, Zeke, we'll go after them together, but I want you to promise me—here and now—you'll leave Homer to me and won't try to stop me from giving him what he's got coming, like you and Betsy did last time." Will begin hurriedly dressing.

"I'll do the best I can, Will, but I'll not promise to stand by and see you hurt—or killed."

"Fair enough. What are we waiting for? Let's get after the bastard."

Always the cavalryman tactician, Zeke began to plan out loud. "Ain't no hope of following their trail in the dark. We best get our gear together and be ready to go after them come first light. It'll just be you and me this time. We'll leave Skeeter to guard my place. Betsy, Moses, and the hired hand can watch out for things over here. Let's ask Betsy if you can ride her Indian pony. She'll be faster and more durable on the trail than anything we've got—now that Natty's gone."

Will winced at the sound of his beloved horse's name. Hated Homer hadn't just killed two valuable horses; he had raised the ante on the blood feud to the limit. Somehow, that dumb bastard had known how to hurt both him and Zeke way down deep!

While Mary helped throw together supplies for their pursuit of the horse killers, she tried to reason with Zeke and Will.

"I know how badly you both feel about this terrible atrocity because I feel bad too, but can't we let the law handle this? Each time you've gone down into the Territory looking for someone, Zeke, you've ended up killing men. I know that weighs heavy on your heart and soul because you're a God-fearing man."

"This is a job we'll have to take care of ourselves—and the sooner the better because Homer won't stop harassing us until he's dead! It could just as easily be one or more of us he takes down next time. The kid is crazy."

"Zeke's right, Mary," Will confirmed. "He's got to be stopped. Zeke and me aim to do that!"

"I guess you're right, but I hope the time comes soon when no one has to take the law into their own hands. This won't be a decent place to live and raise a family until that happens," Mary replied with a sigh of resignation.

They stayed up for what was left of the night, and at false dawn, Zeke and Will were ready to leave.

"Please be careful. I don't know what we'd do if anything happened to either one of you—and we almost lost you last time, Zeke!" Mary said with trepidation.

Betsy remained silent while the rest of the family discussed the matter, except to agree when Will asked to borrow her horse.

"Yeah," she said before Zeke could reply to Mary's admonition, "you sure needed me last time, maybe you'd best reconsider about letting me go with you now—just in case!"

"You may be right, Betsy. It ain't that we don't appreciate your offer, but this time it's personal for Will and me. We have to take care of this ourselves." And then he spoke to Mary, "I understand your concern. We won't take any damn fool chances."

The family shared hugs all around. Mary kissed Will on his lips, which he thought unusual, but enjoyable, and then the man hunters were on their way.

As the first pale light pushed the darkness westward, Zeke found a spot down on the bank of the Walnut where six horses had been held. The horse tracks led them across the river ford a few miles up river, and then southeast into the broad expanse of the Osage Nation.

At first, they had no trouble following the trail of six horsemen in rain-softened soil because one of their mounts had a broken shoe. About noon, they became confused at a place where the riders entered the rocky bed of a substantial creek. With painstaking, time-killing searching, they finally determined the marauders rode in the water for a couple of miles and exited on rocky ground. After they found the trail again, Zeke was perplexed when their prey veered to the west, back toward the Arkansas River.

About ten miles south of the Indian Territory–Kansas border, their quarry found a place to cross the Arkansas. On the west bank, Zeke discovered where they entered the freight and stage road that ran from the new tent town of Arkansas City, across the Cherokee Strip, and then to points further south.

Zeke speculated that the horse killers were headed to a hideout in the lawless area called The Unassigned Lands. The two pursuers searched south for an agonizing hour, hoping to find a broken horseshoe hoof imprint among the mingled tracks on the well-traveled wagon trail. The sun was low in the west, and both men were frustrated and discouraged when they stopped at a stream to rest and water their tired mounts.

"Where you think them bastards are headed?" Zeke asked rhetorically. "I can understand a dimwit like Homer taking a chance on killing two of our best horse for revenge, but it makes no sense that a gang of six wouldn't at least try to steal some of the other horses."

"Well, logically they'd head south, away from Kansas, and deeper into the Territory. But it don't make sense that men trying to keep out of sight would use a well-traveled road," Will replied.

"Damn, I wish we'd brought Betsy with us. She'd probably figure out which of this bunch of tracks are the ones we want," Zeke lamented. "I hate to admit it, but I think we've lost the bastards' trail."

Will shook his head in bitter disappointment, but he had no suggestion about what they should do next. A horrifying thought popped into his mind.

"My God, Zeke! Could it be possible they decoyed us down here to get us outta th' way, and then doubled back to run off a bunch of our stock—or do some harm to our *people*?"

"That's just what those low-life sons of bitches would do," Zeke shouted, as he mounted. "They left a deliberate trail so we'd be looking for them down in the Territory, and then doubled back. I got a gut feeling the women are in dire danger!"

He spurred his horse up the trail toward Mary's place. By the time Will mounted, Zeke had a substantial lead. He pushed Betsy's tough little mare to catch up. As the horses loped abreast, he shouted to be heard.

"I can see Homer shooting our horses, but I don't think he's mean enough to mess with our womenfolk."

"Homer did some terrible things to Joan and Ester. He may be looking for them. God only knows what the damn fool is capable of doing," Zeke shouted back."

"Maybe they're just out to steal our stock," Will shouted hopefully.

"If they've doubled back, I hope to God that's all they're after," Zeke offered.

They pushed their already tired horses unmercifully, but the old cavalryman realized that even though they were mounted on strong horses, the animals required periodic breathers.

"Damn, why are we stopping?" Will grumbled when Zeke called a halt at a small stream. "At this rate, it'll be midnight before we reach Mary's place. That may be too late!"

"We'll be a lot later if we kill these horses." Zeke's voice was shrill. "Best we can do is pray we've got this figured all wrong."

CHAPTER 42

KIDNAPPED

◆

Skeeter ate supper with the family at Mary's place, but returned to Zeke's house shortly after dark. It was a somber meal. They were distressed over the senseless killing of the horses, and worried sick about Will and Zeke's safety.

By 10:00 PM, they were all in bed. It seemed to Mary that she had just fallen asleep when the sound of boots on the porch awakened her. Thinking Will and Zeke had returned, she got out of bed and searched in the dark for a wrap to cover her nightgown, intending to go out and greet them. Before she could get the wrap on, someone lit a lamp in the kitchen. She saw the light under the door, and then her bedroom door flung open, nearly hitting her in the face. A big, shabbily dressed man with a tobacco-stained blond beard stomped into the room and grabbed her around the waist. The putrid odors of an unwashed body, tobacco juice, and a rotten breath nearly caused her to gag. She struggled helplessly in his strong grasp.

"No use to fight it, you little bitch. Your tight little ass is mine now!" his rough voice snarled in her ear.

She kneed him in the groin and clawed at his evil face. He struck her with his ham-like fist and she mercifully lost consciousness.

Betsy's Indian-trained senses brought her awake at the first sound of footsteps on the porch. Instantly, she knew something was wrong, and cursed silently that she didn't keep a gun in her room. But from habit, she slept with her sheath knife under her pillow. She had removed it from the scabbard before she heard scuffling from Mary's bedroom and a man's gruff, depraved voice.

From the sounds of the footsteps, she judged there were at least three invaders in the house. One was obviously in Mary's bedroom and the other two were likely still in the kitchen. Instincts told her one or more of the raiders would burst into her room at any moment. When they saw a half-breed Indian woman, clad only in her nightgown, rape was inevitable, and only God knew what else!

Betsy's mind functioned coolly and rapidly. She had to figure a way to keep them off of Mary and Jeanie until help arrived. But then, where would help come from? Moses and the hired man wouldn't be up to fighting hard case outlaws. Based on what she heard coming from Mary's bedroom, at least one of them was a gruff sounding, ruthless bastard. It's probably the same bunch that killed Natty and Mendy's colt, she reasoned. That was likely a decoy to pull the men away long enough for them to do what else they had on their filthy minds. Skeeter was their only hope, if she could only get word to him somehow.

Her heart dropped to her toes when she heard muffled gunfire from the direction of Zeke's house. My God, she thought, some of them must be raiding Zeke's place, too. Skeeter probably has his hands full. At that moment, she felt an urge to jump out of the window and run, but it soon passed. There was no way she could leave Mary and the girls to the mercy of these beasts, whoever they were. My best bet is get one of them into my bedroom, hopefully their leader. She slipped the knife back under her pillow.

When she opened her bedroom door and boldly walked into the kitchen, her heart missed a couple of beats and her knees went weak. Jeanie and Anne were huddled together beside the stove. They stared with big, frightened eyes at a young, longhaired man standing near them, who looked out of place in such a situation. Neither of the stoic youngsters were crying. Blind anger nearly caused her to rush to the girls, take them in her arms and protect them with her life. Harsh reality dispelled that foolish impulse before she could act on it.

Through the open bedroom door, she saw Mary lying naked and unconscious on her bed. Two large, despicable men hovered over her, arguing about who was going to have her first. Betsy thanked God the girls couldn't see what was happening to Mary from their vantage point, even though they could hear the vulgar discussion.

The man with the fat belly and scraggily blond beard seemed to be the leader. He was winning the argument.

When Betsy spoke, all heads snapped in her direction. She felt depraved eyes scrutinize her nightgown-clad figure. Her knees felt like jelly, but she reached down deep for courage. I've faced worse than this, she reminded herself sardonically.

"Why are you men wasting you're time on an unconscious white woman when there's a hot-blooded Indian girl here that can give all of you more than you can handle?" she taunted.

A gap-tooth grin, more like a leer, curled the big man's thin lips..

"Well by God, ain't you the saucy one," he roared. "I've had me some hot squaws in my time. I'll just take you up on that offer. Always better to have it given to you, than having to take it, I say."

He lumbered around the bed and out of Mary's room toward her.

"Don't you touch that pretty little white gal while I'm taking care of this here squaw 'cause I want to be first on her, too," he snarled at his lecherous companion. "Throw a blanket over her bare ass. Don't want her gettin' sick on the way south. You can have the Injun when I've finished with her."

In three or four eager strides, the beast was beside Betsy. It required all her willpower to keep from shaking when he gripped her bare arm in a huge claw-like hand. Obviously, he intended to hurt her while he raped her. Her mind flashed back to the Blackburn Trading Post, but she didn't cry out or flinch.

"Light that lantern over there. I'm taking this lamp 'cause I like to see 'em quiver," he snarled to the bug-eyed youngster that was standing near the girls. "And take them kids back into their room and find something to bar the door. Then go out and keep watch with Homer. There might be some hired men bunking in them buildings. Set fire to that near haystack so you can see if anyone tries to sneak up on us. Anything moves, shoot it."

The intimidated young man scampered to comply with his leader's instructions. Dirty-beard upholstered his pistol and placed it on the table. Betsy lamented having lost any chance of grabbing his gun while he was distracted by passion. The brute grabbed the base of the lamp in his free hand and pushed her ahead of him into the bedroom. Once inside, he kicked the door closed with his foot and set the lamp on the dresser. He used both filthy hands to rip off her nightgown before flinging her shivering naked body onto the bed.

"Lets see what you got, you Injun bitch," he snarled, while unbuckling the belts for both his gun holster and pants and letting them drop to the floor. He kicked out of the pants without removing his decrepit boots. A pitifully small, erected penis peeked out the open fly of his dirty underwear. It looked so ludicrous under that big belly Betsy had to stifle a giggle, even in the stress of the moment.

He mounted her like a clumsy bear, knocking the breath out of her for a moment. As he frantically worked at entering her with his small penis, her right hand found the handle of the knife. She endured the rutting until the monster was at a critical point, and then with a mixture of glee and malice in her soul, she plunged the ten-inch blade upward, into his big gut just under his left rib cage. Her other hand covered his slobbering mouth to stifle a dying scream. When his body quit quivering, she knew the blade had found its mark. The loathsome animal that reminded her of the hated Blackburn Trader, McClure, was dead.

She shuddered as his warm blood gushed onto her bare stomach. It took all her strength to push him off. The dead man fell between the bed and the wall. Her violated body trembled, feeling dirty and debased. Frantically, she wiped the blood off with her nightgown. Shots rang from outdoors. She looked up to see flames from her window. Oh my God, she lamented, they're likely shooting at Moses and the hired man. I hope they both have sense enough to run, knowing full well loyal Moses wouldn't run away. He'd die defending his womenfolk. Maybe the hired man would get away. She didn't think he had a gun.

A frightened, high-pitched male voice came from outside. She had heard it before down on Bird Creek, and recognized it as belonging to Homer Sommers. He must have stayed outside with the horses.

"Hey boss, someone shot at us from down by the cow shed. I think I got him though. There was another one running toward the barn. I had to get him too, 'cause ol' Billy didn't even fire his gun."

"Better come outta there, Luke. Sounds like we got some trouble," a more mature voice shouted from the kitchen.

Betsy guessed Luke was the dead bastard lying beside her bed. It made her feel good that the filthy monster wouldn't be answering, ever again. Expecting the other scumbag to burst into the room at any moment, she managed to grab her boots and a heavy coat before slipping out the window and running naked into the bushes some fifty feet away. Most likely, she could help the others better from the outside than inside.

After pulling on her boots and coat, Betsy carefully worked her way to the tack shed where Moses slept. She could hear three of the raiders talking loudly and excitedly near the house. To her relief, none of the buildings were in immediate danger of catching fire from the burning haystack unless the wind changed direction.

Groaning noises led her to where Moses sat leaning against the tack shed. Light from the briskly burning haystack revealed poor old Moses holding his bleeding left arm with his right hand.

"It's me, Moses," Betsy whispered. "Don't make any noise and maybe they won't come checking on you."

"I bad hit in the arm, but I be all right, Miz Betsy," Moses moaned. "One of then shots done busted my old rife, too."

"Damn," Betsy replied, louder than she intended. "You have any idea where Boris is? Maybe he has a gun."

"I think them bad men done shot him, over by the barn. I don't think he got no gun."

"You hold on, Moses. I'm going to check on Boris. Then I've got to find a way to help the others in the house. Those bastards are going to be madder than hornets when they figure out I killed their leader. No telling what they'll do to Mary and the girls."

"Please hurry, Miz Betsy. I bleeding something bad."

She took time to cut strips from Moses's shirt and fashion a compress and crude tourniquet for his severely damaged arm before she slipped away. Soon she found Boris, the hired man, lying face down a few feet from the barn door. Unlucky kid probably never knew what hit him, she lamented when she turned him over and saw the ragged hole in his tattered coat directly over his heart.

At that moment, two more riders galloped into the yard. One of them was leading Zeke's prize thoroughbred stud. They dismounted and rushed into the house with the other three.

"Oh God!" she prayed. "Please don't let them have killed Skeeter, too."

Before her shocked mind could formulate some desperate plan, the raiders came hurrying out of the house. They must have panicked when they found their leader dead and me gone, she guessed. Looks like they're going to hightail it out of here. She counted five in the confusion around the horses. That's all of them, she concluded, except the monster I killed.

Her heart leaped into her throat when she saw Mary being dragged toward the horses by one of those beasts. Apparently, she had regained consciousness because the spunky gal was putting up a valiant fight. Thank God, they had allowed her to put on some clothes, her boots, and a coat. Betsy moaned in desperation and gritted her teeth in frustration. Without a gun, she was helpless to stop them. They were obviously very nervous now. Likely, they'd shoot at any shadow or sound. Best wait and trail them.

It took all her willpower not to scream at the top of her lungs when she saw Mary forced to mount a horse. One of the bastards tied her hands together and then her feet, with a rope strung under the horse's belly. There was still enough light from the dying haystack fire to recognize Homer Sommers leading Mary's mount as the gang galloped away into the night.

"Hang on, Moses," she shouted. "I'll be right back, soon as I check on Jeanie and Anne."

"I be okay, Miz Betsy. Y'all see to them little gals!" he replied, his voice strained from pain.

Betsy dashing toward the house, praying the girls were all right. Thank God, they left them!

CHAPTER 43

BETSY'S DILEMMA

◆

Betsy's impulse was to saddle a horse, chase after the raiders, and rescue Mary. On reflection, she realized her first responsibilities now were to Moses and the girls. Also, there was concern about Skeeter. Fearing him dead or wounded after hearing gunfire from the direction of Zeke's place, she'd check on him after settling the girls and tending to Moses.

Greatly relieved, Betsy found the girls huddled in their room, emotionally shaken but physically unharmed. After getting them busy stoking the cook stove fire to heat the internal water system, she fetched Moses. Weakened from shock and loss of blood, the stoic old black man was barely able to walk by leaning heavily on her.

Resilient little Anne soon went back to sleep. Jeanie insisted on helping care for Moses. My, how she's matured, Betsy thought. Her womanhood was just beginning to show. Thank God, the raiders hadn't seemed to notice how pretty she was.

The outlaw's bullet had done a wicked job of shattering the bone in Moses's upper right arm. Betsy could do little beyond bandaging the wound and fashioning a temporary splint to stabilize the jagged break. She judged Moses too weak and fragile to survive a rough wagon ride into town. Come first light, she'd send Jeanie for Doctor Haggerty, who had recently arrived in Winfield. Jeanie had her own little horse and was a good rider.

After settling Moses into Mary's bed and quickly pulling on some clothes, Betsy was searching the kitchen cabinets for some of Zeke's whiskey to serve as a painkiller for Moses, when her keen ears picked up the distant sound of a running horse headed toward them. She quickly snatched the spare Winchester from over the fireplace, blew out the lamp, pulled Jeanie to her side behind the stove, and waited in the darkened room for the rider to reveal himself. The stalwart female Indian warrior put her arm around frightened Jeanie's slender shoulder, steadied her own stressed nerves, and tightened her grip on the Winchester. If one of those monsters was coming back, he'd be a dead man before he crossed the threshold.

Betsy identified the sounds of one loping horse sliding to a stop near the backyard gate, hesitant footsteps on the porch, the squeaky screen door being cautiously opened, and then the doorknob turning. The door pushed open a crack. With both hands now on the Winchester, Betsy's finger tightened on the trigger. A hoarse whisper from a strained male voice penetrated the darkness.

"Mary, Betsy, are you all right?"

"Whew-w-w! Praise the Lord!" Betsy's exhaled breath made a hissing sound, as it escaped through her taunt lips. "Is that you, Skeeter?"

"Yeah, it's me," was the comforting reply. Skeeter stepped into the room and Betsy relit the lamp.

The likable young man was as welcome to the nervous females as a troop of cavalry, or a band of angels. They nearly bowled him over with their enthusiastic greeting. While administering some whiskey painkiller to Moses, they shared experiences.

Skeeter told about hearing two raiders trying to rope Zeke's prized thoroughbred stud. He shot at them from cover in the house. One pinned him down while the other got the horse. After shooting a few more rounds in the direction of the house, they slipped away with the valuable stud.

About the time the two outlaws rode out, Skeeter explained to Betsy that he had seen the reflection of flames against the sky in the direction of Mary's place, and heard the gunfire. The thieves had let Zeke's other horses out of the corral, he said. Figuring he'd need a horse to run the raiders down, he had lost critical time catching one. After finally succeeding, he rode bareback, hell-bent on checking on the women.

"I'm sorry it took me so long to get here," the conscientious young man lamented with tears in his eyes, when Betsy told him the raiders had kidnapped Mary.

"Don't blame yourself, Skeeter," Betsy consoled him. "Sounds like you had your hands full. There were six of them altogether. They killed Boris and wounded Moses, and likely would have killed you, too, if you'd ridden up on them."

She pulled the grieving, self-condemning young man into a hug and gently patted his back for several seconds.

"I got their filthy leader with my knife," she announced calmly. "Would you do me a favor and remove his flea-bitten carcass from my bedroom? He doesn't deserve burying. Let's burn the pile of crap in what's left of the haystack fire they set."

"Of—of course I will," Skeeter said.

Skeeter dragged the hated carrion outside on an old blanket, along with Betsy's bloody nightgown and bedding. With considerable effort, he managed to roll the outlaw's body into the embers of the now smoldering haystack fire. After piling on some old corral poles, he watched the flames begin to consume the earthly remains of the monster that had raped his friend. Betsy walked up behind him while he worked. Her unexpected voice startled him.

"Burn in hell, you slimy bastard," she snarled. "I told you I'd give you more than you could handle!"

"Why would they take Mary with them?" Skeeter wondered out loud. when they were back in the house

"I don't know, but Homer Sommers is one of the depraved men that took her. As you know, Zeke killed his pa, and he and Will are mortal enemies," Betsy replied. "It sets my teeth on edge to think what might happen to her. Before he died, the gang leader said something about not wanting her to get sick on the way south, like they had this all planned. We've got to find them and get her back—damn quick."

"We will, Betsy. When it's light enough to track them, I'll take two of Zeke's thoroughbred mares and ride day and night until I catch them bastards."

"I wish I could go with you, Skeeter, but one of us has to stay with Moses and the girls," Betsy replied. "I plan on sending Jeanie to Winfield for the doctor come first light. I have no idea where we might find Will and Zeke, or when they'll be back," she said with a note of despondency in her voice.

Jeanie had refused to go to bed; she explained to Betsy that she wanted to help and was too keyed up to sleep anyway. When the conversation paused for a moment, she volunteered some troubling information.

"If you don't stop those horrible men, Skeeter, they're going to *sell* Mary," she blurted out with tears in her eyes.

"What makes you think that, sweetheart?" Betsy asked.

"I heard them say that's why they came," Jeanie answered. "They were mad as wet hens because Mrs. Koster and Ester weren't here, too. Homer had promised them four women to sell to someone called Com-man-chair-ro."

"Oh my God!" Betsy exclaimed, putting her hands to her mouth. "Not Comancheros?"

Jeanie was near hysteria, but she had more to tell.

"The young one that was guarding Anne and me wanted them to leave Mary, but that hateful Homer Sommers said he was taking her. Said she could cook for them, they could take turns having fun with her, and that she'd bring a lot of money from Com-man-chair-ro, down in Unassigned lands in Oklahoma Territory. Homer wanted to take me too, but the other young man said I was too young. They were going to fight about it, but Homer backed down."

Betsy pulled Jeanie's head to her bosom and stroked her hair.

"Good Lord what a terrible thing for a twelve-year-old girl to experience," Betsy moaned. "I wish I'd let Will kill that polecat when he had the chance down on Bird Creek."

"This here ain't your fault, Betsy," Skeeter consoled her. "Anyway, it's a long ways to the Unassigned Lands, if that's where they're headed. I'll get the bastards 'fore they're out of the Osage Nation."

CHAPTER 44

GUN FIGHT

◆

As they crested a small hill, Will's young sharp eyes picked up a dim light against a dark horizon to the northeast, probably about three miles away.

"Good God! Looks like the bastards are burning one of the places," he shouted.

"Yeah, they're burning something alright—not big enough for a building, maybe a haystack at Mary's place," Zeke answered, sick at the thought that they were too late.

The moon broke through the clouds, and Zeke recognized that they were very close to the south bank of the Arkansas ford. He pulled his heaving horse to a stop at the water's edge, blocking the narrow, brush-lined trail.

"We've got to give these horses a short breather, or they won't make it to Mary's place," he ordered, as he dismounted.

Will tried to force Betsy's strong-hearted, but winded mare past Zeke's horse. "I'm pressing on, even if it kills this little horse," he shouted.

"Just a minute," Zeke replied. "Keep still. I think I hear something."

Soon they both could hear approaching hoof beats from across the quarter-mile wide riverbed.

"I'd say five or six horses are coming this way at a full gallop," Zeke, the old cavalry scout reported. "They got to be up to no good riding hard like that in the dark. Let's ease our mounts into the bushes on each side of the trail and pull down on whoever they are when they're a few yards from this side."

"Okay, Zeke, but it'd be a miracle if it's the critters we're after," Will replied calmly while also dismounting.

"I've seen bigger miracles in my time," Zeke said. "Just be ready for anything."

Seconds later, they heard horses splashing in the water, perhaps two hundred yards away. A rough voice spoke loud enough to be heard clearly in the crisp night air.

"God damn it, Homer, who the hell made you the leader? Slow down, you damn fool. That gal's about to fall off her horse, what with her hands and feet tied."

"To hell with her," a cruel, high-pitched voice that both Zeke and Will recognized as Homer Sommers's replied. "If the bitch can't hold on, I'll just let the horse drag her. We got to put some distance between us and them damn Curtises 'fore daylight."

"Those are the raiders all right," Zeke confirmed in a loud whisper. "Select your target careful 'cause they got a woman captive with them—but shoot to kill!"

Will tightened his grip on his pistol. His fighting blood ran hot. The lead rider was nearly on top of them in seconds. Rather than shoot the unknown, unsuspecting man out of the saddle without warning, Zeke fired his first shot over their heads, still not sure where the woman was.

"Stop where you are you robbing bastards!" he bellowed.

All the outlaws' horses shied and reared as the riders yanked on the reins, making it ever harder to determine which one was the hostage.

"I'm over here, Zeke," an alert Mary shouted.

Homer dropped the reins of her horse for a moment while he fought to control a rearing mount and draw his pistol at the same time. Mary desperately tried kneeing her horse away from the others.

Hearing her shout, Homer wheeled his big black horse and scooped up the reins of Mary's horse with lighting reflexes. Will recognized the distinctive black horse and got off a couple of rounds toward it that whizzed by Homer's head. As Homer pulled Mary's snorting mount back across the ford, she became her captor's unwitting shield. Livid he couldn't take another shot and that Homer's and Mary's horses quickly disappeared into the darkness, Will's impulse was to ride after them, but the next moment he realized he couldn't do that. He and Zeke still had a hot gunfight on their hands.

In seconds, the odds changed. Zeke shot two of the raiders out of their saddles and Will accounted for another. When the shooting started, the man in the rear turned his horse downstream. Zeke's mind registered an impression that the rider was leading an unsaddled horse. The horses and rider blended into the dark foliage before he could get off a clear shot at the man.

"Damn it to hell, Homer and another of them varmints are getting away," Will shouted while mounting his tired horse. By the time he was in the saddle, Zeke and his horse blocked the trail again

"Get your horse out of my way, Zeke," Will demanded.

"Whoa there, you'll never catch them critters on that worn-out pony," Zeke ordered his willful nephew. "We'll go to the farm for fresh mounts. At first light, I'll go after Homer and Mary. You round up that other polecat. I think he's leading one of my horses."

"Get out of my way, Zeke. I'm going after Homer and Mary, right now!"

"You can't trail them in the dark. At least take time to get a fresh mount. Homer can't travel very fast pulling that horse Mary's tied to. Since we messed up whatever plans he had, maybe he'll get scared enough to just let her go."

"Like hell he'll let her go! If you'll get out of my way, I'll catch one of the horses that those guys we just shot was riding."

"Those horses are going to be worn out too, and there's no need to stumble around in the dark," Zeke replied. "That fool could take off in any number of directions and we'll need some light to identify them tracks."

"*Step aside, Zeke. I ain't gonna tell you again!*" Will's voice was commanding, powerful, and menacing.

There was no other person on earth Zeke would take that kind of guff from, but it was like he was trying to reason with himself. How could he blame the youngster for being like him? Much of the same blood flowed in their veins and he'd helped raise Will that way.

"Okay, Will, just simmer down," he condescended. "You can have Homer, but I'm going to forget about the horse and go with you to help save Mary. Now let's quit jawing and give these poor horses some water."

While Zeke's horse drank, Will dug his spurs into the side of Betsy's tough little Indian pony, and pushed past Zeke, hell-bent after one of the dead men's mounts. All three horses had followed Homer and Mary's horses back across the river.

Will was hoping one of the loose horses would have stopped soon after it reached the other side of the river, but he wasn't that lucky. He'd ridden past the junction where the route to Mary's farm forked off the main trail before he spotted a saddled horse grazing in a small open area. Preoccupied with munching the dried grass, the animal allowed him to catch the bridle reins before it shied. He took time to switch saddles because he wanted his Winchester scabbard, bedroll, and supplies with him, anticipating a long chase.

He was tightening the girth, when he heard a horse approach on the trail behind him. The sounds turned off toward Mary's place. There was a slight pang of guilt at being pleased Zeke missed him. As much as he respected his stalwart uncle, this was his fight.

Will turned Betsy's mare loose, certain the smart horse would find her way back to the farm, only two a mile away. He had mounted the other horse when it dawned on him: he'd gone off half-cocked, and had no idea where to go or how he was going to pick up Homer's trail in the dark.

Damn, he chastised himself; I'd have saved time by going on to the farm with Zeke and accepted his help in working out some strategy. Stubborn pride prevented him from doing that sensible thing now.

"Use your head, Will," he muttered to himself. "Mary's life may depend on it!"

CHAPTER 45

MARY'S ORDEAL

◆

After Homer's horse stumbled a couple of times and nearly threw him, he slowed the gait from a lope to a trot. Mary's feet dangled a foot above the stirrups. Desperately gripping her legs against the horse's sides and with her hands on the saddle horn, she still swayed and bounced like a cork on the waves of a wind-swept lake. Her insides and rump had taken a beating by the time she and her kidnapper reached the Maple City ford on the Walnut.

Homer pushed his horse into the river. The high water made it necessary for him to raise his feet to keep from getting them wet. Mary's feet, being tied with a rope under her horse's belly, could not be raised out of the water. Boots soaked through with cold river water added to her discomfort. Once across the river, Homer stopped, dismounted, and checked the tightness of his water-soaked saddle girth. Mary had little hope of getting sympathy from the volatile, embittered youth, but felt she should try.

"Homer, I'm bouncing all over the place in this saddle. Would you please shorten the stirrup straps and loosen these ropes on my wrists?"

"Th-that's too damn bad, you—you stuck-up bitch. You damn Curtises always looked down at the likes of us—an-and it's sure as hell past time you got your comeuppance."

The squeaky voice and slurred words revealed a mixture of vindictiveness, fear, and uncertainty. Her instincts told her that he was both dumb and unstable—therefore, a very dangerous youth.

"I'm truly sorry you feel that way, Homer," she replied sincerely. "I sure don't recall ever putting you down."

"Well, it—it was the way you looked at us and were always dressed up so high and mighty," Homer snarled. "An-and, that damn Zeke and Will always acted like their shit don't stink."

Mary tried to keep her composure in the face of those ridiculous comments, but she couldn't resist trying to reason with the redheaded dummy.

"That just isn't so, Homer," she replied desperately trying to keep her voice calm. "You and your pa made it hard to like the two of you. We got along fine with Joan and Ester." It was no sooner out of her mouth, than Mary regretted she mentioned his worthless pa.

Homer dropped the saddle girth strap and was beside Mary's horse in a flash. He reached up and grabbed the front of her coat, along with a painful pinch of an unprotected breast. With her feet tied under the horse's belly, her body was twisted sideways. When she reached the limits of her restraining ropes, her face was close enough to his to smell the vile breath. There was enough moonlight for Mary to realize she was staring into the eyes of a madman. For a moment, she feared it was all going to end, right then and there. Her body trembled uncontrollably.

The snarling redhead drew back his arm and slapped her across the face with the full force of his fury. She saw it coming and turned her head away from the blow. Even so, it sounded like a pistol shot. Stars swarmed in her head and her teeth rattled. Only the restraining rope prevented her from being knocked out of the saddle because he had turned loose of her coat for a full swing at her face.

"Shut your mouth, you dirty whore," he shouted, slobbering like a mad dog. "You goddamn Curtises killed my pa. I'd put a bullet in you right here, if I didn't intend to screw you blind, then sell what's left of you to the Comancheros."

Spittle spewed from his gapping mouth, spraying her face. She wanted to scream, cry, and cuss defiantly at this stupid oaf, all at the same time. But she wisely didn't make a sound beyond grunting when the bony hand had hit her face. God, how it hurt!

Homer continued to stare at her with hate-filled eyes for several more seconds before abruptly snatching up her horse's reins, and mounting his horse. He took off south on the well-used trail at a jarring trot.

As full consciousness returned, Mary shrugged her shoulders and shook her head until her loosened headscarf fell off and landed in the middle of the trail, unnoticed by Homer. She had faith that her men wouldn't be far behind. The scarf would assure them that they were on the right trail.

Please hurry, she prayed. The thought of this vile animal being the first man to have her was repulsive. Oh, how she'd fancied about Will being the first one. From what she garnered from her captives' frenzied conversations after she regained consciousness at the house, Betsy had saved her from a similar fate earlier this night by killing the gang's leader. Maybe it was asking too much of God that she would be saved from such a horrible degradation twice in one night.

Mary shook her head to clear it of those frightening, self-defeating thoughts and admonished herself; settle down, girl, you can handle this. Homer may be a monster, but he's also an ignorant bastard; just use you head and don't panic. She turned her thoughts to outsmarting dumb Homer. It made her feel better.

The first rays of the morning sun were peeking over the hills when Homer turned east on a dimmer trail. Mary wished she had waited until they made this turnoff before dropping her scarf as a marker, but she had confidence in Zeke's tracking ability. Maybe they had stopped off for Betsy; she would certainly be able to follow their trail anywhere.

Then a fearsome thought pushed the optimism aside for a few minutes. How long would it be before Zeke and Will came back from the wild goose chase? But there were Betsy and Skeeter—that is, if Skeeter hadn't been killed. Thank God, Betsy would see to the girls. Get those negative thoughts out of your head, she lectured herself. You can beat this miserable moron on your own.

For over three hours, they rode on through rolling hills and brush-choked creek valleys without a break. The horses were stumbling tired and Mary's bowels were in distress when Homer stopped by a small creek. He said nothing to Mary while he watered his horse and took a long drink from the creek. And then he rose, unbuttoned his pants fly, and relieved himself in the creek, seemingly oblivious to Mary's presence.

Mary looked straight ahead, keeping a blank expression on her face. Before Homer finished his endless piss, her horse moved forward on its own, trying to reach the water. Homer stepped aside to let it drink. Mary was parched, but relieving her bowels and bladder were her most pressing needs. The urgency caused her to chance speaking. Be damned, if she was going to beg.

"Homer," she said, doing her best not to sound intrusive or antagonistic. "I've got to have a privy break or I'll mess up this saddle."

Her calmness and levity seemed to disarm Homer. His sneer wasn't nearly as severe when he replied, almost civilly—dumb, but civil.

"Hell, that ain't gonna hurt that there saddle none. I can wash it off. We ain't got no time to waste."

"Well now, I don't think traveling with a stinking woman is going to be pleasing, especially if the wind changes to our backs," Mary lightheartedly replied.

Homer's narrow brow wrinkled. He concentrated on that possibility for several seconds. It seemed forever to Mary before he solemnly shook his head in the affirmative.

"You got a point there. I don't want you stinking up the place, but you got to hurry," he spoke somberly, as though he'd just made a monumental decision.

It was monumental to her.

"Just let me down. As bad as I've got to go, it won't take long," she chuckled.

Apparently disarmed by her cheery demeanor, Homer quickly untied her legs. When she slid down from the saddle, her legs were so numb and wobbly she had to support herself by leaning on the horse while stomping feeling back into them. Homer made no move to untie her hands. She expectantly held them up in front of him and he absentmindedly untied the rope. After warmly smiling her thanks, she moved toward some sumac bushes near the trail. Homer recovered from his distraction before she reached them.

"No, you don't! You're not gonna hide behind them bushes. I want to keep you in my sight. Go right there in the trail."

Mary seethed inside about the indignity of the situation, yet she calmly took a few more steps down the trail, squatted with her back to him, and relieved herself. This was no time to argue about niceties, she reasoned. After all, that vile varmint intended to rape her; maybe it would cool him down to see her take care of her bodily functions.

But—but the rape just wouldn't happen, she reassured herself. Her men would surely rescue her before he had that chance. A horrifying image of that foul-smelling, redheaded scarecrow panting on top of her flashed into her mind. She nearly vomited.

The practical problem of what she could use to clean herself pushed aside that dreadful thought. If she had been thinking ahead, she should have collected a handful of leaves, even though they were dry this time of year. She was almost reconciled to staying soiled when she noticed the wide hem of her dress. It flashed into her mind that tearing off a piece of the wide, turned-under hem to use for wiping and then dropped it in the trail could also work as a marker.

At first, her hands were too weak from being tied to rip the threads or to tear the sturdy fabric. It had to be from her dress because the raiders hadn't given her time to put on a petticoat or any other underclothes.

Clandestinely, she moved the hem to her mouth and bit through the thread. By holding the material between her teeth and pulling with both hands, she managed to rip off a sizable piece. The rip wouldn't show from the outside. After she used it, she dropped it between her legs, and pushed a little dirt over a corner with the toe of her boot.

She looked over her shoulder before standing up and was relieved to see Homer preoccupied with the horses. Apparently, he thinks the show is over, she concluded. She took the opportunity to rip another strip of fabric from the hem, and tucked it into the top of her dress—another marker for further down the trail.

"Hurry it up," Homer shouted gruffly.

Mary stood, smoothed her dress, and took another quick look to see if the torn hem showed. Relieved that it didn't, she walked leisurely back to Homer with a wide smile.

"That's much better," she said. "Thank you, Homer."

It took him a moment to respond to her bold action when Mary stepped around him headed toward the creek.

"Where—where the hell are you going?" she heard him say behind her with uncertainty in his voice.

"Just to get a drink of water," she replied in a matter-of-fact tone.

"Well—well, hurry up, we got to go." The voice was sharper and worried now. Figuring she had delayed him about as long as she safely could, she knelt and quickly took a deep drink, deliberately leaving footprints and a handprint in the soft creek bank. Mary had come up for air, but wanted more, when she felt his grimy hand grip her shoulder. In a purposeful manner, she rose, walked back to her horse, and mounted.

Homer picked up the tie-ropes. "Stick out your hands so I can tie them," he gruffly demanded.

"You won't need those. I couldn't get away from a smart man like you even if I wanted to." She gave him one of her most radiant smiles while fighting down her feelings of disgust and revulsion.

Seeing his chest swell, Mary thought, thank God it isn't difficult to flatter the revolting slob, but I've got to be careful, he's like a stick of dynamite with a short fuse.

"Okay," he said, deliberately making his voice sound deeper. Mary fought her impulse to cringe when he put his hand under her skirt and moved it up past her knee. "You're gonna like rolling in the blanket with me."

Mary cleared her throat to steady her voice and with great effort, continued to smile.

"Well now, Homer, I'm sure you've had enough women to know that its lots more fun if the woman is willing. Treat me well and perhaps I'll be more willing to show you a good time."

"Hell, I know that. I'd have been gentler with you from the get go if you weren't one of them damn Curtises."

"I'm sure you would have." She faked another smile and his reaction showed that Homer was at least temporarily under control. She decided to push a little more.

"How much further have we got to go? I'm getting mighty hungry."

"Just a few more miles. We'll get there around dark, and then you can show me what you got for me," he said with a lecherous leer that caused a cold chill to run up her spine.

She felt a little victory when he took time to shorten the stirrups on her saddle and gave her a piece of fatty, half-cooked ham and a hard biscuit from his saddlebags. It tasted like a gourmet meal to the hungry woman.

Being an accomplished horsewoman, Mary rode much more easily. With her boots in the stirrups, she could concentrate much better on exploring her options. It was a hard reality that she could only put off the gullible redhead for just so long. There was also the fact that he was dumb, cowardly, and volatile—*a very dangerous combination!*

Late in the afternoon, Homer and Mary came to another small creek. He dismounted and told her to do the same. After drinking from the clear inviting water, he removed his hat, submerged his head, straightened up, and let the cold water run down his shirt collar. Mary saw that he was practically asleep on his feet. It was understandable, considering he'd probably been on the move for over twenty-four hours. She was darn tired too, but not too tired to escape if she saw him dosing in the saddle.

He motioned to the stream, indicating she could take a drink, which she hurriedly did before he changed his mind. With water still dripping from her chin, he forced her to remount. As though reading her mind, he tied the reins for Mary's horse to thongs on his saddle and spoke to her gruffly.

"If I doze off some, my horse knows where the grain is. He'll follow the trail. You try to get away, I'll strip that coat and dress off you and tie you in the saddle naked."

Mary judged it best not to reply. There was no doubt in her mind that he was capable of doing what he threatened. She nodded her head, indicating she understood.

The sun was sinking low behind them when Homer turned left on what seemed little more than a buffalo path. Mary surreptitiously dropped the last piece of cloth she had torn from the hem of her dress onto a bush beside the trail. As she did so, a strong premonition that Will wasn't far behind gave her courage.

The path wound upward into a cliff-bound canyon that pinched down narrower as they proceeded. At dusk, they reached a cabin tucked into the end of the box canyon. There was a dilapidated horse corral behind it and a spring-fed stream flowed nearby. The path they followed appeared to be the only way in.

Homer dismounted stiffly and roughly pulled Mary from her saddle. He removed the bedrolls and saddlebags from both horses and handed them to Mary. His eyes were bloodshot and his voice raspy when he spoke.

"Take these in the cabin and start fixing some grub."

When he appeared in the cabin a few minutes later, Homer carried an armful of firewood. He lit a kerosene lantern, started a fire in the fireplace, and went to the stream for water. Mary had been busy, best she could in the poor light, laying out a slab of bacon, a can of beans, and the makings for corn bread from the supplies she found in the cabin and saddlebags.

While she continued preparing the meal, Homer lounged on his bedroll, eyeballing her through heavy eyelids like a lecherous tomcat. It made her feel dirty more than frightened. She realized time was running out before the unspeakable would happen—unless he fell asleep or she found a way to protect herself.

Working as slowly as she could, in about an hour, she had the food ready.

CHAPTER 46

ZEKE'S STRATEGY

◆

Skeeter was untying the reins for the bridle of the horse he'd ridden bareback from Zeke's place when Zeke arrived at Mary's farm.

"My God, I'm glad to see you," Skeeter exclaimed as Zeke wearily dismounted. "Them damn raiders doubled back. They done run off with Mary and your prized stud horse."

Zeke put his hand on the excited youth's slim shoulder.

"Yeah, I already knew that," he interrupted. "Will and me had a shootout with 'em at the Arkansas ford. Killed three, but Homer Sommers got away with Mary, and another one still has my stud. Come back into the house and we'll talk about how best to hunt 'em down."

They'd never seen Betsy cry before. Zeke was surprised when she rushed into his arms, clung to him like a frightened child, and sobbed out a litany of what had happened to them. As she wound down, she noticed that Will wasn't there.

"Oh my God, where's Will? Is—is he all right?" she asked, her voice trembling again.

"He was okay, last time I saw him," Zeke replied. "But no telling where he is by now. The hotheaded youngster took off in the dark, by himself, after Homer Sommers and Mary."

"How'd he know Homer had Mary?" Betsy asked.

Zeke related what had happened at the Arkansas River ford and started making plans. He figured Will would be riding around like a chicken with its head cut off, and of no help to him. His nephew's headstrong actions disappointed Zeke, but he realized Will's all-consuming hatred for Homer and concern for Mary had dulled his judgment. Of course, saving Mary was also Zeke's first priority. During the ride from the ford, he had given the problem considerable thought.

Considering Homer wasn't very bright, Zeke narrowed down his options. He'll either make a run for his gang's hideout, or find some place nearby where he can lay low until he's sure we're off in the Territory looking for him. Then again, he may go to wherever they planned to take Mary and my stud.

From where we last saw him, Zeke reasoned, he'll have to cross either the Arkansas or the Walnut to do any of those things. I'm betting he'll come back to where we had the shootout, trying to hookup with some of his buddies that might have survived. The Arkansas ford is the place to start, Zeke decided. If I don't cut Homer's trail there, I sure as hell can track down the varmint that got away with my stud. With a little persuasion, he'll lead me to Homer.

Zeke slept about three hours and woke, clear-headed, just before first light, eager to begin the search. Skeeter pleaded to go with him. Zeke persuaded him to stay and guard what was left of the family.

"Stay alert. No telling what that crazy Homer might do," he reminded them.

Betsy was also fervent to enter the fray. Zeke reminded her Moses needed her more than he did.

Soon after first light, Zeke's fresh horse was high stepping downstream from the ford, through the shallowest water he could find in the rain-swollen Arkansas. Zeke scanned both banks for signs of where the raider that was leading his stud might have left the riverbed. It wouldn't have been easy for the fugitive, riding in the dark and leading a strong, stubborn horse. Both high banks were lined with dense stands of sumac and black oak underbrush.

About noon, Zeke spotted a grassy delta on the west bank, created by a small creek converging with the Arkansas. Closer inspection revealed the tracks of two horses leaving the riverbed, crossing the delta, and entering the creek bed headed upstream.

This is where the dumb bastard left the river leading my horse, Zeke assured himself. He was likely damned wet, cold, and near tuckered by the time he spotted this way out. A mirthless smile spread under Zeke's bushy mustache and his hard eyes narrowed.

"I'll bet you the farm that bastard stopped nearby to rest and dry off," he said to his horse. "Hell, he's probably even dumb enough to build a fire. I'll have him in my gun sights before dark!"

Zeke cautiously worked his way up the creek. He'd traveled about a half-mile when he came to a small clearing where he discovered the ashes from a recent fire that were now cold. He must have stopped here at least long enough to dry out some, but I've missed him by a few hours. The poor fool is leaving such a clear trail it's only a matter of time before I catch up with him. Problem is, I don't have a hellva lot of time, Zeke lamented.

Evening shadows were lengthening when the trail Zeke followed crossed a substantial creek. He smelled the pungent odor before he saw the smoke coming from a thicket a few yards down creek. After tying his mount's reins to a bush, he quietly stalked the smoke with his pistol drawn. Soon, he came upon a smoldering campfire in a clearing. A snoring, blanket-cocooned body lay beside it. His stud, tied to a nearby tree, whinnied in recognition. Another horse, with a saddle still on him, was tied beside the stud.

The form in the blankets wasn't disturbed by the loud whinny. Zeke stared at it for a few seconds with his anger rising to a fever pitch. That unknown sleeping lump represented all the horrors his family had suffered from the heartless raiders and what Mary must be enduring at the hands of despicable Homer. He felt justified to shoot the bastard where he lay. But it was not in Zeke Curtis to kill any man in cold blood. Even if he could, he reminded himself he needed this skunk to help him run Homer to ground. What he didn't know was that the sleeping man was the "Billy" who pleaded Mary's case and risked his life to protect Zeke's two little nieces.

Zeke quietly approached, knelt on one knee beside the sleeper, put the gun muzzle against his exposed temple, and shouted in his ear.

"Wake up, you scum, and face the music for what you've done to me and mine."

The man sprang to a sitting position, wild-eyed. His right hand reached for his pistol and it nearly got him killed. Zeke's trigger finger tightened and he pushed the gun nozzle harder into the hated man's temple.

"Wha-what—don't shoot!" the stranger stammered.

Zeke swiftly moved his gun from the man's temple and roughly pushed about two inches of the barrel into the horrified man's flapping mouth, cutting his upper lip in the process. It was then that he noticed his prisoner was just a youngster, probably no older than Will and Skeeter. But it didn't soften his raging anger, which was only marginally under control. Given the slightest provocation, he could shoot the man without remorse.

"If you bat an eye or even fart, you mangy son of a bitch, I'll blow your worthless head off," his voice projected as cold as the north wind in December.

Both of the man's arms shot up in a surrender gesture, his eyes filled with fear, and he tried to speak. Zeke mercilessly pushed the gun barrel a little further into the trembling youngster's mouth. The bugging eyes reminded Zeke of a hooked fish. That was about as much regard as he could muster for his prisoner.

"Only thing I want to hear from you is where I can find Homer Sommers," Zeke snarled. "If you can't tell me that, I got no reason to let you live!"

The frightened man grunted and nodded his head slightly, trying not to disrupt the gun barrel pressing in his mouth with a nervous finger on the trigger. Zeke eased the gun barrel from the trembling man's mouth. The young raider went to his hands and knees, spitting blood and gasping for breath.

"Stay right where you are!" Zeke ordered. "If you want to live another minute, start telling me where I can find Homer and his captive."

After a false start, the youngster choked up, cleared his throat, and frantically tried again.

"I—I tried to talk him out of taking the woman. I didn't know he survived the shooting at the ford," he said with a raspy voice.

"Well, I'm telling you, he got away with one of my girls! Now quit wasting time and tell me where you bastards were headed when we dry-gulched you?"

"Honest, mister," the petrified youngster pleaded almost in tears, "I don't know exactly where we was headed. Only Luke, the guy what got killed trying to mount that Indian gal, and Homer knew where we was to meet up with some Comancheros to sell the four women they thought they were getting on the raid. All—all I know, it's somewheres down in the Unassigned Lands."

"Well, assuming I believe that, where have you bastards been hiding out between jobs?" Zeke demanded, figuring that would be the logical place for Homer to hole up.

"Yeah—yeah, that's where Homer would go. I was going to head there myself, soon as I found a buyer for this here horse." The raider's voice brightened.

"It's an old trapper's cabin near the Caney River—northeast of here, on the border between Kansas an' the Osage Nation. Luke left supplies stashed there saying we'd be back after we settled up for this raid that Homer thought up."

Because the kid was scared to death, Zeke was inclined to believe him.

"How far is it?" he asked impatiently.

"Probably about twenty-five miles, as the crow flies, but I'm not exactly sure just where we are now. I'd know how to get there from your place though, or from the ford across the Walnut." The pleading outlaw babbled on, not realizing his story was rubbing Zeke's open emotional wounds raw.

"It took us about twelve hours, hard riding, to get to there the time Homer shot them horses. Then we wandered around down in the Osage Nation for a while and rested part of the day before we went back on that raid.

"I'd just as soon help you catch that damn Homer. I wasn't in favor of his idea for capturing women and I never liked that crazy bastard anyway. Tried to tell him he shouldn't take that gal with us. Did stop him from messing with the little girls. Damn near had a shootout with him over it. I got sisters about their ages," the youngster eagerly volunteered. "I'll take you there, mister, but it's hard to find 'less you know the trails."

"What's your name, kid?" Zeke asked through clinched jaws.

"Billy—Billy Howell," he muttered.

"Well, Billy, you better pray you're right about where Homer would hole up because your life depends on it. Now mount your horse and let's get going!"

Zeke transferred his saddle to his stud and took the horse he'd been riding with them as an extra mount. He thought he could find his way back to the Walnut in the dark. About midnight, disgusted with himself, Zeke realized he was lost. He'd have to wait until daylight to get his bearings.

At dawn, he and his now seemingly willing guide were on the move again, riding fast on rested horses. They reached the Maple City ford on the Walnut River about mid-morning. It was mid-afternoon before they arrived at the turnoff from the main trail. Riding hard, when darkness fell, they were only about an hour's ride from the outlaws' hideout, but they were stymied. Billy pleaded that he needed light to locate the dim trail that forked off into the box canyon where the cabin they were looking for was located. He assured livid Zeke that they were close.

We're two days behind that bastard, Zeke tortured himself. Only God knows what crazy Homer is doing to Mary, or the whereabouts of Will. He was too worried to sleep. Damn, he wished his boy was with him—that is, his nephew, Will, he corrected his mental slip.

CHAPTER 47

RITE OF PASSAGE

◆

Will's cerebral wheels began to turn. Those cutthroats were likely headed for the Cherokee Strip for some reason when we jumped them, he thought. Even stupid Homer is probably smart enough to figure we'll keep the ford across the Arkansas covered to prevent him from doing that. The only other way south with a safe crossing of the flooding rivers is to use the Maple City ford on the Walnut, and that's where this trail leads.

"Yeah, that's it," he muttered into the night air. "It'll be light in a few hours and I'll cut his trail at the Maple City ford. I shouldn't have any trouble picking out the fresh tracks of two horses traveling in tandem. Maybe I'll get lucky and one of them will be the horse with the broken shoe."

Satisfied with his logic, he spurred the strange horse into a trot and headed toward the Walnut ford with a sense of urgency and renewed confidence. After nearly twenty-four hours in the saddle, Will was dozing as the plodding horse found its own way along the well-defined trail. He awakened with a disoriented start when the animal stopped at the bank of the Walnut and tugged at the reins trying to get its head down far enough to drink. The moon had set and the far bank was obscured. Recognizing the rock outcrop on his right, Will was confident he had reached the Maple City ford.

Frustrated by having to wait for enough light to check for fresh horse tracks, he dismounted and allowed the horse to drink. He also drank a few swallows from the muddy river himself. Easing his weary, saddle-sore body to a sitting position beside a tree, it was his intention to rest his burning eyes for just a minute. Within seconds, he was sound asleep.

About the time Homer and Mary turned east off the main trail, Will was snapped awake by his restless horse tugging on the reins that he had fortunately wrapped around his wrist. His unfocused eyes blinked at the first rays of the morning sun and it took a few seconds before the urgency of his desperate quest registered. He lunged to his feet.

"Damn you, Will Curtis," he chastised himself. "You were sleeping while that bastard Homer is making off with Mary. Zeke would've never allowed that!"

The horse shied at the sudden movement and sound. Will nearly lost his grip on the reins. Cursing the nervous animal for causing delay, Will soon brought him under control, mounted, and gave him an angry scrape with his spurs. The goaded horse leaped into the water, and Will was suddenly ashamed for having taken his frustration out on the hungry, innocent horse. Zeke always said to be kind to your horse, and it will take care of you. He ought to know, having had three horses shot out from under him during the war. Gosh, how he wished Zeke was here with him!

On the other side of the swollen river, Will dismounted and closely inspected the trail. His spirits improved when he discerned a damp area on the bank. There were signs that two tandem sets of hoof prints left the water. They looked fresh, but he couldn't be sure they were made by the horses he was after since neither had a broken shoe.

While holding his mount to a slow walk, he searched the rocky trail closely for collaborating signs. Damn, he thought, all bets are off if I'm fool enough to follow a false trail. Discouraged, he had about decided to go back and check the river banks at the ford again when he spotted a bright piece of cloth in the trail ahead. In seconds, he was beside it, had dismounted, and snatched the cloth from the ground. Instantly, he recognized it as Mary's headscarf. He'd seen her wear it many times.

"They came this way all right," he confirmed to the disinterested horse. "God bless Mary; she marked the trail for us. Considering the ground is still damp where they left the ford, they're not far ahead."

Quickly swinging back into the saddle, Will nudged the mount with a spur and gave it verbal instructions.

"Get a move on, horse. Let's catch that bastard before he hurts Mary. I pray to God we're not too late!"

Concern for Mary caused him to chance loping his horse. However, he realized he'd have to check each side trail or clearing where Homer might have turned off the main trail. That necessity caused lost time. A maddening sense that he was dropping further behind his prey gnawed at his guts.

The frustration nearly reached a breaking point about midmorning. He lost the distinctive tandem tracks. Rationalizing they had turned off on some obscure side trail that he had missed, he had no alternative but to backtrack and search for it. An hour later, he found one that looked promising. The dim trail was overgrown and hard-packed. Yet, smashed grass indicated it had recently been traveled. He'd follow it for a couple of miles and turn back if he didn't see clear tracks by then.

He stopped to drink and water the horse at a clear-running creek. Because he took his drink from the other side of the trail, Will missed the fresh footprint and handprint. He would have missed the partly covered small piece of cloth lying near a pile of fly-covered excrement if he hadn't been studying the trail carefully on both sides of the creek. There was enough print on the cloth for him to recognize it as having come from one of Mary's dresses. The disgusting picture of what had probably happened there formed in Will's mind. But he was elated about finding verification that he was on the right trail. He quickly remounted and pressed the tired horse hard. He felt vibes from Mary, telling him that she wasn't far ahead, but please hurry. That polecat Homer would soon be paying for debasing his Mary, Will vowed!

The sun was only about ten degrees above the western horizon when Will arrived at the creek where Homer had stopped for their second drink. He detected two sets of boot prints in the soft earth beside the creek this time, one small and the other much larger. They were fresh, making him feel confident Homer and Mary made them, and he wasn't far behind. He reached out and tenderly touched one of the smaller imprints.

"Hold on, my darling, I'm coming—I'm coming!" he uttered, praying that somehow she would get his message. But there was anguish in his voice, reflecting fear that he'd be too late to prevent her from being violated.

The tired, but surprisingly durable, horse caught its breath and drank while Will studied the signs. After Will finished a quick drink, he remounted and pushed the horse hard, fearful he'd lose the trail when it got dark.

As though by providence, a big harvest moon rose in the southeast shortly after the sun sank, otherwise Will wouldn't have noticed the faint path his quarry had taken to the left. Some unseen force directed him to check it out. He soon spotted Mary's dress material dangling from a bush as it marked the trail.

"We're damn close, horse. I feel it in my bones," Will said softly, while he snatched the precious piece of cloth from the bush and put it in his coat pocket.

Even in the bright moonlight, the seldom-used path was difficult to follow. Will walked, feeling his way along, leading the horse. In about half an hour, he detected a whiff of wood smoke and knew his destination was nearly at hand. He tied the horse, secluded in a clump of blackjack brush, and carefully continued on the path until he saw a cabin outlined against the dark cliff.

No telling how many outlaws are holed up in there, Will reasoned. I better check it out before I go barging in. He detected light and guessed there was a window on right side of the one-room cabin. Pulling his pistol, he moved quietly to the window, looked in, and went berserk at what he saw.

Homer and Mary were grappling on the floor. Homer's pants were down around his ankles. Mary's dress was up under her armpits. She was trying to reach a piece of firewood while clawing, kicking, and biting Homer. He tried to pin her down and mount her, but she seemed to be winning the battle, if not the war.

A sea of red flashed before Will's eyes. The wail of a banshee came from deep in his gut as he dashed around the cabin toward the door, giving Homer a few seconds warning. Will stumbled over something. The fall momentarily knocked the wind out of his lungs, providing his enemy a few more seconds.

After regaining his footing, Will burst through the cabin door just as Homer crashed out of the window. Will snapped off two hasty shots in Homer's direction and dove after him. Outside, Will stopped for a moment, trying to determine which way Homer ran. From the back of the cabin, he heard whinnying and the milling of nervous horses.

"You lucky son of a bitch, you ain't getting away again!" Will screeched in desperation as he ran toward the sounds.

The big black horse nearly collided with Will at the corner of the cabin when it cleared the low corral fence with Homer riding bareback. Will got off one more clear shot. He saw Homer fall forward on the horse's neck, just before horse and rider disappeared down the trail.

His impulse was to dash after his archenemy and make sure he was dead, but concern for Mary overrode that idea. *I hit the worthless varmint at least once*, he consoled himself. *If he's alive, he has no weapon. I'll find his worthless carcass in the morning. I'm not leaving Mary alone.*

Mary straightened her tattered dress as best she could, and had regained much of her composure by the time Will returned to the cabin. The moment he stepped inside the door, she rushed into his strong arms and wept.

"I knew you were coming. I knew you were coming. I love you, Will. I love you so much!"

An image of the first time she hugged him flashed into his mind. He was just thirteen years old then. His face had been buried in her breasts by the exuberance of that hug. Now, her head nestle under his chin. He felt her firm breasts pressing against his flat stomach.

"I love you, too, Mary—always have—since the first time I laid eyes on you," he whispered in her ear. Then louder, "Did—did that varmint hurt you?" He couldn't bring himself to use the word rape, but she knew what he meant.

"No, nothing that won't heal. But you came just in time. Did—did you kill him?"

"I think he was hit hard, but he rode off into the dark on that big black horse of his. I figure he won't get far. I'll look for what's left of him in the morning."

They sat close together on the stone hearth, held hands, and talked about the events of the stressful day.

"Are you okay to be alone for a few minutes while I take a look around and see to my horse?" Will asked after a few minutes.

"Yes, I'm fine now," she replied, giving him another hug and kiss on the lips, "except for feeling filthy from that animal putting his hands on me. I know it probably sounds silly, but I'd like to take a bath as soon as possible. There's an old washtub over there in the corner, would you put it by the fire and fill it with water for me?"

"You bet I will," he said.

While the water heated, Will went after his horse and searched the area for some distance around the cabin to make sure Homer wasn't sneaking back. He found a substantial smear of blood on the top corral pole, which made him more certain Homer wouldn't be coming back.

Before starting her bath, Mary hung an old blanket over the window and warmed some food for Will. While he ate, with his back turned discreetly to her, she scrubbed herself with a reasonably clean rag and the sliver of soap she'd found, until her skin was pink. And then she washed her filthy, frayed dress. Her pretty, auburn hair was still damp when she moved over to sit beside him with one of his bedroll blankets around her. She combed it the best she could with her fingers.

The cabin was cozy, and he was tired. Even with his true love beside him, clad only in a blanket, Will had to fight to stay awake. He knew she was also tired and suggested they get some sleep. Come first light, he wanted to start tracking Homer.

"I'm exhausted, Will, but I don't want any blanket from those filthy outlaws touching either of us. Let's share your blankets."

That was fine with Will. They were soon sound asleep next to each other. The sun had been up for over two hours before they woke the next morning.

Mary was sore and stiff from her rough treatment. They had plenty of supplies. Will suggested they lay over at the cabin until the next day, even though he knew the family would be very worried about them. Over Mary's protest, he cooked their breakfast and insisted she rest while he searched for Homer's body. Midafternoon, he found the black horse nibbling dry grass in a little meadow about half way to where the path to the cabin forked off from the more distinct trail. Blood matted his mane.

Backtracking, he found Homer's body lying in tall grass near the trail, about a mile from the cabin. There were two bullet wounds in the body, either lethal enough to have killed Homer. The gangling redhead's stork-like legs protruded six inches beyond the cuffs of his outgrown pants and there were holes in the soles of his dilapidated boots, which he obviously hadn't bothered to remove before he tried to molest Mary.

"Damn," Will lamented out loud, "he is a pathetic sight."

It's too late to do anything with the body tonight, he decided. If I can find something to dig with at the cabin, I'll bury him before we leave in the morning.

Will was very pensive about Homer's death by the time he returned to the cabin.

"As much as I hated the guy, I can't help feeling sorry for him," he told Mary. "Poor devil never had a chance, considering the kind of pa he had."

"You feel remorse because you're a decent man, Will," Mary said, "and I love you for it. But what you did had to be done. That monster was dangerous and beyond redemption. He never would have left us alone!"

"You're right, Mary, it had to be done, but I can't say it gives me much pleasure for having killed him. Now I know what Zeke meant when he told me that killing a man is a hard thing to live with."

"It's not easy to take another person's life," Mary agreed. "Only God should make those decisions. For whatever his reasons, he put poor Homer on a path that had to end this way. In that respect, it was God's will."

After supper, Mary took another bath and soaked in the old washtub with her knees up under her chin until the water got too cold for comfort. She also washed her tattered dress again, trying to cleanse away the memory of her horrifying experience.

With her dress still wet, she remained wrapped in one of Will's blankets. He removed his boots and outer clothes, blew out the lantern and rolled into the other blanket next to her. He had no sooner settled in when he felt her hand reach over, find its way into his blanket, and slide between the buttons of his long johns to rest on his firm stomach.

Her soft, warm touch brought him fully awake and created an immediate erection. Soon she lifted the side of his blanket and slid up against him. Even through his underwear, he felt the softness and warmth of that wonderful body cuddled next to his.

"Will," she whispered, "please make love to me."

God how he wanted to, but he worried it would be unfair under those circumstances.

"Are you sure you want that, Mary, considering what you've been through?" he whispered back with passion in his voice.

"That's part of why I want you, *now*," she replied, a little louder and breathless. "I'm twenty-three years old and have been saving myself for you. In the last two days, I've almost lost my virginity twice to horrible animals. I don't want to take a chance on that happening again. And—and I love you. I want you, Will, with all my body and soul."

Mary gave him a squeeze and began to unbutton his underwear. He frantically helped with the buttons, slipped out of the long johns, and turned toward her. In this, Will became the teacher. There was excitement as never before, but no wild groping—just tender love as he caressed and kissed her. She responded passionately. When he sensed she was ready, he entered her gently at first, and then with a plunge of uncontrollable pent-up desire.

She uttered a little scream, and then he felt her passion take possession of her body. She rose to meet him and pleaded for more. When they reached orgasms at the same time, he felt their souls merge, never to part again. Mary sighed deeply and pulled him closer. At that moment, Will realized what Betsy had meant when she spoke of finding that one special love. He was holding that love in his arms, and intended to hold her there forever.

"I love you, Mary," he whispered in her ear.

"I love you, too, Will. I've love you since the first day I saw that bashful little boy twisting his battered straw hat in his hands," she uttered, clinging to him, not wanting to break the spell of ecstasy.

It was an adult love they declared, with all its pleasures, depth, and ramifications. The tensions and fears of the past few days melted away in their second lovemaking. They drifted into a blissful sleep, cuddled in each other's arms.

Tired as he was, Zeke hadn't slept. He and Billy had eaten cold ham and biscuits, washed down with creek water, and were back on the trail by first light. The sun was in their eyes when they reached the path that Billy told him led to the gang's cabin, hidden in the box canyon.

With high hopes of finding Homer and Mary at that cabin, Zeke guided his horse up the faint path. They had traveled about a mile when Zeke's horse shied. He reined him in and took a hard look along the trail to determine what had spooked the mount. He spotted a body that was nearly hidden in tall grass.

Zeke dismounted and turned it over. He recognized the carrot red hair, styled in a round bowl cut, and those long, skinny legs protruding from pants that were always too short. It was Homer Sommers, with two bullet holes in him.

"Damn," Zeke said, "the poor dumb bastard looks more pathetic dead than he did when he was alive." As much as he despised Homer, he found himself saddened at seeing the pitiable redhead's dead body abandoned out in the middle of nowhere. He judged it would be the same for Will if he saw the wretched body.

Could Mary have somehow managed to have killed him, Zeke wondered.

"Is it possible that some other member of your gang killed Homer and took Mary?" he demanded from trembling Billy, after giving the mystery some more thought.

"It—it couldn't of been none of our gang what done it. There was only six of us. We was all on that damn raid. That Indian gal killed Luke, and you guys killed three more. That left just Homer and me. Now—now, it's only me."

Billy looked like he was going to cry. Perhaps he sees himself ending up just like Homer, Zeke thought, feeling a little sorry for the youngster.

"Well, assuming you're telling the truth, I'm gonna tie you to a tree over there and go take a look up that canyon. If it don't work out right, I'll be back for your hide."

When Zeke spotted the cabin, he tied his horse out of sight and scouted around to get the lay of the land. He noticed three horses in the corral. From a distance, one looked like Homer's big black horse. There was a blanket over the only window so he cautiously approached the door. Hearing no sound from inside, he slowly pushed the door open, with his pistol in his hand.

A smile, so big it turned the tips of his bushy mustache up into a U shape, spread across Zeke's rugged face. His penetrating hazel eyes sparkled with relief and happiness. Two of the people he loved more than life itself were blissfully asleep on the floor, cuddled in each other's arms. Mary's dress was spread over the hearth and one of her bare legs protruded from under the blanket. Will's clothes, including his underwear, were piled next to their cozy pallet. He guessed what had happened between Will and Mary, and he was pleased. While observing the intimate scene, Zeke Curtis' heart overflowed with love and pride. In his mind, Will had passed his rite of passage into adulthood with flying colors.

Zeke only hoped Will and Mary wouldn't tie the knot too soon. Will had a lot of wanderlust in him. He knew from his own experience it would be best if the youth got it out of his system before he settled down to have a family. He shouldn't wander too long though, and miss out on his true love, like Zeke had done. But wise Mary would know what he needed, and she'd sense when to reel him in. If she didn't, ol' Uncle Zeke would tell her.

The affection and serenity of the two lovebirds snuggled together in peaceful sleep brought Joan Koster to Zeke's mind. It was high time he asked her to marry him. Right then and there, he resolved to do so, just as soon as he could get to Winfield—no excuses this time! Marge would understand.

It seemed a shame to wake the lovers, but he needed a cup of coffee, and they should start for home as soon as possible. The rest of the family would be worried sick. Zeke made a move toward the sleeping beauties, and then thought better of it. Hell, they don't need me—I should just sneak on back home.

In a magnanimous mood, he thought that since Homer was dead, Mary was safe, and he had his stud horse back, he might even let that pitiful, dumb kid, Billy Howell, go free. The big smile was still on Zeke's face as he carefully closed the cabin door and quietly walked away. It would stay there for a long time because it sprang from a joyful heart.

"Marge, darling," he uttered, speaking to Will's departed mother, "*our* son has matured into a fine man and he's in love with a pretty little gal that's darn near as wonderful as you were! We done good after all, didn't we, my love?"

In his heart, he knew Marge heard him, and that she was pleased.

About the Author

Len Custer was born and raised on farms near Pawnee, Oklahoma. His father was a farmer, who at times held elective county offices. His schoolteacher mother imbued her son with an inquiring mind, by encouraging his natural interest in reading and creative writing.

While still in school, Len held part-time and summer jobs as farm hand, construction laborer, printer's helper, school bus driver, feed store clerk, surveyor's assistant, pipeline welder's helper, car washer, and ball rack boy in a pool hall. He managed to hold down the three part-time jobs of school bus driver, feed store clerk, and ball rack boy at the same time, while in his senior year of high school.

Joining the navy at age seventeen, he served a two-year enlistment in the regular navy. As a reservist, he was called to serve for another eighteen months in the Korean War.

During a thirty-year career in the marketing department of Chevron Corporation, Len rose through twenty-one positions at nineteen different locations—from Service Station Attendant to Area Marketing Manager, in charge of Chevron's marketing in four states.

He is also the author of two previously published books: *Goodbye Old Friends and Other Stories*, a collection of fourteen short stories on a variety of interesting subjects, and *Called to Serve: A Historical Novel of the Korean War*.

Printed in the United States
149591LV00003B/1/P